KD WENTZEL

DARK FRIDAY

AN AURORA WINTER THRILLER

DARK FRIDAY

Copyright © 2021 by KD Wentzel

Library of Congress Control Number: 2021912335
Print ISBN 978-1-7374459-1-3
Ebook ISBN 978-1-7374459-0-6

Dedication

I want to thank my dear friend, Dennis, who has been my collaborator since kindergarten, a critical sounding board, and someone who calls bullshit if I get too far afield. You've always been my hero.

To Harlan, who always finds adventure without even trying. You didn't think writing stories was a waste of time and assumed I would keep doing it. So I did.

To my mother for reading big novels to a little boy. Melville and Twain were my favorites. Thank you for setting me on the path. I hope you enjoy this book despite the racy parts.

Finally, thanks to M for your love and tolerance. Our life is a first draft, but we'll keep editing together until we get it right.

PART ONE - BORDERLAND

CHAPTER 1

WINNIPEG

The rear door of the Musalla Al Islam opened and two men emerged into the night. They struggled with a roll of sodden carpet between them, the center like a distended belly, holding the corpse of Imam Osama al-Qadhi. Before they could cross the landing to reach the stairway to the alley, a motion security light flashed on, catching them in a tableau, the vapor of their breath smoking in the harsh glare. Halil quickly dropped his end of the carpet and seized a rusty snow shovel from the landing, smashing the bulbs in a shower of sparks.

Mohammet held his end of the bundle tightly and looked around in a near panic, fearing a light would come on in a window facing the alley or someone would challenge them from the darkness. They both waited for a moment, but nothing changed. Their eyes adjusted to the dim light and they cautiously started down the stairway, the body swaying between them. Halfway down, Mohammet slipped and sat down heavily on the concrete steps, wincing with pain, trying to keep his grip on the rough carpet. He swallowed hard, enduring the touch of the dead man's hair against his hands. He was relieved he couldn't see the Imam's scalp matted with blood.

"Are you all right? Can you manage?" Halil tried to mask his frustration. *They needed to get off these stairs and into the shadows!*

"I'm fine." Mohammet was sweating and his face glistened in the glow of a streetlight at the end of the alley.

"You're fine?" Halil muttered. "It's bloody obvious you're not!" Halil started to lower his end but Mohammet leaned forward and stood up, gritting his teeth to hold on long enough as they made it down the last steps to the alley. Mohammet dropped the carpet and staggered back to the steps, sitting down again.

Halil noticed but didn't say anything. There was a lot of blood, and Halil could smell it even in the cold. He wiped his nose on the back of his sleeve and began dragging the corpse to the side of the building. Mohammet started to get up, but Halil waved him back. "I'm just getting it out of sight until Ahmed gets here with the car."

"It?" Mohammet reproached. "He was an Imam and a good father following the word of the Prophet...Perhaps we should have reconsidered..."

Halil bristled at the sanctimonious words, straining to be patient. "I wish this hadn't come to such a turn, but this *Imam and father,* this *fool,* couldn't keep his mouth shut. I did the right thing and you know it!"

"Imam al-Qadhi is in paradise now," Mohammet said, trying to avoid looking at Halil.

Halil had heard enough. "That's a proper way to look at it, but right now, his salvation should be the least of your bloody worries!"

Mohammet knew he had said too much. Halil was hardened, but he was his friend and shared the same sensibilities. They were both vexed by this turn of events and he shouldn't fault his oldest friend for making such a hard decision. "I'm sorry, Halil. It must be Allah's plan."

"You mean the plan that doesn't end in our arrest and torture for plotting against the United States?" Halil was struggling not to slap Mohammet into reality.

"I didn't mean that. I meant..."

"I know what you meant," Halil said, kicking Imam Al Qadhi's body through the sodden carpet. "This fool isn't a martyr fallen in battle! He tried to stand on our shoulders and tell the world that he helped foster the great attack on America. I warned him, *you warned him,* but he couldn't bloody help himself! This fat asshole would have posted us on YouTube if we'd given him more time!"

"I know, Halil, but we should mourn him...Not judge him so harshly."

Halil shook his head and stroked his stubbled chin, pacing in front of the body, trying to contain his anger. There was no practicality in Mohammet and never would be, but they had come too far for this incident to matter in the least. "To hell with it. It's done." Halil said with finality. The two remained silent, dreading any more surprises.

"Sorry I took so long," Ghazi said, coming out of the back door and going down the steps to stand next to Mohammet. "It was a lot to clean up."

Halil glared at the boy, his mind dreading what could happen if he were able to make a call or signal someone. "You were left alone?"

"No," Ghazi replied quickly, "the other man, your friend, walked me to the back door and locked it behind me. He is coming around with your car, I think."

Mohammet looked at Halil and knew this could be bad. "Ahmed wouldn't let him do anything, Halil. I'm sure…"

"Mohammet! Shut up and think before you speak!" Halil was at his wit's end. *What a balls-up!*

"Sir," The boy Ghazi said in a soft but steady voice, "I know you don't know me, and you're upset, but I assure you, I only want to help the cause however I can." Ghazi stood silently, awaiting a rebuke or worse. Halil was about to reply, but a vehicle turned into the alley from the side street, the headlights playing across the rough buildings on either side. All three shielded their eyes as Ahmed, Mohammet's elder brother, drove a Honda Pilot SUV to where they waited, stopping next to Halil near the imam's body.

Ahmed got out of the Honda and sensed the tension between his brother and Halil. "Let's go!" He said, glaring at Halil. "Get the carpet into the back. I have his computer and cell phone."

Halil glowered at Ghazi. "Come help me load our holy warrior into the boot!" Ghazi hesitated but stepped around Mohammet and took up the carpet roll with Halil, careful not to touch the body. Mohammet remained on the steps, not speaking while the two loaded the Imam's corpse into the SUV.

Ahmed closed the rear hatch and began kicking snow over the blood spots in front of the steps, his eyes scanning the alleyway. He noticed that Mohammet was keeping his distance. It was too late to have second thoughts, but Mohammet brought another person into their circle tonight. Maybe it couldn't be helped, considering the boy witnessed the Imam's execution.

Halil had cut the Imam's throat with a practiced stroke of his knife, catching most of the blood in a towel he'd brought for that purpose. Ghazi had come to Imam Osama al-Qadhi for his nightly janitor instructions and halted in the doorway, mouth open in shock as Halil wiped his commando knife in a glistening streak on the dead Imam's tunic. Before Halil could cross the room to silence his only witness, Mohammet intervened and hustled the boy away from the office, determined to prevent another killing.

Ahmed marveled that his brother Mohammet had not only prevented Halil from adding another body to his tally but had actually drafted the boy into abetting murder! Ahmed remembered the boy as a harmless fixture at the Mosque but allowing Halil to take care of the only witness was prudent. Mohammet thought with his heart, but this was a stretch even for him.

Mohammet had led the boy through the former thrift store now converted into a Masala, the floor covered in rugs of all designs, the ceiling a patchwork of water-stained tiles and flickering fluorescent lights. Mohammet guided the boy into a small side room used for ablutions and motioned for him to sit on a wooden bench along the wall. "What is your name, Brother?"

"Ghazi."

"Warrior," Mohammet replied. "A good name." Mohammet knew time was ticking away but did his best to show patience. "How old are you?"

"I'm seventeen." The voice was soft but confident.

"Be assured, Ghazi, we mean you no harm," Mohammet said, sitting down and taking the boy's hand in his. "You may not understand, but this is the will of Allah. You must trust me that what happened here tonight with Imam al-Qadhi was necessary and done with no hate or malice. We took his life for a larger cause. Do you believe me, Ghazi?"

"I understand," Ghazi said gravely, letting go of Mohammet's hand and standing up. "He was a stupid loudmouth."

Mohammet frowned, struck by the callous response. "Perhaps, but it's still a bloody horrible turn of events. We didn't..."

"I want to help," Ghazi interrupted, dark eyes showing something like hunger. "I want to be part of what you're doing."

Mohammet's eyes widened, "What we're doing?" *Halil was right. Al-Qadhi might have told too many people already!*

"Your jihad...Crossing the border. I'll do whatever you need me to do."

Mohammet rose from the bench and looked closely at the boy. Ghazi's face was plain and clean-shaven. He was slight of build and his clothes were ill-fitting and loose. Perhaps they were given to him by the Mosque. Only Ghazi's eyes made an impression with thick lashes and dark irises that shined with intensity. Mohammet found no hint of deceit or cunning and sensed that the boy could be trusted. To a point.

"Mohammet!" It was Ahmed. "We have to leave!"

Mohammet had to decide. He wanted to probe more about the boy's motivations, but that would have to wait. "Come with me," Mohammet said, the issue settled. "We must be sure the Imam is taken care of with proper reverence. Will you help me?"

Ghazi nodded and went to a nearby closet and produced a mop and bucket. "I'll clean up, but I don't want to touch him....Is that okay?"

Mohammet nodded with consternation and watched the boy roll the bucket down the hall to the office while softly humming or perhaps praying to himself. *What the bloody hell just happened?* Mohammet shook his head and went to tell the others there would be another on their journey. He hoped they would understand.

They didn't, but they indulged Mohammet, convinced that having the boy close to them in the following hours would ensure he couldn't connect with the RCMP or Winnipeg police. Ahmed and Halil agreed they would let this play out. Ghazi could be pressed into service for the crossing, but if he became a liability, his body would be left somewhere along the way.

One thing was sure, Imam al-Qadhi would be missed, and their window of opportunity was closing fast. It would have to be tomorrow night.

CHAPTER 2

WALKING GHOST

Despite its size, Winnipeg is relatively quiet at night, and Ahmed and Mohammet were almost alone traveling through the city. They drove past homes clouded in a white haze, the SUV's passing muffled by the first snow of the season. Halil had taken Ghazi to meet the others and prepare them for the journey. They were down to hours now and the planning was over.

Mohammet wished to stop for cigarettes and bottled water for the journey south. They pulled into a 7-Eleven and parked at the edge of the lot. Ahmed waited in the car, the engine idling, watching his brother walking with an effort to cross the lot. He sighed and lit his third cigarette since they loaded the body. Mohammet was still weak from his bout of flu and he wasn't sure how he would manage in the coming hours.

Ahmed watched his brother leave the store. He seemed to be in pain as he returned, his gait stiff and slow. Mohammet got back into the car with his shopping bag and smiled at Ahmed as he buckled his seatbelt. "All set."

They drove southwest on Main Street, passing Kildonan Park on the left, the golf course already covered with a dusting of snow. Mohammet watched the silent landscape as they traveled along an iron fence surrounding a sparse field, the amber of sodium street lights casting across acres of tombstones and monuments. They passed one of the entrances to the cemetery, a pair of white brick columns flanking an ornate iron gate.

Mohammet pointed to the right and murmured, "Shaarey Zedek."

Ahmed couldn't hear him and he reached to turn down the heater fan. He was too hot anyway and starting to sweat. "What did you say?"

"We just passed Shaarey Zedek Cemetery. Did I ever tell you about a man named Louis Slotin?"

"No, who is he?"

"Who *was* he?" Mohammet rolled down his window and threw his cigarette out into the wind. "Louis Slotin was part of Oppenheimer's team working on the Manhattan Project during the Second World War."

Ahmed wasn't interested in the story until he heard the words "Manhattan Project."

Mohammet continued, his eyes staring straight ahead. "Slotin was working with criticality testing, establishing critical mass values. Of course, this was all a new frontier, and protocols for controlling the hazards of radioactivity were still being developed."

"So what happened?" Mohammet had Ahmed's full attention.

Slotin was conducting experiments on a plutonium core, I think to be used in a third atomic bomb, but I don't remember. Anyway, he made a terrible mistake handling a beryllium hemisphere…"

"What the hell is a *beryllium hemisphere?*" Ahmed interrupted.

"It's like a bowl…half of a sphere made for reflecting neutrons into a radioactive core to enable it to go critical," Mohammet explained. "Slotin caused it to release gamma radiation and couldn't stop the reaction until he was exposed to a lethal dose." Mohammet swallowed hard and continued. "Slotin knew he was a dead man. His hand burned, and he fell ill almost instantly, vomiting soon after the exposure. "Mohammet was staring at his own hand, extending the fingers as they lay on his thigh. "Slotin was ill for a few days, then strangely, he recovered."

"So he lived?"

"No. Slotin died just over a week after the accident."

Ahmed frowned, not understanding. "How could he become so ill and then improve before dying?"

"It's the latent phase of radiation poisoning," Mohammet said quietly. "After the initial wave of damage, the victim experiences a period of relative wellness that can last for days before the body begins to hemorrhage internally. His colleagues thought of him as a *walking ghost.* He was already dead, but his body lived on." Mohammet took another camel from the pack. "Now you know I won't be dying from smoking these."

"What are you saying?" Ahmed dreaded the answer.

"I'm saying I made a mistake and did much the same thing. I don't have the flu, Ahmed. I'm dying from radiation poisoning. I am like Slotin. I am a walking ghost."

Ahmed's mouth became dry and he felt as though his insides were suddenly hollow. "Why do you tell me this story now?"

"Because Louis Slotin was born here in Winnipeg, and he's buried in Shaarey Zedek, the cemetery we passed back there."

Ahmed said nothing to his brother and in the silence that followed, Mohammet retreated into his thoughts. It had been four days since the exposure, and though he knew his remission was temporary, he truly felt all right. He was a little tired, as though with the flu, but otherwise, he was still effective and his mental capabilities weren't impaired. Mohammet knew he could carry on and get through it. This business with the Imam was more serious, and they had to press on soon before things unraveled completely.

He put his hand on Ahmed's shoulder. "I will miss these times alone with you, my brother." Mohammet stifled a cough, turning away. "But Allah makes no requests; he only demands that we serve him, blessed be his name."

The walking ghost of Mohammet had no more than five days before the latent phase passed, and he wouldn't be able to raise his head above a hospital pillow.

But he had less than 24 hours to live.

CHAPTER 3

ORIGINS

"What we now know is that Ahmed Ibrahim and Mohammet Abu Sharim were born in Birmingham, England, in the mid-1970s. Their English mother lectured at the University of Birmingham and their Lebanese father practiced internal medicine at Selly Oak Hospital in its final days. The brothers were brought up in an affluent yet austere household, avoiding social traumas or real class oppression during their childhoods. Former classmates described Ahmed as a clever student whose charm offset his weak academic performance. His younger brother, Mohammet, was studious and introverted, shunning activities outside of the classroom, focused on mastering physics and mathematics.

By all accounts, the brothers weren't exposed to a fundamental religious agenda, and though observant Muslims, their parents were far from strict. The boys grew up without much of a legacy from their quiet mother or pedantic father, who believed in honor, service, and fealty to one's fellow man. 'Deeds and service,' he would admonish his sons, according to family friends. 'Not materialism and vanity.' Doctor Abu Sharim wasn't much different from his staid British colleagues. However, his Levantine roots may have been a barrier to advancement, and he failed to rise in the new Health Service, becoming a static component of the system. Real or imagined, the institutional discrimination Doctor Abu Sharim experienced set itself into the lore of their family and likely became a touchstone for Ahmed and Mohammet's views of British society."

Excerpted from "Fallout – Surviving in a Dark New Age" by Miriam Glenn - published in the St. Paul Pioneer Press

At university, Ahmed's dark features and ready smile won him many friends and he took part in all of the traditions practiced by students at university. He streaked naked across the soccer pitch, played Fuzzy

12

Duck, and bedded an impressive number of young women. Like many ambitious young men, Ahmed had his eye on the future and understood the benefits of networking, cultivating many superficial yet important contacts among his peers. His web of association would help immensely to succeed in business.

One of his acquaintances, Halil Jobrani, grew to be a close friend. They shared a similar worldview and often pursued their vices together, daring the other to attempt the outrageous. Halil was less refined and enjoyed the lifestyle Ahmed afforded. In return, no one ever bothered his wealthy friend. Ahmed didn't have any ex-girlfriends or bitter rivals. Halil Jobrani saw to that.

In contrast, Mohammet paid no attention to his appearance or social status, devoting an obsessive amount of time to his studies, becoming even more withdrawn. Ahmed visited him regularly, often with Halil, and the three enjoyed their time together. Ahmed and Halil would try to coax Mohammet out of his ascetic environment, but he was happy to pore through a scientific journal or be alone with his thoughts. Ahmed didn't know what to make of Mohammet at times, but he didn't mind his brother's forbearance; it was a natural component of Mohammet's personality and didn't alarm Ahmed in the least. In time the three were conferred degrees and left their universities behind.

Doctor Jobrani and his wife passed away not long after, and the brothers never returned to Birmingham or thought to stay in the UK after that. They were left with a sizeable inheritance and could live well on their annuities if they wished. Ahmed invested their money wisely and let the accounts grow as they continued on their separate paths.

Ahmed gained a position as a sales representative for a large petrochemical corporation and built an easy rapport with clients, no matter how diverse. He also had an ear for languages. In his travels through Europe and the Middle East, Ahmed gained a surprising vocabulary in several dialects, carrying him aloft in the organization to a lucrative executive situation in North America. When he was secure in his position and able to manage work and leisure, Ahmed leased an expensive flat in Toronto's urban center, enjoying the life of a bon vivant, cultivating expensive tastes in tailored suits, fine wine, and exotic women.

Mohammet drifted away from academia, uninterested in teaching or research. His mind sought solutions to problems and he gravitated to engineering, applying theory to practical use. He was uncanny at rendering complex challenges into simple components and solvable steps. His approach wasn't novel, but Mohammet's consistent and reliable performance made him a valuable commodity for any number of employers.

As the European Union became more inclusive to compete with America and Asia, Mohammet's client list grew in stature. Clients initially engaged him to control costs or boost production, but as he progressed, so did his work's complexity. His introverted personality began to work to his advantage. He naturally avoided personal attachments and shunned attention, making it very easy for him to remain discrete. Mohammet became the perfect consultant, working long hours, tolerating hazardous work environments, and eschewing monetary gain in favor of the challenge. Mohammet was rewarded handsomely for his efforts, but sometimes his compensation was in strange forms that spoke of his eccentric clientele. Automobiles, limitless credit cards, services of women (and men) offered and rejected, expensive toys and what he liked best, exotic equipment he could employ on the next project. A few patrons treated him as family, taking him under their wing and advising him on everything from proper social behaviors to security precautions. Mohammet once mentioned in passing that he sometimes awoke in a hotel and forgot where he was, and the next day the keys and title to a small apartment in Podgorica, Montenegro appeared in the post.

Then came a paradigm shift that altered almost every facet of Mohammet's life.

The September 11, 2001 attack on the World Trade Center caused much of Mohammet's clientele to withdraw from commitments that might anger a vengeful America. Close business associates became targets of the U.S.-led coalition, and Mohammet knew his non-disclosure agreements could never survive a war. Lines were drawn between former allies, and as the Gulf Wars raged, alliances were made and broken over the years, adding to the instability of the Middle East. Iraq fell, and like many agents peripheral to conflict, Mohammet prospered. He studiously avoided bringing attention to himself and carried on, walking the tightrope, avoiding ideological entanglements, and choosing his projects carefully.

In time, Saddam Hussein hung from a rope, Al Qaeda and the Taliban morphed into ISIS. The new brotherhood swore to restore the Caliphate and rid the infidels from all of Asia.

In late 2017, Mohammet's careful dance came to an end.

If one had asked him at the time, Mohammet would not have appreciated his importance in the drama playing out between the Gulf States, Iran, and the United States. He felt that he was working unnoticed and didn't attract attention that would bring trouble. He tried to be neutral in a struggle that targeted the moderates above all else. He was steadily pushed, even as he thought otherwise, to declare an allegiance.

The West or the Caliphate. *Scylla or Charybdis?*

It came down to a woman.

He barely got to know her. She was Iranian and assigned to assist him as he worked through a deviling challenge he'd taken on for a company he later learned was a particular holding of the Saudi royal family. They had commissioned his firm and he hadn't challenged the assignment, savoring the chance to dabble in nuclear technology.

Isa was not beautiful, but she had treated him kindly and displayed competence and fresh intellect that impressed Mohammet far more than any physical attraction. They worked together closely. Though they never physically consummated their relationship, Mohammet felt at ease around Isa and spoke to her often in the casual way he'd only experienced with his brother Ahmed. They made each other laugh, and the experience was like light showering a dark room, making Mohammet's life bright for the first time.

And then she was dead.

Mohammet grieved and blamed a feckless America lashing out like a blind giant in its prolonged war against the people of Afghanistan, Iraq, and Syria. She was killed along a desert highway in the company of associates who had risen in the struggle to achieve a place on the kill list kept by American and Israeli Intelligence. She was likely an operative for the Iranians, but Mohammet had lived so long without emotion or caring for another that the loss of Isa caused him to come undone. The guilt of knowing he had only realized her value after she was dead just fed his rage. Whether he had loved Isa or not, the unfairness of snuffing out such a brilliant, righteous woman struck him to the core.

Mohammet's demeanor changed. His eyes were opened to the unfairness of his Muslim brothers' struggle against the mighty Americans and their sycophantic allies. In time, his mourning became a grim resolve that would not allow him to tread the middle line, and he began to think of, then crave retribution against such a decadent culture that would project global destruction without consequence.

Mohammet had chosen. He would devote his efforts to the Caliphate.

The West would pay.

CHAPTER 4

MOTIVATIONS

"Halil Jobrani, the brother's old friend, resurfaced at some point and made contact with Mohammet Abu Sharim. It is thought that Jobrani had procured a nuclear core, likely stolen from the Pakistani government. Abu Sharim and Jobrani began working together to develop the core into a functional atomic weapon, later enlisting the help and financial resources of Mohammet's brother, Ahmed."

Excerpted from "Fallout – Surviving in a Dark New Age" by Miriam Glenn - published in the St. Paul Pioneer Press

On a sunny afternoon in early October, Mohammet answered a Skype call from one of his benefactors. Mohammet brightened at the sight of his friend through the video feed. The two men shared pleasantries, then spoke about the difficulties they would encounter after the Iranian pact with America failed and the conflict in Syria continued. Libya had fallen, Iraq was stabilizing, and much of what was known as "IS" had been routed from Afghanistan. The new Caliphate was exiled to isolated enclaves, struggling to mount a meaningful counteroffensive.

Mohammet's patron didn't mince words. "My friend, even if we destroy every record of our relationship, we know too damn much."

Mohammet was alarmed that his friend was talking like this. "You have associates to vouch for you, and I've done nothing that would put you in danger."

The man on the computer screen smiled but shook his head. "Mohammet, there are a host of functionaries investigating us as we speak."

"But why?" Mohammet replied. "You've been an honest broker, and what am I to these people?"

"You and I and many others are to be silenced within the next week. I am leaving tonight with my family, and I implore you to do the same."

"Why would Mossad want us dead? " Mohammet asked sincerely.

"My friend, if Mossad wanted us dead, we would already be so."

"But what about the security men you have in place?"

"There isn't a security firm on earth that will stand against the Pakistani ISI when they decide to tie up loose ends. Do you still have the package we prepared for you?" Mohammet nodded into the webcam. "Good, get it and do as I taught you."

Mohammet became more agitated. To be intimidated by the bloody Americans and their mercenary coalition was a bitter pill to swallow, but to be threatened by agencies of nations they had worked with for years was ridiculous. "What is this?" He shouted at his computer monitor, his friend staring at him from his office in Ankara. "We've worked hard for this! We've done nothing wrong! I've never let you down or failed to complete a contract, and now I'm to abandon everything and go to ground like a hunted rabbit?"

The man cleared his throat and, in a steady voice, told Mohammet that his association with Halil Jobrani had not gone unnoticed. "My friend, I know what you've pulled off, and though I am impressed and sympathetic, I must leave you to your fate. I cannot hide you in my shadow any longer. You know what I'm talking about, and I implore you not to insult me by denying it."

Mohammet tried to communicate his regret in not being forthright about his avocation and explain his motivations but his friend had muted the transmission and couldn't hear his words. The man held up his hand to Mohammet. "A large sum of money has been deposited at Credit Suisse, UBS, and Julius Baer on your behalf. Go with God, my friend. Please do not try to contact me or any of your other associates. Just retrieve that package and follow it to the letter." The camera feed ended, and Mohammet Abu Sharim was left staring at a black screen.

Mohammet's rage faded as he sat alone in his flat, adrift for the first time in his life. The sudden loss of his friend's support and the prospect of ending relationships he'd built over decades weighed heavily on his heart. For the second time, it was a challenge to keep his emotions under control. Isa's death had pushed him into a covert Jihad, and now this exile tore at him as he considered his next moves. He could go to his other clients and forge on, but he was pragmatic and knew his patron was right about cutting ties, making him even more resentful of the Americans and the fear they caused among his brothers.

An hour later, he stood in front of a small counter in a private carrel at Atlas Mont Banka, peering at the contents of a safety deposit box he'd stored years before. The package was assembled when his friend had recognized the volatility of Mohammet's work environments and had insisted on engaging a consultant to provide him with false passports, credit cards, and information he might need at some point. Mohammet had scoffed at the precaution, but now he saw the wisdom of forethought. He transferred the items into his backpack and returned to his apartment to plot his disappearance.

He placed every personal or sensitive document he had in his possession into a metal dustbin and lit them on fire. He burned an array of USB drives, ID badges, photos, two of his favorite cell phones, and the hard drive from a laptop he'd smashed to bits against a doorframe. He made sure it was all reduced to a useless mass of charred plastic before leaving his apartment.

His EuroRail pass among the ashes in his flat, Mohammet paid cash for a seat on the B433 train to Belgrade, rehearsing his new identity. He rode through the darkness, unable to view one of the most picturesque routes in the world, falling asleep somewhere between Budapest and Vienna, waking when the train arrived at Wien Hauptbahnhof.

There was only one person Mohammet wished to speak with, and he phoned his brother from a kiosk next to a Yorma's delicatessen on the station concourse. As he waited for Ahmed to answer, he was unsure what his elder brother could or should do about this upheaval in Mohammet's life.

Ahmed was not surprised by his eccentric brother's early morning call, but when he heard Mohammet refer to himself by a name that was an alias, he sat up in bed, pressing the phone close to his ear. The caller said he wanted to visit and spend time with his old friend, Ahmed.

At Ahmed's level of business dealings, with industrial espionage a constant threat, engaging on an open line just wasn't done. Ahmed rose and quietly left his bedroom, shrugging into his bathrobe. Despite the fall chill, he went onto his small terrace and leaned against the ornate balcony railing, the sun rising above the skyline of Toronto as the murmur of traffic played below.

"You know you are welcome any time, my friend!" He said brightly, assuming the call was monitored. "What's your flight schedule?" Ahmed listened then said in the same cheery tone, "right then, I'll pick you up at Pearson and we'll have a proper holiday!" Ahmed ended the call and sighed. This impulsive move was out of character for Mohammet and that made Ahmed uneasy. He retreated inside and climbed back into bed with the Croatian beauty he'd met at an Art Gallery of Ontario gala the night before. She stirred as he laid his head on the pillow but soon fell back to sleep. Ahmed remained awake and stared at the ceiling, listening to the girl breathing softly in his ear.

What have you gotten into these days, little brother?

CHAPTER 5

THE DEVICE

The refugee population of Sweden has tripled in the last ten years, and though many assimilate, some do not, challenging a homogenous population used to cooperation and secularism. Critics point to a smugness in Sweden's ethos that resists measures encouraging assimilation, and radical elements have taken advantage of the nation's benevolence to sow discord. Ahmed and Mohammet Abu Sharim found the country to be an ideal haven for readying the nuclear device for shipment to North America."

Excerpted from "Fallout – Surviving in a Dark New Age" by Miriam Glenn - published in the St. Paul Pioneer Press

Ahmed and Mohammet devised a plot to divert an intermodal container of Volvo automobile replacement parts, including several S90 engines. Halil, the bold one, pulled a black balaclava over his face and hijacked the lorry and its Volvo cargo bound for Moscow, growling in virulent Russian that the driver would be hunted down and gutted if he went to the authorities. The driver had a Russian mother-in-law and understood perfectly. Halil left the man on the side of the road with a bonus in Euros to maintain his silence and drove the truck and container to an abandoned bondgård where Mohammet went to work.

Global security changes place as much emphasis on cargo leaving Europe as examining goods entering North America. Mohammet's first challenge was to devise a method of shipping the package without drawing suspicion to the ship, its cargo, or the individual container itself. Second, the package must pass close physical inspection, and third, no radiation could be detected during the shipping process. To meet those three conditions, Mohammet knew the device could not deviate in appearance from any other item of cargo, including a neutral radiation signature.

With the help of Halil, the brothers removed the shipping container's contents and selected one of the Volvo S90 engines for their purpose. They disassembled the engine down to its aluminum and steel core and took extensive measurements for the following process. Using a CNC mill that employs a drill bit mounted on a head that moves in three dimensions, they shaped five-centimeter thick lead plates to carve a digitally-modeled replica of the Volvo engine powerhead. After machining, the ingots were stacked into a sandwich of shaped lead identical to the engine block. Their "layer cake" was then disassembled, and they used the CNC mill to hollow out a chamber tailored to fit the device's nuclear component. Once reassembled and painted in the same factory high-temperature coating, the lead replica appeared identical to the S90 core.

Halil and Mohammet placed the false engine block on a heavy steel trolley and added all the parts they had taken off the original engine. The plastic shrouds, oil pan, pulleys, belts, and wiring were laboriously attached to emulate a Volvo engine. Warning tags and instructions were affixed to the various appurtenances. Their "Trojan Horse" unit was packaged like the original, carefully wrapped and crated with the same care used to protect an expensive engine for a long sea voyage.

They lifted the assembly with a forklift and positioned it in the shipping container's center, repacking the other Volvo parts around it. Mohammet checked his radiation detector and nodded as the digital readout didn't change. "It's acceptable," he said to Ahmed and Halil.

"Brilliant!" Ahmed said with a brief smile. "Now we have to get this to our ship for the trip west."

In Torslanda, Gothenburg, Sweden, the Volvo plant ships new Volvos and replacement parts via container ship to the North American continent each year. Shipments leave the factory and are loaded at Goteborg's port on the River Göta, flowing into the North Sea from Lake Vanern.

The purloined container housing the false engine was sealed appropriately and logged into the database by a trained officer of the port authority paid not to ask questions. His Islamic sympathies encouraged cooperation, and he took quiet satisfaction that his brothers were active and pushing back against the haughty Europeans and mighty Americans.

He would have assisted anonymously without the gift of Euros placed in his desk drawer, but the sum would help with his living expenses, which was only practical. He changed the stolen container's identification code to explain its reappearance, arranged the necessary documentation for the unit to be slipped into the loading queue with other cargo, and made sure it was trucked to the port without incident.

The container was lifted off the lorry's running gear and hoisted aloft by a dock crane, then lowered and stacked among 2,276 others to form a massive, multi-colored block of steel boxes towering above the deck of the Ultra Class container ship *Mørsea Stavanger.*

The *Stavanger* unwittingly carried the weapon of mass destruction down the Göta River, into The Kattegat, and around Grenen Bank through the Skagerrak, one of the busiest shipping lanes on earth. In two days, the ship traced a route through the English Channel and turned west, 32 nautical miles from England's south coast. She made revs for 19 knots and in a matter of hours, put Europe astern, bound for Halifax, Nova Scotia.

The giant ship varied its speed to avoid arriving too soon or late, holding to the Halifax Port Authority's tight schedule for off-loading. Their docking window was between 02:30 and 04:30 on the 16th of October. The sea air had a biting frost as the colossal ship reached Chebucto Head and rendezvoused with a yellow and black utility vessel emerging from the darkness. The boat's navigation lights illuminated the gigantic ship's steel wall as the harbor pilot boarded for the final leg into Halifax via the main channel.

Mørsea Stavanger went under the Angus L. Macdonald Bridge just after 03:00 coming abreast of the Fairview Terminal pier marks and shutting down her 26,000HP diesel engines after 13 days at sea.

The container with the Trojan horse and Volvo components did not register on any radioactivity sensors. After a cursory inspection, it was cleared for crane retrieval and lowered onto a semi-trailer rig headed west. In 22 hours, the container arrived at a freight yard close to the Toronto airport in the suburb of Brampton. The truck left the yard after dropping the sealed container for local assignment. Ten hours later, the Volvo parts and false engine were delivered to McGladrey Auto Center in Mississauga. There, glittering Volvo sedans and polished SUVs waited under brilliant LED lighting to be sold by nattily attired men and women building on the motto, *"Volvo for Life."*

The Service Manager of McGladrey, Mr. Assam "Sam" Al Bayoumi, accepted the assorted Volvo factory parts, including one turbocharged, intercooled DOHC 16-valve 2.0-liter inline-4 cylinder motor that encased something far more powerful than any internal combustion engine.

Mr. Bayoumi directed his forklift operator to unload the container contents while he bantered with the truck driver, sharing ribald jokes about the Canadian Prime Minister and the American President. The Volvo parts were stored in the tidy warehouse across the tarmac between the repair shop and the modern sales floor.

After a quiet night at McGladrey, the false S90 engine had disappeared from the warehouse, unrecorded in inventory. Other than Sam Al Bayoumi and a disinterested forklift driver, no recollection of the engine existed.

CHAPTER 6

THE MISSION

Halil joined Muhammet and Ahmed at a rented farm near Portage la Prairie, a small town just west of Winnipeg, Manitoba. Halil complained about being too conspicuous in a small community, arguing they should be in the heart of the Muslim community in Winnipeg proper. Mohammet assured him that the farmhouse was isolated and he could work without intrusion. Winnipeg had a Muslim population, but few were amenable to Jihad, and there was a greater chance they would be exposed there.

Halil reluctantly agreed, but he and Ahmed took steps to make sure they weren't discovered or taken by surprise. They installed passive security devices and were conscientious in following strict protocols that didn't expose their activities to outsiders. Halil worried over the security and allowed Mohammet to focus on their ultimate task.

Mohammet carried on uninterrupted, converting their precious acquisition into something more than a static munition, too stable to be triggered but robust enough to transport through harsh conditions. He worked steadily to perfect the device, and though there was no deadline, all agreed there were preferable times for detonation that would maximize the number of Americans they could kill.

Mohammet's task was to create something as powerful as any western democracy possessed. He was determined to develop a weapon fit for Saladin or Mohammed himself! His bomb would become the sword of Islam, and he reveled in every step forward.

Mohammet ran into a setback in the second week and fell ill. He stopped work for a few days to recuperate, but soon continued, Halil aided him in crafting a reliable trigger mechanism using an untraceable cell phone as he had for countless IEDs in the war zones of Afghanistan and Syria.

There remained the challenge of transporting the bomb. Ahmed and Mohammet had always assumed they would use a power vehicle of some sort to move quickly and carry more cargo. Halil, with the most field experience, counseled that any incursion would have to be on foot. The terrain was too thickly wooded to trust a snowmobile or ATV to navigate the heavy brush and dense woods. "ATVs and snow machines make noise, give off a heat signature and leave a clear trail," Halil told them. "They also break down and strand their riders. Simple is better."

"But how can we carry the device through miles of forest?" Mohammet was still recovering from his virus and sounded exhausted.

"Perhaps a cart or dolly we could use to support it?" Ahmed suggested.

"No," Halil said, shaking his head. "Mohammet is right, we can't carry it, and anything with wheels isn't practical in such thick cover." Halil paused a moment, then continued. "We'll have to drag it on a sled we can maneuver with simple manpower."

Ahmed leaned back in his chair. "' Simple manpower'? There is no such thing! And I suppose we'll have to wait for snow?"

"Snow would certainly help such a long trek," Halil replied. He noticed Ahmed's criticisms were becoming more pointed.

Ahmed shook his head. "Even with snow, I don't know how the three of us can manage, and it's too late to recruit anyone trustworthy. There must be an easier way."

Halil shrugged and sat down at the table. "If it were easy, the bloody Americans would have built a wall on the border and not rely on trees. We know two men who will help us."

Ahmed looked at Halil warily. "You mean the two that delivered the Volvo engine to Winnipeg." It was a statement, not a question. "Nadeem and…."

"Waleed," Halil finished.

Mohammet put his arm on Halil's shoulder. "If Halil is satisfied with these men, we should be as well."

Ahmed looked skeptical. "Transporting a container with no knowledge of its contents is one thing. Crossing the American border is another."

Halil shrugged. "I think the crossing will be physically demanding, but the remoteness of the terrain will keep them close. We have a plan for the bomb after we reach America. After that, Waleed and Nadeem won't be needed. We needn't become close friends."

Ahmed knew what Halil was implying, but he focused on their plan and how it could be carried out. "Alright. Contact them."

Halil nodded, "I will use Osama al-Qadhi. He is supportive of Jihad and..."

"Imam al-Qadhi!" Ahmed interrupted, "I'm sure the RCMP would never think to infiltrate his Mosque, especially with that fat Al-Qadhi spouting shit while others do the fighting. No, you'll contact them yourself."

Halil bristled at Ahmed's tone but shrugged it off. "As you wish, I'll make it happen. Halil stood and went to the sideboard in the kitchen and retrieved an outdoor sports catalog. He thumbed the pages and folded them open to show the others. "This might be a good way to transport our weapon."

Ahmed glanced at the page. "A portable fishing shelter," he said, sliding it across the table to Mohammet. "Yes, that could work."

Mohammet looked at the catalog and nodded at Halil. "Brilliant, my son! We'll take the guts out of it and nestle our egg in foam packing! That will withstand the trip and won't draw attention when we transport it to the final destination. What could be more bloody Canadian than one of these silly things? It's almost as clever as my hollow engine that got us this far."

Ahmed and Halil were surprised at Mohammet's rare show of vanity.

Mohammet stood slowly with a tired smile on his face. "It's coming together, boys, but I am now going to bed."

They watched Mohammet walk stiffly to the back bedroom. "Get some sleep, Mohammet!" Halil called after him. "You look like hell!"

CHAPTER 7

RED RIVER FALLS

Axel Winter stood behind the stone mausoleum, out of the wind, tamping his pipe in the weak November sun. He bit down on the pipe stem while he unbuttoned his American Legion dress uniform jacket and fished out a battered Ronson lighter. Axel flicked it open, and a rich yellow flame made the tobacco glow cherry red. He snapped the lighter shut with a metallic click that had comforted him since his father had sent it to him during his second tour in Vietnam. He took a moment to run his thumb over the familiar image of a grinning skull engraved on the lighter; its gold-plating wore away years before. Axel was nineteen in 1968 and lived through that tour and one more before he got nailed hard and they sent him home for good. Axel stood six feet and four inches, maybe more, but he was old and on the back end of things. His chest was a keg of muscle, and although the crisp white shirt of his uniform stretched over a paunch, it didn't invite anyone to think him unfit or lazy. His face was weathered with a tight mouth that rarely smiled and ice-blue eyes that had never lost their intensity.

Dale Lindquist came around the corner of the tomb to get out of the wind, nodding when he saw Axel.

"Hello, Dale." Axel still found Dale's ponytail and beard unsightly, but Axe had mellowed with the times, and Axe had to admit it was goddamn hard to judge a book by its cover these days. Everyone seemed to sport tattoos or had jewelry hanging off them like a Christmas tree. Dale was a good man but the fact that his hair was as gray as Axel's didn't mean he wasn't just a kid. "I see you still ain't cut your hair, you goddamned hippie."

Dale shook his head, the ponytail lolling along his back like a cat's tail. "Nope. Ain't planning to either."

"Figured as much."

Dale shook out a Kool from a wrinkled pack and patted his uniform pockets for a light. "We're still burying them from World War Two, but there aren't many left."

Axel held his lighter out to Dale. "Gone, but not forgotten," Axel said, staring off past the highway and into the distance.

Dale took a deep drag of his smoke. "You know, I remember joining this outfit," Dale said, putting his hands in his pockets and leaning back against the white marble wall. "When I got back from Vietnam in 71, you were the hard case, and I was the new guy. Shit, me and you and Arnie are the only ones who show up anymore." Dale knew the other men were in heavy combat, and he knew all about that. He wiped his nose with the back of his hand and looked down. "How are you doing, Axe?"

Axel continued to stare into the distance. "I'm alright," he finally said.

Dale was uncomfortable in the silence. "How are your boys? You hear much from them?"

"They're doing okay," Axel replied. "They use that email and texting stuff but don't call their old man much. I don't have a computer, but my granddaughter lets me know the important stuff."

Dale stole a glance at Axel. "I could get you set up…With a computer, I mean. It isn't too hard…"

"No," Axel shook his head, looking off into the distance again. "It's…Not for me." Axel almost said it's too late for me. He had about six months left, and he was damned if he'd waste it on Facebook or tweeting like an imbecile. He wasn't able to get his fill of the old ways he loved, and texting and all that computer bullshit were just walking in place and thinking you've gone somewhere. "I'm taking Aurora up to deer camp over Thanksgiving," Axel said, changing the subject.

"Your granddaughter? I thought deer hunting was over for the year?" Dale knew Axel was in the hospital doing his chemo during the regular season and it was the first season he'd missed since coming back from Vietnam.

"The DNR opened a special hunt starting tomorrow to thin the herd. The boys, Phillip and Kurt, are coming up there with me. He didn't say for my last season. Aurora wants to join in, and I think that will be good for her. She needs to get her hands dirty. Get away from her mother and see there's another side to her family."

"Sounds like you're on a mission, Axel," Dale said with a smirk. "I feel sorry for her."

Arnie Callan appeared around the corner, his round face raw from the wind and his limp more noticeable than the past few times they'd turned out. He nodded at Dale and Axel. "It's time, fellas."

Axel shouldered his M1 rifle. "And I feel sorry for you, Dale, you goddamn hippie." He slapped Dale's back as he passed. "Cold enough for ya, Arnie?"

"Not as cold as Korea in 51," was Arnie's stock answer. Arnie just turned 83, and Axe wondered how much longer he could do this. Axe felt like hell, but as long as Arnie was up to the job, he would hack it too. Arnie earned his limp. A Chi-Com round splatted into his shovel as he was chipping at the frozen ground, shattering the steel and sinking two pieces into his hip. Arnie was a tough little bastard, Axel guessed they all were, but times were changing, and it wouldn't be long until Axel Winter was beyond making much of a difference to anyone, living or dead.

Dale took one last drag and bent low to grind his cigarette into the brown grass. He pocketed the butt as always, then picked up his rifle and followed the others. Dale would never embarrass Axel with open admiration, but Axel was both a brother and father figure to him.

Dale got drunk, mean drunk, one Saturday night in the summer of 1973 at a bar that isn't there anymore, screaming at people he didn't know about what he couldn't remember. No one would slow down to comprehend what he and so many others had gone through, and his anger and anguish had exploded that night. He took on three farm boys while their girlfriends shrieked and tried to pull him back from pounding them senseless.

At some point, Mel Erickson, one of Pendleton County's older deputies, appeared at the edge of the dance floor, his hand on a holstered Colt Python .357. Deputy Erickson saw the situation for what it was;

Dale Lindquist was one of their own who had returned from God knows what and had earned some slack. He held back, nodding at the bartender to make a call.

Dale drifted in and out of his drunken stupor but still loomed above the boys he had laid out and ranted gibberish at them until Axe Winter was in the doorway, his massive figure unmistakable in silhouette. Without a word, Axel laid his bear paw hand on Dale's arm, and Deputy Erickson watched as Axel frog-marched Dale out the door of the bar. He pushed and pulled Dale across the parking lot like a child, then yanked open the passenger door of his truck, took Dale by the collar and belt, and heaved him into the front seat.

Dale raged in Axel's truck as they drove out of town, the yellow headlights casting out over the gravel roads leading away from Red River. Dale talked about the friends, real friends he'd lost in dirty battles over shit ground that had to be re-taken over and over again with another body count every time the NVA made another push.

Axel listened to all of it. His face grave and stoic in the dashboard light.

Dale ran out of energy and he crashed down in silence, his chest racked with sobbing and years of guilt and anguish he couldn't control. Axel slowed the truck and pulled over into an abandoned farmstead choked with weeds. The headlights were stark against the remnants of a gray pioneer cabin built when the land was first settled.

"You done whining?" Axel didn't look at Dale as he turned off the ignition, and all was suddenly dark and quiet.

Dale turned his head and looked at Axel Winter with a baleful stare, his eyes sore and unfocused.

"Dale, listen good," Axel began. "In what other country are we going to live? What other town? The entire country is full of good and bad people who didn't share in our war. They'll never get it and after it's all said and done we lived through it and some didn't. There isn't anywhere else for us."

Dale was silent, swallowing the rage and frustration that had come so violently to the surface. "Why do you even want to make it work?"

Without hesitation, Axel replied, "I embraced the pain because it's all there was and I dreamed that someday I'd float above the hurting and put it behind me. My wife loves me and I love her for that. I have three boys that make it worth getting up in the morning, and every day that I act like things are normal, they become normal."

Now, so many years later, Dale couldn't count the many men and women he shepherded through their time of anger or doubt at coming back to a place they longed for in their darkest hours but wasn't the same as before and never would be. Dale Lindquist healed as he healed others. The way Axe Winter had healed him.

The three veterans walked into the wind, taking take their place near the grave. Axel nodded to the priest and to a boy who stood with a cornet waiting to play taps while two younger boys took their positions with the Minnesota flag and Old Glory, the fluttering colors vivid against the gray sky.

Before the minister began and while the family gathered near the fresh grave, Axel's mouth moved in a silent whisper, his words unheard heard by the living:

…And under his wings you will find refuge; His faithfulness will be your shield and rampart. You will not fear the terror of night, nor the arrow that flies by day, nor the pestilence that stalks in the darkness, nor the plague that destroys at midday. A thousand may fall at your side, ten thousand at your right hand, but it will not come near you."

Axel always left off the last line:

"You will only observe with your eyes and see the punishment of the wicked."

CHAPTER 8

THOMAS AND SAEED

Saeed Alghamdi sat in the passenger seat without speaking. He didn't have much choice; Thomas was talking enough for them both. Despite the Chevy Suburban's space, Saeed's back was stiff from the long drive. He needed to get out and walk or at least get away from Thomas for a time. He glanced at his companion for the first time since they started the trip. Thomas Duchamp's oily brown hair hung down like rat tails from the black knit cap he wore year-round. His patchy beard whorled around his throat like a smear of dirt under a necklace made of shells and worn beads. Aviator sunglasses, a black hooded sweatshirt, and expensive skinny jeans finished off his Antifa hipster look. As long as someone else continued to pay for his lifestyle, Thomas would go on fighting the one-percenters.

Saeed squirmed in his seat, trying to get comfortable. "We'll stop in Red River for petrol? I believe we're ahead of the weather, and we'll need fuel, right?"

Thomas stared straight ahead and scratched his scalp through the cap. "It's a shitty little town, but I guess we'd better," he replied.

Saeed had learned to ignore Thomas's foul language. It had become like an accent or unique dialect to be accommodated. "Why do you hate it? You have no good memories or loved ones there?" Saeed knew Thomas's father had died and left his only son a small farm near the Canadian border, and that was what mattered.

Thomas snorted at Saeed's question, shaking his head. "It's a good place to be from," he said finally, patting his chest pocket and making an unconscious show of searching for cigarettes he'd run out of miles before.

Saeed pulled a package of Camels from his jacket. "Here," he said, shaking out a cigarette and holding out the pack for Thomas. "I think you will be buying me more of these when we stop."

"Sure," Thomas said, snatching the cigarette from Saeed and slipping it between his lips in one fluid movement. He again patted his chest and pockets until Saeed produced a lighter and tossed it into his lap. "Thanks, SA," Thomas said with a wink. He lit the camel and inhaled, the cigarette glowing red in the gray November light. Exhaling smoke out of his nose, Thomas cracked the window and wondered how his Saudi friend could go so long between smokes, but SA was nothing but cool.

Saeed was aware of his striking differences to the Americans. He kept his appearance very American, wearing ball caps and casual clothing that didn't stand out to avoid Middle East stereotypes. He also shaved every morning, leaving a neatly trimmed mustache. Thomas had called him a preppy once, and though initially offended, Saeed found out its meaning and tolerated Thomas mocking him. Saeed accepted the moniker as evidence of friendship, and he would be a preppy as long as he fit in and didn't draw negative attention.

Thomas took a long drag then waved his cigarette as if to describe the world. "Welcome to Pendleton County, Minnesota -The only place in the state without a fucking lake. Just woods and swamps between here and Canada. And from there, more woods until you hit Hudson Bay.

"There's Winnipeg." Saeed interrupted.

Thomas exhaled smoke from his nose. "Yeah, there's Winnipeg."

"You've been there?" Saeed was fascinated that such a vibrant city could thrive so far north from this place.

"Shit yeah, it's very Canadian." Thomas took another puff and flung the butt out the window. "Let's see. You can get decent chronic up there, and the beer's excellent. Did you know the Canucks always screw doggy style?"

Saeed frowned, not sure what Thomas meant. "Why always doggy style?"

"So they can both watch the hockey game!" Thomas laughed at his little joke, starting a coughing spasm full of phlegm and tobacco.

Saeed shook his head and looked out the passenger window. *There's nothing like a long trip in a small space to try one's patience, virtue, and bladder.* Saeed's father had said that once when they traveled to Riyadh from Jeddah. Saeed was a teenager and beginning a protracted rebellion against his family. He feared his father then, but Saeed feared him more in the years since his death.

There were oceans between them then as now. Saeed's father was both righteous and obedient, traits a younger Saeed detested. Their family was of the House of Saud on his mother's side but with no real stature or influence. On that same trip, traveling back to Jeddah, his father described waiting hours in the receiving line to pay respects to a bloated prince and wealthy entourage. Like others, he clasped hands with the royal for the briefest moment, whispering a shortened request in the most apologetic of manners, then being shuffled aside for the next merchant, or barrister, or minor relative needing a favor.

"But that is how it is done," his father answered when Saeed reproached him about groveling before the royals. "You needn't fill your voice with contempt, Saeed. You are young and don't possess the only truth in this." The rebuke chastened Saeed, and it was all the more effective in its quiet delivery. Saeed didn't look at his father, instead watching the landscape on the long journey back to Jeddah, the sun only a brighter glow in the golden haze above the dull apricot of the desert. "It is easy for you to heap your scorn on me, the father who has been so lenient with such a willful child. But it is you, Saeed, who will learn that pride will only carry one so far. Our circumstances have tempered my pride, and with you soon in university and your mother expecting the happiness I have provided for so long, there are considerations I must take into account, or all will fail." That is what made Saeed fear him most; exposing Saeed's shortcomings without malice, only contrasting his son's weakness with his strengths. Saeed was becoming more like his father, or at least complacent and apathetic, but that would soon change.

Now another long trip, but this land seemed more of a desert than the Rub' al Khali. Perhaps it was the darkness of the cultivated fields or the deadened bristles of brown and gray trees crowded under the steel gray sky. *I'm becoming maudlin*, he thought. *It is just the climate and this insufferable trip. I need to focus on the task ahead.*

Saeed tried to relax, watching the land pass by, dotted with farms both small and large. Cross-like telephone poles along the highway seemed not much different from those in the old western movies he'd seen. Billboards appeared for an insurance agent and a credit union, then the low skyline of Red River Falls appeared, the tallest building, a grain elevator, stood like a tombstone on the landscape. As they neared the outskirts, there was a scattering of houses closer to the highway, and then the businesses consigned to the fringe; used cars for sale under a multi-colored rope of faded pennants fluttering in the wind. A small movie theater with a dirt parking lot showed two new releases, one with a mis-spelled title. A sprawling lumberyard came into view, then an apartment complex in a sea of brown grass next to a senior living complex and a hotel in need of renovations. Finally, the green and white sign posted at the city limits. *Red River Falls Pop. 9,240.*

Soon the buildings crowded nearer to the highway as though begging for attention. A convenience store appeared. Saeed leaned forward in anticipation of stopping, but Thomas accelerated, and Saeed glared at him with an annoyed expression. "Too many people there," Thomas said, a new cigarette bobbing in his mouth, one eye winking from the smoke. "Check that out," he said, gesturing toward a field of tombstones nearby where a small collection of women and men clad in dark clothing milled around an open grave. Saeed saw it was a veteran's funeral with three uniformed men, old men, standing in line with blue jackets and hats with white belts and puttees. Two boys stood nearby, holding flag standards. The aged soldiers raised their ceremonial rifles and released a volley of shots as Thomas and Saeed passed.

Thomas grinned. "Another fascist bites the dust!" He said, rolling down the window. "Enjoy that dirt, motherfucker!" He yelled across the cemetery.

Saeed was alarmed by Thomas's actions. "Don't do that!" *They didn't need any negative attention!* "Why do you say they are fascist?" It bothered him that Thomas acted on impulse and lacked a belief system other than being a radical. Whatever that meant in such a comfortable nation.

"Because he was in the military, SA!" Thomas rolled up the window and took a deep breath as if he'd settled the matter.

Saeed sank back into his seat and crossed his arms, thinking again of his father, the end of life, and what legacy might be left behind.

CHAPTER 9

AURORA

Aurora "Rory" Winter sat in the backseat of Jenny Tieg's car, next to Anna Johnson, while Kelli Swenson rode shotgun in the passenger seat. Rory wasn't sure when she was relegated to the back seat, but it was Jenny's car and Kelli was her new BFF. It wasn't a contest because Kelli was perfect. Her blonde hair was beautifully toned with ivory highlights and auburn lowlights that didn't come from any local salon. Rory listened to Kelli's French manicured nails dancing on her smartphone in a frenzy of texting. Kelli was popular, and that meant she had a killer social network demanding constant feedback. Rory tended to ignore her phone and that meant not fitting in. Her lack of social standing made her a little sad, but the effort to match the whims of her classmates was too exhausting.

Jenny unwrapped a lollipop, pinching it between her fingers and sucking noisily. Rory noticed Jenny's nail polish was chipped. They had painted each other's nails last weekend while binging on Netflix, but Rory knew she wouldn't ever be asked to do them again. Kelli turned her head toward Jenny and stared until Jenny flicked the candy out the window and returned her hands to the wheel. Rory couldn't imagine Kelli binging on anything or doing another girl's nails. Anna chewed her thumb while watching the street over Jenny's shoulder, oblivious to the hierarchy that had developed since Kelli's arrival. It was only a matter of time before Kelli commented on Anna's shock of electric green hair or the red gauges in her earlobes or caustically mentioned she needed to lose weight.

Rory wished she had a car, but she wanted many things these days, mostly to get on with her life. It was her senior year and fall was sliding into winter. Everyone had their college or tech school plans, but not Rory. She looked out the window at the slate clouds and stark trees, their leaves skittering across the ground, rippling like waves in the north wind.

"Rory, wake up." Jenny was looking at her in the rearview mirror.

"What?" Rory leaned forward in her seat and caught the light floral scent of Kelli's hair. *Jesus*, Rory thought, *she still smells like summer!*

"I asked if you wanted to hang with us Saturday. Kelli's parents are down in The Cities and she gets to stay home over Thanksgiving."

Rory shook her head. "No, I can't. I'm going up to our cabin over the holiday."

Kelli pretended not to listen. She looked up from her smartphone but kept her thumbs on the screen. "I'm texting Barry to see what he's doing."

Anna frowned and stopped chewing her finger. "You don't even like Barry."

Kelli rolled her eyes. "True, but his brother will get him beer and weed, so he's invited."

Rory sank back into her seat and resumed looking out the window. They crossed the bridge over the Red River that gave the town its name, the dull brown water flowing below. Comparisons to Kelli Swenson aside, her classmates would describe Rory as tall and pretty in a wholesome way. They might comment on her ice-blue eyes or the golden hair she usually kept in a thick braid, but they might also mention that she didn't stand out. Rory would agree, but given a chance she would rock the shit out of a little black dress.

"I didn't know you had a cabin," Kelli said to everyone, turning her head to make sure they knew she was talking to Rory. "What lake is it on?"

"It isn't on a lake," Rory replied. It's just a hunting shack on some land up north." Kelli had a real cabin on a lake. And a dad who was one of three lawyers in Red River Falls.

"Ew!" Kelli was wrinkling her pert little nose in the front seat. "You don't hunt, do you?"

Rory remembered that Kelli was a vegan, whatever that meant. "Yes," she said, looking at the back of Kelli's beautiful head. "Deer."

"Ew!" Kelli turned to face Jenny, looking for support. "That's shitty! Meat is murder!"

Anna's eyes flickered between Rory and Kelli while she chewed the nail of her pinky finger. Jenny looked at Rory in the mirror again with something between sympathy and shame.

"Murder is the unjust taking of a human life," Rory said to the front seat. "Meat is food." It sounded lame, but sharpening her argument wouldn't phase Kelli Swenson in any way.

"Fucking murder," Kelli continued. "Especially hunting! How can you do that?" She was looking back over her shoulder, trying to catch Rory's reaction.

Anna's eyes flickered toward Rory, a pensive look on her face.

Aurora's throat tightened and she could feel her face turning red. "This is far enough, Jen." Rory pulled her backpack onto her lap and put her hand on the door handle. "I'll walk the rest of the way."

Jenny turned to Rory as if to argue, but she was already pulling over. "You don't have to walk, Rory," she said in a voice that sounded very relieved.

"Yeah, I do." Rory opened the door and started to get out.

"Awkward!" Kelli said absently, looking back down at her smartphone.

Rory looked at Anna and Jenny. They were both waiting for her to get out. Instead, Rory leaned far into the car and, grasping Kelli's perfect blonde head, buried her face in that mane of luxurious hair and stuck her tongue deep into Kelli's ear.

"Ew!" Kelli shrieked, trying to squirm away. "You fucking psycho! What the hell is wrong with you?" Rory held her for a moment longer, then let go and pushed her away. Jenny looked straight ahead as Rory slammed the car door and shouldered her pack. Anna, mouth open wide, stared at her through the rear window as the car pulled away. Rory stoically watched them leave, her eyes welling with tears. When Jenny and her friends were far enough away, she wiped her eyes, zipped up her coat, and began her long walk home.

Rory jammed her hands into her pockets and trudged into the wind, hurt turning into anger. It was so unfair to be verbally ambushed and judged by someone like Kelli Swenson. There was no room for differences -it was all emotion and righteous anger.

Rory felt a bitterness rising in her like a black cloud. Her father died years before and she lived with a mother who had lived in a twilight of depression for what seemed like forever. Now, the only person in her life that she could count on was dying. Axel Winter was more than her grandfather; Axe was her best friend and mentor, always there like a benevolent giant, protecting her and smoothing out the rough spots. Rory feared a future without him and the crushing emptiness it would bring.

Rory realized she was crying again, and the hot tears made her hate the other girls for getting to her. She wiped her face with the back of her hand, pulling herself together. Axe wasn't gone yet, and she wanted to be strong for him. There was so much more significance to this Thanksgiving, and it bothered her that she couldn't make people like Kelli and Jenny understand that her grandfather's last season at camp would be her first, and that was a rite of passage that transcended any high-school bullshit. She did her best to swallow the hurt and anger, switched the pack to her other shoulder, and kept walking.

CHAPTER 10

PHILLIP

Phillip Winter waved goodbye to his neighbor, Paula, as she left the repair shop. Phillip had allowed her to use his Subaru the day before while her vehicle was getting work done and he'd finally dropped her off to blissful silence. He tried to adjust the driver's seat to a comfortable position, but he just couldn't seem to get it back where it was before Paula wedged her bulk into place. She also left a haze of stale perfume behind that would take days to dissipate. Phillip knew Paula as the pleasant woman from the condo next door, but enough was too much.

Paula's jovial face had stared at the side of his head the whole time they were traveling to the dealership, never ceasing her banter. He supposed his good deed made her overly gracious or something, but it had gotten irritating. As they neared their destination, she produced a troll doll keyring with purple hair and a bare butt. The metal jingling along with her prattle put him on edge, but he nodded at appropriate times and listened patiently, unconsciously speeding up to end the torment.

Phillip watched Paula's SUV, a moving carbon footprint, swing onto the frontage road and head south. Phillip left the lot, turning in the opposite direction. He was heading north, out of Minneapolis, to Red River Falls, the town of his birth, then on to the family deer camp on the Joshua River North of Roseau. Phillip detested hunting and loathed guns but agreed with his brother that they should have this one last time with Axel. As far as Phillip was concerned, once Axel was in the ground, it would be the last trip north of the metro. Ever.

Philip never hunted, but his father had dragged him to the Joshua River cabin many times in his youth. Being a middle child was Phillip's cross to bear. Elder brother Brian, the overachiever, football jock, U of

M standout, and ROTC grad while it was still acceptable on campus. Then tours with the Marine Corps in Kuwait and later Iraq and Afghanistan while Phillip protested the Middle East wars, weakly, from his Minneapolis echo chamber.

Brian was dead now and all of that was in the past.

Then there was little brother Kurt, twelve years younger than Brian and six years junior to Philip. After Brian's death, Phillip perceived Kurt became Axel's favorite, probably because he didn't make waves and was a go-getter like Dad. Staying in Red River and marrying a local was another mark in his favor, and Kurt's success wore on Phillip because it was so jejune and yet so natural.

Philip was something else entirely. A widower of many years and father of two grown children, Susan, his daughter, legally changed her name to Ravenfyre two years before and spent most of her time bouncing between hotel cleaning jobs and cosplay. From the pictures she'd shared with him, her characters were always morbidly obese versions of comic book heroines. He could imagine her at a convention, parting the crowd like a Macy's parade balloon run amok, chuffing for air as she stomped to the next symposium, a sweaty cape clinging to her backside.

He tried not to think badly of her, and generally supported her attempts to find her way, but Ravenfyre had issues.

Merrill, his son, was another disappointment. He was an engineer, successful, married to a gorgeous woman, and a goddamned Republican. They didn't have kids and that made it easier for Phillip to remain distant. A Christmas card appeared in the mail every December with a printed recollection of exploits during the year, and that was enough. Merrill lived in Kentucky, of all places, and seemed happy. It made no sense to Phillip, and he shut him out of his mind.

The family line will have to go on without me, he thought, picking up speed as he hit I-94 in Maple Grove. He absently turned on the radio, resigned to the long drive. *"GODDAMMIT, PAULA!"* He swatted at the power button like it was a hornet. *"SEAN HANNITY?"* He calmed down in the silence, glaring at a passing van with a child in the back staring at him with an open mouth. *Seriously, Paula? How could anyone listen to that asshole?* Shaking his head, Philip turned the radio back on and quickly tuned in to Minnesota Public Radio. He sighed and listened to the low drone of the NPR news feed and readjusted his seat again. He vowed never to let anyone drive his car again.

CHAPTER 11

THOMAS AND SAEED

Thomas leaned against the Suburban and let Saeed fill the tank. It was much colder here than in Minneapolis, and Saeed was chilled to the bone despite his Carhart parka. Thomas seemed immune to the cold, no jacket, only his black sweatshirt with a worn screen-print of a young Johnny Cash gripping his guitar in one hand and giving the finger with the other. Saeed didn't know who Johnny Cash was but thought it was childish and antagonistic. Saeed turned his collar up against the freshening wind and looked at his Rolex. They had left the university campus early in the morning and now it was almost noon. The snow would come soon, which was good, but they must be mindful of it and reach the farm before it made things difficult. Saeed clicked the automatic fill lever and stretched, bearing the cold rushing up his back as he lifted his arms. Thomas stared at the gas pump numbers as they clicked past, his mouth closed for once. There weren't any other customers at the pumps, but Saeed noticed the attendant inside watching them.

Saeed knew he should be avoiding the locals as a stranger in town, but Thomas was so unpredictable that when Saeed finished filling the tank, he decided to go inside himself. He had to urinate anyway and wanted something to drink.

"You got it, SA?" Thomas made a half-hearted effort to push away from the truck to follow but then leaned back again and cracked his knuckles as Saeed stepped past the pumps and walked toward the store.

A plain young woman behind the counter stood with her hands at her sides, watching Saeed as he entered. Saeed nodded a greeting and went towards the restrooms. After three years in the states and one in Minnesota, he was accustomed to the reserved responses he encountered.

They were tolerable people, but many behaved like sheep. He went into the lavatory, urinated and washed, but there were no towels. He grunted with irritation and went into the toilet stall, pulling a wad of tissue off the roll and dabbing his hands. He flung the wad at the trash can and missed. *I always seem to miss! Perhaps my depth perception is off. I'm a decent pilot, the flight instructor said so, but maybe the kind of depth perception needed to land a plane is different?* He pulled his sleeve over his hand and opened the door without touching the handle.

He scanned the glass coolers along the back wall and was about to select a quart bottle of water but thought better of it. He didn't want a full bladder on top of Thomas and that unbearable truck. He went to the coffee station and poured a small cup. He paid for the gas and coffee with cash, then, thinking of Thomas, asked for five packs of cigarettes. He almost asked the cashier how far it was to the Canadian border but caught himself. That would be a big mistake.

There were two strange men, and one asked about the border, the attendant would tell the police.

Saeed said nothing more to the woman, paid, and left. The attendant said nothing in return and neither thought anything of it. It was easy to avoid communicating in Minnesota.

"Not far now, SA," Thomas said brightly, ignoring the chiming seatbelt alarm as they left the station and started on the final leg of their journey. "You'll be farting through flannel in a few hours! In the North woods, off the grid, no one to fuck with us. But no one to fuck, unfortunately." When Thomas stopped talking, it was like a horn running out of wind. Saeed was constantly amazed that Thomas related every personal experience to sex and drugs. Saeed was uncomfortable when Thomas overtly described his addictions, but he knew he was not one to point a finger.

Saeed didn't drink often but couldn't seem to stop once he started. That was a scar from the war with his father. Even in the pious state of Saudi Arabia, a rebellious Saeed could break the taboo against alcohol in the private company of young royals. With over 10,000 princes in the kingdom, Saeed knew several at university and was able to fuel his paternal rebellion with sadiqi or bootleg vodka. The drinking blossomed into other vices and had become a real problem once he came to America. That would have to change soon, *but would there be an opportunity to change?* He was part of a plan set in motion over a year before, and second thoughts were dangerous. Maybe it wasn't such a bad thing to be distracted by Thomas and his annoying chatter.

As if to punctuate his dark thoughts, it began to snow.

Saeed handed Thomas one of the cigarette packs, keeping the rest in reserve. Thomas nodded and put it on the dash, then leaned forward and plucked out a joint from under the seat, lighting it and inhaling. Holding his breath, he held it out for Saeed, giving him a wink. Saeed hesitated but took it and pulled deeply. *Just to help get through this,* Saeed rationalized.

"You'll probably hate it, my friend."

Saeed exhaled and looked at Thomas for the second time of the trip. "What will I hate?"

"The cabin…The woods…*Fucking nature, man!* But you won't know that till you're up there shitting in the bush. We'll be all alone with the wolves and bears!" Thomas chuckled until he started coughing again.

Saeed didn't say anything more, but he knew something Thomas didn't. They wouldn't be alone for very long.

CHAPTER 12

THE AXE

Axel kissed his wife goodbye as he always did, whether going to the store, on a long trip, or what would be his final deer hunt. Ellen smiled at him, the laugh lines around her eyes erasing the years and making her the shining jewel he had married so many years before. It was only her photograph, but he needed to say goodbye as he always had.

Axel wasn't one to shy away from words but lately, every conversation, no matter how short, dissolved into a pity party and it had become tiresome. He stopped going to the café for morning coffee with his friends and decided to let them write him off as his illness got worse. A few treated him as usual, with no sympathy or pity, making him feel normal and alive. It was bad enough to have an expiration date handed to you but to wallow in sorrow long before cancer took you was hard to justify.

It was good he was leaving. He tried to put things out of his mind and focus on making the best of things. Ellen was a good woman, and he couldn't have asked for any better. His mind didn't take to nostalgia, and the tempering he went through growing up and in Vietnam made him pretty damn thick-skinned. But it was different when your wife and partner of over 50 years was only a memory, and looking at her photograph caused a queer feeling like seeing heaven through the cracks of your coffin.

He left the house and walked down the lane he had carved out of the woods with his own hands towards the mailbox he'd visited a thousand times. Oak and maple trees he'd planted and nurtured towered over him as he passed, their leaves a patchwork of gold and red. The sky was a bruised slate blue, but it was so vivid and real it made his eyes sting with tears. They say when you are close to death, everything becomes more colorful, more sensual, more everything. They were right.

He hoped Kurt and the kids would be by soon. He had come to realize he dreaded the time he spent alone these days and longed to be with his sons and grandkids. The wind rose in the trees; aspen leaves swirling in the air before they blew across the road and gathered in the woods. He arrived at the mailbox and set down his gear and gun case.

Axel could smell the coming snow, like the smell of rain but with the crisp finish of winter. The clouds grew darker and the sun would be just a memory until the snow had passed. The damp air penetrated his jacket and heavy wool shirt and made him shiver. He began to think he'd made the trek to the mailbox too soon. Kurt was punctual and Axel wondered why his son was late but caught himself. The boy had a million problems, and his old man wasn't one of them. Not yet, anyway. Besides, they hadn't set a time, and Kurt had to wrangle Jordan and Aurora, which was not an easy task. He smiled at the thought of his grandchildren. They made him proud, and he wished Ellen could see them now.

He was played out by the funeral and getting ready for the hunt. Now even walking to the end of the goddamned lane was getting harder. He leaned against the mailbox and packed his pipe, searching the gravel road winding toward town, looking for Kurt's truck. The sun broke through the clouds for a moment, shining across the land, bringing the fall colors to life and a memory of summer, but there was no warmth in it, and the air had the bitter chill of winter. He shivered and buttoned up his battered field coat. He lit his pipe, drawing in the hot cherry tobacco, and felt a bit better. The blue and gold patch of sun and sky closed and the world was gray again. He took a long pull off his pipe and exhaled slowly.

To Axel, it didn't matter. It was still his sky and his air to breathe. It would do.

CHAPTER 13

RORY

"Aurora, you're home already?"

Brie Winter, Rory's mother, came out of the living room's shadows where the TV flickered with the volume too high. Her lined face and pale complexion looked like a mask in the weak sunlight coming through the curtained windows.

"Yeah, we got out early, remember? It's Thanksgiving tomorrow." Rory hung her backpack on a kitchen chair and shrugged off her coat. Rory noticed the half-empty wine glass on the counter, red lipstick on the rim. She went to the kitchen sink and opened the cabinet below, seeing a freshly emptied bottle of chardonnay lying on top of a full wastebasket. Rory pulled back the curtains and took down a small plant from the window sill to water it under the faucet.

"I didn't hear Jenny's car drive up." Her mother rubbed her eyes and Rory noticed she was in the same too-tight sweat pants she'd been wearing since Sunday. Rory knew her mother wouldn't have heard Jenny's car if it had crashed into the house, but she said nothing. She brushed past her mother and went to the basement door to go down to her room. "Remember, I'm going up hunting with Grandpa Axe over Thanksgiving."

Her mother dropped her hand from her face and looked at Rory for a moment, then nodded, took the wine glass from the counter, and went back into the living room.

Rory clicked on the light and went downstairs. Her bedroom was a corner of the basement nearest the furnace. She kept the basement as comfortable as she could and left the upstairs to her mother. Rory knew she should engage her mother about her drinking but lacked the energy to try again. She pulled a duffel bag from under her bed and started to pack for the long weekend. Her hunting coat and outdoor gear were already in a plastic tote box in the garage. Collecting her things from the bathroom, she caught her reflection in the mirror. Her mother's face seemed to be looking back. Rory peered at herself for a moment, almost expecting the image to say something. She brushed her brown hair behind her ears and leaned into the mirror, staring into her ice-blue eyes. "*Are you a psycho? What the fuck IS wrong with you?*"

The reflection stared back and said nothing.

She looked as deeply as she could, staring into pupils wide and dark. "How would we know?" No reply. Both of them blinked, and she almost smiled.

Rory finished packing, and the last thing she did was go to the back area of the basement, near the drawing table and artist's easel she hadn't used in a while, and found her shotgun leaning in the corner. She got the soft gun case from a shelf above the washer machine, then sat down on the bed and looked at the shotgun in the yellow light of the naked bulbs hanging from the ceiling. It was a Remington 870, 12 gauge from Grandpa Axe, but it was her father's before that. It kicked hard, but she was proud that she could handle it and didn't suck at shooting. She could hit a grouse if it wasn't flying too crazy, and she'd done okay with clay pigeons, although you needed something more sophisticated for serious trap shooting. Someday maybe, but she was saving for other things.

She pressed the release, pulled back the foregrip to make sure the chamber was unloaded, then slipped it into the case. She laid it on the bed and knelt to get a wooden ammo box from beneath, another prize from her father via Grandpa Axe. She opened it and took out the rifled slug rounds. Only six were left from earlier in the fall when Grandpa had made her shoot a paper target in a gravel pit south of town. It wasn't hard to hit the target, but like Axe, she was thorough and had focused on his directions and corrected her technique until they both realized she had nailed the center of the bullseye four times in a row, two shots in the same hole. She asked him if she would need more shells for hunting and he looked at her with a frown. "Aurora," he said in his deep voice, rough with age and tobacco, "you're gonna kill your deer with one shot. No need for more."

She shut off the lights and propped her bed pillows against the head-board, and laid down next to the shotgun in the dim light from the small basement windows. Above her were concert bills for *The Dandy Warhols* and *The Black Keys*. On the wall to her left were Beyoncé and Taylor Swift posters and a framed photo of her father. She had mentally trained herself not to dwell on the picture of her father in his dress blue uniform and guileless stare caught by the Marine Corps camera. His eyes were a dark threshold leading to a feeling of sadness and loss. She was mature enough to know Brian Winter wasn't a saint, but she could never shake the feeling that things would have been a whole lot better if he had lived.

Under Beyoncé and Taylor, she had put up some minor school awards and a matrix of photos she'd taken on a trip to Disney World she'd earned in Girl Scouts. It was the only trip she had ever taken out of the state since moving back from Maine, but it reminded her there was a big world beyond Red River.

She pulled her phone out of her jean pocket and swiped it open, the screen lighting her face with a soft blue glow. A text from her cousin Jordan said they were on their way and would be there soon. She checked her Facebook page and tried to watch a cat video someone had posted, but it didn't hold her interest. She went back to the main screen and saw a text from Jenny. She felt as though a door was slowly closing in her life, and she was being ushered forward in an unknown direction. She didn't have a plan and it bothered her that she didn't care enough to make one. She deleted Jenny's message without reading it and went upstairs with her bag and shotgun to wait for the others.

CHAPTER 14

KURT AND JORDAN

Kurt Winter tried to decompress enough to calm down and focus on the trip to the camp. Stroking his blonde and gray beard, Kurt sighed. He'd been dealing with bad clients, bad employees, and horseshit sales all year, and it was time for a vacation. He backed out of the driveway and his wife, Jennifer, waved goodbye to both him and his son, Jordan.

"Are you ready for your first deer hunt?" Kurt glanced at his son and smiled. "This is a big deal, Spud." He ruffled Jordan's brown hair and patted the boy's shoulder.

"I know," Jordan replied. "I get to go to deer camp and stay up there with you guys!"

Jordan had been to camp many times but never during deer season. That was reserved for men, and that usually meant the magic age of thirteen. He knew his dad was bending the rules, letting him come up a year early, but Grandpa Axe was sick, and this was a time for everyone to see him off. Besides, his cousin Aurora was coming too. It was a little weird to be up there with a girl, but she was Grandpa's favorite, and Jordan didn't mind. He liked her and was glad to have another newbie at camp so he didn't get ragged on as much.

Kurt was glad that Jordan would be able to share camp with his grandfather. It wouldn't be the same without Axel, and he knew next season would be tough without his father. They will have a long weekend with the holiday, and it was going to be quite an adventure for his son. Kurt knew he shouldn't be leaving on the busiest shopping weekend of the year, but this hunt was the last he would spend with his father.

Thanksgiving weekend was great for some people. You gorged on food, watched football if you weren't napping, and enjoyed the first goodwill of the holidays. If you were in retail, you just thought of Black Friday and the shit you would endure to break even. That's if you were a decent businessman and moved some product. He had started a general store back in the '80s, and later it evolved into a hodgepodge of hardware, paint, power equipment, and appliances. He didn't like the winter, but he liked to sell shovels and snow blowers.

Thanksgiving Day for Kurt usually meant sitting through the awkward time between peeling potatoes and clasping hands for the blessing, enduring the quiet discomfort of in-laws who never drank and a wife who became their baby daughter all over again. Kurt would smile through dinner while they pissed and moaned about soybean prices and how the cornfield north of the home place flooded in the spring. He wanted to stand up and let his in-laws know he didn't give a damn about their problems. The north field flooded every other year and if you can't appreciate farming life, quit and get a job punching a time clock with a real boss!

But Kurt always held back because he loved his wife, and her parents were good folk who worked hard, and if they whined, they weren't the only farmers who did. Besides, the hypertensive diabetic shaking salt on his third helping of mashed potatoes was a decent man and the grandfather of his son.

While Jennifer prayed for health and happiness during the blessing, Kurt always gave thanks that the in-laws would be heading south to their double-wide in Scottsdale for the winter. He wouldn't have to listen to their country Christmas music and watch them slurp virgin egg nog and stare into space like dead fish.

"There's Rory," Jordan said, looking up the street where his sister-in-law Brie lived with his niece. Brian had died over six years ago and his wife and Rory moved back soon after.

Brian was part of the military SERE program at Kittery, Maine, wherever that was. Kurt knew it was Survival Escape, and…He couldn't remember the rest of the acronym. Kurt just knew Brian was a survival expert and had a small home off-base with Brie. One day, he returned from a week-long course and found her in bed with her boss, an attorney in nearby Portsmouth. Brie told Kurt the whole story one night a few weeks after the funeral when she had settled back into her folk's place in Red River. Brie was sloppy drunk, and Kurt was hungry for the story of how his big brother died.

"He didn't say anything," Brie told him. "My boss got off me, and I pulled the sheets over my face like I was a little girl. I waited for Brian to explode, but all I could hear was my boss pleading with Brian while he got his shit and left. I was shaking under the sheets, waiting for Brian to rip them away and then tear my head off, but nothing happened. I cried and shouted at him to say something but there was nothing. I finally pulled the sheet off my head, but he wasn't there. The house was totally quiet. That was the worst part of the whole thing."

Kurt was fascinated yet repulsed. This woman had done about everything she could to trigger him, but Brian kept it together. Until he had turned inward that night, and whatever ran through his mind caught up with him, and he was gone.

Brie told him what happened after that, but her version held no more insight than anyone else's. Brian had left the house and drove into memory. He died in an accident, swerving across the median, missing a car with two shocked high school kids catching on the shoulder and flipping the vehicle into the air. Brian was half out of the driver's side window and folded under the rolling vehicle, snapping his neck. Other than Brian not wearing a seatbelt, it was never determined to be a suicide, and it became just another car accident, and it didn't go deeper than that.

Kurt didn't know his big brother very well. There wasn't much of a connection, Brian being the eldest and twelve years his senior. Kurt distantly loved him, but lately, it was getting hard to keep the real memories apart from the daydreams of what might have been. He sometimes felt guilty growing up when he thought of Brian and Brie and how he should have helped somehow. His wife, always pragmatic just to the point of coldness, made it clear he was too young at the time and should just quit stewing about it.

"Your memories of Brian are no more clear or real than Brie's or Rory's or mine, and I never even met the guy."

He resented her viewpoint at first, but gradually he came to understand. We focus on what might be instead of truth because that's what gets us through a bad day, being screwed over, or maybe even a shitty marriage.

"I wonder if the whacko will come out," Jordan said, bringing Kurt back to the moment.

"That's Aunt Brie to you, Jordy," Kurt said automatically. Jordan looked at him with some surprise but said nothing.

Kurt was ashamed that he was hoping Brie didn't make an appearance. He tried to be a good person and not think badly of her, but he couldn't bring himself to seek her out and draw her deeper into their lives. They pulled into the driveway in front of Rory, sitting on her duffel bag. "Aurora has her act together, as usual," Kurt remarked.

"Whatever," Jordan scoffed, "I had to get ready earlier than her." Jordan opened the truck door and jumped out, slamming it behind him.

Kurt got out and stood by the truck. "Jordan, go help Aurora load her gear." He watched the window curtains for any sign that Brie might come out for a rare appearance. He smiled at Aurora, and she gave him a quick wave.

Jordan walked up the short driveway, watching his cousin sling her gun case over her shoulder and pick up what looked to be a heavy duffel bag. "*What up, Beeyatch?*"

Rory grabbed the back of Jordan's collar and pulled him close. "Listen, taint stain," she hissed in his ear. "If you think you're going to troll me all weekend, I'll dick punch you out of puberty!"

"Holy shit," Jordy said, stepping back in surprise. "That was *fucking savage!*"

"Jordan!" Kurt bellowed, "On what planet do you think you can use that kind of language?"

Rory smirked as Jordy's face turned red. "Sorry, Dad," he muttered, knowing he would pay for that later.

"Get Aurora's gear and let's get rolling. Grandpa's waiting, and the snow's coming!"

Jordan picked up the plastic tote with effort and barely made it back to the pickup without dropping it.

Kurt glanced at the big living room window and saw the curtains move a bit. Brie was still alive. He shook his head and thanked God that at least his niece was a keeper.

CHAPTER 15

THE JOURNEY NORTH

"I call shotgun!" Jordan jumped into the front seat of Kurt's pickup and quickly put on his seatbelt to ensure he wasn't stuck in the back seat. Rory ignored his taunt and climbed into the truck to sit behind her uncle.

"Okay," Kurt said, backing out of the driveway. "Next stop, Grandpa's place!"

Jordan slapped his thighs with excitement. "Then we get to go hunting! I still wish we could hunt bucks instead of just getting a stupid doe."

Kurt glanced over at his son. "Jordan, we've been over this. Every deer is a trophy and a gift. You've got plenty of years ahead to shoot big bucks. A few females under your belt won't hurt. Besides, this hunt is about your grandpa getting up to camp since he missed the regular season. I told you why it's doe deer only, right?"

"Because the herd is out of balance and more does need to be harvested so they don't exceed their sustainable habitat," Jordan said. "That's why we can't shoot any bucks this year."

"Wow," Rory said, genuinely impressed. "You sound like a wildlife manager!"

"No, Dad just keeps harping about it when I talk about shooting a big buck." Jordan looked out the side window. "It's hard to get a set of antlers when you can only shoot females."

"Well," Kurt answered, "I suppose a huge buck could attack, and you could kill it in self-defense."

"Really?" Jordan looked at Kurt with renewed hope.

"Not a chance in hell," Kurt replied. "You'll shoot a doe and like it."

Aurora tried not to laugh at her cousin. "I'll let you shoot my deer, Jordan."

"Really?"

"Not a chance in hell," Aurora said flatly. She and Kurt burst out laughing, and she reached forward and tickled Jordan until he started laughing too.

They didn't talk much as they crossed through town, over the river bridge, and past the city limits to the home place. Kurt had good memories growing up in their old house on the river. There was always something going on, and it wasn't so far out of town that he couldn't bike in to meet up with his friends and get into trouble. Red River was changing, and like every other small town in America, Kurt wasn't sure what would be left for the next generation. Jordan would probably strike out on his own after graduating, and unlike his old man, he would not be staying to work in some little hardware store. It would be nice to pass the business on and watch Jordan take it to the next level, but Kurt wasn't about to set any expectations. Too many parents had their children's academic and career trajectory planned while they're still in the womb. Jordan could find his own way.

Kurt watched the aspen trees quaking, their golden leaves beginning to disappear. November had been kind this year, but winter would be here tonight, and if the forecast was accurate, they wouldn't see bare ground again until spring. He sighed and hoped they had enough savings this year to go on a real vacation. He'd been promising Jordan they would go to Florida one of these winters, but usually, they just went to some hotel with a water park and let him splash around while he and Jennifer watched from a patio table next to the pool, resentful that this was as good as it gets.

Kurt made a right turn onto a gravel road and started up a low hill. The home place was just over the rise, and he hoped his dad was still feeling up to this. Between the kids and Marty and brother Phillip, it was going to be lively up there. He supposed Axel would rather deal with their antics than sit around eating turkey and making conversation, knowing he'd missed his chance at one last hunt on the Joshua.

Kurt's truck crested the small hill and saw that Axel was already at the mailbox, smoking his pipe, his gear neatly stacked at his feet.

"Hey!" Jordan sat up in his seat. "Grandpa's already at the mailbox!"

Aurora smiled. Her grandfather was wearing the red plaid jacket and red wool cap he did every winter.

Kurt pulled over next to Axel and put the truck into park. "Jordan, go help your grandpa get loaded. You can let him sit up front." Jordan frowned but undid his seatbelt and hopped out of the truck. Axel tousled his grandson's hair and opened the back door of the pickup. "How's my Rory?" Axel asked, smiling as he placed his gun case next to hers under the seat.

"I'm good, Grandpa. How are you doing?"

"Still kicking." Axel winked at Aurora and went back to help Jordan carry his gear to the back of the truck. He returned in a moment and opened the rear door.

"Dad," Kurt said, "you can sit in the front. The kids can be in the back."

"Nope," Axel replied, climbing in next to Aurora. "I'm sitting next to my smokin' hot granddaughter." He gave Aurora a brief hug and settled in, closing the door.

"Sweet!" Jordan couldn't believe his luck. He got back into the truck and sat proudly next to his father. "Let's go hunting!" Jordan said, clicking his seatbelt on for the trip to Joshua Camp.

"You heard the man, Kurt!" Axel said, squeezing Jordan's shoulder. "Let's go hunting!"

The snow was starting to fall, filling the air and casting a white shroud over the landscape. Visibility dropped and Kurt made sure his headlights were on. They had about two hours to go and he hoped Phil and Marty left home soon enough to reach camp before dark. "Winter is here," Axel said absently, wishing he could light his pipe. Kurt would skin anyone that dared to smoke in his vehicle. "I can't say I'm looking forward to six months of this stuff."

Kurt sighed at the realization that spring would be here just in time for them to bury his father. He cleared his throat. "Let's just hope the deer are moving in the morning. This storm could be a blessing or a curse."

"They'll be moving," Axel said with authority. "Besides, I'm sure the Swede will come to plow us out sometime over the weekend."

"Who's *The Swede?*" Jordan asked.

"Owen Swenson," Kurt replied. "He's our only year-round neighbor up there."

"I'm in no hurry to get back anyway," Aurora said, crossing her arms and leaning her head back.

"Me neither," Jordan added. "I wouldn't mind living at the hunting shack all year long."

"Ha!" Kurt slugged Jordan on the arm. "No texting? No Facebook or TV? I'd like to see that!"

"I could do it," Jordan said, his voice trailing off.

"We wouldn't want to, Jordan." Rory said, "It wouldn't be special anymore. It would just be a place you lived."

"Well, said Aurora," Axel replied. "Special things are just that. Most folks don't appreciate the good in life unless they've experienced the worst. Jordan, this will become your special place, and when you get older, you'll treasure it even more." Kurt slowed the truck as they came to the highway crossroads just out of town. A single traffic light hung above the intersection, swinging in the rising wind.

"Last call for a pee break! Anyone need anything in town before we head north?" No one replied, and Kurt turned onto the highway that would take them to Joshua Camp.

"So your big brother's coming up?" Axel knew Kurt and Phillip were about as opposite as they could be. Kurt didn't reply, so Axel continued. "Martin will be up too, right? What the hell is he doing these days?"

Kurt kept his eyes on the road, raising his voice to be heard in the backseat. "Still selling real estate in Detroit Lakes, I guess. He's still married to my sister-in-law and still goofy as hell."

"That's for damn sure," Axel snorted. "He's nuttier than squirrel shit." Jordan and Aurora snickered at that one but tried not to be too apparent that they were listening to every word.

Kurt shrugged. "He's a good guy. He just needs to let his brain catch up to his mouth once in a while."

"I haven't seen Phillip for a long time," Axel said, changing the subject. "When was the last time he was home?"

"Mom's funeral," Kurt said, quickly adding, "When was the last time he was up at camp?"

Axel thought about it for a moment. "Hell, I guess he was still in his teens. You were probably still in kindergarten." Jordan laughed, quickly slapping his hand over his mouth. He was on thin ice after dropping the F word earlier.

Kurt had never been at camp with Phillip. He'd started when he was Jordan's age, hunting with his father and brother Brian. Phillip wanted nothing to do with hunting, and Kurt was still surprised that Phillip even responded to his email, let alone called him back to say he would come up for Axel's last hunt. Marty even bet him Phillip would be a no-show. They'd know soon enough.

"Well, it's good that he's making the trip," Kurt said. "He's bringing the groceries for the weekend, including turkey and fixings for Thanksgiving dinner tomorrow."

"He always had a flair for cooking," Axel said.

And eating. Kurt thought to himself. Their conversation dwindled as the miles passed, and in time Kurt was alone with his thoughts. *Joshua Camp wasn't the end of the world, but you could see it from there.* His father was right. As he got older, he appreciated the wild places disconnected from anything that could change them. There were hundreds of deer camps nestled in the north woods from Minnesota to Maine. Every November, work was postponed, school let out, and vacations revolved around deer season. Joshua Camp was no exception and Kurt felt pride that Jordan was old enough to join in their tradition.

He tried not to think about Phillip. He was a moody bastard, and you never knew which Phillip would show up that day. He hoped he and his brother could set aside their baggage long enough to enjoy the weekend. Marty was a wild card, and it might be a damn tinder box with him up there with Phillip. *Just add alcohol for instant assholes.* Axel and Kurt had welcomed Marty to camp the season after Brian died. Marty knew there was an unspoken probation period, and he wasn't always an asset, but despite his douche moves, he did all right. Axel never said anything good or bad, but that was enough to keep Marty around.

Kurt willed himself to relax and enjoy the moment. He was never one to compartmentalize his thoughts, and it was damn hard to put aside so many pressing things and live in the moment. He looked forward to, cherished, deer camp every year. He honestly felt sorry for any American who wasn't grounded with a wild retreat that reaffirmed their roots. A golf weekend or Vegas trip just didn't cut it. It wasn't about the boozing or card games or just getting away from the rolling pin. It was a time to recharge your batteries. Once you got sick of shitting outdoors or freezing on a deer stand, you knew you were ready to go back. How long that took each year, depending on what was waiting at home. He watched the fields and woods pass by and felt the stress leave him with each mile and he would do his best to make this a good weekend.

Chapter 16

Marty

The wind across the prairie was forming finger drifts jutting out from the snow in the ditch, and when Marty Johnson hit them at driving speed, the pickup shuddered and jerked to the right. The last one damn near pulled the wheel out of his hands, so he reluctantly slowed down and switched over to four-wheel drive. Half an hour later, he pulled into the Outpost Bar on the western edge of the town of Roseau. It was the same old log siding with dark-tinted windows glowing with neon beer signs. The wind was steady out of the northwest when Marty parked, the truck rocking with each gust of wind. Maybe it would be best to head directly to camp. *I could get stuck here all night*, he thought. *Axe and Kurt will be on my ass if I'm not at deer camp by supper.*

"Screw it," he said aloud to himself. "One or two won't hurt. " He shut off the engine and jumped out before he changed his mind.

He couldn't believe there were this many cars in the lot. A jukebox pounded from inside, and Marty pulled his head low into his parka, squinting against a nasty gust of snow. He pulled open the door to the bar with effort and went in, the wind slamming it behind him. The entire bar stared at the newcomer, and Marty gave an embarrassed smile and stomped the snow off his boots. He shivered as the stuffy air of the bar washed over him. About thirty people were milling about, sitting in booths and at the bar. Four guys in worn Carhart bibs and grimy orange safety vests were playing pool on the far end, the balls clacking over their dull murmuring.

He shrugged off his coat and took a corner stool, listening to jukebox country while waiting for the bartender to make it back to his end. He looked above the window line and surveyed the deer heads, decoys, and a lonely moose head hanging from fresh pine half-log walls. There were multiple TVs and a gas fireplace surrounded by fake fieldstone. A mounted bobcat perched on a shelf with its mouth open and teeth bared. Marty couldn't tell if it was supposed to be fierce or just yawning.

"What can I get ya?" The bartender had a round, friendly face and was about as local as they came.

Marty hadn't thought about it, but he quickly looked at the tap handles and ordered some local microbrew. He gulped about half the glass and felt the familiar warmth in his belly, radiating to his head and making him feel calm and sharp at the same time. He swiveled on the stool and did a visual tour of the place. Mostly college types, home on Thanksgiving break catching up with the local kids who stayed to fight it out. There was a nest of lovelies in the corner with a blonde beauty with huge tits and big brown eyes. He lingered on her face a bit too long and she busted him, giving him a look that shut down any fantasies he might have had. He felt his face redden and turned to face the bar again. He caught his reflection in the mirror behind the bottles of liquor. His short stature didn't allow much to show above the bar, and his elbows jutted out like a child sitting at the family table. His hair was receding, and his face was slack with a shadow of beard matching his dark eyebrows. His eyeglasses were out of date, and he took them off and set them next to his drink. It didn't help. Marty looked away, uncomfortable with what he was becoming.

A handwritten sign behind the bar with a color copy picture of a Polaris ATV and *"WIN ME"* in bold blue letters, *Raffle courtesy of the Roseau Fire Department.* The bartender was close again, so he waved him over. "What's with the raffle?"

"Ten bucks gets you a ticket for the 4-wheeler or $30 for four tries. Money goes to the Fire Truck Fund. How many do you want?" The bartender was reaching for the ticket book.

"Like I have a hope in hell of winning," Marty snorted. "I'm from out of town. The second you see my tail lights, my ticket's in the shitter."

"Nah," the bartender replied with mock offense. "We wouldn't do that."

"I'll think about it. In the meantime, shoot me another one." Marty glanced at the TV above the bar, too embarrassed to check out the college girls again. There was a basketball game on, but Marty didn't follow the sport. He read the crawl of words across the bottom of the screen blaring winter storm warning—another reminder to get back on the road.

"You need another?" The bartender was already clearing his glass and moving toward the tap.

"Wait, hold up," Marty said, scanning their selection of whiskey behind the bar. "Give me a Windsor water on the rocks."

Whiskey in hand, knowing he wasn't leaving for a while, Marty spun around and looked back at the girls in the corner booth. The blond priestess eyed him again, but this time he held her gaze and she looked away, putting her hand to the side of her face. The other girls at the table weren't half bad, but she was still the best choice. The bar had an ebb and flow of sound that allowed snippets of conversation to be heard clearly above the clink of glass and the deep bass of country music thumping in a steady beat. He tuned in to some of the talk filling the air.

"If it has tits or wheels, you're gonna have problems..."

"I guarantee the fucker won't do that again..."

"I didn't know whether to shit or go blind..."

"Hey," Marty's speech was just a bit slurred as he spun on the stool and motioned to the bartender.

"What can I do you for?" The bartender was always impressed by how much booze the runty guys could put away.

"One more." Marty tinkled the ice in his glass and pushed it across the bar.

"Windsor water," the bartender replied. "You ready to buy a raffle ticket yet?"

Marty smiled and shook his head. "I'm telling you, man, I'm from out of town and you're just going to tear it up the minute I leave."

"That's illegal." This from a stocky young guy with a thick beard and a greasy Cenex cap. He was sitting next to Marty but Marty hadn't noticed the kid until now. "They got to honor it. If you buy a ticket, they gotta enter you no matter where you're from."

"See? This kid don't lie." The bartender was pouring another deep glass with Windsor. "One for ten bucks, four for thirty. You gotta try, man, and it's for a good cause."

Marty sighed and squinted at the sign behind the bar. "Tell me again who's giving this thing away?"

"Roseau Fire and Rescue," the big kid said hopefully. "We're trying to get a four-wheel-drive pump truck we can take out in weather like this."

Marty gave him a skeptical look. "Okay, but only one. I won't win anyway." Marty took the blank ticket and a pen from the bartender and started to fill out the stub.

"It's a sweet machine," the big kid was looking at him and smiling. "I'm on the volunteer squad and a first responder."

Marty was nearly drunk now and wasn't interested in hearing about Cenex cap's civic contribution. "Good for you." He said it with more sarcasm than he intended but continued to fill out the entry ticket in silence, letting the kid hang out there.

He sensed the kid looking at the bartender, wondering what he'd done to deserve that, but Marty shrugged it off. The bartender took Marty's ten, gave him the ticket as a receipt, dropped the stub into a goldfish bowl next to the cash register, and then turned to watch the basketball game.

Marty sipped a bit more, regretting his rudeness. A joke would make amends. "Hey, how do you make three pounds of fat look pretty?"

The bartender looked back over his shoulder. "Don't know."

"Put a nipple on it!" Marty slapped the bar and cackled, a few turning to see what was so funny.

Cenex cap next to him smirked into his beer, but Marty didn't notice no one was laughing at the joke.

Marty looked down and saw he was empty again. "One more, please."

The bartender turned to face him and cleared his glass. He gave him the old once-over but made the trip to the bottle rack.

Marty swallowed his last whiskey without talking, holding the glass tilted to his lips for longer than he had to. It was an old habit, drawing it out and stalling his trip home to reality. The Leinenkugel beer clock over the door said it was almost five and Marty knew he'd cause a stir if he didn't make it the rest of the way to camp.

"Better roll…" He carefully slid off the stool. His legs and feet felt like he hadn't walked for a very long time. He left what he thought was a generous tip and turned to go, struggling with his coat. "See ya!" He gave a sloppy wave and tried to keep it together long enough to walk to the door without looking too shitfaced.

"Thanks and drive careful." The bartender had his hands on his hips while Marty pulled on the door handle before realizing he had to push. Marty stumbled out into the wind, and the door again slammed behind him. Wiping up the water ring left by Marty's glass, the bartender paused for a moment, watching the door. Cenex cap looked at him curiously as he turned, slung the bar towel over his shoulder, and dug into the goldfish bowl.

"What are you doing?" The kid asked.

"Finding his ticket stub." The bartender pulled out Marty's entry and held it up for the kid to see.

Cenex cap frowned. "What're you going to do with it?"

"I'm tossing it."

"But you told him it was a fair drawing…I said we couldn't do that."

The bartender dropped Marty's entry into the trash, picked up the remote control, and began flipping through TV channels. "Fuck him. He's from out of town."

Chapter 17

Winnipeg

When they rendezvoused at Winnipeg International Airport, the plan was for Ahmed to meet Halil in a remote section of the long-term parking lot where they could abandon the Honda and al-Qadhi's corpse. There was no better place for a vehicle to remain undisturbed for an extended period than airport parking.

Waleed and the two others arrived first and parked near the entrance to the service hangar areas, waiting in a black Toyota SUV, snow already building on the windshield. Waleed didn't want to be in this situation, and Nadeem was openly frightened at this turn of events. They both wondered how it came to be that a plan to cross into America should require killing one of their own. Then there was this Ghazi kid sitting in the backseat, dumped on them the night before by Halil. He gave them a stern warning to keep an eye on the boy until they met the next day. Waleed protested, but Halil ignored him and walked out the door to his white Jeep idling in the driveway.

"When is Halil coming?" Nadeem asked, looking through the back window of the Toyota.

"When he gets here," Waleed replied, turning on the wipers to keep the windshield clear.

"I understand that we need to keep our journey a secret, but what good is it if they've killed Imam al-Qadhi?" Nadeem continued, obviously upset. "It's the Americans with their Hollywood and fucking attitudes I would want to kill!" Nadeem's heart was beating faster, and he took one last cigarette, crumpled the pack, and rolled down the window to throw it out.

Halil suddenly loomed next to the SUV and grabbed Nadeem's arm. "Don't drop that here," Halil said, meeting Nadeem's eyes for a lingering moment to make his point. "Stay put until you see Ahmed and I leave, then follow us out. But not too close." Halil returned to his Jeep, leaving the others shaken.

"How the hell did he sneak up on us like that?" Nadeem muttered to the others. "Halil's a fucking devil!" He put the cigarette between his lips and lit it, closing his eyes and leaning back in the seat. "I don't like this." He didn't say that he wished he'd never gotten involved with this scheme.

"I don't give a damn if you like it," Waleed said to Nadeem, looking back to make sure Ghazi was listening. "This trip is more important than all of us, even the two brothers or that asshole Halil. Nothing has changed. We're going to meet soon and leave all of this behind. We need to look ahead and not go to pieces."

Nadeem opened his eyes and glared at Waleed. "I'm fine. You don't need to lecture me."

Waleed said nothing more as he stared past the windshield into the dark afternoon.

Ghazi watched the two men from the back seat. Nadeem had short-cropped hair under a faded ball cap. His beard was full and dark and reached down to his chest. His green plaid jacket smelled like diesel fuel and cigarettes. Waleed didn't have a full beard, but his chin was dark with stubble below a thick mustache. His eyebrows met in the middle of his forehead and gave him a menacing look. He was wearing a red warm-up jacket, and Ghazi thought perhaps he was an athlete at one time. "There are Ahmed and Muhammet," Ghazi said as the Honda Pilot passed them and went into the lot where Halil waited. They all thought of Imam al-Qadhi's body resting in the rear of Ahmed's SUV.

Ahmed and Mohammet turned into the parking area and passed Waleed and the others in the black SUV. In a moment, they spied Halil, his Jeep sitting across the lot, the wipers making arcs across the windshield in the new snow. Ahmed pulled even with the Jeep and turned off the ignition. Halil nodded in greeting, his cigarette glowing red in the darkness.

Mohammet leaned toward Ahmed as he reached into the backseat to retrieve his overnight case. Ahmed quickly seized Mohammet and thrust a steel shiv deep into the back of his brother's skull, grinding it in a circle, severing the spinal cord, killing him instantly. Mohammet convulsed for a moment, then his body relaxed.

Ahmed's eyes welled with tears as he withdrew the spike and pulled Mohammet's face to his, and kissed him for the last time. "Goodbye, my brother. Go with God, my beloved Muhammet."

Ahmed was grateful he didn't look into his brother's eyes and see the confusion and sadness of betrayal. To Ahmed, it was almost crueler to deny Mohammet the fulfillment of his work, but they could not afford Mohammet's weakness at this stage in their plan.

Halil watched from the other car as Ahmed pulled Mohammet close and rocked him in his arms. Halil held his breath, stunned at what he saw until the cigarette burned down to his knuckles. He stubbed it out in the ashtray and rubbed his fingers.

Ahmed gently lowered his brother's body back onto the seat and got out of the car. Standing outside, he leaned in and arranged the body to lay across the front seat. He gently placed Mohammet's delicate hands in repose, one atop the other, and covered him with a blanket from the back seat. Ahmed backed out of the tomb created for his brother and Imam Al Quadi and closed the door softly until it locked with a dull click. In the darkness, the blanket would cover Mohammet's body enough to pass casual inspection, and no one would notice the dark streak of blood left in an arc across the passenger seat. The snow would soon coat the windows, and it could be weeks before the frozen bodies were discovered.

Halil looked straight ahead as Ahmed slid into the passenger seat. Halil put the Jeep in gear, and as they left the parking lot, he felt he had to say something. "I am sorry that this happened, but I don't...."

Ahmed cut him off with surprising venom, tears streaming down his cheeks. "I do not want to hear your comments! Don't mourn him or pity me! Just be as Mohammet and die as a Martyr with no sin and no regret! Thank him for his sacrifice and know that he has given all Islam a hammer to strike the Americans in their homeland!"

Halil said nothing more, but his friend was dead at the hands of his own brother. Halil should demand an explanation, but Mohammet's illness had to be the reason. Ahmed's ruthlessness shocked him almost as much as Mohammet's death. He would grieve for his old friend in the coming hours, but this brutal side of Ahmed was troubling. *I wonder if our ties are strong enough for both of us to survive the next few days?*

Waleed and Nadeem sat silently in the front seat of the SUV, feeling uneasy as they watched Ahmed leave the Honda behind and get into the Jeep with Halil. Ghazi leaned forward and voiced what they had all been thinking. "Where is Mohammet? I thought he was coming with us?" Ghazi wasn't close to any of the men in this group, but Mohammet had been kind and his absence was troubling.

"I don't know," Waleed snapped at Ghazi. "We'll find out soon enough." His bluster aside, Waleed began to share Nadeem's reservations. *If Mohammet wasn't making the crossing, what did that mean for the rest of us?* He shifted the SUV into gear and turned on the headlights, following Ahmed and Halil at a distance as they left the airport heading south.

CHAPTER 18

PHILLIP

"What a fucking mess," Phillip whispered at the road ahead. The wipers were keeping up, but the snow and wind were building to a real blizzard. The Subaru had four-wheel drive, but it was white-knuckle no matter what you were driving. He was nearing Red River Falls and could make out the dull red glow of radio tower beacons in the gray sky ahead. It had been so many years since he'd been here. The home place and his mother came to mind. He wasn't nostalgic, but being in his hometown gave him a peculiar feeling. Not many good memories, but maybe he didn't want them or need them now. As he put the town behind him, Phillip fell back into staring at the gray ribbon of frozen road, the rhythm of the wipers lulling him into a trance.

The year he left Red River Falls, he met a girl named Molly Kearns. They were drawn together as much by mutual loneliness as any physical or spiritual attraction. Phillip loved her in a platonic sort of way, but what was love? It was just one step ahead of chocolate on the biochemical reaction scale. Molly was plain and not very assertive, and that was fine with Phillip. He liked the way she listened to the intellectual rants that set him apart, and he could comment incessantly on the conspicuous consumption flashing across the TV screen without interruption. He explained to Molly in great pedantic gasps how the American military had wrangled its way into the fabric of sports, and it was intolerable for anyone with an awareness of American jingoism to take it seriously.

They married, and for a time, they were comfortable. Phillip got a job at a well-funded non-profit, and Molly graduated as an RN and worked at Hennepin County General in downtown Minneapolis. They had a few dollars and were able to make ends meet, unlike today when graduates are saddled with six-figure debts, and no one is doing a thing about it except maybe Bernie Sanders. They found themselves pregnant twice. The boy they named Merrill and the second, a girl; they called Susan. They were all Molly. Phillip took the stance that having children with a new millennium approaching was for abject sadists conferring a life of hardship due to corporate greed and a damaged environment lashing back with global warming.

He took some pride in them but didn't click with the whole fatherhood thing. He would feign sleep when the children woke in the night and always find a way to delay a diaper change or feeding until Molly was handy. He was moving up the ladder in the non-profit community and took himself very seriously. Phillip had a gig on a local public access channel from the basement of an alternative music station in Mid-Town. He would sweat under the small studio's lights and discuss politics every Sunday at five am. It was the only time he could be motivated to get up that early. Molly seemed proud of him, and she still asked about his day, but now, looking back, it was clear she was falling away at that point. The establishment was getting to her, and he could feel her waiver from the path they shared.

She wanted a new car and mentioned moving to a suburb. He had a real problem with that. How were they to stand in solidarity with the disfranchised and voiceless? It would be like hiring a stockbroker or a tacit vote for George Bush. He tried reasoning with her when she mentioned leaving downtown, but their discussions always devolved into Phillip ridiculing Molly's point of view, and in time she stopped sharing her thoughts with him.

He compromised on a new car for her, researching vehicles with a singular emphasis on social awareness. They decided on a pea-green Subaru Outback, the same one he was still driving. He added bumper stickers, *"Wellstone!"* and *"Hate is Not a Family Value,"* among others, to offset any appearance of affluence elicited by a new vehicle.

One January, they drove the Subaru to the Minneapolis airport on a trip Phillip reluctantly agreed to and parked it in the ramp at 22 degrees below zero. When they got on the plane, they had been married for ten years. There were newlyweds in the seats ahead of them, and Phillip felt pity that they didn't get it. They were too exuberant, and that made

Phillip suspicious. Molly read the Sky Mall magazine, even after she caught Phillip's disapproving glare, and just before they touched down in Nassau, she ordered a rum and Coke! He looked out the window at the turquoise water and hoped this trip killed whatever wanderlust she'd harbored over the years.

They did the usual things, beach walking, sipping too-expensive tropical drinks, and riding in crowded buses around New Providence. Phillip felt uneasy around the natives of the island, his white privilege making him very self-conscious. He watched from the windows of the bus as they bumped along, passing Bahamians standing in front of jerk chicken stands while tan Potcake dogs lolled in the shade. He didn't notice that they seemed happy, and it bothered him that he wasn't more in tune with their culture and social causes.

Molly ganged up with a woman hawking goods in the straw market to make him try on a Panama hat. They both flattered him until he bought it, and Molly made him wear it through the morning. Phillip began to think it might look good on him until he passed a mirror in one of the expensive shops on Bay Street. The reflection took him by surprise, and he almost gasped at such a ridiculous figure. The hat topped a ruddy, bearded face with thick glasses and a sweaty polo shirt clinging to flabby tits and a massive belly. His cargo shorts were too large, and his hairless, sunburned legs led to white socks and brown leather sandals. He looked away and almost felt ill. He'd lost his intellectual and social credentials in this environment and looked like any American tramping around the island. He took off the hat, claiming it was chafing his scalp and didn't wear it the rest of the day.

In contrast, Molly seemed to blossom in the sun's warmth and the island's colors and experienced a sea change that left Phillip behind. He goaded her at lunch or started minor arguments in the afternoons, subconsciously souring the mood to avoid going out to dance or spend time with fellow visitors to the resort. Molly made time for herself by cleverly finding things for Phillip to do that didn't involve her, and they ended up spending time apart as their vacation wore on. He found he didn't mind and soon was immersed in a book or doing crosswords while she wandered the resort or went down to the beach and waded in the ocean.

On the sixth day, he had gone to the front desk to check on their taxi for the next day's departure and ended up catching up on CNN in the lobby. The primaries were underway, and it looked like Hillary was falling behind Obama. Phillip wished there was a more progressive candidate, but anyone would be better than *Bushitler*.

Heedless of the ozone layer, he poured free coffee into a foam cup and shuffled back to their villa across the resort, looking forward to the air conditioning and absence of sun. He opened the door and noticed a pair of pants crumpled on the floor near the bedroom and heard something strange. Setting his coffee on a side table next to the orphaned hat, he went across the living area to the darkened bedroom. More clothing littered the floor and he walked cautiously to the bathroom. The door was slightly ajar, and when he pushed it open to peer inside, he saw Molly's reflection in the mirror.

He had never seen such a look of sexual ecstasy on Molly's face. She was bent forward over the vanity, her hands gripping the marble with fingers white with effort while she breathed heavily, her eyes closed tight and mouth open in a silent moan.

Phillip opened the door further and the musky smell of sex and sweat roiled around him as he watched the Bahamian bartender from the resort lounge thrusting into her from behind, his dusky thighs flexing and lifting her with each stroke. Molly's legs splayed wide, and her knees trembled as she pushed back on tiptoe, her breasts wobbling with every thrust. Phillip watched in silence, aghast, his amazement delaying any rage or embarrassment.

The bartender leaned his head back as he released, uttering a long sigh and gripping Molly's hips tightly as they orgasmed as one.

Phillip pushed open the door until it hit the wall, and the man opened his eyes. Phillip expected fright or shame, but the man smiled and pulled out of Molly, his dark member wet and flaccid. The man said nothing but let go of Molly's hips and backed away from her. He raised his hands with fingers splayed wide as if Phillip was holding him at gunpoint. Phillip backed away as the man approached him, hands still held high. He smiled and brushed against Phillip as he passed, leaving a damp streak on Phillip's khaki shorts.

Molly remained at the sink, leaning forward with her chin on her chest, breathing deeply, her eyes still closed as though in a trance. Phillip watched in fascination as his wife raised her face, opened her eyes, and focused on her reflection in the mirror.

"Molly..." He whispered.

She didn't turn towards him. She only moved her eyes to meet his dull stare in the mirror. He became aware of their reflection as a stark photo - man and wife posed in the sterile white of the vanity lights - her face moist with sweat, skin flushed, and an animal fire in her eyes. He, cuckolded and impotent, an insignificant person lost and forgotten.

He was vaguely aware that the man who had just screwed his wife was putting on his clothes and leaving the villa, closing the door behind him.

Phillip went back into the living room, the air conditioning causing him to tremble as he made his way to the rattan chair in the corner. Throwing his crossword book against the wall, he angrily turned the chair so he could watch the sun going down over the resort through the patio door. Brushing away tears with his fists, he steeled himself as Molly cleaned up and dressed in the other room. Phillip prepared his bitter recriminations and braced to rebuff her pleas to forgive her spontaneous moment of weakness. He couldn't fall back on their marriage vows, that was just a construct of the church, and the government went along with it. There were the kids to think about, but they weren't really in danger of anything they couldn't come to terms with if given years of proper counseling.

He was suddenly unsure, adrift with nothing to cling to. Maybe this whole scene was just an embarrassment to be tolerated and forgotten.

When Molly came out of the bedroom, he knew there wouldn't be any biting indictment of her behavior, and she would not be seeking forgiveness. She went to the kitchenette, and he could hear her pouring a glass of wine. She returned to the living room and, without looking at him, seized the TV remote and started flipping through channels. Phillip was an uninvited spectator and would remain so until they went their separate ways.

The next day they packed in silence and left the resort behind. The Panama hat remained on the side table next to the cold cup of coffee from the day before. The plane ride home was excruciating with Molly three sections up, chatting up an old couple, sharing stories, and acting as nothing had happened. Phillip and Molly split up officially soon after, selling the house and dividing a decade of shared possessions. Phillip attempted to dominate the divorce process but was swept along by Molly's sensibilities, and he meekly followed the proceedings until the paperwork was final and the attorneys high-fived on their way to the bank.

Leaving the courthouse was the last time he saw Molly Winter, nee Kearns.

Lost in the single world, Phillip was shocked at rental costs and how little he could afford on his salary. He engineered an efficiency apartment run by one of the advocacy groups he shilled for, likely displacing someone more deserving. He didn't care and felt entitled to lick his emotional wounds. He began drinking heavily, clipping liquor store coupons and lowering his standards to alcohol under twenty dollars a bottle. He spent even more of his time hating Molly and resenting the kids. After two months, the shelter board suggested he either move on or calls would be made, jeopardizing his gig as a paid community organizer.

Two more months passed, and he existed. Seeking validation for the great injustice he'd endured, Phillip put aside his distaste for Christian dogma, attending a divorce support group in the basement of a church on Marquette Avenue. It was his second session joining men and women sitting in a circle of steel folding chairs sharing their stories, sipping stale coffee, and wondering what hit them. The moderator, a harsh woman, so long divorced she could only be doing this for entertainment, nodded at Phillip to begin. Phillip adjusted his glasses and delivered a moving tale of his betrayal in the Bahamas, eliciting surprised gasps and sympathetic looks from the women in the circle until an athletic black man in a mechanic's jacket with *"Andre"* embroidered on an oval patch sighed and shook his head.

"So what we hear for the second time is you watched while a brother did your wife and you just stood there? *What the fuck, dude!*"

In the stunned silence, Phillip groped for words and looked at other members of the circle to come to his aid. *Andre* took a sip of coffee and sneered at Phillip. The moderator cleared her throat and said something about tolerance, but Phillip didn't hear it. Indignant, he put his jacket over his arm and went up the stairs to the exit. He stood outside for a few minutes, fuming and feeling the same weakness he endured watching Molly's romp. Surely one of the women in the group would come to console him, to ask him back, but like Molly, he hadn't made any real connection, and he went to his car defeated and alone.

When he unlocked his apartment and flicked on the light, he noted a single message on his answering machine. He didn't recognize the number but pressed play.

"Phillip, this is Lucille Kearns." His former mother-in-law sounded in distress. "Molly went into the emergency room tonight. She's had a seizure, and you should come for Merrill and Susie." A pause as someone spoke in the background. "We're at Hennepin Medical Center...." She began to say something more, but the machine cut her off.

Molly had a large brain tumor that put her into a coma and killed her the following day.

Phillip felt sorry for her and a bit of remorse that he didn't medically put two and two together. It all fit. Molly's "sea change" was only a tumor and her infidelity was nothing more than the pathological equivalent of a hurricane that ravaged their marriage.

That was over ten years ago, and in the bending of memory, there is satisfaction in vindication, and gradually his confidence returned. He fell into the role of a stolid widower and single parent, helped a great deal by his in-laws who couldn't get enough of their grandchildren. There was insurance, Molly hadn't yet removed him from her policy, but an inheritance from the Kearns family would bypass Philip and go to the children. It surprised him how much he had been counting on that inheritance to offset his disdain for financial planning and allow him a soft retirement. At least the kids wouldn't bother asking him for money.

Amber streetlights glaring into the car roused him like a sleepwalker finding himself standing next to the bed instead of in it. He was coming into Roseau, and he took his foot off the accelerator, letting the car slow itself as he passed The Outpost Bar. He noted the many vehicles clustered around. *Thanksgiving weekend, and what the hell else was there for the yokels to do here besides drink?*

Phillip slowed his speed and watched for the turn north to take him to the Joshua River and Winter Camp.

CHAPTER 19

AHMED

Waleed drove the Jeep while Ahmed walked ahead on foot. Halil followed in the black Toyota, likely to make sure Nadeem and Ghazi didn't stray. It was snowing thickly, with heavy flakes obscuring his vision. Waleed couldn't see more than the hazy edge of the gravel road in the twilight, but now they were near the final turn to the jumping-off point. The darkness was closing in, and without headlights, it was getting difficult to stay on the road. Ahmed's red ski jacket stood out enough for Waleed to follow, but the wipers were barely keeping up. Waleed rolled down the side window and reached out to clear the ice for the third time since Ahmed went out on foot.

Ahmed held a GPS receiver in his hand, raising it aloft like a torch, hoping the signal would hold and lead them to the turn-off. They must be close; the coordinates would soon match up to the waypoint Halil had programmed last March. The snow was getting deeper, and his feet were getting cold. *It must be here!* He wiped the snow off the GPS unit and squinted at it. It showed they were at the turn-off, but holding his hand to shield against the snow, he could see nothing. He changed the GPS output to tracking and zoomed to the maximum setting. The programmed trail started within the next few meters. He cautiously walked to the side of the road, the deep ditch barely visible.

Waleed lost sight of Ahmed. He inched the Jeep forward, and for a moment, the tires whined before gaining purchase in the snow. As he crept along, there was only the sound of snow crunching under the tires and the frantic sweep of the wipers. They had misjudged the intensity of the storm, and soon it would be too deep and heavy for them to travel. If they could just get to the damn jump-off point, the snow would swallow them, and they would cease to exist until they reappeared on the other side of the border. The car crept along another twenty yards, but Waleed could not see Ahmed. He nervously rubbed his chin. "Ahmed!" he whispered fiercely, slamming the wheel. "Where the hell are you?" He leaned forward, squinting to see something besides the darkness. Waleed decided to risk turning on the headlights. They only illuminated the reflected glare from the snow, whipping past the car in the rising wind. He couldn't even see Ahmed's footprints! Now he had lost the road, and Waleed started to feel a rising panic. *Where was Ahmed?* He tried to think. *Was he ahead, or did he fall into the ditch, or had he found the trail and I've missed him? No, Ahmed must still be in front!* He unconsciously revved the engine to catch up, the Jeep fishtailing as it hit a snowdrift. Waleed cried out as a dark shape loomed at the passenger window and struck the door with force. *A trap!* He hit the accelerator, the wheels spinning, his knuckles white on the steering wheel.

"Open the door, you fool!" It was Ahmed, pounding on the window with his gloved fist. "The turn is here!"

Waleed caught his breath and let off the gas, fumbling with the door lock. Ahmed swung open the door and leaned in, the cold air sharp and damp.

"Turn off those bloody lights! They do no good and show our position." He slammed the door and moved to the front of the Jeep, glaring back at Waleed, motioning him to follow.

Waleed turned off the lights and gripped the wheel, following slowly behind Ahmed as he led the way off the road, seeming to dissolve into the storm. Waleed turned the wheel, following obediently, trying to keep the Jeep moving, trusting Ahmed that they weren't going to drop off into the ditch. He could feel the SUV edging downward, but before he could panic, the Jeep leveled off, and he could see the darker shapes of trees on either side of the trail. The wind wasn't as strong here, and though the snow was fierce, Waleed could see where he was driving. He rolled down the window to clear the wiper. "Ahmed, get in!" He called. "I can see enough now for you to be inside!"

Ahmed turned and glared at Waleed, brushing past the driver's window and walking back to the others. They were not far behind, following

Waleed's trail. In a moment, Ahmed was back inside the Jeep, turning up the heat and stamping his feet.

"It isn't far now, "he said, putting the GPS unit on the dash. "Go faster so we keep our momentum."

Waleed wiped his brow and pressed the gas pedal. The Jeep responded, and they began moving south at a steady pace, the car bouncing softly on the old logging trail, winding south through brush and trees.

"Don't slow down." Ahmed was looking at the GPS unit, his face lit by the tiny screen. "It's close, but we must get the autos into the area Halil cleared of brush before the snow gets too deep!"

"How far?" Waleed's voice sounded raspy, his throat dry.

"Less than two kilometers," Ahmed replied, twisting in his seat to look back to see if the others were following. He could see nothing, but he didn't dare make a call on the cell phone. If the Toyota wasn't behind them, they would just have to go back. Ahmed was on edge. The weather should discourage satellite surveillance, and drones were too precious to be flying around in this shit, but the Americans always had a way of getting around problems.

Waleed was thinking the same thing. They were very near the actual border, and the sureness about getting across undetected he felt back in Winnipeg was gone now. He felt as though there was a huge target painted on the car, and at any moment, a missile would come streaking down from the clouds, and they would be immolated in a ball of flame. "Will this weather be enough to keep us safe?" He blurted out, chancing a glance at Ahmed.

"The Americans can probably see through this, but our best protection isn't the weather or the remoteness of our crossing point; it is the bloody laxness of their attitude. You don't plan to defend against something that doesn't exist. " Ahmed seemed very calm as he spoke.

"But I believe they know we exist." Waleed's voice sounded childlike.

"Yes, Yes! They know we exist!" Ahmed snapped. "I mean, they know we are out there, somewhere, but it's been decades since the twin towers and devoting the resources to guard the Canadian border is a low priority. They know we exist, but does the threat of an incursion in this weather exist? They are rich and lazy gamblers, and the odds aren't enough for them to make an effort to close every gap." Ahmed looked again at the GPS unit. "This is it. Stop and let me get out to find the clearing."

Ahmed got out of the car, the cold air sending a chill down Waleed's spine. Ahmed turned suddenly and leaned in. He met Waleed's eyes. "You worry too fucking much. Stop it." Ahmed slammed the door and disappeared again into the darkness.

Waleed wondered why Ahmed mentioned the twin towers. *What does that have to do with us crossing the border?*

CHAPTER 20

MARTY

Marty knew he'd cut it pretty close leaving the bar. The blizzard was here, and if he'd screwed around any longer, he'd be stuck in the parking lot. The headlights barely penetrated the snow, and it was slow going. He did not want to be ass-deep in the ditch, explaining how he got there to the Sheriff. Or worse, Axe Winter.

He cracked the window to get some fresh air and wake (sober) up before arriving at camp. It was going to be awkward with Axel this year. The guy had always terrified Marty, and though Axel allowed him into their camp, Marty still felt he didn't belong with the traditions Axe had built over the years. Marty was impulsive and flippant and Axel was just the opposite; Well read, well respected, and tempered by a life Marty could only imagine. Marty was determined not to say or do anything that would disrupt this last time at camp.

He closed the window and checked the odometer. The camp was only a few miles more, and he relaxed slightly, knowing his drinking hadn't brought disaster. He'd grown close to Kurt in the years since they'd married sisters. Marty thought Kurt got the better of the two with Jennifer. She was pretty and aging well, even after having Jordan.

Then there was his Pamela. He constantly fought an itch for freedom from her, but he knew she was a good woman, and he probably couldn't do any better. They argued over money or lack of it, but lately, she was nagging him to cut back on the drinking and focus on their marriage. Of course, he resented her demands, but at night, when sleep was far away, he wished he didn't feel so trapped and just appreciated what he had. Maybe she had a point. He'd been drinking more, and though part of it was stress at work and home, it had become a nasty habit. It might be time to get some help. But not this weekend.

There were wheel-ruts in the snow, probably Kurt's, and Marty followed them to the narrow road buried in aspen woods that split off to camp. Strangely, the tracks of a lone vehicle kept going, continuing past the turn-off into the snowy darkness. Marty knew the road dead-ended at Tom Duchamp's place across the Joshua River about a half-mile away. Since Tom Senior died, no one stayed there anymore, and it was strange anyone would be on this road on a night like tonight.

Marty's headlights illuminated the vehicles parked in front of the cabin, then reflected off a collection of Nash, Studebaker, and Packard hubcaps hanging along the porch. A few bullet-riddled road signs hung on the rough-sawn walls above rows of split oak firewood. The cabin wasn't much bigger than a small garage and made of white pine logged off in the 1930s and could only be described as "rustic." A gray swirl of wood smoke rose from a blackened metal chimney jutting above cedar roof shakes already coated with snow, and the yellow glow of gas lights came from a small window next to a stout oak door. No palace could look prettier.

Kurt's pickup was alongside a green Subaru, and Marty realized he'd lost ten bucks. Marty bet Kurt that Phil would never show up, figuring it was money in the bank. Marty couldn't believe the asshole didn't just order his dad some gluten-free tobacco from *guiltyoffspring.com* and call it good. *Damn. Ten bucks out the window!* Phil could make a train take a gravel road, but Marty knew Kurt was trying to do the right thing by his old man.

He shut off the truck, opened the door, and was nearly shocked sober by the wind whipping through the trees. He stretched, looking at Phil's snow-covered Subaru, and not surprised he was still driving the same car after all these years. Marty walked to the back of his truck and dropped the tailgate to grab his gear. He slung a bag over his shoulder and hauled out a blue and white cooler full of ice and beer. Marty grunted with effort, going around the truck, then stopped as he noticed Phillip's bumper stickers. He could still see the "Wellstone!" sticker outline, but it had faded to just a white rectangle. A new decal had

"COEXIST," spelled in symbols. Shaking his head, Marty trudged through the deepening snow and dumped off the cooler on the open porch. Bracing himself, he opened the cabin door and went in.

"Hey, Uncle Marty!" Jordan was leaning against the wall next to the door and put up his hand. "Hello, Spud," Marty replied, ignoring Jordan's high five, and instead batted his hat down onto his face.

"Whoa! Rory's here too?" Marty said, genuinely surprised. "Look at you, all grown up!"

Aurora rolled her eyes. "Hello, Marty."

"Kurt. Axel," Marty nodded, skirting past them to put his duffel on an upper bunk.

"Martin," Axel replied, barely glancing at him as he puffed his pipe. Kurt just nodded to him and made a show of checking his watch.

"What's new with you guys?" Marty asked just as he noticed Phillip at the stove, wearing the same thick glasses and shitty attitude he had the last time they were together. "Hey, Phil! I didn't see you there! You made it, huh?"

Phillip pushed back his glasses and eyed Marty warily. "Yes, I'm here."

"Well...Good," Marty said, going back to the door to finish unloading his truck. "Looks like they've already made you camp cook!" He hesitated at the door, waiting for Phil to reply, but Phil just nodded and opened the stove to peer inside. Marty gave Kurt a look of contempt and went back outside. Marty was pulling his gun case from behind the seat when Kurt joined him, going to the back of the pickup to help haul gear without a word. Both men went back to the cabin and put their loads down on the porch. Marty opened the cooler and pulled out two longneck bottles, opening the caps with his wedding ring.

"Neat trick," Kurt said, taking a beer from Marty. "I never learned how to do that."

"That's because you're a pussy," Marty replied, taking a deep swallow, then putting his bottle on the porch railing. He pulled out his wallet. "Here's the money I owe you. Hope it was worth ten bucks to have your brother screw up our weekend."

Kurt snatched the bill out of Marty's hand. "Keep quiet! Don't make it worse than it is." He sniffed the bill then pocketed it. "Thanks for the cash. Who's the pussy now?"

Marty shook his head and finished his beer in one long pull. "Okay, enough of your bullshit, let's light the fuse on this bitch and see what happens."

Kurt nodded and opened the door, holding it for Marty as he carried the last of his gear into the cabin.

Kurt went back to his seat at the wooden table next to Axel and across from Aurora. He watched Marty roll out his sleeping bag, wobbling as he reached to straighten it. "I take it you stopped for a few before you came out here?" Axel spared a glance at Marty and frowned.

"Are there mustaches in Mexico?" Marty replied. "Had to check in with the locals to get the skinny on the deer situation."

Kurt took a swig of beer. "So what's the skinny?"

"Only mentally unstable animals will be out in this shit, and we should just sleep in tomorrow morning."

Jordan looked at Kurt with concern. "I thought we were going to hunt. We're going out hunting in the morning, aren't we?"

"Hey, I was just kidding," Marty said quickly. "Geez, take it easy. I also bought a raffle ticket for an ATV, so I've got that going for me. Anyone want a beer?"

"I'll get 'em," Kurt replied, getting up. "Phil, you want one?"

Phil looked up from the stove and raised a wine goblet half full of Chardonnay. "I'm drinking this."

"Dad?" Kurt had his hand on the door.

"I believe I'll have some whiskey in a bit," Axel stated. "There's some rot-gut I stashed under the counter last year."

"Like hell, you will!" Marty interrupted, digging in his duffel bag and producing a bottle of Glenmorangie Scotch. "I brought you a present!"

"That's too damned expensive to waste on me!" Axel said with surprise.

"Live a little!" Marty replied, instantly embarrassed at his choice of words. He set the bottle in front of Axel, feeling his face redden. "Do you want some ice?" He added quickly.

"No ice in single malt, just a hint of water to open the flavor," Axel replied, already undoing the seal with his pocket knife. "Thank you, Martin! Join me in a snort?"

"Noooo," Marty replied. "I hate that sh....Stuff. But I'll get you a glass."

"I'll try some," Rory volunteered.

"Me too!" Jordan chimed in.

Axel hesitated, holding the bottle, one fist around the neck, glowering at them through his pipe smoke. "I doubt you'll like it," he said gruffly, pulling the cork, "But, there's only one way to find out. Three glasses. We'll all live a little!"

Kurt shook his head and went outside to fetch the beer. Phillip pulled an assortment of jelly jars and chipped coffee mugs out of the cupboard. "Make it four...I can't pass up a good Scotch."

"That's the spirit!" Axel beamed. His family was all here, and it was time to celebrate.

CHAPTER 21

HALIL

Halil had done a short reconnaissance when he chose the crossing point the previous March. The snow was almost gone from the countryside, but there were still large swaths covering the forest floor. He found that animals made paths, and over years of use, they were quite passable, even in the thickest areas. He had used the weather then as well, scouting the path during an early spring rainstorm.

Halil crossed the border that day but hadn't gone very far before retracing his steps. The path beyond he only knew from the Saudi pilot's reports and Google Earth. It was about two kilometers to the border from the jumping-off point, and when he reached it, Halil found the line between Canada and The United States was only an east and west swath cut through the forest less than ten meters across. He didn't bother to look for tripwires or sensors. The area was too remote to maintain electronics, and false readings from tree falls and animals made sensors worthless. The forest was essentially a fence several kilometers deep, and he would have to convince Ahmed that crossing on foot was the only way.

Another hazard was crossing the border unnoticed. It would do no good to enter the United States if the FBI or NSA traced their movements and rolled them up along with anyone mentioned during the water-boarding sessions they would endure.

The key was to cross undetected, remain undetected, and strike without warning.

Easier said than done. Many had tried to cross from the south, wading across the rivers or crossing the desert mingling with Hondurans and Salvadorans, only to be exposed or murdered by the very people they were trying to emulate. Some tried to bluff their way across wherever they perceived a weak point, but the border service weren't idiots and only risked some verbal abuse to detain anyone they thought suspicious. Mohammet suggested they cross in winter over the frozen Rainy River, but it was too well monitored to prevent Meth and marijuana traffic. The deep woods was the safest route.

Few in jihad admitted it, but the Americans and their British and Israeli whores had won. Halil's information network didn't lie, or more accurately, wasn't successful in hiding the truth. Key individuals stopped leaving posts. Entire groups fell silent. Operations planned for years never materialized, and across the globe, hundreds of families stopped hearing from their beloved brothers, sons, and husbands. What the West didn't root out, it attracted like moths to a flame. Thousands made their way to Iraq, Afghanistan, and Syria, many perishing without firing a shot. Some were gathered like fish in a net and, after being crushed for what information they could provide, were sent to Saudi Arabia or Kuwait, where they often had their heads removed as a final insult.

With no significant attacks in the years following 9-11, Halil believed the American psyche was again apathetic. To Americans, the Twin Towers was a tragic one-time incident that would never happen again. *What have they done to me lately?* Halil smiled to himself. It was very safe to live in America, but with Ahmed's connections and Mohammet's knowledge, they would change that forever.

* * *

Both SUVs were parked and shut off, the engines ticking softly in the darkness. The woods sheltered them from the wind, but the snow was getting worse, and soon, they were all shrouded in white. They didn't speak as they readied for the trek ahead. They had disconnected the dome and trunk lights days ago, and all of them tried to remember where they had left the items they would need in America. Waleed was putting on a pair of winter boots while Ghazi dug in a duffel bag for warmer clothes. Halil began shoveling snow on top of the vehicles to block any residual heat from showing up on a drone's infrared sensors. The tire tracks were hardly visible after only ten minutes, and the storm showed no sign of letting up.

"Hey, watch it!" Waleed brushed snow off his jacket and dug along his collar where Halil had thrown a shovel-full onto him. "You could have waited until I was out of the way!" He snapped.

"Fuck off," Halil replied, leaning the shovel against the Jeep and walking around the other side. He unzipped his pants and began urinating.

Ghazi joined Waleed next to the Jeep, adjusting the straps on a small day pack. Halil noticed Ghazi still carried his knapsack like a bloody college student and wondered how such a skinny wanker would hold up in the deep snow. Halil turned slightly and aimed a stream of piss at Ghazi's feet. Ghazi looked down and jumped back. Halil giggled quietly, but Ghazi said nothing and stomped around the other side of the vehicle, shuffling in the snow to clean off the urine. Halil could feel the heat of the boy's glare even in the darkness but didn't care. Only he and Ahmed mattered. The rest were just dross with a temporary purpose.

Halil's rough treatment embarrassed Ghazi. These men weren't going to offer a welcome into their circle, which was concerning for the trip ahead. Ghazi suddenly thought of something else and shrugged off the backpack, frantically digging through the pockets. *Were they here, or did I forget them?* Ghazi was trying to think of where the bottle of medication could be when Ahmed called for them to join him at the back of his SUV. Ghazi was uneasy about losing the prescription but could do nothing at this point.

Ahmed opened the cargo door of the Jeep and waited for the others to gather around. In a moment, they all stood looking at the black plastic box. Waleed leaned in and hefted the nearest corner. "It's heavy as concrete! What is this thing?"

"It is an enclosure used for fishing on the ice," Ahmed replied.

"What? I don't understand." Waleed leaned in to look closer.

Halil kicked him in the ass. "He means we put the cargo inside a portable shelter for ice fishing. It's like a clamshell that slides on the snow."

Waleed turned slowly and lunged at Halil.

"Stop!" Ahmed stepped between them. "We are brothers in this! We're all excited, and it is making us tense. Save your energy for getting into the United States!"

Despite the tension, Waleed helped Halil lift the sled out of the trunk and onto the ground. It rested in the snow like a lifeless black hole opening to a dark abyss. "What's in it?" Nadeem asked.

"Things we'll need," Ahmed replied. "No more questions. Let's get going."

Halil took up the front tow rope. Despite its weight, the sled floated over the snow. Mohammet had planned well, rigging a loop of cord on each end of the sled box. One could lead, and another follow, pulling and lifting the sled to steer it through the brush.

Ahmed motioned Halil to join him away from the others. "Do you have your pistol?" Halil nodded, producing his Russian-made Tokarev. Ahmed feared two scenarios; one, an ambush or border skirmish, during which the pistol would perhaps buy enough time for Ahmed to set off the device, or the second scenario that Ahmed now shared with Halil.

Ahmed pulled his stocking cap over his ears and motioned for the others to follow. He held the GPS unit and began to follow the trail Halil had marked seven months earlier. No one looked back. Everything had been left behind, and all focused on the task ahead. Nadeem pulled the sled from the front, and Waleed took up the trailing rope. Ghazi followed, and Halil brought up the rear, Ahmed's second scenario fresh in his mind.

If Waleed, Nadeem, or Ghazi showed any sign of endangering the mission, Halil was to shoot them dead.

CHAPTER 22

THE RITUAL

The cabin was filled with a blue haze of smoke and warming nicely as the heat radiated into the walls and floor. The oak and birch in the woodstove smelled heavenly, but Axel's pipe gave the sweet edge that made Winter Camp what it was.

Axel wrapped his knuckles on the wooden table, commanding their attention. "Time to shit-can your electronic devices."

Aurora looked puzzled but said nothing. Jordan looked at the others with surprise. "What do you mean electronic devices?" He crossed his arms on his chest, and the beginnings of a pout formed on his lower lip.

Axle stood slowly, knees cracking as he pushed his chair back. He went to a pine plank shelf above the sink and snagged an old Hills Brothers coffee can, brushing against an ancient hula girl dash ornament that swayed its hips as though alive.

Axel shambled back and slammed the can in the center of the table with authority, standing with arms crossed. "Put your stuff in here," Axel said through teeth clenched on his pipe. "This is Deer Camp."

Kurt pulled his cell holster off his belt and placed it in the can. All followed suit, dropping their cell phones into the faded can. Jordan was last because he had to go to his bunk and dig in his duffel. Rory noted the items; cell phone, which Jordan carefully turned off to save the battery, an old Gameboy with a rat's nest of wire attached to it, a lime green GPS, a set of walkie-talkies, and finally some sort of survival radio/flashlight with a crank on the side for running without batteries.

Axel watched this with growing alarm, displaying the highest raised eyebrows in camp to date. Jordan held the mass of technology like a litter of puppies and reached across the table to stuff it all into the can.

Axel took out his pipe and blew a thin line of cherry tobacco smoke. "I guess we'll need a bigger coffee can if you keep coming up here."

Jordan was returning to his seat. "If I have to put everything in there, why did I bring it up here in the first place?"

"Darn good question." Axel reached over and seized the can and carried it back to the shelf, placing it between the hula girl and a bleached bear skull.

Watching her grandfather move through the darkened cabin in the smoke and yellow lantern light allowed Rory to see a time long past. The timbers above were dark with age, covered in a patina of smoke and decades of cooking grease. The cabin's walls were only planking, but there was plenty of wood for heat, and she felt warm and secure, all the more when the wind gusted outside and the oak crackled in the stove.

Axel wore the same buffalo plaid shirt his father had when he first hunted deer on the Joshua. Rory's great-grandfather gave it to Axel in 1958, and Axel more than grew into the shirt, but today, it fit the same, tucked into charcoal wool pants held up with blood-red suspenders. Axel's Red Wing boots had been re-soled more than once and carried him through many seasons, the leather supple and dark with Neat's foot oil.

He moved to the woodstove, his boots scuffing on the floor planks logged and sawed during the Great Depression by Swedes and Germans toiling in the woods in camps, not unlike this one. He produced a wooden match and touched it to the black iron stove, braving the heat until the match flared, illuminating more treasures hanging from square cut nails. A deer skull with yellowed teeth and antlers eaten down to nubs by field mice, a collection of grouse tails bound with rawhide lace, a hornet nest fused to a willow branch, and a pair of ancient snowshoes. "Deer camp is the sacrament for continuing our traditions," Axel said after lighting his pipe. "We've got two new hunters this season. Jordan has come of age, and Aurora is our first female. They're young, but I think they understand the greater importance of deer camp." He gave Rory a quick wink. "Joshua Camp is the boulder in a stream, the tree among the ashes and a place that changes by never changing."

The hunters of Joshua Camp understood what Axel was saying and took heart in their sanctuary. Kurt had never heard his father give a speech of any kind, and it surprised him that he had spoken so openly. He was right. Deer camp was more than a place or event. It was the best of traditions.

Phillip silently scoffed at his father's sermon. "Tradition" was just a dog whistle for bitter clingers to excuse gun violence and resist meaningful change. Social justice could never be achieved until men like Axel Winter were buried along with their beliefs. Phillip finished his whiskey and went back to the cookstove.

CHAPTER 23

THE CROSSING

"As with many battles, planning and timing become dependent upon weather conditions. The group made their incursion the day before Thanksgiving, crossing the world's longest undefended border in the twilight. Their movements were obscured by a leaden sky, their path covered by the steady snowfall that continued to accumulate long after they were beyond detection. Nature had allied itself with their effort and allowed a breach that would forever change the United States and its people..."

Excerpted from "Fallout – Surviving in a Dark New Age" by Miriam Glenn - published in the St. Paul Pioneer Press

Waleed had taken Nadeem's place in leading the sled while Ghazi handled the rear. He could tell the wind was freshening, meaning they were close to the cleared area separating the two nations. He stopped and held up his hand. Ghazi dropped the rope and bent forward, panting with effort, watching Halil join Ahmed on the trail ahead.

The screen lit up on the Garmin. "We're under 100 meters from the cleared zone," Ahmed whispered to the others. "We'll have to cross quickly to the American side and then the final leg to the safe house." He had checked Facebook last night, and Saeed would be waiting, but because he didn't have a trail plotted on the American side, he would have to navigate to the spot using coordinates only. Ahmed and Halil had mapped the area on Google Earth and hadn't seen any obstacles. There was a small river, but they shouldn't need to cross it. Ahmed was more worried they would encounter an unfrozen swamp or bog. That would be a disaster if they stumbled into one with the package in tow. Mohammet warned them the sled could not be immersed in water.

Ahead could make out a lighter area silhouetting the trees. They slowed their pace, approaching the cleared border between Canada and the United States with caution. The four looked left and right as though coming to a busy street, the wind rushing along the gap as they stepped away from the Canadian side. No ditch or fence marked the transition, only knee-high grass clotted with windblown snow in both directions.

They crossed.

It was uneventful, but there was a queer feeling of being nude as they broke from the trees and made their way across the clearing. Ahmed led the way and knew they all felt an urge to run as fast as they could, but the high grass snagged their boots, and the heavy sled demanded a slower speed. Waleed and Ghazi put their heads down and pulled the sled across with their hearts beating fast in their chests. Halil thought the grass would be an easy traverse compared to the infernal woods, but it seemed they were walking in slow motion. The image of a drone circling above came into his mind. It would spot their thermal signatures like dark blotches against the grey backdrop of snow. He had seen what American missiles could do. Halil's scalp prickled as he strained to hear something on the wind that would signal danger. He pushed himself harder, lifting his legs as far as he could to clear the damnable grass, knowing a Hellfire missile could shriek down from the heavens and end them on the spot.

Before their urgency turned to panic, they were into the woods on the other side. Inside the United States.

They stopped, and Ahmed went to each of them and patted their shoulders, grabbing Ghazi by the back of the neck and pulling the boy close, their foreheads touching. "We've done it, my young Ghazi! You've done it with us!" They all felt a thrill that replaced the fear and uncertainty, and they began to think they might succeed.

Ghazi was surprised at their leader's excitement and gave a weak smile, trying to stand on rubbery legs. Ahmed released his young soldier and backed away, producing the GPS again and holding it so they could see the icon for the safe house glowing on the screen. "Not even five kilometers to go! Let's have a rest, boys. We've bloody well earned it!"

CHAPTER 24

EVENING IN CAMP

Axel had sipped his way through two fingers of good Scotch, and though Jordan had rejected his, Aurora had acquitted herself well, sipping her Scotch at a respectful pace, enjoying its esoteric taste. Even Phillip had joined their circle and seemed to be loosening up, and as he relaxed, so did their group.

Rory lifted her glass to her lips and tasted the flavor of tradition and the richness of something timeless. This one drink was better than all the beer she'd drank at keggers or the house party shots when parents were away. If she were aware of sophisticated society, she might know that she had *arrived.* Her "coming out" rivaled any Houston debutante with a party dress and a coterie of beaus. Rory knew this was real, and she felt truly at home. *Deer camp wasn't about the deer, it was about the hunt, and the hunt was about the kill, but the kill wasn't necessary for the magic to happen.* She let the Scotch burn deliciously down her throat and was happier than she'd been in a long time.

Axel puffed on his cherry tobacco, and it wafted above the rafters and hung there in a blue-gray aura. Kurt wrinkled his nose unconsciously and went to his bunk, hauling his gear around the table and out onto the covered porch to hang it outside where the smells wouldn't impregnate the cloth and tip off a deer the next morning. Axel noticed but didn't point out that he'd been smoking cherry tobacco in the cabin for over 50 years and never worried about a deer getting his scent.

Jordan sulked at the other end of the table, his Scotch abandoned, leaning his chair back against the wall with his arms crossed over his chest and his baseball hat pulled low on his forehead, the bill at the proper angle. He wanted to text his friend, Avery, or the girl with the locker across the hall. Robin was way more popular than him, but she was nice to Jordan, and it would have been cool to send a selfie with his drink. Jordan watched his dad carry his gear outside and soon went to his bunk and did the same, joining his father on the porch, hanging his clothing on wooden pegs along the outside wall.

Axel shook his head at Kurt and Jordan, but every man hunted differently. Axel used the wind, and that meant his smoke went to the lee side of any deer. His father didn't have hi-tech waterproof crap or super-insulated coats. If he was chilled, he lit a fire, and often as not, a buck would walk by and be hanging on the meat pole that night. Axel got them started, but where they went from there was up to them.

CHAPTER 25

THE PIT

They were almost a kilometer into the United States, and Ahmed felt confident that they were on schedule. It was snowing harder, and the weather didn't seem to be letting up. That was good for covering their tracks, but it was getting more challenging to navigate in the woods. The snow was drifting over the snags and clumps of underbrush that tugged at them and caused them to stumble.

Nadeem and Waleed kept their heads down, tugging at the sled cords as they followed Ahmed's trail. They trudged along in a kind of trance, placing one foot in front of the other and pushing aside branches, trying to keep pace.

Ghazi took up the rear behind Halil and was struggling to keep up. These men seemed to be like animals, built for this sort of thing, especially since they all smoked like chimneys. The boots Ahmed bought for Ghazi caused blisters on both feet, and it was getting harder to walk.

Waleed was tiring too, and he wanted more water. The sled was getting harder to pull, and he had a blister on his palm from the tow rope. He gritted his teeth and continued along, trying to anticipate Ahmed's next move, following his footprints around the snags and trees.

Suddenly, Ahmed stopped ahead, his face illuminated in the eerie glow from the GPS. Waleed slowed, causing Nadeem to ram the sled into the back of his legs, sending him sprawling into the snow. Waleed gasped and quickly stood up, turning around like a fighter who tripped in the ring. "Pay attention, you damned fool!" He snapped.

Nadeem didn't apologize. He just nodded and dropped the rope, his lungs hurting from the cold air. Ahmed was at their side. "Be quiet," he whispered. "We're getting closer to the safe house, and this will be another dangerous time for us." He leaned against a tree and sized up the men. "We'll take a moment to rest but keep your coats on – don't get chilled. You'll just lose your energy that much sooner. Try to drink some water too."

"How much farther?" Ghazi asked, out of breath from catching up.

"Under two kilometers," Ahmed replied, "But with these woods and the weather...." He trailed off, too winded to speak more. Ahmed slipped the GPS lanyard from around his neck and tried to adjust his collar to let some of his body heat escape but keep out the snow. He looked at his watch. "A quarter of seven."

Ahmed leaned against a tree and took a long swig of water before passing the bottle to Waleed. They all wanted to be at their destination, but the possibility that the Americans were waiting for them was real. Ahmed could sense everyone was on edge, trying to detect something that would signal danger, but there was nothing but the woods, the snow, and the wind.

"I know we're about done in, but let's have it over with, Brothers," Ahmed whispered, pushing away from the tree. "This will be the last leg until we get there. Ghazi, you can take the back of the sled; Waleed the front. Nadeem can spell you when you tire. Halil, I want you to bring up the rear."

Waleed thought to protest, but it would be useless. Halil was Ahmed's favorite. They all fell into place, marching through the darkness, almost hypnotized by the light from Ahmed's GPS screen bobbing ahead like a firefly in the trees.

Halil trailed the others, his tiredness overcoming the nervous energy he had felt since they left Winnipeg. He slowed and looked back at their trail in the snow. He was relieved to see it was almost indiscernible in the tangle of fallen trees and thin brush. He started forward again, growing weary of parting the bloody willow branches that snapped back into his face and brought stinging tears to his eyes. There was a sound ahead, and Halil stopped to listen. Something wasn't right.

"Halil!" It was Nadeem calling him in a loud whisper. "Halil, get up here!"

Halil struggled to move faster and catch up. He pushed past Nadeem and almost ran into Ghazi as the little prick stood looking down at something or someone. Waleed and Ahmed were nowhere in sight.

"What is it, you shitheads," he hissed. "What's going on?"

"Ahmed fell down a cliff." Ghazi leaned forward to peer over the edge of a drop-off.

"Are you taking a piss?" Halil snorted. "How could anyone find a bloody cliff in this flatland?"

"Look for yourself!" Ghazi snapped.

Halil stepped forward and almost fell headlong into a dark void, but Nadeem grabbed his arm and steadied him. Halil leaned forward and could barely see Ahmed laying on his side at the bottom of a steep six-meter drop. He could feel the wind in his face and realized they were at the edge of a large excavated crater. Waleed was crouched below, tending to Ahmed's leg. "Waleed," Halil said as loud as he dared. "What's happened?"

Waleed stood and craned his neck to look up at the rim of the pit. "Ahmed's leg is broken! He's not bleeding, but he's in rough shape."

Ahmed muttered something to Waleed, but Halil couldn't make out the words in the freshening wind.

Waleed cupped his hands next to his mouth. "Ahmed says to stay there and make sure the package doesn't slide down on top of us!" Halil pushed Ghazi back toward the sled. "You heard him. Move the bloody thing back before it goes over the edge!" Ghazi hesitated, but before Halil could say more, Nadeem helped pull the sled away from the crater.

Halil tried to see across the ravine, but it was too dark. *This pit must be over 60 meters across, and Saeed didn't warn us about it?* Halil tried to comprehend this avoidable setback. *What was the sense of having that wanker in place if he wasn't able to help them reach the safe house?* He saw Waleed examining Ahmed's leg and was sure it would be on their minds as well. "Waleed," he whispered loudly, leaning forward over the rim of the drop. "Help Ahmed across the opening, and we'll meet you on the other side." Waleed nodded and gave a half-hearted wave.

Waleed sighed and reached under Ahmed's arms, struggling to help their leader to his feet. "Let's get you straightened out and see how bad it is." Ahmed let out a loud moan, and Waleed knew this was bad and going to get worse. He feared this entire venture was a complete balls-up starting the moment they dealt with the Imam. That damned Halil with his temper, and now their leader was fucking crippled. Waleed felt Ahmed tense at his side as he brought him upright. "Put your weight on the good leg, and I'll hold you on this side." Ahmed nodded and put his weight on Waleed's shoulder, trying to make his way on his left leg while lifting the other above the snow as they made their way across the gravel pit.

Waleed looked down and winced. Ahmed's right leg was broken, and his foot was almost twisted backward. Waleed knew what to do to stabilize the leg, even permanently set the break, but they hadn't planned for a medical emergency, and traveling would be almost impossible now. Waleed held him tightly, trying to take as much of the man's weight as he could bear. The pain must be terrible, but Ahmed didn't cry out again. Waleed would cut some willow branches to splint the leg. He had the foresight to bring a roll of duct tape for repairing his boots or something mundane, but maybe he could get this back under control and get them to the safe house before daylight.

"Once we get across this pit," Waleed said to Ahmed, "we'll get your leg splinted and make sure it doesn't get any worse."

Ahmed could no longer lift his useless leg, and it dragged along the ground, sending jolts of pain up to his hip that almost made him faint. "Damn this!" He said through clenched teeth. "This bloody crater didn't show up on the map or the aerial pictures!" He leaned heavily on Waleed as they struggled across the half-frozen ground. "And then I walk right over the edge like a daft cow!" Ahmed had been adjusting the GPS as he took the last step into thin air, and then he was at the bottom of the ravine, gasping for breath, his leg bent under him.

Waleed almost fell too but was able to stop in time. He had carefully slid down the nearly vertical wall of the crater to Ahmed's side.

"What about your man in America, "Waleed muttered, "I thought he plotted the trail on the American side? Couldn't he have steered us around the only pitfall in these fucking woods?" His anger and frustration were bubbling up, and he began to wonder if something darker was at work here. "Maybe he's screwing with us! Maybe he's working with the Americans?"

"No," Ahmed snapped, "this must have been excavated recently. I'm just as foolish as Saeed not having another look before we crossed. Ahmed suddenly sat up. "Oh, fuck all!"

Waleed jumped. "What is it?"

"The GPS!" Ahmed winced at the realization that he should have put the lanyard back around his neck. "It flew out of my hands when I landed." *This compounded foolishness just might cost them the mission!* He could imagine them foundering in the woods and snow until daylight exposed them, and they were rounded up like goats.

Waleed sighed and looked forlornly at the carpet of snow covering the floor of the pit. "I will have to go back to search."

Ahmed pointed to a snow-covered hump ahead. "Get me to that raised spot so I can sit down."

Ahmed felt another shock of pain as he sat heavily on a pile of gravel. He pulled his glove off with his teeth and wiped the cold sweat off his forehead. He was about to tell Waleed to hurry, but Waleed was already halfway back to the other side of the pit.

"What a bleeding mess," Ahmed whispered into the darkness.

Chapter 26

Joshua Camp

Phillip stood in the kitchen, vaguely angry, trying to adjust the old propane stove's burner. The leek soup could burn, and it was a constant headache to bake Beef Wellington with the oven's hot spots and roller coaster temperature. The turkey thawing on the counter was going to be easier tomorrow, but even if he pulled it off, his skills in the kitchen likely wouldn't raise a compliment. "Ouch, goddammit!" He slammed the oven door and sucked on his burned finger.

"Phil," Marty said, "That oven can't make a decent frozen pizza, let alone a gourmet dinner." He smiled at Phillip and waited for a reply. Phil's blood pressure was slowly rising, but he said nothing. Marty should know he hated to be called Phil, and once again, he thought about this damnable weekend with dread.

Kurt and Jordan came back into the cabin and swung the door closed with a gust of frigid air. Jordan went back to his seat against the wall, and Kurt leaned his shoulder into the door to make sure it stayed shut. "I shoulda' been up here in the summer fixing this door latch," he said to no one in particular.

Aurora sat next to Axel, sipping the last of her Scotch.

"It's snowing like a bastard," Kurt said, sitting down across from Aurora. "Phil, are we gonna eat anytime soon?"

Phillip unconsciously gritted his teeth and stirred the soup. He pushed his eyeglasses back on his nose. "In a bit. Have you set the table? I don't see any plates or silverware. We'll need some bowls for the soup too."

Kurt shrugged and pulled a handful of peanuts out of a bucket in the middle of the table. He cracked the first one loudly, let the shells fall to the floor, and winked at Marty.

Aurora sensed where this was headed and went to the sideboard to begin setting the table. "Jordan, you can help me. Grab some silverware."

Jordan hesitated. None of the men were getting up to help, so why should he? When Aurora didn't push it, he relaxed a bit.

"Jordan," Kurt said, "you're the new meat at the cabin. Go help Aurora."

Jordan knew that tone and reluctantly got up and took a handful of silverware from Aurora. He started laying it out on the table while Aurora set down the plates.

Axel puffed away on his pipe and stretched. "How's Susan, Phillip?" He asked.

Phillip cringed at the question. His father was asking sincerely, but to bring up Susan in front of Marty and Kurt was a disaster. "She's okay, Dad," he said just loud enough for his father to hear but not come across too proudly.

Kurt snapped another peanut. "Doesn't she call herself *Ravenhair* or something?" He could almost feel Phillip squirming by the stove.

Axel frowned for a moment, then remembered the name change scandal. "Ravenfyre. I forgot. Glad she's okay, but she could call her old Grandad once in a while." He touched a new match to his pipe."

What's this about? Marty mouthed silently. Kurt shook his head and rolled his eyes. Both of them grabbed another handful of peanuts from the bucket.

Phillip stirred the soup, adjusting the burner control with pliers; the knob lost years before. "Well, Dad, she doesn't call me very often either. She's finding her way, I guess. Kids today just don't want to stay in touch."

Aurora had only met Susan a few times but remembered her as being very unpleasant. She also remembered Aunt Molly having to lock their refrigerator at night so Susan wouldn't devour the contents, butter and all, while they were sleeping.

Jordan was still thinking of Robin with the locker across the hall.

Axel hesitated and finally said, "Funny how it's easier for people to stay in touch than it's ever been, but we still have to make an effort."

Marty cracked another peanut, punctuating the statement.

Phillip bristled. "It's easy for people living in the past to think that way, I suppose. The pressures of modern life carry people along, and it isn't anyone's fault. It just is, and besides, she's an adult and can make her own choices."

Axel looked perplexed. "Isn't that what I just said?" Axel changed the subject. "Merrill calls me every week. He seems to be doing well."

Phillip turned red and looked down at the stove. "Dinner's ready. Is the salt on the table?"

CHAPTER 27

THE PIT

Waleed dropped to his hands and knees and began to search for the GPS, looking for any light showing through the snow from the thing's screen. *It probably shut off after a period of inactivity to save the battery.* Waleed sighed and dug into his coat pocket. Ahmed had forbidden them to bring torches, but Waleed brought one anyway. He clicked on the LED flashlight and kept it close to the ground, trying to recreate the accident in his mind, thinking about where it would have landed when Ahmed hit the ground.

Ahmed waited in the darkness, trying not to move. Even breathing caused twinges of pain from his injured leg, and he tried to think about the next move. Halil and the others were skirting around the rim and would be behind him soon. If this excavation wasn't on the map or satellite, it must be recent. He could make out the tire tracks left by heavy vehicles. That meant there would be a road into this crater and maybe a faster way through these woods. Especially with his broken leg. This could be a good thing! He hoped Mohammet wasn't watching this utter balls-up from his seat in the afterlife.

A glimpse of light from across the pit caught his eye. *Waleed was using a torch, damn him!* He watched the narrow beam of light from across the crater, and his anger subsided. Waleed did the right thing. It was more important to find the damn GPS and get moving than to worry about being detected. Ahmed also knew if he had been more aware, he would not have fallen, and this delay would not have occurred. *If I'd thought this through, I would have told Saeed to fly over again for a final look.* He adjusted his position and winced as his leg shifted. He embraced the pain as payment for being a fool.

* * *

Halil could vaguely see the pit's edge to his left as they pulled the sled through the trees. He could hear Nadeem and Ghazi gasping behind him and knew both of them were losing strength fast. They would have to haul Ahmed up the other side of the crater, and it was going to be a bloody challenge. *Stupid fool,* Halil thought. *Ahmed had to be the leader, and he led himself into a fucking hole!* He hoped it wouldn't be as steep a grade on the south end.

Waleed had found the GPS and handed it back to Ahmed. He waited while Ahmed put the thing around his neck and confirmed it was still working. Waleed wiped his nose on his sleeve and took out his pocket knife. "Try to stay still," he said to Ahmed. "I'll get something for a splint, and we'll get you fixed up." He didn't say that 'fixing him up' would involve setting the bone and a massive amount of pain.

Ahmed heard Waleed move off behind him into the night. Another sound came to his ears, and he hoped it was Halil finally reaching the other side of this damnable hole. He tried to breathe evenly and fight against the throbbing pain below his knee. The ache was exquisite, and he just wanted to lie down and forget everything. *A footfall behind him!* His heart beat faster, but before he could react, Waleed was next to him, kneeling in the snow. "How are you doing, Ahmed?" Waleed seemed as pained as Ahmed felt.

"I'm ready to get moving."

Waleed shook his head. *Ahmed was tough, but that only takes you so far.* "We have to set this leg of yours before we can go anywhere." He had the duct tape ready and trimmed the willow branches to length. *Where were Halil and the others? Fucking assholes. We should be in a warm house by now, eating hot food and getting ready to sleep!* He sat back on his haunches and wiped his nose with the back of his hand. "Once the others show up, we can set your leg." He waited a moment for that to sink in. "You know what that means, eh?"

Ahmed said nothing.

Waleed craned his neck, looking into the darkness. "I can hear the shitheads but can't see them yet. I'll guide them in."

In a moment, they were all there, standing gravely at his side. He couldn't see their faces, but he could hear their labored breathing and felt he should say something. "This is just a setback. Waleed will get this leg mended, and we'll be off again." Their silence told him they weren't giving him much of a chance. "Oy! If I can handle it, so can you!" A fresh wave of pain washed over him, and he clenched his jaw.

Waleed put his hand on Ahmed's shoulder. "Enough talk, let's see this through." He gave Ghazi the torch, motioning for Halil and Nadeem to take positions at Ahmed's side. Waleed knelt in front of his patient, looking at the gruesome leg and foot 180 degrees out of place. Halil and Nadeem seized Ahmed under the armpits, holding him tightly. Waleed gripped the broken leg, and Ahmed moaned like a lost soul, dreading this new hell to come. Waleed pulled and twisted at the same time, and Ahmed released a tormented howl into the sky. His scream echoed through the crater and beyond, filling all of them with a feeling of dread and foreboding.

CHAPTER 28

DINNER

The hunters sat down to eat Phillip's meal with fear, knowing how sensitive he was about his cooking. Axel placed his pipe in an ashtray next to his plate, a slender line of smoke rising in a gray string, only ruffling and dispersing well above their heads.

Phillip strained to hear any thanks for their upscale dinner. Maybe a frozen pizza was what he should have made. Something cheap and inedible. He used to eat them in college once in a while, but he'd rather have the cardboard tray now.

Everyone ate in silence except for Marty. He was too drunk to be sensible. "Do we have any ketchup?"

Phillip stopped chewing and set down his fork. "Ketchup? Why would you want ketchup on Beef Wellington?"

Marty looked around the table for help, but no one met his eyes, so he forged ahead. "Well, I think it needs…Something."

Phillip leaned back in his chair and looked at the ceiling. "Hmmm…Let's see, aged prime beef, Parma ham, shallots, red wine…and *morel mushrooms* for Christ's sake!"

Marty waited, fork hovering above his plate, pretty sure there wasn't going to be any ketchup coming his way.

Kurt sipped on his beer, Jordan stopped probing the dish to see what was in it, and Aurora started eating faster. Axel ignored everything.

"Phil," Marty began…

"It's Phillip, and if you want ketchup, you'll have to drive back to town." He took a draught from his wineglass (the first the camp had seen) and slammed it down without the drama of a beer bottle or shot glass.

"Geez, Phil...Um, Phillip, I'm just sayin'...."

Kurt cleared his throat, "Phillip, Marty's a dumbass. He would put ketchup on ice cream! Don't get so bent out of shape. The food's fine!" The others were grateful that someone would break this condiment stalemate.

Phillip Winter knew something about Minnesota argot, and *fine* usually meant *fuck you*. "Fine?" he said, pushing back from the table. "Fine? I think you guys need to experience something more than McDonald's or Marge's Café! Christ, you all think the height of cuisine is the Red Lobster in Fargo!"

Aurora blushed. She liked Red Lobster. *Where else were they supposed to get seafood around here?* "Uncle Phil, the food's good!" She reassured him. "I mean, the soup tasted great and the....Beef Wellington seems like it's just right!"

"I could use some ketchup too," Jordan said absently.

Kurt shook his head and nudged Marty under the table. "The food's fine, Phillip. Look, we're all eating. We're cool. Just drop it!" Marty went back to his plate and picked up where he left off.

Phillip fumed silently, pushing his eyeglasses back on his nose, glaring at everyone through the thick lenses, daring anyone to say something more. The table was silent except for the renewed scraping of silverware against the plates. He drained the last of his wine and finally began to finish his plate. It was cold now, and everyone knew that Beef Wellington had to be served piping hot.

Thank God this would be the last time he would ever be up here.

* * *

Aurora and Jordan did the dishes. They were new at camp, and that was the deal. Besides, Grandpa Axe was sick, and neither of them could imagine Marty or Kurt doing dishes. Uncle Phil made dinner, so he was off the hook according to camp rules, leaving the two of them. Jordan was irritated that his dad wouldn't let him sit with the men. The cabin wasn't big enough to have any particular sitting area, but there was a definite man zone, and it wasn't at the kitchen sink.

Kurt sipped his beer, and Axel sipped his whiskey, both trying not to piss off Phillip. Marty was at the woodstove, poking at the logs, trying to make room for one more.

"Marty, stop irritating that stove and sit down! It's warm enough in here already." Kurt loosened his shirt collar and rolled up his sleeves.

Marty squinted into the flames and shrugged, closing the iron door and leaning the poker against the wall. Sensing the tension, he cleared his throat. "I have to go drain the lizard. Can I get you guys anything? Phillip, you want a beer or something?"

"No thanks." Phillip didn't look up from his crossword puzzle, trying to ignore Marty.

"Bring me another one, Marty," Kurt said, stretching his arm out to put the empty onto the table. He'd weathered many of Phillip's emotional storms over the years, and his big brother was just as much a stranger as he'd always been. They should knock off giving Phillip the needle, but it was going to be tough. The guy just begged to be jerked around.

When people drink alcohol, even the expensive kind, tongues loosen, and the primitive self takes over. Marty had managed to down four bottles of cheap beer since arriving at the cabin. He handed Kurt a bottle and sat back down at the table to start on his fifth.

"So Phil," he began, a virtual grenade in a plaid shirt, "I see you're still driving that green Subaru? You know, they make cars for men now, right?"

Kurt put down his beer and couldn't believe Marty had gone there.

"It's still in good shape," Phillip said defensively, missing the jab. "What should I do...Get rid of it because it's not the newest model?"

Marty ignored Phillip's reply. "And what's with the 'COEXIST' sticker? I mean, talk about a useless platitude...Why not 'PUSSY WAGON' or 'HONK IF YOU'RE HORNY'?"

Phillip stared at Marty. "What?"

"Never mind," Marty said, leaning back in his chair. Under his breath, he whispered, "Maybe you should get one that says 'MY OTHER RIDE IS A FIST.'"

Aurora and Jordan didn't know what they were talking about, and Axel just stared at his glass of scotch as though it might speak to him.

Kurt stepped in like a fool. "It's all good, Phillip. It's your car! If you want to put useless platitudes on it, then more power to you."

Phillip pushed his glasses up on his nose and pulled a strand of hair away from his face. "You guys are bathed in unexamined privilege and don't even know it!"

"Dial it down, Boys," Axel cautioned halfheartedly. He knew this would be a real blow-up, but maybe it was best to let them go at it and vent a little. He glared daggers at Marty for starting this whole shit show.

Kurt called Phillip a socialist moron. Phillip told Kurt he was a closet racist and an entitled asshole. It went on for a while longer, Marty goading them on until Phillip let loose with a screed that left the cabin in silence. None of them would be able to remember his message exactly, but it included concepts like "patriarchy," "white centrism," "xenophobia," and "the disenfranchised people in the shadows." Their consternation rivaled a freshman on the first day of *Intro to Sociology.*

Jordan and Aurora watched the fray like a tennis volley, trying to follow the conversation by its emotional pitch.

Marty leaned back in his chair. "Bathed in unexamined privilege? Patriarchy? Wow, Phil, you're woke as fuck, aren't you?"

Phillip glared at his antagonists but felt ashamed he was baited into an argument.

"So, Phillip, what exactly do you do these days?" Kurt asked in a voice as cold as snow, ready for round two.

Marty broke into the conversation. "Yeah, Phil, still doing the rent-a-mob thing for Antifa? Grant whore? Unitarian grief counselor?"

Phillip began, pushing his chin forward, "I'm a public advocate for...."

"Public advocate?" Kurt interrupted. "Is that like a community organizer?"

"Well, not really…" Phillip replied in a wavering tone.

"Good, because you couldn't organize a new box of pencils!"

Marty chuckled and crossed his arms, rocking in his chair with glee. Phillip was apoplectic. "Shut up, you goddamn wingnuts!"

"Enough!" Axel slapped his hand on the oak table, silencing them with his rumbling voice. "I won't have this place tainted with politics or arguments between family! Shame on all of you! Wasn't I just talking about tradition and leaving the outside world behind? This cabin is my sanctuary, and if you three came up here just to patronize me, you can all go to hell! I should kick your asses out into the storm and let you sleep in your cars because you're not welcome here with that political bullshit!"

Aurora stood with her heart racing. Axel's threat booming in the small cabin.

Jordan leaned up to whisper in Rory's ear. "Holy crap! Grandpa's pissed!"

"No shit," she replied, "I think I just peed a little!"

"Lights out!" Axel growled at them, rising and slipping off his suspenders. "We've got an early start in the morning." He went to his bunk and began taking off his boots.

Marty went around the table and started through the door, his face white. "Gotta pee one last time before bed," he muttered.

Phillip and Kurt wouldn't make eye contact as they walked outside and went in different directions. Aurora waited for the men to shuffle out before taking a flashlight and heading to the outhouse.

She went into the privy and closed the door, setting the light on the bench next to the toilet seat. She pulled down her jeans and underwear, gasping when she hit the wooden seat, but in seconds it was tolerable, and she relaxed. Her head was swimming from the scotch, but more from the tension in the cabin. The rift between her uncles was enormous, and she wondered how they would keep it together until Sunday. They'd go their separate ways for the morning hunt, but tomorrow night would probably be epic. She finished and swung the door open, clicking off the flashlight to let her eyes adjust to the dark. The sky was just a little lighter than the woods and ground, and she picked her way back to the cabin carefully. The lanterns were off, and Rory thought she would stay outside for a little while and let things settle down. Like men, they would worry and come out looking for her if she dawdled too long, and like men, they would probably forget all of their harsh words by morning. Rory climbed the porch steps and sat down on the cooler by the door. The cold and snow were gratifying as she leaned back against the rough wall of the cabin.

"Are you going to sleep out here?" Axel stood in the darkened doorway wearing his red union suit and a pair of worn slippers.

"What are you doing up?" Aurora asked, startled by her grandfather the second time this night. The others must have retreated to their bunks.

"Doing my business," Axel said, closing the door behind him. "It just takes me a while to get organized lately."

Aurora smiled in the dark. "That's okay. I'm just trying to process everything."

"Don't waste time processing anything," Axel replied, starting down the steps. "Phillip and Kurt have been fighting since Kurt could talk. Politics is just the latest subject. Right or wrong, they're both sincere, and that's the tragedy of the whole debate. There isn't any middle ground anymore, and that's too bad."

"Grandpa, was there a middle ground when you were younger?"

Axel gave a short laugh, remembering the late sixties. "No, I guess not. Most things are better now, but some are worse."

Aurora wanted to ask him more questions, but it wasn't the time. She stood up and opened the door to the cabin. "Goodnight, Grandpa."

"Goodnight, Rory. I'm happy you're here. Don't let the boys bother you. Tomorrow will be better."

Aurora smiled and hoped he was right.

CHAPTER 29

ARRIVAL

The five rested at the edge of the woods surrounding a clapboard house in a small clearing. There was no sign of activity besides two dim gas lanterns swaying from the branches of a tree. Ghazi was gasping for breath, leaning against a tree. Halil took Ahmed's arm from around his neck and sat him on a tree stump. He scanned the trees surrounding the house for danger. Waleed still held onto the sled rope with one hand, his other undoing his collar and pulling open his coat while Nadeem leaned forward with his hands on his knees, panting like a dog.

Ahmed tried to get comfortable. Waleed did a bang-up job on the splint, but his leg was numb, and Ahmed didn't know if it was going dead from lack of circulation or just the cold. He counted the dulled pain as a blessing. All of them were still breathing heavily, and steam was rising from their heads and shoulders. It was a tougher chore than it had to be, and Ahmed cast an embarrassed glance at Halil, knowing the balance of power would shift if he didn't keep control of the mission.

Ahmed put his finger to his lips to ensure none of them spoke. "Waleed," Ahmed whispered, handing him a Walther pistol. "This is the most dangerous time. Take this and go round to the front of the house and see if anything seems amiss." He didn't share that Waleed was expendable and wanted Halil at his side if something went wrong.

Waleed nodded and took the pistol, surprised that Ahmed was armed. The automatic was warm from being inside Ahmed's coat, and Waleed felt better investigating the house with a weapon. They planned for this rendezvous, but now that he was leaving the forest's safety, it seemed far more dangerous. He put the thought out of his mind and left the others with the sled.

The wind pelted him with snow once he left the trees, and Waleed kept his head down, glancing up with squinting eyes to see if anything was moving. He approached the back corner of the building and stretched up, chancing a look into one of the dirty windows. He couldn't see anything inside but thought he could hear voices around the front. He moved in the shadows along the wall, following the footprints of whoever had placed the lanterns in the tree.

Edging around the front corner with the pistol in a ready position, Waleed spotted a man standing in a pool of light thrown from the front doorway. The man was looking towards a driveway approaching the house from the front. It was as though he was trying to make contact with someone in the darkness. Waleed suspected a trap, but he could see no weapons, and the man's light clothing and wild hair were nothing a soldier or policeman would tolerate. Waleed moved away from the house and stood in the open, The Walther at the ready. The man sensed Waleed's presence and turned around.

Thomas had stepped out to get some fresh air and urinate. He was high from two bowls of Hindu Kush and reacted slowly to Waleed's appearance, stroking his beard absently as the gaunt figure materialized out of the darkness. "Fuck...Who are you?" Thomas asked in a slurred voice.

Waleed quickly moved forward, cocking the pistol's hammer and pressing it against Thomas Duchamp's chest. "Where is Saeed Alghamdi?" Waleed hissed, grasping a fist full of Thomas's wispy beard and moving the pistol to Thomas's throat.

"Hey man, what the fuck?" Thomas stammered, stumbling backward.

"I asked you a question!" Waleed was beyond frustrated after what he'd endured getting here. "You cannot be Saeed...Where is he, asshole?"

"I am Saeed," the Saudi spoke from the open doorway of the house. "Please calm down - Where is Ahmed?"

Waleed quickly let go of Duchamp's beard and backed away, aiming the pistol at the silhouette in the doorway. Thomas coughed and rubbed his throat.

"Saeed Alghamdi? Thanks to you, the whole fucking program is messed up!" Waleed left Thomas standing in the snow in front of the cabin. He climbed the porch steps, still aiming the pistol at Saeed. "Who the hell is that, by the way?" Waleed growled, nodding over his shoulder.

"That is Thomas, Saeed quickly replied, putting his hands up. "He is a friend. We thought you might be coming from the road."

"Yeah, dude, where the hell did you come from?" Duchamp was approaching the steps, shivering in his Johnny Cash sweatshirt. "How the fuck did you get here?"

Waleed frowned and looked back at the bearded American. Before Waleed could say anything, Saeed gently touched his shoulder. "Calm down and tell me your name."

Waleed glared, still aiming the pistol at Saeed. "Later. Are you two the only ones here? Anyone else?"

Saeed shook his head. "No, we're alone." He glanced at Duchamp. "Thomas, this is one of the friends I spoke of." Saeed gave a nervous smile to Waleed. "Please bring Ahmed and the others, and we'll all meet inside where it's warm."

Waleed said nothing but turned to go back down the porch steps and almost ran into Thomas. Waleed was disgusted by the glassy, unfocused stare as he shoved the fool out of the way. Ahmed would not like this new development, but it would be his problem to sort out. The others would be getting very uneasy, and he needed to let them know he had made contact.

The four had been watching and waiting for Waleed to reappear, and Ahmed was becoming edgy, already thinking of his contingency plans. He knew it had only been a few minutes, and he forced himself to control his emotions. Ahmed checked his watch for the sixth time, sensing the fear rising in his companions. They were like coiled springs, and he knew he would have to remain in control. This was when he envisioned an American ambush ending with their capture and the waste of all their efforts.

He saw a figure rounding the house through the snow to the tree with the lanterns. "Easy, mates," Ahmed cautioned. "If it's a trap, they won't see us. We'll have time to fight or run."

"You can't run, and neither can we," Halil whispered in a hoarse voice. "If that isn't Waleed coming round, we're well and truly fucked!" As if to punctuate the statement, Ahmed heard the sound of Halil cocking his Tokarev. The four held their breath as the figure pulled one of the lanterns out of the tree.

Waleed held the lantern next to his cheek, the heat warming his face, the snow hissing on its metal shroud. He waved with his free arm to show them all was clear.

"It's Waleed!" Ahmed growled at Halil, projecting his own fear and doubt. "Put that damned pistol away, and don't be so bloody quick to think the worst! You might get your chance to face the Americans soon enough." He hoped Halil still knew who was in charge.

Exasperated, Halil moved out into the open yard to speak with Waleed. Ghazi went to Ahmed's side, and they both waited for help getting him into the house.

Halil gave a tense nod to Waleed as he crossed the open yard. His feeling of relief vanished as Waleed reached him, and Halil saw the look of concern on his face. "What is it?"

"Nothing," Waleed replied, his voice too loud.

"Where is Saeed Alghamdi? Halil asked, looking beyond Waleed, expecting their contact to help them after so much trouble.

"Right where I left him," Waleed replied bitterly. He was about to tell Halil that Saeed wasn't alone, but that would be obvious soon enough. "It's clear. Let's get Ahmed into the house."

Ahmed forced himself to calm down as he watched Halil speaking to Waleed. "Ghazi, Nadeem," Ahmed said, "You watch over the package while they get me to the safe house. I'll send for you as soon as I know nothing is amiss."

The two didn't respond, hanging back while Halil and Waleed struggled with Ahmed between them, leaving Ghazi and Nadeem to stand at the edge of the forest.

"I hope it won't be long," Nadeem whispered. The cold was already chilling the sweat on his back and arms. "I'm sick of this bullshit. I want to rest and have something to eat."

Ghazi leaned against a tree. "Careful what you wish for, Nadeem. We'll be in that house soon enough."

"What do you mean by that? You think they are going to kill us?" Nadeem stepped closer as if meaning to shake a response from Ghazi.

Ghazi pushed away from the tree and faced Nadeem. "I mean, we don't know these men very well, and things haven't gone smoothly so far. How is that going to change now that we're at some farmhouse in the middle of nowhere?"

Nadeem moved back a pace. "I don't know, but they have guns, and we don't."

"Exactly." Ghazi sat down on the sled and stretched. "Just relax and wait. Besides, we made it to America, didn't we?"

Nadeem sat on the stump Ahmed had occupied, and in the silence, Ghazi began to hum in an irritating monotone. "Do you have to do that?" He said in a harsh whisper.

Ghazi didn't seem to hear him, humming quietly in the dark.

Chapter 30

Night at Camp

Rory lay awake, reliving the day. She needed the dark and solitude to put aside distractions and see things as they are. The time between climbing into bed and falling asleep was when she thought most lucidly. Her grandfather was dying. Her mother was an alcoholic and mentally unbalanced. All she could do was love them both and contain her emotions until she could release them in manageable stages to find joy again. She was still thinking about the argument between her uncles and the rift between them. She wasn't sure what she could do about it, but now she understood what was meant by *irreconcilable differences.*

She thought of her ancestors and their Norse traditions. She was a voracious reader and absorbed every book she could find on Viking culture. The Norse lived in one of the harshest regions on Earth, in villages clustered next to glaciers and fjords, not just surviving but thriving as they set out to conquer lands and gain knowledge of the world beyond their own. In the cabin, with the wood stove's dying flames flickering against the walls, it wasn't hard to feel their presence. Not unlike Aurora's clan, they gathered around their hearths with glowing embers and licking flames centered in great wooden halls with their fathers' war shields adorning the rafters with woolen banners shifting slowly in the currents of heated air. They would relate the sagas of their history and celebrate the victories and deeds of the fallen.

But the Norse were fatalists, and for proof, one only had to observe their afterlife. A berserker felled in battle was born up by the Valkyries and taken to Valhalla to war anew each day in paradise. The ichor from the celestial bodies of the defeated bloodied the grounds of heaven until they were resurrected for a great feast each night. But all knew that paradise was not eternal and the dreaded Ragnarök would come. Odin and

123

the Aesir's gods would perish from treachery and seal the fate of Yggdra-sil, the tree of worlds.

Aurora thought she understood the dark and stoic resolve of their ethos and the flinty existence that created such a dour afterlife. Their land could be cold and bitter, culling the weak and forging a people strong as iron who crafted their salvation from ships that bore them to new countries and freed them from the shackles of their homeland.

Aurora sighed. Viking maiden or not, the cabin was getting colder, and the chill was going to be too much for her sleeping bag. She thought about getting up to stoke the fire but didn't want to be the weak little girl who couldn't take it. She shivered and tucked her legs up, trying to conserve heat, berating herself for not bringing an extra blanket. Nevertheless, Rory refused to get cold on her first night in camp and closed her eyes, willing herself to sleep.

"Jesus, it's cold!" Kurt whispered loudly in the darkness, throwing back his sleeping bag and struggling out of his bunk. "Time to throw some more oak on that fire!"

Aurora smiled in the darkness. *Maybe we Vikings aren't so tough after all.*

CHAPTER 31

THE SAFE HOUSE

Ahmed panted with effort even as Halil and Waleed supported him up the steps and through the open door into the yellow light and heat of the safehouse. He entered the room like a wounded Caesar, his adjutants flanking him, their worried faces betraying the disaster that was unfolding.

Saeed stood useless with his hands at his sides, eyes wide as the men came in with a scuffling of boots and a rush of cold air. He had never met these men, but there was no question which of them was Ahmed. Saeed was shocked to see one of the man's legs bound with a splint and beads of sweat on his forehead.

Ahmed surveyed the darkened room without meeting Saeed's eyes. "How long have you been here?"

Saeed flinched at the man's tone. "Several hours," he replied.

Ahmed glared at Saeed without really seeing him. "Several hours? What the hell does that mean?" Saeed could feel Ahmed's anger from across the room. Saeed cleared his throat and came forward. "We arrived around three this afternoon," Saeed said as quickly as he could. "Everything is secure, the weather is in our favor, and no one will be traveling for at least the next twelve hours. We barely made it here in the blizzard, and there is no one else around!" He cast a furtive glance at Thomas sprawled on the threadbare sofa, his head nodding on his chest. "We have the vehicle ready to travel. With the four-wheel drive, it will be able to get out and onto the main road."

Ahmed glared at Thomas and a coffee table strewn with cigarette butts and the remains of their dinner. A pink glass bong half-full of dirty water completed the scene. "We?" Ahmed's voice boomed in the small room, and Saeed looked at the floor, his face burning, knowing he hadn't followed their plan.

Ahmed shook his head in disgust. "Put me somewhere I can get off this bloody leg."

"Hold him," Halil said, ducking away from Ahmed and leaving Waleed to manage. He went over to the sofa and slapped Thomas in the face. "Get up, you bloody wanker! Bugger off and let Ahmed have a rest!"

Thomas awoke with a start and rubbed his cheek, trying to focus on Halil's face. "What...."

Halil slapped him again. "Get up, ya twat! Move!"

Thomas rolled away from Halil and fell off the sofa onto his knees. "Christ! Okay, I'm moving!" He crawled over to one of the chairs in the small room. "What the fuck?"

Halil glared at him and went back to Ahmed and helped Waleed place him on the sofa. The two carefully lifted Ahmed's legs as he grimaced with pain. Ahmed pulled off his sodden gloves and threw them onto the floor. He opened his collar and arched his back, his muscles stiff after the long haul across the border.

Saeed watched from across the room, his hands in his pockets, wanting to help but knowing this was not a time to speak. These men were of a different culture and mindset, and he cursed himself for thinking this would go as planned. *I truly must have lost my mind to think these men would tolerate softies like Thomas and me!* A trickle of sweat rolled down Saeed's back, and he began to rehearse his excuses.

Ahmed fought to block the pain and gather his thoughts. This entire venture was spiraling into failure, and it was time to get control! He gritted his teeth and shifted onto his side so he could face the others. "Halil, Waleed, help Ghazi and Nadeem put the package in Saeed's lorry." Ahmed didn't speak forcefully; he was tired of explaining everything to these asses. He waited until the two had closed the door behind them before he glared at Saeed in the dim light. "Get the men some food and ready a place for them to sleep when they get back!"

Saeed Alghamdi clasped his hands together and nodded vigorously in acquiescence. "If I may ask, what happened, Ahmed?" Saeed tried hard to sound concerned. "How were you injured?

"My leg is broken. I fell into a bloody gravel pit on the way here that you failed to mention the last time we went over the route!"

Confused, Saeed opened his mouth to reply, but Ahmed had laid back on the sofa and closed his eyes. Saeed tried to signal Thomas, but his friend nodded off again in an old plaid recliner next to the oil stove. Saeed hurried into the small kitchen and found a box of wooden matches. His hand was shaking, and it took three tries to light the burner.

"Saeed Alghamdi," Ahmed called from the other room, waving his hand in the air. "Open a fucking window. It stinks in here!"

* * *

Halil and Waleed went down the porch steps, relieved to get out of that pig's den. Halil tucked his hands into his coat pockets. "I'll see if the truck is ready. You go help Ghazi and Nadeem drag the sled so we can load it for the morning."

Waleed stared at Halil with contempt. "Why don't you go drag the sled, and I'll check the truck?"

Halil pushed Waleed away and pointed to where Ghazi and Nadeem were waiting. "Piss off and go get the sled!" He turned and left Waleed standing in the snow. Waleed fumed as he followed the tracks back to the wood line behind the house. Ghazi and Nadeem were invisible in the darkness, their figures blending with the trees. Waleed's boots crunched softly in the deepening snow, and he wondered if they would be able to get out of here in the morning.

"Well, you two aren't the only pain in my ass on this adventure!" Waleed said in a loud whisper.

Ghazi stood up from sitting on the sled. "What's wrong?"

"Saeed's fucked up twice already, and we've only just met him!" Waleed replied. "He brought a friend."

Ghazi wasn't sure what he was talking about but knew that Saeed was a pilot and the only friend they had in America.

"There is someone here other than Saeed?" Nadeem asked, his fear rising again.

"Probably not for long," Waleed replied.

Ghazi was shifting from foot to foot in the snow. Waleed noticed Ghazi was shivering, and he considered that maybe he had been too hard on the boy. Ghazi had held his own with the others, and with Ahmed's injury and Halil's brutality, the hazing had to stop. "Give me a hand with this damned sled one last time, and we'll haul it around to the front," he said in a softer tone, leaning forward and touching Ghazi's shoulder. "Just a little farther as sled dogs, and we're done for the night."

Nadeem took the front, and Ghazi handled the trailing end. Half-way across the yard, Waleed noticed Ghazi stumble and took up the rope, pushing the boy aside to let him rest. "Thank you, Waleed," Ghazi whispered, wearily following behind. They rounded the house to the front, where a tan Suburban was parked. Halil was rearranging items in the back to make room for the sled. Nadeem and Waleed dropped the ropes and went to sit on the porch steps.

Ghazi thought their exhaustion might be something more serious. There was a sense of defeat in the others that didn't seem right. *Why should they feel this way? Yes, Ahmed was injured, but hadn't they already beaten the Americans? They had crossed the border and got to this place safely, and that was the hardest thing. Now there was this feeling of unease?* Ghazi thought hard on this as they helped Halil load the sled into the back of the Suburban. It took all four of them to lift it, and after it was safely inside, Halil slammed down the cargo door. "Come on, you lot," Halil said as he turned and trudged past them up the porch steps. "Let's see if there's anything to eat around here."

* * *

Saeed Alghamdi couldn't fall asleep. He let the others take the two bedrooms and sat in a moldering chair in the living room. Not that he had a choice. Halil, the most fearsome of them, was apoplectic with Saeed and would probably take it out on Thomas. His friend was sleeping like a child while Saeed sat awake, worrying for him. *Why did I think this would go smoothly?* He fumed. *I knew this could happen, but thinking of something in the abstract is easy. Taking action to affirm your convictions is much more difficult!*

He wasn't that worried about Ahmed punishing him. Saeed was too valuable, and his contribution was almost as crucial as getting the bomb to America. He knew he was just a part of something much larger but still felt he held the upper hand with the men. He was a trained pilot and would deliver the bomb at the right location and altitude to do the most damage.

And that brought him back to Thomas. His friend shouldn't have to die. He liked Thomas despite his lack of religion or faith in anything. Thomas was essentially an empty vessel, and Saeed felt he could be trusted, perhaps not with the whole truth, but enough to excite him and allow him to help them now and in the future. Saeed felt an icy jab under his heart. *What future? I will be dead within a week, and what did Thomas matter then?* He knew he should pray for guidance and, most of all, forgiveness for his prideful acts. He felt an emptiness that he had never experienced before, even when he'd drank himself to sleep, struggling with his decision to sacrifice himself in jihad. He thought somehow he would become closer to God, not adrift in doubt.

He leaned back and closed his eyes. Today was a hard day, and tomorrow would be worse. Much worse.

CHAPTER 32

AXE

Axel lay staring at the bottom of Kurt's bunk in the dark and listened to the stove ticking as the fire waned and the metal contracted. He was tired, but his mind always struggled with bad memories just before sleep. Lately, it was thoughts of death and the afterlife. He'd seen heavy combat and been in his share of scrapes, but with cancer, no cleverness, no personal skill, no bravery could protect you. It was like being strapped on a conveyor belt to nowhere.

He felt Ellen's absence suddenly, and he was surprised to feel a tear wet his cheek. He hadn't done well with his two boys tonight, and she would have handled things better, especially with Phillip. He hoped Aurora wasn't too upset by what she'd seen and heard. She had asked if there was a middle ground in his younger days, and he considered that again.

Today the right and left were seeking different Americas. Even at the height of Vietnam and as the nation became aware of its darker history, both sides desired health, happiness, and the opportunity for the future, only differing in the means to achieve them. To Axel, no matter the strife or issue, America was still America. It was the framework for all to participate, and injustice could be righted within that framework. White or black, south or north, left or right, it housed us all. Axel wasn't against protest, even violent protest, but to stab at the heart of the country and constitution was to burn down your house with you in it.

There was another time in America that split the country. PFC Axel Winter served in Vietnam with the 1st Battalion, 7th Marines. He grew up fast, hauling dead and wounded from the battle zone on bloody stretchers on his first day in-country. He would never forget the smell of opened human viscera and the stench of blood and shit so strong you couldn't help but puke until your chest ached.

In-country, Axel rides a Huey chopper with six other Marines heading for a landing zone in the central highlands. A salty Corporal with a red handlebar mustache in a boonie hat sits on his helmet, smirking at them while they play grab-ass and talk shit. They're enjoying their grand adventure as the veteran suddenly stands in the door and cycles the bolt on the M60 machine gun mounted at a downward angle to aim at the heavy jungle canopy below. Corporal mustache turns and smiles at Axe and the other newbies. "Just thinkin' out loud here...." He yells over the turbine engines, "But you cherry motherfuckers might want to put mags in your rifles and accept Jesus as your personal savior because you are about to land in a world of shit!"

Axel and the others look at each other, half smiling, half frowning, then the Corporal looses a burst of fire from the waist gun at some target below, and all hell breaks loose.

The chopper does a swooping slowdown that couldn't be called a landing, and all seven tumble from the Huey, Axel last. Three are killed outright, victims of a distant DShK machine gun raking the LZ, but Axel and three others make it to a slit trench and roll over the ragged sandbags along the edge. They land on top of their new Gunnery Sergeant, his black face shining with sweat in the midday sun.

"Whoa, look at all you beautiful little babies!" He laughs over the noise of battle, his teeth white against his blue-black skin. "You guys just lay right here! Protect my black ass! That's it, baby! Stay between me and Mr. Charles!"

Axel is more confused than scared. To go from such an idyllic flight through azure skies over a patchwork of lush green and brown to a howling storm of battle is surreal. Axel crawls past the Sergeant and pushes his back against the cool dirt of the trench. His rifle is gone, and he puts his hands over his ears, the thumping of mortar rounds numbing his brain.

"I'm done with this!" Axel shouts, his voice lost in the maelstrom of battle. "I'm cold, and I'm getting up!" He stands and boosts himself, working his boot tips into the soft earth, trying to climb out of the trench and get warm. The DShK rounds strike his back like hammer blows, passing through him and bucking him off the ground with their impacts...

131

Axel awoke with a start, unsure of where he was. He lay panting, the sweat on his forehead cooling in the darkness. The phantom dream retreated, and he let the nightmare drop back into his subconscious. The fire had gone out, and it was getting cold in the shack. *Aurora will probably be freezing,* he thought. He was about to climb out of his bedroll when he heard Kurt mutter something above him, then crawl down from the top bunk and feel his way in the dark to tend the stove.

Axel put his arm across his eyes and tried again to sleep. *I can't stand the past, and I have no future.* He prayed there would be no more dreams so he could cling to what was left.

* * *

"Daylight in the swamp!"

Joshua Camp came to life.

For the first time in decades, Kurt was the first to rouse the cabin. No one had ever needed an alarm clock at the camp. There was always someone too excited to sleep, or had gotten too cold or just had to hit the outhouse. The group lay in the dark and listened to Kurt slip on his leather boots and clunk across the plank flooring, the laces slithering behind him as he crossed to the table. Then the familiar sound of the matchbox opening and the sudden scratch and flare of flame.

Aurora, her sleeping bag pulled around her head like a hood, watched Kurt's determined face as he maneuvered the flame up to the lantern. There was a low *woof,* and with a soft hissing, the lantern glowed brighter and brighter. Kurt squinted against the glare and ran his hand through his mop of yellow hair. He blinked and rubbed his eyes, looking around at his campmates.

"What the hell?" He said with a deep morning voice. "Time to get up!" He scratched his crotch a bit and caught sight of Aurora watching him from the corner bunk. "Welcome to camp, Rory!" he winked at her and went out to piss off the front porch, letting a blast of icy air wash through the cabin.

Aurora glanced at Axel laying in his bunk with the sleeping bag open, his arm across his eyes. "You okay, Grandpa?"

Axel lifted his arm and squinted at her for a moment. "Yep. I suppose we better get up if we're going to get anything accomplished today." He threw back the sleeping bag and slowly swung his legs out of bed, and began fumbling with his pants hung on a peg next to his bunk. Aurora tried not to watch him dress. He looked weak and vulnerable and seeing him like this frightened her. Watching him falter was like looking into a deep chasm, and she felt the dread of losing him forever. She began to tear up and turned away to the wall, afraid he would see her crying.

"Hey, Rory," Jordan whispered loudly. "Did you hear that buck grunt?"

Before she could reply, Jordan released an enormous fart, even for him. "There he is! Sounds like he's inside the cabin!"

Aurora rolled her eyes. "Nice, Jordan." She was secretly glad she could think of something besides Grandpa's sickness.

"Jordy!" Kurt said, returning just in time to catch the deed. "Do that outside! Besides, you're going to kill yourself if you fart like that in your sleeping bag." Kurt went to the sink to pump water for coffee.

Phillip began snoring softly.

Jordan flipped back his sleeping bag and made a big show of waving the smell towards Aurora.

"Dammit, Jordan!" Aurora screeched, pinching her nose.

"Good rip, Jordan," Marty said from the top bunk. He was lying on top of his bag in his long johns. "Damn, it was hot up here until about an hour ago," Marty said. "Kurt must have stoked the fire after we went to bed."

Marty watched Axel slide his arms in the sleeves of his red plaid shirt and struggle to get his suspenders over his shoulders. Marty was going to ask him if he needed help, but he knew Kurt was pretending to be busy at the cookstove while keeping an eye on his old man. No one said anything as Axel stepped into his boots and shuffled to the wood stove in the corner.

"Let's get that fire going, eh folks?" Axel opened the stove, and the hinges made the same metal screech they always had. Axel fed some kindling into the dying embers, followed by two heavy pieces of split oak.

He closed the door and fiddled with the damper and air vent, confident it would flare back to life as it always did, season after season. He turned around and perceived that the others were watching him. "You heard the man, daylight in the swamp!" He shook his head and went outside to do his business.

Aurora and Jordan got out of bed and started to dress while Marty carefully swung his legs over the side of the top bunk, trying not to snag his scrotum on the rough plank as he gingerly lowered his feet to the floor. He checked his watch under the lantern. "*4:50 AM!* Jesus Christ, did we have to get up this early?"

Kurt farted mightily. "That's my answer to that."

"Nice one, Dad!" Jordan said, smiling at Aurora.

Aurora thought this was going to be a very long weekend.

Phillip slept on.

CHAPTER 33

RORY AND AXEL

Rory was uncomfortable with Axel exerting himself so early in the morning. Even worse, he'd insisted on leading the way to the deer blind in the woods to the south of the cabin. There was a faint trail winding through the brush, but it was clear her grandfather knew just where they were going. She tried to relax and just follow his red plaid jacket in the dark.

Axel walked carefully through the woods, not needing a flashlight but still cautious of deadfalls or the branch that would slap your face or poke out your eye. He hoped Aurora was keeping up and still enthused by this sport. Talking about hunting and doing it are very different, especially when you have to get up early and be alert. *It was a lot like work for some people.* Axel held a branch aside while Aurora caught up. She ducked down, and he let it snap back, a spray of fresh snow clumping onto the ground. "Thanks," Rory whispered, but The Axe was already ahead of her on the trail again.

It seemed like a long time, but soon she was at her grandfather's side while he dusted the snow off the roof of their ground blind, opening the side door and beckoning her inside. She was grateful it wasn't a tree stand and went into the pitch dark shelter, sitting down on a wooden bench, her shotgun across her lap. Axel opened the front of the blind and let the cover hinge down out of the way. She thought it was dark outside, but now that she was in the shelter, it was easy to see into the woods. Axel appeared at her side and closed the door behind him, sitting down on the bench and leaning his rifle against the wall. "Let's get some heat in here," he muttered, leaning forward. She heard the click of his old lighter, and the tongue of yellow flame lit up the deer blind. She had a moment to look around inside. A neat row of over 50 empty 30.06 rifle

135

casings lined a shelf above the door, and she noticed a squirrel nest on the floor and cobwebs in each corner. She would bring along a broom tomorrow and clean this up a bit.

Axel lit a small stove and rubbed his hands. "There we go," he said in a quiet voice. "We'll be toasty in no time!" He stood up as far as the low ceiling would allow and took off his coat. Rory thought he looked a lot younger suddenly. *Hunting was truly his element.* "You want me to hang up your coat?" He asked. "There's a hook on the wall next to you."

"No way, I'm not that warm yet!" Aurora held the collar of her coat. Axel smiled and sat down. He produced a vacuum bottle and spun off the cap. "How about a cup of joe?"

"That sounds good," Aurora replied. He handed her a cup, and she took a sip. It was strong, and she savored the taste. At home, she usually added stuff to make it drinkable, but this was just right.

"Coffee's supposed to stunt your growth if you're still a teenager," Axel said, slipping shells into his rifle and closing the bolt.

"So is Scotch, but that didn't kill me." Rory was scanning the woods in front of the blind. "What if a deer walks behind us?"

"Then we look stupid until it comes around the front."

Rory didn't reply, but she handed the cup back to Axel and loaded her shotgun with slugs.

Neither said anything more. Both waited and watched, sharing the coffee and letting the heat from the tiny stove take the edge off the wind and snow that swirled in from the window. There was no other place they would rather be.

* * *

Kurt and Jordan sat in silence in the morning darkness. All save for Phillip had left the cabin and went in separate directions. Marty went northwest, and Rory and Axel had taken the south trail to Axel's ground blind. Kurt and Jordan went to the east, trudging through the snow until the wooden tree blind materialized in the beams of their flashlights. They'd built it two summers before, constructing the frame around a sturdy birch, then making the walls and roof large enough for two to sit side by side out of the weather. Jordan thought it was cool and like the watchtower on a fort. He went up the ladder first and pushed the door open while Kurt held their rifles. Once Jordan was inside, he reached down from the doorway and took the rifles, careful not to ding them against anything. His dad was real touchy about that.

Kurt climbed up into the blind and quietly closed the door behind him. After they opened the gun ports (Jordan thought they were like the ones on a pirate ship), they sat on upended five-gallon buckets, loaded their rifles, and settled in for what could be a long wait.

Jordan sat in the darkness, glad his dad was with him. The woods made him uneasy, but especially in the dark. He pictured something huge lumbering through the woods towards them, snapping branches and parting the trees. *It would be gigantic and hairy, with glowing eyes appearing out of the whirling snow. Before they could react, it would be upon them, bellowing like a dinosaur, then smashing the wooden stand to matchsticks and seizing them by their legs and smashing them against the frozen trees!* Jordan blinked, scared out of his daydream by his imagination.

"Dad," he said more to break his mental image than curiosity, "Do you think there are any Sasquatch around here?"

Kurt rolled his eyes in the darkness. "No."

"But they say they've seen them in almost every state. Even Minnesota! " Jordan wanted to believe in Bigfoot, but not right now. Not in the woods, and for sure not in the dark.

Kurt looked at his son, and in the growing light, he could see Jordan's eyes peering into the woods, nervously turning his head to look out the windows of the shelter. "Knock it off, Spud. You're getting too old for that crap. Sasquatch is the last thing you're going to see today. I've been around these woods my whole life and haven't seen one yet!"

"Why couldn't Bigfoots be here?" Jordan wanted to be sure they weren't living in these woods while convincing his dad they existed.

"Because I said so," Kurt said, making a mental note to curb Jordan's TV and internet and get him into the woods more. "Grandpa Axe grew up here, hunted here since he was your age, and hunted all around the country. If he had seen one, don't you think you'd have heard about it?"

"I guess." Jordan thought of Grandpa growing up here, working, hunting, *living* in the woods. Jordan felt reassured that if Grandpa Axe hadn't seen one, there probably wasn't any around. "They probably just have them in Oregon and Washington." Jordan equivocated.

"There you go," Kurt said, relieved he could refocus on hunting. "Pay attention and try to keep quiet, or we aren't going to see anything with hair, Bigfoot or not."

Jordan noticed it was getting lighter. He could see deeper into the trees, and it wasn't so dark inside their shelter. He stole a glance at his dad. "When is Grandpa going to die?" Jordan hadn't been thinking about that, but he was scared to think of Axe being gone. Even more scared of that than Sasquatch.

Kurt turned away and watched the trees sway in the wind and snow. He pulled up his collar and shifted uncomfortably in his seat. "We're not sure. The doctors said six months, but I'm afraid that he will be really sick before that."

"What do you mean?"

"I mean, he may live six months, but he'll be sick and probably in bed for quite a while before he's gone. He won't be the same old Axe, and you need to prepare for that, Spud."

Jordan remained silent, and after a moment, Kurt could tell he was crying. Kurt didn't say any more but put his arm around his son as the woods became a lighter shade of gray.

CHAPTER 34

MARTY

Marty struggled up the tall Norway pine on the neighbor's land. He wasn't supposed to hunt over here, but he knew old Duchamp wasn't around anymore, and his numb-nut son, Thomas, would rather sit in a Starbucks in Dinky Town. If Axel bitched, he'd deal with it later. Marty paused for a moment, his head pounding. He had to catch his breath, but he was also thinking of Axel tearing him a new asshole for hunting the neighbor's property. *Oh well.* He panted in the darkness, clinging to the rough ladder cleats nailed into the tree, the weight of the rifle slung over his shoulder, tugging him backward. He was getting too fat for this tree climbing shit. He looked up at the old stand swaying in the darkness above him like a crow's nest. The falling snow stung his eyes, and he leaned forward, his forehead against the rough bark.

Marty climbed the rest of the rungs and heaved himself up onto the wooden platform. He unslung his rifle and leaned it against the railing made of scrap wood nailed into an old pallet wedged into a crotch of the tree. He scraped away the snow and adjusted his glasses, smearing them with water and sweat, making it almost impossible to see anything. *Shit!* He forgot to bring toilet paper for wiping his glasses and his rifle scope. Or his ass if it came to that. He backed against the tree trunk and brushed snow off the small bench seat, sitting down and struggling to remove his gloves. They were already too wet to keep his hands warm, and after he pulled them off with his teeth, he tried to get his wet hand into the pocket of his coat for the...

Dammit! He had left the flashlight on in his pocket, and a small disc of light was showing through the orange hunting coat. A surge of frustration caused him to tug the light out of the wet pocket, and in one final pull, the light came free, flew from his cold fingers, and fell into the snow at the base of the tree. Marty leaned over and looked below him. A faint ivory glow emanated from a flashlight-shaped hole in the new snow, and he closed his eyes, leaning back against the tree. *Whatever,* he thought.

He could feel the sweaty steam rising from his open collar, and though it well below freezing, he unzipped his coat and took off his hat, careful not to let it fall and join the rapidly dimming flashlight. He did what he could to clear his glasses and rifle scope and sat still for a moment, trying to wake up. His head was throbbing from the beer and lack of sleep. It was way too early for this shit. *Goddamn deer hunting. You had to navigate through the woods in the dark like a fucking ninja, rupture yourself climbing a tree, then perch five hundred feet in the air like a blind man on a flagpole. Golf was looking better all the time!* He shivered as snow whispered down through the branches and landed softly on his neck.

He slipped rifle cartridges out of his shirt pocket and quietly levered them into his Marlin rifle. The brass clinked as he slid them into the magazine. *You can't shoot one of God's furry creatures with an empty gun,* he mused to himself. He thought maybe Phillip should have one of these shoved up his ass. *That constipated douchebag might enjoy it!* He smiled to himself in the darkness and ran his hand through his hair, putting his now wet hat back on his head. Marty zipped up his coat, shoved his hands into his pockets, and waited for enough light to see a deer stupid enough to be walking around in the ass-end of a blizzard.

CHAPTER 35

THE SAFE HOUSE

Saeed Alghamdi opened his eyes and tried to focus, momentarily confused by his surroundings. Remembering where he was, his heart began to race, bringing him fully awake. He sat up in the chair and rubbed his eyes. In the weak light from an overhead bulb in the kitchen, he could see Thomas was still on the chair he had been in the night before, snoring softly, his legs pulled up under him like a child. One of Ahmed's group was sleeping on a cot near the kitchen. Saeed stood slowly, his body aching from a fitful sleep on a recliner with more mouse droppings than padding. He went into the kitchen, careful not to wake the man on the cot. Saeed poured out the batch of coffee from the night before into the dirty sink and ran the water from the faucet until it went from rusty orange to something like weak brown tea. He poured two handfuls of coffee grounds into the kettle and put it on the stove.

"What time is it?" The man on the cot asked from the living room. The voice startled Saeed, and he dropped the box of matches he was holding. He looked at his watch. "Just after six."

Waleed muttered something, and Saeed could hear him getting up from the cot. In a moment, the man that pointed a pistol at him the night before came into the kitchen. "Not ready yet, eh?" Waleed said, squinting at the coffee pot. Before Saeed could reply, Waleed brushed him aside, looking out the kitchen window, snowflakes still rushing past in the wind. "Fuck! It's still snowing." Waleed went back to where he'd slept and began to dress. "I have to take a shit," he said. "Where's the bathroom?"

Saeed was almost afraid to answer. "It's outside," he replied, "next to the small shed. You passed it as you came in from the woods last night?"

"Great," Waleed answered. "You got ass-wipe out there?"

"Yes," Saeed replied, bending down to retrieve the matchbox he'd dropped. He heard the front door open and slam closed as the man went outside. Saeed cringed, and a chill rolled down his back. *That did it. Ahmed would be awake now, and the recriminations would begin where they left off last night!* He thought of Thomas sleeping on the chair and wasn't sure how this would play out. Like the night before, his hand trembled as he lit the gas stove and set the coffee to boil.

Ahmed woke from the sound of a door slamming and tried to sit up, but a lightning bolt shot up his leg, and he fell back against the pillow, gritting his teeth against the pain. *It's a damn sight worse this morning,* he thought. *I am bloody worthless to this venture!* It was still dark outside, and the cabin was inky black. He barely remembered the men putting him to bed and tried to recall where the hell he was. *The back bedroom of a derelict house in the middle of fucking nowhere.* Ahmed groped in the darkness and brushed against a lamp chain next to the bed. He pulled it, and with a dull click, the bedside light came on, and he could see. The room was small, with wooden paneling covered with an array of ancient taxidermy. Dead fish and animal species he didn't recognize hung from the walls, their glass eyes dull with dust and grime. He shifted to sit up higher in the bed, wincing with pain as he moved the pillow against the headboard and leaned back again. He threw back the covers, dreading what he would see, but his leg looked the same as the night before.

There was no blood, but his mates had left the crude wooden splints in place, and the willow branches looked out of place in the bed linens. He felt his forehead. *He had a fever.* He flexed the toes of his damaged leg, but they didn't respond. *This is not good.* He thought of getting out of bed, but that wasn't practical and might cause him to cry out again. He'd shown his weakness enough, and he had to remain in charge. He covered his legs again and tried to make himself comfortable. "Halil!" He called in a hoarse voice. "Come in here!"

Here it comes, Halil thought to himself. *Ahmed is already giving orders.* Halil lay below Nadeem in a bunk bed in the bedroom next to Ahmed's. He finished the cigarette he'd lit when he awoke to the door slamming in the other room. He stubbed out the smoke on the floor and left the butt to smolder, getting out of bed and pulling on his trousers, still damp from the night before. Ghazi was lying on a crumpled pile of clothing with a coat for a pillow. Halil was surprised the little bastard hadn't complained. Halil pulled a heavy wool military sweater over his head, tucking it into his pants and adjusting knife sheath on his belt as he left the room.

Saeed heard Ahmed's voice calling to the one they called Halil, and he felt as though he would throw up. *A condemned man about to place his neck on the chopping block must feel this way,* he thought. Pragmatically, Saeed was too valuable to eliminate, but logic may not apply to these sorts. He feared for Thomas, and Saeed doubted he could defend his friend in the face of everything that had transpired. They all blamed him for Ahmed's accident in the gravel pit. He'd been delusional to think that Thomas could take part in this, even passively. Saeed now realized he should have just left Thomas behind and make the rendezvous without his knowledge. *But it was too late now.*

Halil appeared in the doorway to Ahmed's room, looking worse for wear as they all must. "What's happening?" Ahmed asked, "Is everything secure?"

Halil shrugged. "I believe so, we locked the device in the back of Saeed's truck last night, and after some food, we went to sleep," he replied. Halil masked his irritation with a yawn.

Ahmed shook his head and threw the covers back, struggling to sit on the edge of the bed. "Help me up so I can speak with that bloody Saeed." Halil went to his side and supported Ahmed as he swung his legs onto the floor, almost fainting as the blood rushed to his broken leg. It seemed the skin would burst open, and he cried out in pain.

"I'll get the Saudi and bring him in here," Halil said. "Just lay back. No need to make things worse for yourself." Halil pushed Ahmed back onto the bed with more force than necessary and lifted his legs back onto the mattress. "It's after six in the morning, and if we were in danger, we'd know it by now."

Ahmed took a deep breath, fighting the pain from his shattered leg, ignoring Halil's rough treatment. "Perhaps, but I don't trust that fucking Saeed. Is his bloody American still with us?

Halil frowned. "I'm not sure. I haven't checked on him."

"Don't you think you'd better?" Ahmed glared at Halil and pointed at the other room. "The bastard might be halfway to a town by now!"

Halil's anger flared at Ahmed's tone. He didn't appreciate being ordered about, but he nodded and left the room.

Saeed heard voices in the backroom and dreaded what they might be saying. Halil's footsteps were coming from the hallway and into the living room. Saeed listened as the footsteps went to where Thomas was sleeping. He almost jumped when a voice came from the darkness. "Saeed, go talk to Ahmed. He's waiting for you."

Saeed wiped his hands on a towel and went into the darkened room, stopping as he saw Halil in the dim light. "Is everything all right?" He tried not to sound frightened but knew it was no use.

"You'll find out, *ya sharmouta*," Halil replied flatly. "Ahmed's waiting." Saeed met Halil's cold eyes, the Arabic insult hanging in the air. He was in no position to protest, so he said nothing and went to see Ahmed.

Waleed came into the house with a gust of cold air and slammed the door behind him again, heedless of anyone trying to sleep. He started when he caught Halil's silhouette in the kitchen light. "Everyone is up?"

"Thanks to you, you clumsy ass." Halil's voice seemed to come from a shadow.

Waleed felt a wave of dread. *The bastard is going to ride me again today!* "Fuck off," he said, instantly regretting it.

Halil was on him in a blur, seizing him by the collar and pushing him back against the door. "What's that, mate? Did you say something?"

Waleed gasped in surprise but quickly recovered. "You heard me," he gasped, "Give it a rest, you asshole! We're all on the same team, remember?"

Halil slapped Waleed with a vicious backhand. "Listen, you bloody poseur, I'm not on anyone's team, and you're not in my league. Your part in this is over, and as far as I'm concerned, I could slit your throat and have done with it. You're on time borrowed from me, and that means I own you!" Halil let go of Waleed, and the younger man sagged against the door. Halil patted Waleed on the cheek. "Don't speak to me that way again, mate, or you might lose your head."

Halil left Waleed to simmer in anger and went down the hall to Ahmed's room.

Ahmed had a moment to collect his thoughts. The sleep helped, and he could think clearly again. Saeed was still critical to their success, and replacing him at this point would delay their timetable even more and add another missing person to draw suspicion. He was aware that time was still ticking, and at any moment, someone could discover Moham-met and the Imam in the field of autos parked at the airport. He would try to hold his temper with Saeed and reason with him, but that courtesy didn't extend to Saeed's companion.

"Ahmed, you are feeling better?" Saeed tried not to show his fear as he entered the bedroom.

"Yes, I do feel better, but I'm still fagged-out from the trek, and my bloody leg is giving me fits!" Saeed nodded and wrung his hands to-gether. "Saeed," Ahmed began, "I know the gravel pit wasn't your doing. I was just as oblivious, but who in the bloody hell would think there could be a chasm in such flatland, eh?"

Saeed smiled hopefully.

"But when we arrived, you were not alone."

Saeed's smile disappeared, and he looked at the floor. "I felt Thomas could be....Can be trusted. I think he could be useful in the future. Even after I'm gone!" Saeed wasn't about to explain himself without weaving in a reminder of his crucial role in this mission. "Perhaps he can maintain this portal across the border...You could use him to...."

Ahmed raised his hand. "Saeed, stop talking. Your companion is nothing but a distraction and has served his purpose."

"But, Ahmed," Saeed pleaded, his voice rising like a child, "Why must we kill him?" He felt strange saying the thought aloud.

Ahmed smiled patiently, "Saeed, listen to yourself! You have committed to flying over an American city and triggering a device that will kill thousands *and yourself*, but you fret over some drug-addled fool? I think you've adopted the wrong child!"

Saeed said nothing.

Ahmed changed his tone. "We all have to make sacrifices to this effort, and you're no exception."

"It seems I'm making all the sacrifices," Saeed replied indignantly, "I will be a martyr soon, and now you wish me to kill my only American contact? The man I've cultivated for years!" Saeed approached the bed and looked into Ahmed's eyes. "What can I say to change your mind?"

Ahmed's face darkened with rage. He thought of Mohammet, his beloved brother, resting under snow in such a lowly tomb, while this whining Saudi tries to impress him with a martyr's boast. "You miserable bastard! I've heard you out, and now you're going to solve this problem. Halil!" Ahmed shouted past Saeed, "Come in here!"

Saeed trembled with horror. "What are you going to do?"

"I'm not going to do a bloody thing!" Ahmed snapped. "You are! Halil will make sure you do what's proper so we can put this shit behind us without loose ends!"

Saeed jerked as a cold hand gripped the nape of his neck. Halil leaned in, resting his chin on Saeed's shoulder. "Come, *aleahirat al-saghira*," Halil whispered another Arabic insult in a soothing voice that was all the more chilling. "Let's have a walk outside and discuss our situation with your American."

Halil released his vice-like hold and spun Saeed around, shoving him out the door and propelling him down the hall, putting on a wool stocking cap and gloves as he followed the Saudi. Saeed rubbed his neck. "Don't call me a bitch again."

Halil remained silent and prodded him out into the living room. Waleed and Nadeem were in the kitchen with Ghazi waiting for the coffee to brew. Halil's glare was enough to send the three out of the kitchen and into the side bedroom. None of them wanted anything to do with whatever Halil was planning.

Thomas slept on, oblivious to the court that had sentenced him to death. Saeed stood frozen as Halil went to the chair and leaned over Thomas. Halil raised an open hand and slapped Thomas in the face, knocking him off the chair onto his side. Saeed reached out to stop Halil from further violence, but Halil brushed him away and stood with his arms crossed, observing the American.

Thomas stood awkwardly, backing against the wall and rubbing his face. "What the fuck?" His voice was fearful, and Saeed could tell his friend was close to tears. "You guys come to my house and treat me like this?" Thomas spluttered with emotion. "You can all just get the fuck out! You too!" He yelled at Saeed, the betrayal apparent in his voice.

Halil was on him before he could say more and yanked him away from the wall with an iron grip. "Come, we're all three of us going for a walk!"

"I…I'm not dressed," Thomas stammered. "I don't have any shoes on!"

"Oh, by all means, get your shoes," Halil said in a playful tone. "Grab your coat too while you're at it. It's cold outside!"

Thomas looked at Saeed pleadingly, but his friend looked away, going to a coat rack next to the door, taking down his tan parka, and tossing it to Thomas. "Here, you can wear mine," Saeed said weakly. "I'll get your shoes."

Thomas stood with the coat grasped in his hands, beginning to shake as Halil stared at him with a stone face. Saeed placed his friend's shoes on the sofa table next to the beer bottles and bong. The tension increased as Halil and Saeed waited for Thomas to step into his shoes and tighten the laces with trembling fingers. The moment he finished, Halil took him by the arm and pulled him toward the door. "Aren't you going to put on your coat?"

Thomas's face was swelling, and his left eye was almost closed. His pathetic appearance touched Saeed to the core, and he brushed a tear from his cheek, going to his friend and helping him with the heavy jacket.

Halil watched the two with interest. He thought perhaps they were homosexual, but it didn't matter now. The American would soon have a bullet in his brain, and the Saudi loverboy would have to watch. Halil slipped the Tokarev out of his pocket and took two steps forward, aiming the muzzle subtly between Saeed and Thomas. "Out the door! Now!"

Saeed placed himself between Halil and Thomas, gently prodding his friend out the front door and onto the porch. Before they could take another step, Halil shoved them across the porch, and they lost their footing and fell down the wooden steps into the snow next to the Suburban like two drunks bounced from a pub. Halil slowly walked across the rough planks of the porch then deliberately stomped down the front steps. At the bottom, he hauled the two to their feet and shoved them into the clearing. Thomas fell face-first into the snow. "Good thing you're wearing a coat," Halil goaded, "you might catch your death!"

Saeed and Thomas found their footing and stood side by side, both near shock at this sudden turn of events. Halil produced the large knife from his belt and threw it at Saeed's feet. "Take it," Halil said calmly.

Saeed backed up a step, looking at Thomas, then Halil. "Fuck you!"

"Fuck me?" Halil transferred the pistol to his left hand and quickly stepped forward, delivering a vicious punch to Saeed's stomach. The younger man staggered back, turning away in pain. "You'll do as you're told!" Halil commanded. "Take the blade and cut this fool's throat!" Saeed said nothing, appearing to be in shock. "Do it, ya sharmouta!" Halil shouted, prodding Saeed with the pistol.

Instead of leaning down to pick up the knife, Saeed lunged forward and delivered a right uppercut into Halil's chin with all his strength. The blow staggered Halil, and he fell back into the snow, stunned that the Saudi faggot could surprise him. He leaned forward and rose in the snow and heavy grass to his hands and knees. "You fucking *kos omak!*" He bawled at Saeed. Halil realized he had dropped the pistol when Saeed struck him, and he flailed in the snow trying to find it to shoot their Arab pilot and his bloody American friend. His mouth throbbed like a new heart, and he spat out a wad of blood. "You're dead, *kos omak!*" Halil raged, trying to rise to his feet.

Saeed quickly stepped forward and kicked him in the chin. Halil's head became a black cloud filled with brilliant stars. He came to in seconds and lurched to his feet, ready to strangle the Saudi, but Saeed had found the Tokarev and was pointing it at Halil. *"Kos omak!"* Saeed hissed. "Now, who's the twat?" Saeed backed away, holding the pistol at arm's length, knowing that at this moment, Halil wanted to kill him very badly. Saeed thought about shooting the fucking demon, but that would likely guarantee his own death.

Halil realized Thomas was gone, and he looked wildly around the clearing, trying to spot the American. "You bloody fool! What have you done?"

"He's gone," Saeed replied, keeping the pistol trained at Halil. "Just leave it! Thomas can't hurt anyone! There are only trees and snow out there. Nothing more!" Saeed shouted.

Halil wiped the blood off his chin and smiled at Saeed. "You're dead. You just don't know it yet."

Saeed chanced a look at the tree line, knowing even a short delay could allow Thomas time to escape. He may perish in the forest, but perhaps he could return to the house and warm himself after they'd gone. Ahmed would know Saeed forced his hand, and they would have to get the bomb to his plane as soon as possible.

Ghazi came upon them in the clearing. "What are you doing?" Ghazi shouted, getting between the two men. "What are you thinking?" Ghazi looked around for Thomas. "Where is the American? Ahmed is going to kill both of you when he hears what you've done!"

At the mention of Ahmed, Halil realized they were continuing a folly with this standoff. Halil turned away and stooped for a handful of snow. He held it against his swollen mouth and gestured over his shoulder. "This bloody queer let the American slip away like a rabbit! You can tell Ahmed that the little bastard is on the run to who knows where!"

Ghazi sized up the situation and stepped up to Saeed, looking into his eyes while gently gripping the pistol and firmly tugging it out of Saeed's hand.

"Let's go," Ghazi said, glaring at Halil. "We'll go tell Ahmed. He'll know what to do."

"Fuck you, boy!" Halil snapped. "I know what to do! I can follow his tracks. You two faggots can tell Ahmed I will take care of the American. Give me the gun!" He held his hand out to Ghazi and snapped his fingers. "Give it to me and take this bloody fool inside and tell Ahmed what's happened!"

Ghazi hesitated but knew Halil was the only one who could catch the American. Trying not to think about what would happen to Thomas, Ghazi tapped Saeed on the shoulder and motioned for him to go back to the house. Saeed kept away from Halil and staggered toward the house, looking over his shoulder, worried Halil would shoot him in the back.

Halil snapped his fingers again and thrust his hand impatiently for the pistol. Ghazi made sure Saeed was a safe distance away and, with a look of contempt, handed the gun to Halil, barrel first. Halil snatched the Tokarev out of Ghazi's hand and examined it as though it was a mistreated pet. He was about to start after Thomas but paused. "Tell Ahmed to deal with that bloody Saeed, or I will!" Ghazi watched Halil melt into the gray forest, then went to tell Ahmed how things had gotten out of hand.

* * *

Thomas worked steadily through the brush and gray aspens. He knew there wouldn't be anyone at Axe Winter's place, but he could probably find something he could use to get out of this mess. He needed to get away and find a weapon to defend himself or a safe place to wait them out. Thomas hoped they wouldn't follow, preferring to let him freeze in the woods while they escaped to wherever the hell they were going. He kept his pace steady, not hurrying, knowing there was too much snow falling for them to see or hear him unless they were right on his ass. The property line was close, and he could just stay on this side of the river until the footbridge. Thomas would cross the Joshua and make his way to Axel's cabin.

The Joshua materialized out of the early gloom, and without stopping, he turned to the left and began to slog along the riverbed, keeping it close on his right as he followed its curves and bends. The footbridge spanning the Joshua would be just ahead, and Thomas sped up as much as he could, wanted to put the river between him and the assholes trying to kill him. He noticed it was getting light, and his eyes caught something brightly colored in the gray woods ahead.

* * *

Marty heard the deer long before he saw it. It was hauling ass and didn't seem to care how much noise it was making. Must still be in rut, he thought. The season wasn't open for bucks, but he knew he'd take one if it was sporting a decent rack and figure out a way to get the antlers home later. He carefully took up his rifle and raised it to his cheek, ready for the deer to break cover. It was going to cross in front of him—*There!* A brown and tan shape appeared from down the river bank. It was moving fast, and Marty could only see snatches of color and texture through the weaving branches. He peered through the scope and silently cursed the droplets of melted snow on the lenses. Despite the blurry image, Marty decided to shoot. He pulled the hammer back, instinctively tracking the animal as it loped along past his stand. He cleared the safety and, with a steady squeeze, pulled the trigger.

Thomas was still stumbling along at a steady pace, trying to make out what the hell was in that tree. Hunting season was long over, and though it looked orange or fiery red, he didn't want to stop to see what it was. *Probably something those asshole neighbors left in the tree from the last season. Figures they would hunt on Dad's land when no one was around.*

A sharp flash of yellow lightning erupted in the tree, then a jolt like a baseball line drive hit the side of Thomas's chest. The bullet pierced his right lung and clipped his spinal column before exiting. In the second it took for his momentum to carry his paralyzed body face forward into the snow, he couldn't believe Saeed's friends had caught up with him so quickly. He grimaced as he fell into the brush and powdery snow, clenching his teeth as he smashed against the ground. He struggled in his mind to turn over, to get his face above the snow and breathe. There was no pain, but he became aware he'd been shot and was dying. In a few heartbeats, he quietly suffocated in the new snow.

Marty didn't celebrate the kill because he was always a little surprised and grateful when he harvested a deer. The rifle blast faded, replaced by a high-pitched whine in his ears. He began to shake, quivering with adrenaline and the excitement of making the shot. The deer had dropped right where the bullet caught up with it, which meant less work getting it back to camp. With the snow still falling, he could drag it back across the footbridge and avoid explaining why there was a blood trail from Duchamp's property.

I can have my cake and eat it too!

He put the scope back to his eye and checked the brown and tan lump just thirty yards from his stand. It wasn't moving. *There isn't a cleaner kill than that!* He unloaded the rifle and climbed down with a much better attitude than when he'd climbed the tree an hour before. He slung the rifle on his shoulder and went to see if he'd killed a buck or doe.

* * *

Halil stopped suddenly, holding his breath, wondering who could be shooting. He stood as still as he could, his senses taut as a wire, hearing nothing but the wind in the treetops and seeing nothing but the light snow falling in the gray forest. The gunshot was that of a large-bore, and the sound came from just in front of him. Halil instinctively moved against a tree to break up his silhouette. He strained to hear or see anything ahead and tried to think. *Was someone shooting at me?* Halil hadn't heard the whine of a bullet or any sign that he was the target, but who else but Thomas could be in these woods? The bastard must have found a gun, he thought. *If this is a trap, that bloody Saeed must be in on it!* Halil didn't wait any longer. He had to warn the others that they might be in real jeopardy. He turned and started back along the trail to the safe house, looking over his shoulder, hoping he wasn't someone's target.

At the safe house, Ahmed tried to make sense of what had happened, rubbing his stubbled chin and wondering how they had fucked up so badly when the distant report of a rifle sounded in the woods to the northeast. *Who could be shooting a rifle?* His mind raced. None of their group had a long gun. The forest could play tricks with sound, but Ahmed sensed something was wrong. "Saeed! Ghazi! Come here!" Ahmed pushed himself off the bed and limped to a wooden chair near a murky window near the door.

Ghazi came in first, standing in the doorway, eyes dulled with exhaustion. Saeed stood behind the boy as though he was a shield to protect him from Ahmed's wrath. "Tell me again what happened."

Ghazi stepped away from Saeed and looked at the Saudi with tired contempt.

"Halil went mad," Saeed began in a plaintive whine. "He attacked me! He threatened to…"

"I've already heard that part, you stupid twit!" Ahmed was fighting waves of pain, and his face was red and beaded with sweat. "What happened after that?"

Ghazi stepped forward. "Halil took the gun, that pistol of his, and ran to catch the American- Saeed's friend."

Saeed looked down at the floor, knowing they would blame all of this on his friendship with Thomas. Ahmed shook his head with disgust. "Saeed," Ahmed growled, "Get out of my sight! Think of your role in this and how you will make things right!" Saeed bowed his head and backed out of the room, surprised at the reprieve.

Ghazi turned to follow, but Ahmed leaned forward and tugged on the boy's sleeve. "Stay here a moment," Ahmed whispered. "There is something inside the package we brought here last night. I want you to go to the truck and retrieve it for me."

"Is it a secret?" Ghazi's said in a subdued voice. "I'm to hide this from the others?"

"Yes," Ahmed replied, "but before you get it, take this and give it to Waleed." Ahmed produced the Walther PPK he'd carried across the border. "It's loaded and ready. Tell him not to use it unless there is no other way." Ahmed sighed and looked at Ghazi with something like desperation. "Tell Waleed and Nadeem to find Halil and help him eliminate the American and come back immediately." Ghazi nodded, holding the pistol with reverence.

Ghazi turned to leave but stopped at the bedroom door. "So once Nadeem and Waleed go to find Halil, I am to bring an item you want from the sled?"

"Exactly, young Ghazi." Ahmed flashed a smile despite his pain and their precarious circumstance. "It seems you're the only sensible one in this bloody place!"

Ghazi melted away, leaving Ahmed alone. The stark fear of being caught or killed welled up in Ahmed's mind. The boy would obey, and it was a blessing he'd joined them. Mohammet continued to show his wisdom even in death. *We cannot fail!* Ahmed told himself, his mind burning with thoughts of failure, death, and betrayal. Ahmed considered Halil and how the mission had deteriorated since they'd arrived. Saeed was a fool, and the others were simple men, but Ahmed's rising suspicions about Halil were the most painful. *A broken leg does not make me expendable!*

The wooden chair creaked as Ahmed leaned back to take pressure off his injured leg. He sighed and crossed his arms, waiting for Ghazi to bring him what he'd secreted in the sled they'd towed across the border. The bomb wasn't the only weapon Ahmed packed for the mission. He only hoped it wouldn't be needed to defend against the Americans.

Or one of their own.

CHAPTER 36

THE HUNTERS

The rifle shot startled them both, and Jordan looked at Kurt with surprise. "Who was that?"

Kurt couldn't place the direction of the shot. "I don't know. It sounded like Marty, but it could have been Axe. Or maybe Aurora."

"Dang it," Jordan said. It would suck if Rory shot a deer, and he didn't.

"Probably Marty, though," Kurt quickly added.

"Marty's always lucky," Jordan said, sounding almost as resentful of his uncle. "He always gets a deer. I hope it's not a big buck!"

"Pipe down," Kurt said, shooting him a glance. "This isn't a competition! We just started hunting, for Christ's sake. Besides, he better not have shot a buck, or your grandpa will leave the deer and hang Marty on the meat pole!" Kurt looked at his watch. "It's only 7:20. It's called hunting, not shooting, Jordan. There are plenty of deer in the woods. You'll get your chance." Kurt was glad there was something to take their mind off Axel's cancer. He'd been thinking of hospital beds and funerals and the hollowness that would come after.

"It's a good sign, Jordy," Kurt said, punching his son in the arm. "This means the deer are moving. I wasn't sure anything would be out in this weather!"

* * *

Aurora and Axel followed Marty's tracks along the trail to the footbridge. There was a rifle shot, and not long after, Rory thought she heard someone shouting for help. She followed Axel as he surged through the

155

brush, his red plaid coat weaving deftly through the willow and around the tangled popple branches. The snow was deep enough that they had to pull their feet clear with each step, and Rory was starting to sweat. The shotgun seemed too heavy as she swatted away branches whipping back from Axel, the snow wetting her face. They crossed the footbridge over the Joshua and caught a glimpse of Marty's orange coat. As they neared, they could hear Marty crying out in anguish. Aurora hung back, dreading what they would find.

"What the hell's going on?" Axel roared. Marty was kneeling next to the man he had shot, and he turned to look at Axel. The tears in Marty's eyes and look of terror on his face spoke more than words.

Axel immediately knew what happened. The man on the ground was wearing a brown parka, and as he leaned closer, he could see blood seeping into the snow. He stripped off his gloves and knelt next to Marty. "You thought he was a deer?"

Marty nodded, trembling. "He was wearing a brown coat..." His voice trailed off, and he met Axel's eyes in a plea of understanding.

The man was face down and didn't seem to be breathing. Axel gently reached across the body and turned it over. He opened the man's coat and winced at the extent of the wound. The eyes were open but caked with melting snow. He was probably dead before he hit the ground. Axel sighed and looked at Marty. "There's not much to be done for him." Axel leaned forward and gently brushed the snow away from the dead man's eyes and mouth. Marty and Aurora watched Axel hesitate, then, after a moment of recognition, saw him close Tommy Duchamp's eyes for the last time. Axel leaned back and wiped a smear of blood on his wool pants. Marty rocked slowly back and forth, holding his rifle in his lap. Aurora put her hand on his shoulder, but he didn't seem to notice.

"Who is he, Grandpa?" Aurora asked quietly.

Axel sighed. "That's Tom Duchamp's boy, Tommy Jr." He found his gloves and slapped them together to shake off the snow. "We'll have to get back to camp and use one of the goddamned cell phones, I guess."

Aurora stepped back and looked at the dead man with a fresh wave of dread now that she recognized the name. She looked away and tried not to be sick, staring into the endless gray. A glimpse of movement in the trees caught her eye. Three men were coming toward them, the snow crunching under their feet and the willow branches whipping against dark jackets and blue jeans. Something about the men caused Aurora to hold her shotgun tighter and step behind her grandfather. "Grandpa, someone's coming," Aurora said, her voice shaking with tension.

Axel slowly rose and retrieved his rifle, turning to face the men as they approached.

PART TWO – WAR ON THE JOSHUA

CHAPTER 37

CONFRONTATION

The first thing Aurora noticed was the three men were dressed in street clothes, just like Tommy Duchamp. The second was that they were all dark-haired and seemed middle-eastern. A man in his forties with heavy beard stubble and was leading the other two through the brush. He wore a black sweater and watch cap like commandos she'd seen in the movies. The men slowed as they neared, and Aurora nervously watched them survey the scene.

Marty wiped his eyes and got to his feet next to Axel.

The man in black who appeared to be the leader stopped on the other side of Tommy's body. "What is this?" He barked. Aurora was surprised to hear a British accent.

Marty started to say something, his voice cracking, but Axel cut him off. "You fellas with Tommy Duchamp?" Axel's voice had an edge to it that Aurora had never heard before.

One of the three, a lean young man with a thick beard and green plaid jacket, stepped forward. "Yes," Nadeem replied, trying to appear as non-threatening as he could. These people had weapons, and at the moment, they only had Halil's pistol and whatever Waleed was carrying. Nadeem took off his ball cap and smoothed his hair back before putting it on again. "What's happened here?"

Axel spit and took a step forward. "He got shot, that's what. Tommy looked like a deer wearing that goddamned brown coat. You guys aren't hunting, so what the hell are you doing up here this time of year anyway?"

Aurora saw that the older man who had spoken first was visibly trying to control himself and began edging off to the right as the third man split off to the left.

Nadeem answered quickly. "We were with Thomas at his place in the woods." He gestured toward the Duchamp place. "Thomas left, and we came to look for him and heard the gunshot." Nadeem could hear Waleed and Halil moving somewhere behind him. He hoped they wouldn't try anything because Nadeem was in front and likely the first one to join Thomas in the next life. *The situation was getting out of hand.* "What can we do now?" He asked sincerely.

"You have a cell phone?" Axel asked.

None of the three answered. Axel knew this was escalating into something much worse. He slowly brought his rifle up, pointing at the men. "I asked you a question. I expect an answer."

Nadeem glanced first at Waleed and then Halil and saw steel in their eyes. "We don't have one. Maybe back at Thomas's place? We can go there to call for help."

Axel's eyes narrowed, and his hands tightened on the rifle. His finger slowly moved inside the trigger guard, and his thumb released the safety. "How about if I go back and make that call." He nudged Marty and made a subtle motion with his head for him to start back to the camp. Marty came out of the fog of shock and noticed that Axel was pointing his rifle at the men.

"I didn't murder him!" Marty sobbed with a fresh wave of guilt. "I didn't mean for this to happen....It was an accident!" Axel brought his elbow up and gave Marty a sharp jab in the ribs. "Shut up, Marty. These guys don't care much about Tommy, and I can tell they don't want to deal with this any more than we do." He focused on the oldest of the three. "Isn't that right, you son of a bitch?" He had seen hard men like this before.

Halil flinched at the insult. He knew this kind of man as well. They didn't run from a fight or hesitate once they'd found a weakness. This man was old, but he held the advantage. Halil knew the Tokarev pistol inside his pocket was no match for the high-powered rifle the old man was aiming at them. The younger ones weren't a threat. The simpering idiot that shot Thomas did them all a favor, and the younger one with the pink cheeks was too frightened to move. Halil decided they would need to deal with this problem before returning to the safe house.

Nadeem quickly spoke up, his hands shaking. "Please, sir, there is no need to talk like that! We were friends of Thomas, and we only want to go and call for help." He started to back up slowly, trying to place his feet carefully so he didn't fall and trigger a reaction.

"Alright," Axel said, "you go get help." He didn't move from the spot.

Aurora watched the older one glaring at Grandpa Axe motion for the other one, the one in the red jacket who hadn't spoken, to go back the way they had come. The leader reached out and grabbed the shoulder of the one in the green jacket who did the talking, and all three began to back away. Aurora's heart was racing, and she felt scared. She had never seen Grandpa Axe react like this, and it made her sick to her stomach.

Axel watched the men retreat a few more steps then turned to Aurora. "Do you think you can find your way back to camp?"

Aurora was still watching the men walk back the way they had come. "Yes, I think so."

"Then go back and get the sheriff out here. Joshua River Camp. If they're not sure, tell them Axe Winter's place. They'll know how to get here." He glanced back at the men and saw they weren't moving very fast. "Get going, Rory, and make sure your shotgun's loaded."

Aurora frowned and hesitated, but then she looked at Thomas Duchamp's body resting in the snow and turned to leave. She got two steps back along their path when she heard the sharp reports of a pistol.

She froze, startled, a cold chill running down her back. She turned to Grandpa Axel, and he was catching Marty, who seemed to be falling backward in slow motion.

"Rory, go!" Axel yelled, "Get back to camp and get help!"

Aurora turned and began to run as fast as she could in the snow, her boots like lead as she pushed through the branches on the trail. She didn't look back, and in a near panic, distanced herself from whatever was happening behind her.

* * *

Halil had waited until the old man in the bright orange coat turned to speak with the young one and pulled the Tokarev from his jacket pocket, aiming at the old man and snapping off two wild shots. He hit the one they called Marty, the man's knees buckling as he staggered back.

"You fucking idiot!" Waleed hissed, but he didn't have time to say anything more before the old man turned, brought his rifle up in one smooth motion, and shot Nadeem between the eyes.

Nadeem's head bucked backward, and the pressure of his head expanding from the heavy round popped his hat into the air like a cork from a bottle. His body followed the energy of the bullet and lazily dropped back against a small tree, folding like a rag doll and resting in the snow between Halil and Waleed.

Waleed had the Walther in his hand instinctively before the echo had died from Halil's pistol, diving to the ground and firing two rounds at the figures in orange, missing, but trying to buy precious seconds before the old man was able to fire again. *This can't be happening!* Waleed's thoughts raced. *To come all this way for a fucking disaster like this! Nadeem was dead; they had alerted Americans to their presence and now to be killed before we're in America for less than a day?*

"Waleed!" Halil said through clenched teeth, already lying prone in the brush and snow. "Go after the kid before he can get away!"

Halil fired again but missed. The old man and his wounded friend had reached safety behind a deadfall. "I can rush them," Waleed said, starting to rise to his knees. " I can kill them before they can get off another shot!"

Halil grabbed his arm and pulled him back. "No, you bloody idiot, go after the young one!" Halil pointed toward the river. "He will get help before we can get out of here. I'll keep these two pinned down while you go round and take up the boy's trail. Kill him and then come back from behind the other two, and we'll have this over so we can get back to the safe house and continue south! Go damn you!"

Waleed meant to protest, but he saw the logic. Once the old man recovered, he would pick them off when he chose while the young one made his way to reinforcements. Halil was right. If they couldn't catch the one who ran away, all was lost. Waleed stayed low and moved around the scene in a wide arc, staying low along the riverbank and only swinging back to cross the bridge once he was out of range. *He had to catch that kid before he could get help!*

* * *

Axel was breathing heavily, and the struggle to pull Marty through the snow to a fallen oak tree had sapped him of energy. He could feel a fluttering in his chest, and his vision was darkening at the edges. Marty had balled himself up behind the log and was groaning softly. A feeling of desolation washed over Axel. *Gunfire, blood, and death.* The Axel Winter who had shot the man in the green coat minutes ago was the Axel of 1968, reacting to survive. He rubbed his eyes and tried to make the rush of emotion recede. He didn't remember aiming the rifle, let alone pulling the trigger. It was instinct honed over years of battle and a lifetime of reliving the moments. He pulled back the bolt of his Winchester to make sure a fresh round was in the chamber, then closed the bolt as quietly as he could. Axel felt despair that he would be on the firing line and forced to kill once more. He dropped to one elbow. "Marty," he asked patiently, "where are you hit?" Marty groaned in reply. "Goddammit, Marty, where were you shot?" Axel prodded him on the shoulder.

"In the stomach," Marty replied weakly.

"I know you don't want to, but you gotta let me see," Axel whispered, trying to sound calm. He again felt that sense of surreal unfairness that they would be put in this position. "Hurry, Marty," he said more urgently.

Marty struggled to turn toward Axel in the snow. He opened his coat and turned his head away, too frightened to look.

Axel pulled back Marty's coat roughly and saw the hole in his shirt. *Might have hit the liver,* he thought, *or maybe just the intestines.* He felt under Marty's waist. No exit wound. Axel knew from harsh experience Marty would already be dead from hydrostatic shock from a rifle round. With a pistol bullet, he had a chance, but he needed medical attention.

"Marty," Axel said in what he hoped was a soothing tone, "I know it hurts like a bastard, but it isn't that bad." Axel took one of Marty's hands and placed it over the wound. "Leave your glove on and press as hard as you can stand."

Marty promptly screamed in response to pain like a hot poker rammed into his abdomen.

"Quiet!" Axel said in a harsh whisper. "We don't want them to zero in on us!"

Marty clenched his teeth and nodded.

"Okay," Axel continued. "We have to keep the bastards pinned down so Aurora can get back to a telephone. Do you get me?" Marty nodded again, trusting his fate to Axel Winter.

* * *

Aurora ran for as long as she could before she had to stop, lungs aching from the cold. She could barely take in enough air to remain conscious and hugged a tree to keep from collapsing into the snow. She opened her coat and let the wind and cold wash around her in a bracing chill. The woods didn't look familiar, and their tracks from the morning were half-filled with snow. Aurora pushed away from the tree and turned in a complete circle, sensing that she may be lost. *They're counting on me,* she thought, *and I don't have a clue where I am!* "Jesus," she whispered, finally getting her breathing under control. "If I get out of this, I will lose weight and exercise!"

She had run like a scared cat and probably screwed up big time. *I have got to get a grip,* she thought. *I can't be far off the trail. As long as I keep going, I should hit a side trail or even run into camp.* She tried not to think of the expanse to the north leading straight through Canada to Hudson Bay. She hadn't brought a compass either. *What a brainless idiot!*

A sound, unnatural to the woods, caught her attention. She held her breath and listened. *There it is again!* She realized it was the subtle swish of cloth passing over a branch. *Someone's coming!* She went around behind the tree, crouching as low as she could, careful to keep her shotgun out of the snow. Aurora strained to see who it was, but the sounds grew fainter as the phantom went slowly past, just beyond her vision. She waited for several minutes and decided to keep going.

The person must be on the main trail. Was it Grandpa trying to follow her? She didn't know what to do. *Should I call out? Surely Grandpa wouldn't just leave Marty behind.* She had to find the trail but keep her distance, at least until she found out who it was. She zipped up her coat and began weaving around trees and trying to quietly move through the willow and aspens toward the origin of the sounds.

* * *

Axel reached into his coat and pulled a brass cartridge from his breast pocket. Four rounds left. He had never needed more than one shot to take a deer. Never. But he always carried more ammunition. "Better to have it and not need it than to need it and not have it!" Sergeant Dixon had screamed about a hundred times out on the rifle range. His drill sergeant in basic would pace behind them as they fired their weapons, hovering over them like a guardian angel in starched fatigues, cramming the fundamentals of combat into them before they faced the Vietcong and NVA.

"Got your tit in the mangle this time, Axe!" Old Dix would have cackled seeing this clusterfuck. Axel almost smiled, but then he thought of Marty and his granddaughter and knew he was the only one standing in the way of a massacre. He slipped his hat off and raised his head above the rough bark, surveying the cluster of trees beyond Tommy Duchamp's body. Holding his breath so the vapor wouldn't show his position, Axel decided if he was hiding over there, the mound of snow just to the left of fallen aspen was a likely spot. He leveled his Winchester and pulled the trigger.

Halil felt as much as he heard the whine of the rifle bullet explode in the snow, just missing his head and peppering his face with ice and dirt. He rolled to his right and tried to lay as flat as he could. *How did that old bastard know where I was?* He held the pistol over his head like a periscope and fired two rounds in the American's direction. He wasn't sure how many shots he had fired and ejected the Tokarev's magazine, holding it to the gray sky to count what was left. He stared at the clip and tried to focus on counting them for the third time. *Fucking Saeed! He sucker punches me and lets his boyfriend escape! Now Nadeem is dead, shot down like a bloody criminal, and Waleed's off on a bloody goose chase!* Halil's face darkened with rage, and he considered charging at the Americans. It seemed there were nine rounds in the magazine. *Did it matter?* He thought bitterly. *The old bastard had a scoped rifle and knew how to use it!*

It was a simple choice; he could wait for Waleed to reappear or, Halil could go back to the safe house and escape with the others. *The plan was shit anyway with Ahmed down.* He reasoned. *I'm the only one left who can complete the mission.* Halil slipped the magazine back into the Tokarev and pulled the slide back quietly to seat a fresh round. *To hell with this!* He began to crawl back toward the safe house. *Waleed is on his own!*

* * *

Axel knew that Marty was settling into a kind of stasis brought on by shock and loss of blood. He would be going numb, as much from blood loss as the cold, and would no doubt die within a few hours. *Not too long ago,* Axel thought, *I would have carried Marty back to camp, but now I couldn't drag him ten yards.*

Aurora was their only hope.

CHAPTER 38

PURSUIT

Waleed trudged through the snow, his chest starting to ache from the cold and exertion. The fact that he smoked two packs of cigarettes a day didn't register. *Halil deserved to have his balls cut off for this!* Waleed thought. *They were in deep shit now unless I can stop the kid from calling for help. I don't plan on spending the rest of my days in an American prison! If I can get things back under control, I'll make Halil pay for Nadeem!* Waleed pushed on, almost in despair. He could imagine the boy excitedly relating the shooting to the sheriff or whoever's in charge of this fucking wasteland. *Then what?* He thought. *He and the others hole up in the safe house and have a stand-off with the police?*

Waleed had come too far for that. Any witnesses to this fuck-up in the woods will have to die.

* * *

Rory finally found the main trail cut through the woods, but there were no fresh tracks. Either the phantom had given up, or the sounds were just her imagination. She must be getting close to the cabin, but she didn't know how much farther it was. She had to rest for a minute. Leaning the shotgun against a tree, Rory bent forward, putting her hands on her hips, trying to catch her breath.

A branch snapped behind her. She gasped, her heart beating in her ears. The phantom again...*She must have gotten too far ahead!* She waded over to a huge pine tree, its snow-covered boughs touching the ground. There would be a hollow under the branches, where she could hide. She dropped down and crawled through the lower limbs, trying to be silent but knowing she was seconds from being spotted. Snow fell off the branches and went down her neck. She winced and hunched her shoulders, crawling as fast as she could.

It was dry and warmer underneath. There was no snow around the massive trunk, and the dead needles made a soft carpet. *I'll have to ditch this orange clothing. Talk about the worst thing to wear if you don't want someone to see you!* Still, she wouldn't last long in the cold with just her sweatshirt. She quietly shrugged off the coat and *turned it inside out, the gray lining better than blaze orange. It didn't fit right, but it was warm and would blend into the trees.* She pushed aside one of the branches trying to catch sight of her pursuer.

She was shocked to see one of the men from the confrontation approaching the open trail from the other side. He was holding a pistol in his left hand, deflecting branches with the other, searching the woods, slogging through the willows and snow, turning to look behind him about every ten steps. He hadn't spotted her yet, but her heart was beating so loudly she thought it would give away her hiding place. Rory was getting a cramp in her leg, and she tried to lie on her side, keeping the man in sight. Her movement frightened a cottontail rabbit hiding nearby, and it exploded out of the snow, scrambling away from Aurora, bounding directly toward the man with the pistol. She gasped and almost cried out but held tight, her heart thundering in her chest.

The rabbit saw Waleed and changed direction at the last second. Startled, he brought up his pistol but lowered the gun when he saw it was only an animal.

Aurora watched in terror as the man seemed to ponder the rabbit, watching it disappear into the white fog. He must be wondering what spooked it to run at him like that. The guy was alert now, scanning the woods more intently. He stood motionless, only moving his head, peering at the trees and brush. Turning to face Aurora's hiding place, his eyes focused on the tree.

She held her breath. *Can he see me? Did I drop something?* She scanned the snow between her and the trail. *There was nothing, but could he see where she crawled under the tree?* She didn't think it would be that obvious from where he stood, but now she had a horrible thought; *would she have to use the shotgun?* She probably didn't have a hope of getting a shot off before he took his time firing his pistol into her hiding spot under the tree.

Then he started walking again, toward camp. In less than a minute, he was gone from sight, and soon after, she could hear nothing but the wind.

She sighed with relief. *Now what? I should follow him, try to see what he's doing. He's got that automatic pistol, but my shotgun has a longer range.* She cautiously crawled out from under the tree, tolerating the snow clumps that dropped onto her head. Once clear, she stood, looking for any sign of danger. As before, there was only the mono-chrome gray of the trees and the sighing of the wind.

CHAPTER 39

WALEED

Waleed could feel the ice building up on his pants, chafing at his ankles, the melting snow seeping into his stockings. *These shoes aren't warm enough, and this fucking jacket is too thin!* He thought of his heavy coat drying by the oil heater next to his soggy boots. *They still would have been better than wearing these damn light clothes!* Waleed was starting to believe this was something that Thomas and Saeed had planned. *How did these others appear so conveniently in such a remote place? Maybe Ahmed and Halil are setting me up too! Halil demands we go with him out into the woods to chase that damn American, and we run into a trap! Now Nadeem is dead, and I'm shoved out of the way chasing some kid.* The thought of everyone planning to leave the two of them to die while they escaped seemed a certainty and filled him with rage. *It's not fair!*

It seemed an eternity since he'd left the safe house and he must have walked half a kilometer from the spot Nadeem died. He tucked the pistol into his pocket and blew on his hands. He wondered if there were any wild animals about besides the rabbit that had startled him. *Bears? No, they slept in winter, didn't they?* He couldn't remember the term to describe it. Wolves could be a problem, but probably Americans with guns were the only wolves in these woods. *The others abandoned me,* he thought. *They've already fled the safe house, leaving me behind to deal with the fucking consequences!* He felt the beginnings of panic and tried to stay calm. *Where did that kid go?*

* * *

Phillip sat in the outhouse, planted firmly on the bench, his pajama bottoms scrunched around his ankles, trying to focus on a crossword puzzle. He was miserable in this icebox toilet and constipated from the long drive and drinking too much the night before. Phillip heard shooting and surmised the old man had bagged another Bambi. *As if he hadn't shot enough deer!*

Phillip finally and painfully defecated and opened the door for some air. Finishing up, he tucked the crossword book under his arm and stepped out into the wind, letting the door slam shut behind him.

* * *

A door banging! The sound snapped Waleed out of his panic. It was near, and he strained to see through the gray lattice of trees. If there was a building, there could be a telephone or radio, and that meant trouble. He had to move fast. He came to a clearing and a rustic shack with two pickup trucks and a small car parked outside, all covered with snow. A steady cloud of smoke rose from the chimney and swirled around the clearing.

Phillip tiptoed through the snow back from the outhouse, trying to stay in the footprints he'd made on the way out. He foolishly wore his bedroom slippers out to the privy, and snow filled them with each step. Phillip heard a branch crack, and he looked up to see a stranger at the edge of the clearing in a red jacket. The young man looked bedraggled and shocked to see another person in these woods. "Hello," said Phillip heartily as he reached the cabin steps. The man stopped but said nothing. "Are you lost?"

Waleed was startled at the appearance of someone other than the kid he'd been tracking. He ignored the fat man's question and approached the cabin. Waleed cleared his throat. "Are you the only one here?" He gripped the Walther in his jacket pocket, scanning the area for the one who had escaped.

Phillip frowned. "Um…right now, yes. There are other people with me, but they're all out hunting. Do you want to come in and have a cup of coffee?"

"Yes," Waleed replied warily, following closely behind Phillip as he went into the heat of the cabin. Waleed stood in the doorway, letting his eyes adjust to the dark interior. He squinted and looked at the walls and ceiling, leaning in as if afraid of what he would find.

"Come on in," said Phillip brightly, "Let's close the door – it's cold out there!"

Waleed hesitated a moment but stepped inside, leaving the door ajar in case he had to escape what could be another trap. He rubbed his hands together, looking for anyone hiding in the cabin. "Why aren't you out hunting?"

Phillip had rinsed his hands and was reaching for two cups. "I don't hunt," he said, in the same tone one would say *I don't molest children.* "This is a forced family weekend, and I'm the camp cook," he said, pouring the coffee. "Say, where are you from? You don't sound like a Minnesotan!" With his dark complexion and heavy mustache, he looked too foreign to be a local. "Are you staying over at a neighbor's?"

Waleed ignored the questions. He hadn't eaten a decent meal since Winnipeg, and his stomach growled. He reluctantly took the cup of coffee from Phillip. "What are you cooking?"

Phillip recited a menu he never dreamed would offend anyone. "Buttermilk biscuits – with lingonberry jam from a little shop on Grand Avenue, scrambled eggs, bacon…"

Goddamned Americans! Of course, they would have bacon. Waleed slammed the cup onto the sideboard and strode into the cabin, scanning the bunks, looking for anyone in hiding.

"What's wrong?" Phillip was finally alarmed. "I said something to offend you! Oh, I am sorry. I didn't mean…."

"Shut the fuck up, asshole!" Waleed pulled out the pistol and leveled the gun at Phillip. "Where's the telephone?"

"There isn't one! There isn't electricity here. Um, we just have cell phones!" Phillip raised his arms, his coffee spilling over his wrist.

"Where!" Waleed barked.

"On that shelf," Phillip stammered. "In that coffee can!"

"Give it to me!" Waleed's voice was jarring in its intensity in the small space. Phillip set down his coffee cup and reached up, taking the can off the shelf.

"Slowly, or I'll blow you away!"

Phillip was shocked that this man, this stranger he was trying to befriend, had suddenly turned violent. *What was this, some sort of robbery?* "Here," Phillip said, his voice breaking a little as he slid the can down the counter. "What do you want? I have some money, but my wallet is in my other pants. I'm sure the others will have some cash as well." He started to put his hands down and move toward the bunks.

"Stop!" Waleed was peering into the coffee can and the jumble of devices. "What is this all about?"

"It's a ritual," Phillip stammered. "We don't use them up here!" Phillip's voice was shaking now, and he felt pressure from his bladder. "They may not work up here anyway....There are no towers...Um...Cell towers!"

Waleed pulled the can off the counter and tucked it against his chest, keeping the pistol pointed at Phillip. "Move! Away from the door!"

Phillip backed away as Waleed went to the wood stove and opened it, the burning oak lighting the room as he shook the contents of the can into the flames. When the electronics started to smolder, he turned back to Phillip.

"How many of you are there?"

Phillip was unsure of what he meant. "There are five of us...No six! Six with Marty! There are my dad and brother and...two others. They'll be back any minute!"

"Do they have cell phones or radios?" Waleed was glancing furtively out of the dirty window next to the stove.

"You just burned the cell phones...There are no radios! Is this about drugs? I mean, we aren't going to tell..."

"Shut up, asshole! Waleed swung open the cabin door; illuminating Phillip backed in the corner of the kitchen. "Are these the only vehicles you have?"

"Um…" Phillip was trying to process this obtuse question while staring at the pistol. "Yes, I guess so."

"You guess so? What the hell does that mean?" Waleed was suddenly furious. The intense frustration and paranoia that had grown over the last 24 hours erupted like a volcano. *This situation isn't fair! The others set me up, and now I'm left to deal with another witness!* With no more hesitation, he thrust the pistol forward and pulled the trigger. The flame from the muzzle blast enveloped Phillip's head and spattered the wall behind him with blood.

Waleed became unhinged. The high-pitched whine in his ears from the gunshot enraged him further. "You asshole!" He grunted as he kicked Phillip's corpse over and over. "This shouldn't have happened! It isn't fair!" He finally stopped and leaned against the kitchen counter, panting and trying to calm down. "It just isn't fair…" He whispered to himself. Waleed went to the bunks, using the pistol's barrel to sling the bedrolls onto the floor and search under the mattresses. He saw no way of communication, so the fat guy told the truth. He tilted his head as he looked at some clothing crumpled on the floor. *A bra? The kid I chased must be a girl!* He was not so scared now. *He could still intercept this girl and get back to the safe house before they left him behind!*

The plastic and electronics burning in the stove were making his eyes water, and Waleed went back to the open door. *No loose ends!* He discovered a fuel can under the counter. He opened it and smelled kerosene. Waleed splashed some fuel on Phillip's body and poured a trail of kerosene across the floor and down the outside steps to the parked vehicles.

* * *

Aurora stopped when she heard the muted gunshot from the trail ahead. She could smell wood smoke, and that meant she was close to camp. Maybe it was Kurt shooting, but it didn't sound right. Looking down, she realized she was standing in the fresh footprints of the man that was tracking her. He must have reached the camp, and her stomach felt queasy knowing he was ahead, waiting for her. She continued forward for a few more paces, keeping her finger on the shotgun's safety button. She wanted to run back to Axel but had to get to a cell phone!

She continued to creep forward until the clearing came into view, and she could see the trucks and the cabin.

Suddenly, a bright orange explosion flashed in the clearing, followed by a basso thump as the fuel ignited and the cabin and vehicles became an inferno. Oily flames turned into gouts of black smoke billowing up and carried off by the wind, and Aurora knew she was too late. Flames engulfed the cabin, and the trucks were burning like torches. She felt lost and hopeless, their chance for getting help evaporating with the smoke blending with the iron-gray sky.

* * *

"Wake up, Spud." Kurt shook Jordan, and something in his dad's voice brought Jordan fully awake, his heart pounding. He scanned the area around their deer stand but didn't see anything but the same woods and snow.

"What is it?" Jordan asked, sure he had missed an opportunity at his first deer.

"I don't know," Kurt said. "I think I heard a gunshot from back at camp."

Yuck," Jordan said, wrinkling his nose. "What's that smell?"

Kurt started to unload his rifle. "That's smoke, but something's not right. We have to go back."

Both scrambled out of the blind and began the hike back to camp. After they had traveled halfway, Kurt halted and dug in his pocket for ammunition. "Why don't you reload your Browning, Jordy? We might jump a deer on the way." He knew they weren't going to see a deer, but he felt uneasy. That goddamned Phillip probably burned the cabin down trying to flambé some waffles or something. "You know the drill, Jordy. Keep your gun pointed down or to the side. Don't shoot me in the back, okay?"

"Okay." Jordan carefully loaded his Browning rifle and held it across his chest, following in his father's footsteps. More gunfire came from the camp's direction, and Kurt hurried his pace, Jordan following as best he could.

* * *

Aurora could feel the heat even from where she stood transfixed by the orange flames consuming the camp. She wasn't sure what to do. She couldn't go back to Axel and didn't know where to find Uncle Kurt. Rory took one tentative step towards the clearing, and the whip-crack of a bullet grazed her ear. She dropped to the ground and frantically crawled behind a tree, huddling with her arms protecting her head. *Oh shit! Oh shit! Oh shit!* She looked at her hand and saw the bullet had drawn blood.

CRACK! Another bullet snapped through the trees, the echo absorbed by the white forest. She had to buy time to get away! Aurora reached around the tree with the shotgun, aimed it toward the clearing, and pulled the trigger.

Waleed ducked at the booming shotgun blast and heard the slug sizzle past him like an angry wasp. He backpedaled on the trail and crouched down, not sure if he was in the crosshairs. *What the fuck... The kid was shooting back!* Girl or boy, Waleed was sure it was the kid from their earlier encounter. Now that he'd eliminated their cell phones and means of escape, Waleed was having second thoughts about killing again. Still, he had to get to the safe house soon. *The kid is just in the wrong place at the wrong time!*

Aurora bolted after firing the shotgun, running back the way she'd come, putting distance between her and the attacker. The nape of her neck was tingling as she fled through the snowy branches, imagining a hundred figures darting through the trees, dogging her, waiting to attack.

Her side started to ache, and Aurora knew she couldn't keep running. She looked desperately for somewhere to hide, but there was no sheltering pine tree this time. *There!* A snow-covered stump jutted out of a willow clump twenty yards off the trail. Aurora coiled herself and leaped into the snow along the path. She hadn't jumped far, maybe six or seven feet, but it would have to do. Aurora back-tracked to the stump and vaulted over it into the snow on the other side. She lay still, trying to catch her breath.

The crunch of snow underfoot... *He's getting close!*

She shrunk down behind the tree stump, terrified to think she had made a fatal error in hiding instead of running. At least she had turned her coat inside out. The gray lining would blend into the dead bark and...

Her hat! She forgot her hat!

Quickly, too quickly, she reached up and snatched the safety orange cap off her head, snapping off a branch with a dull crack. It was so loud she knew he would hear it.

The footsteps stopped.

Oh shit! Oh shit! Oh shit! Aurora pressed tight against the tree stump, her body rigid with tension, waiting for the crack of a pistol to know he'd spotted her. *Why doesn't he do something?* She peered over the log, moving her head slowly, trying to see through the vein-like branches. *Has he gone around behind me?* She fought the urge to leap to her feet and run.

The man suddenly moved into her line of vision, and she felt a sense of relief that he was in sight. It was the one with the red jacket from the Joshua confrontation. She followed him with her eyes without moving her head. He had the pistol at arm's length and was following her trail. He would soon come to where she had jumped to the side and back-tracked to this spot.

He looked as scared as she felt, but that made him seem even more dangerous. Rory watched him shift the pistol to his right hand, stuffing the left into his light jacket under his armpit. These men weren't planning on spending much time outside. *Who were they?* He was close enough to see his heavy mustache and deep-set eyes under a dark line of eyebrows. He kept getting closer, and Aurora could see his breath.

He stopped where she leaped off the trail.

She couldn't let him get past her. He would come up behind Marty and Grandpa and kill them, and stopping him was up to her. She rested the shotgun on top of the stump and aimed down the barrel. She carefully focused on the front sight, the metal bead covering most of the man's chest as she brought her face tight against the stock. She tightened her grip, her body trembling with fear. She felt cold and burning hot at the same time, and her entire body began shaking. She clenched her teeth and blinked hard, trying to gain control.

She clicked off the safety.

It was a sound Waleed had heard before. He turned his head towards her, putting both hands on the pistol, aiming stiffly in front of him.

The man's eyes searched the brush, straining to see her; then, like an animal, he must have sensed her stare. His eyes met Aurora's, and he opened his mouth in surprise.

Waleed aimed the pistol at Aurora, and time stopped.

They both fired at almost the same time, but Waleed missed. Her shot took him in the throat.

Waleed collapsed in the snow in a burst of white. He bucked and arched his back, gasping for air and gagging. He made a mewling sound from his ragged throat, clutching at the wound, his legs flailing, trying to get air into his dying lungs.

Aurora looked on in horror, unable to turn away. She swallowed hard, trying not to vomit.

The man struggled more, rising out of the snow, his eyes focused on something far away.

Aurora racked another shell into the chamber, the spent cartridge spinning into the brush. She awkwardly went around the stump, keeping her eyes on the wounded man all the while. She had to see. To make sure he wasn't a threat anymore.

He was dead by the time she reached him. He was pathetic in death, a young man wearing a red Adidas warm-up jacket and blue jeans with a pair of soggy hiking boots. He died with his hands near his throat, blood spattering his arms and soaking his chest. Aurora was shocked at the amount of blood in the snow, vibrant crimson in the white and gray of the forest. "Who are you?" She whispered down at him. "Why did you want to kill me?" Her eyes blurred with tears, and she found herself sobbing with fear and relief. "Why would you want to kill anyone?" She looked into his dead eyes, half-open, already drying in the wind. A small trickle of blood drained from his nostril and pooled in his eye. She vomited then, still holding the shotgun, leaning on it while she retched.

CHAPTER 40

KURT

Kurt moved as fast as he dared. There was gunfire ahead, and that meant trouble. As he and Jordan neared the cabin, he couldn't believe his eyes. Joshua Camp was entirely in flames! Jordan leaned his rifle against a tree and stood next to his father, coughing from the thick smoke billowing from the pickups and Phillip's Subaru. The melting snow around the vehicles shined like frosted glass, reflecting the orange and yellow flames. The cabin was already burned to its framing, the interior a solid wall of fire.

"Can't we do something?" Jordan pleaded, holding his arm up against the heat. He thought of the cell phones inside the cabin. "How are we gonna call the fire department?"

Kurt shook his head and backed away from the fire, skirting around toward the vehicles, keeping an eye out for anyone that might be lurking nearby. He could see footprints around the trucks, but no one had tried to get inside them. He went around the other side of Marty's pickup and spotted their fuel can lying empty on the ground. *What the hell was this all about?* He looked back and saw that Jordan was starting to follow him.

"Spud, stay there. Don't come any closer until I tell you, okay?"

Jordan nodded, his eyes red and watery from the smoke and heat.

Kurt moved as close as he could to the cabin, holding his arm across his face. His sleeve started to smoke as he got too close. He tried to withstand the heat, to see if anyone was inside, but the roof trusses gave way, and the roof fell into the mass of flames, sending a massive cloud of smoke and embers into the sky.

He retreated, his face stinging from the blaze. *We are totally fucked! Who would do this to us?* There'd been some scrapes with the neighbors, but that was far in the past. He thought of the years he'd spent here and what Axel would feel knowing it was all gone. He suddenly remembered Phillip.

"Phillip!" He yelled, feeling guilty that he hadn't thought of his brother until now. "Phil, where are you!"

He went back to where Jordan was standing, squinting against the heat and smoke. Jordan swallowed hard, trying to be strong. "What do we do now, Dad?" Jordan asked, his voice wavering. "How do we get home?"

"I don't know yet, Jordan," he said, not sure he should tell him someone deliberately torched the place. *And then there were those gunshots. Did we get too close to a meth lab? Did Marty piss someone off at the bar last night?* The more he stood in the heat of the flames, the angrier he became.

Two more gunshots, almost simultaneous, sounded in the woods beyond the camp. Kurt was sure two guns had fired. That wasn't good, but that's where the answers would be. *Should I leave Jordan here, or would he be safer by my side?* He put his hand on the boy's shoulder. "Jordan, we're going to check out that gunfire. Stay quiet and stay behind me." Jordan nodded solemnly and fell into step behind his father.

Kurt and Jordan cautiously followed the trail of whoever had come to camp and started the fire. Kurt wasn't sure what he would do when he caught up to them, but he had to get to the bottom of this. The wind was still harsh, and after standing next to the bonfire that was their hunting retreat, he was starting to shiver. *This weather was going to be more than a nuisance in a few hours.* Kurt knew it was the winter pattern – snow and clouds replaced with clear skies and plummeting temps. But this time, there was no shelter or way to get to help. Jordan began to cough, and Kurt stopped. "Jordy," he whispered, "I know the smoke was brutal, but don't make noise if you can help it, okay? Try to cough into your sleeve."

Jordan nodded and felt another tickle in his throat. He put his mouth into the crook of his arm and coughed as quietly as he could. The cloth reeked of the acrid smoke from camp, and he coughed again. This trip wasn't fun anymore, and he just wanted to go home. Jordan stumbled on behind his father, trusting that his dad would know what to do.

Kurt walked as stealthily as he could, his eyes straining to see into the brush and spot a threat before walking into an ambush. He halted to let Jordan catch his breath when he caught sight of a figure standing in the path ahead dressed in gray. Kurt crouched down and turned his head slowly, motioning Jordan to come closer. "Jordy," he said, "there's someone up ahead. Stay here and don't make a sound, okay?"

Jordan nodded, peering into the distance ahead.

Kurt stood up slowly and started walking forward. As he crept down the trail, he recognized his niece. "Rory!" Kurt said, surprised she hadn't heard him coming up behind her. "Are you okay?" Aurora swung the shotgun around and would have pulled the trigger if Kurt hadn't grabbed the barrel before she could fire. He held onto the shotgun barrel and stared into Aurora's eyes, trying to make sense of what was happening. She pointed behind her to something lying in the snow.

Kurt moved Aurora aside and gasped. There was a dead man in a bed of bloody snow, his face staring at the sky, a gaping wound in his throat. Kurt backed away and turned to Aurora. "What the hell happened here?"

Aurora's lip started to tremble, and she felt a rush of relief that she wasn't alone anymore. "He tried to kill me," she sobbed, her words coming out in gasps. "I had to shoot him…He was trying to kill me!"

"Holy shit!" Jordan said as he joined them. "Is that guy dead?"

"Jordan, be quiet!" Kurt snapped, his nerves raw. He spied something resting in the snow near the corpse's feet and bent down to pick up the Walther pistol Ahmed had given Waleed. "What the hell is this guy doing out here with a goddamned handgun?" Kurt wondered aloud. Pulling open the man's warm-up jacket, Kurt carefully tucked the gun inside. "The sheriff will have to figure this one out." Kurt put his hand on Aurora's shoulder. "Why do you think he was trying to kill you?"

Then Aurora remembered. "Oh my God…" She almost screamed, "Marty and Grandpa!"

* * *

Kurt busted through the brush as fast as he dared. He was mentally going over the contents of his pockets and pack. There was a small first aid kit, but it was for treating slivers or a cut finger. Rory told Kurt about the three men and the shooting. She wasn't sure how bad Marty was injured but was frantic about getting back to camp to call for help. "Three men," she said. "All foreign-looking like the dead guy in the snow." That bothered him a lot. Kurt only had five rounds for his rifle and wasn't sure he was up to this. He thought of the pistol he'd left with the dead body but knew if his rifle weren't enough, a handgun wouldn't make any difference.

He told Aurora and Jordan to head back to camp. Despite the lack of shelter, it was still safer than facing whatever lay ahead. Hopefully, Phillip was hiding somewhere, but Kurt thought it unlikely that the ass-hole that torched the camp spared Phillip. *Hell*, Kurt thought, *Phil probably invited the bastard in for a coffee!*

Aurora did well to defend herself. He hoped Marty and Axel were able to do the same.

CHAPTER 41

KURT

What the hell was happening around here? Kurt thought, working his way to where Rory had left Marty and Axel. *The camp goes up in flames, Rory has a gunfight, and now I hear Marty shot Tommy Duchamp. The whole woods was a fucking circus!*

The footprints were leading straight to the river. Marty must have made a beeline to Tom Senior's property over the bridge. *He'd told Marty more than once not to cross the river!* Even though Tom Duchamp had been dead for two years, it wasn't right to trespass on his land. Kurt checked his rifle for the third time, starting to tremble with adrenalin and fear. He wanted to call out to Axel, but that could end badly for all of them. *I'm not trained for this shit, and I don't have a hope in hell if someone's out there waiting for me!*

The rustic timbers of the footbridge materialized out of the snowy haze.

Kurt brought his rifle to his shoulder, scanning with his scope as he stepped onto the bridge, relieved the snow muffled his footfalls on the planking. He glanced down at the dark water of the Joshua slowly moving below. Stopping in the middle of the crossing, Kurt scanned the woods again, swinging his rifle, trying to spot any threat. He knew the closer he got to Marty and Axel, the more dangerous it became. *Maybe they're already dead, and I'm walking into a trap!* He took a deep breath and crossed the bridge to the other side.

* * *

Halil made his way back to the safe house as fast as he could. The Americans must know he had retreated, but would they pursue him? He heard far away exchanges of gunfire but no sounds since. Waleed must have encountered trouble, and Halil doubted Waleed could survive a brush with the Americans. Whatever the result, they'd delayed too long, and it was critical they clear out the moment he got back. *Ahmed will be furious about losing the American and protest my decision to leave Nadeem and Waleed behind, but Ahmed is just an amateur. With that leg of his, he's dead weight, and I'm not letting his vanity get in the way anymore!*

Halil entered the clearing and went around the front of the safe house and saw the Suburban still blanketed in snow and no effort underway to leave. He stormed up the steps and burst through the door, holding it open as his eyes adjusted to the dim interior. "Of course, you useless twats didn't lift a finger..." Halil's voice trailed off. Something was happening he didn't understand. Ghazi and Saeed were standing in the kitchen, looking at Halil with contempt. Neither seemed surprised to see him. "What the bloody hell is going on here?" Halil barked, his voice hoarse from his flight through the woods. Neither replied, but Ghazi's eyes made a furtive glance toward the back bedroom. "I'll deal with you two soon!" Halil said in disgust. "Where is Ahmed?"

"I'm right here." Ahmed's figure emerged from the back room. He was grimacing with pain, leaning against the door frame, an AK-47 assault rifle cradled in his arms, the muzzle pointed at Halil's chest.

Halil was astounded to see Ahmed pointing a weapon at him. *An assault rifle, no less!* "What the fuck is this?" Halil raged. "You had a rifle all along and didn't fucking tell me? That would have made a big bloody difference out there, you fucking idiot!"

"Idiot, am I? You forget yourself, Halil! I've funded this operation, sacrificed my identity, and lost my brother to this mission! None of this would be possible without me!"

"Fuck you, Ahmed!" Halil raged. "You think I don't know you've hedged your bets?"

Ahmed's face paled. "Shut up, Halil. You don't know what you're talking about!"

"Really, Ahmed? I suspect you'll be shorting the market before the bomb goes off and become an even wealthier man," Halil said viciously.

"Will you bother funding the movement then? Are you going to help build another bomb, or will you just disappear to an island and forget all the fools who paid for your betrayal?"

"Halil," Ghazi interrupted in a nervous voice, "What happened to the others? Where are Nadeem and Waleed?"

Halil glared at the boy. "They're dead, you stupid little bastard! All of them! Even that fucking Thomas—done for by American hunters!"

Ahmed tightened his finger on the trigger. "American hunters? You can't be fucking serious! Why would they kill Thomas? I give you simple instructions to eliminate the American, but instead, you tried to kill Saeed, our pilot, and the American escapes into the woods! You say Nadeem and Waleed are dead, but how is it that you managed to return unharmed?"

"Oh no, Ahmed, this isn't about me," Halil replied, ignoring the question. "This has always been about you!" Halil continued, pointing at Ahmed. "Ghazi, ask Ahmed what he did to his brother, Mohammet!"

Bewildered, Ghazi looked to Ahmed for an answer.

"You bastard, Halil! You know what I did was necessary!" Ahmed stammered. "He...He was dying! I...We couldn't let him..."

"What—Slow us down? You did that anyway, you fucking oaf! I doubt Mohammet could have done any worse!"

Ghazi stepped forward between the two. "If we are the only ones left, shouldn't we just leave?" Ahmed and Halil glared at each other, their confrontation still simmering.

"I mean, if there were Americans, and they killed the others, won't they be coming for us next?" Ghazi's eyes went from Halil to Ahmed, pleading for them to be reasonable.

"If only it were so, Halil," Ahmed said. "I fear you more now than your imaginary Americans."

Halil thrust his hand into his pocket, fumbling with the pistol, desperately trying to fire at Ahmed.

Ahmed simply pulled the trigger and hammered Halil backward with a short burst from the assault rifle, dropping him in the doorway.

Ghazi stood rooted in the center of the room, mouth agape, deafened by the gunfire, sickened and afraid. Saeed knelt on the kitchen floor with his arms covering his head.

The gun smoke from the exchange swirled in the air like a blue cloud as Ahmed finally lowered the rifle. Saeed lifted his head and looked around, surprised to be alive. Ghazi leaned against the sofa in a daze.

"It became necessary," Ahmed said dully. "Please bring him inside and close the door. Be sure to take his pistol. We may need it." Exhausted, Ahmed retreated into the bedroom and returned to the chair by the window.

Saeed and Ghazi dragged Halil's corpse through the living room to the first bedroom, leaving a broad smear of blood across the floor. Ghazi dug into Halil's bloody jacket and retrieved the Tokarev, holding it out to Saeed. Saeed recoiled at the blood-stained gun and backed out of the room. Ghazi shrugged and shoved the pistol into a back pocket, joining Saeed in the hall. They stood side by side, looking at Halil's corpse sprawled on the floor, neither believing Halil could be dead. It was easier for them to imagine Halil's eyes opening and his body springing up with hands reaching for their throats.

Ghazi nudged Halil's legs out of the way and closed the bedroom door.

Saeed saw a tremor in Ghazi's hand, but the boy didn't seem to notice. Ghazi began to hum in a low tone, and Saeed backed away, unsure what might be wrong. *Stress is affecting us all.* Saeed thought. *But I wonder..."*

Chapter 42

Reunion

Axel heard a branch snap under the snow behind him, but before he could react, Kurt was lying next to him, catching his breath.

"Jesus, Boy, am I glad to see you!" Axel said, closing his eyes and leaning back in relief.

"What the hell is going on around here?" Kurt was trying to look over the fallen tree to see across the way. "Marty, how are you doing, man?"

Marty lifted his head and looked at Kurt with tears of pain filling his eyes. "I got shot."

"That's what I hear," Kurt said with a forced smile, trying not to look at the blood staining the snow around Marty's waist. "If it's any consolation, Aurora shot one of the guys you tangled with."

Axel looked at his son with alarm. "Rory shot someone? Is she hurt? Did she get to camp and call for help?" Kurt took Axel's arm and leaned close to speak into his ear. "Someone torched the camp— Cabin, trucks, the works— It all went up in smoke. I couldn't find Phillip, and I sent Jordy and Aurora back to what's left of camp, but I'm not sure it's any safer there."

Axel blinked, trying to process what he was hearing. He pushed himself up to his knees and aimed his rifle where he thought the men would be watching. "Get Marty up and start back. I'll cover us."

Kurt went to Marty's side, and Marty cried out when Kurt got under his arm, stretching him upright and tearing the wound open. Kurt gritted his teeth and ignored Marty's whimpering, lunging forward, holding his rifle, and trying to keep his balance as Marty hung on his neck, dragging beside him. "Marty, come on!" Kurt grunted, trying to get them out of pistol range before a bullet found them. "You gotta help a little, buddy!"

"I'm sorry," Marty replied. "I can barely feel my legs!"

Kurt regretted his words. "Sorry, Marty, I'll take care of you."

Axel scanned for a target while Kurt and Marty started back. He wanted to turn and see how they were faring, but he didn't dare take his eyes off the woods ahead. Axel struggled to his feet, feeling his age and health getting the better of him in the cold. He backed away from the scene in a sloppy stagger, his rifle at his hip, aiming at his back trail. *This is where I get it*, he thought, trying to will feeling into his legs and feet. *Christ, if I can't move faster than this, I deserve to get shot!*

But the bullet never came, and he kept following Kurt and Marty as best he could, trying not to focus on the blood droplets spattering their path.

* * *

Rory stood next to Jordan and watched the last of the cabin being consumed in flickering tongues of orange flame as the falling snow hissed and popped into the ruin. Neither said anything, awash in a dull sense of dread. Rory bent down to scoop a handful of snow. "Here, put this on your eyes; it will help with the smoke."

Jordan pressed the snow against his face and staggered back, shocked at the stinging cold. Aurora did the same and let the snow melt and soothe away the burning.

"Why is all this happening?" Jordan asked.

Aurora sighed. "I don't know, Jordan."

"What are we going to do?" he asked.

Like Kurt, Aurora didn't have an answer. She had to do something to take their minds off the darkness they were feeling. "First of all," Rory said, "I'm thirsty. Let's get some snow melted and see if there's anything we can salvage." The two went around the camp, kicking at any snow-covered lump, looking for something of value. Aurora found an old rake and carried it over to the remnants of the cabin. "Let's get a new fire going away from this mess," she said, pulling embers from the cabin debris over to the campfire pit. Jordan spied the metal bucket they used for the water pump and filled it with clean snow. In a few minutes, they'd started a decent campfire with some oak logs from the woodpile. Jordan dragged a rusty metal lawn chair into the pit and slid the bucket onto it. They watched the flames take hold, and Jordan added snow to the bucket as it melted. In other circumstances, they would have been proud of their ingenuity.

Aurora trudged over to Phillip's Subaru and wiped the soot away from the driver's door window. She yanked hard on the handle, and the door creaked open on its hinges. A puff of greasy smoke made her step back, waving her hand in front of her face as she peered inside. There was nothing but melted plastic, the warped steering wheel, and the metal guts of seats laid bare in the blackened mess. Kurt's truck and Marty's old pickup were in worse shape, and she knew it wouldn't be worth checking them. Jordan watched her with hopeful anticipation, but when she pulled back from the ruined car and shut the door, he knew it was stupid to think they could get it going and drive out of here.

Rory wiped her hands on her pants and went to Jordan's side. "Nothing we can use there. That guy really screwed us."

"What guy?" Jordan asked with fear in his voice.

"The guy that attacked me." She swallowed hard at the memory of the dead man and the blood pooling in his eye. "He's dead now. We're safe." *Am I trying to reassure Jordan or myself?*

"I'm glad you killed him," Jordan whispered. "He deserved it."

He looked utterly defeated, and Rory turned to watch the campfire flicker in the wind and snow. She laid another log on the fire and crossed her arms. *They could keep this fire burning, but how long can we stay out here? Marty probably needs a doctor, and I just want to get out of these woods and put this nightmare behind us.*

* * *

Ahmed sat on the bed and waited for Ghazi and Saeed to redress him for killing Halil. It was true there was no love lost between Halil and the others, but they were a team of sorts, and now it had all collapsed. Ghazi knocked on the doorframe, leaning in. "What do we do now, Ahmed?"

Ahmed thought the boy sounded scared. *Of the Americans supposedly on their trail, or me?* "Bring Saeed. It's time we discussed our next move." Ghazi summoned Saeed, and both stood in the bedroom, looking at their feet while Ahmed spoke. "Nothing has changed, really," he began. "We still have the device, we still have a pilot, and the plan remains the same."

"I think a lot has changed," Saeed said, looking out the window instead of meeting Ahmed's eyes. "The others are dead." He didn't mention his friend Thomas. "I mean, Halil compromised the mission, and it's obvious we have to abandon the plan! What he said…"

Ahmed was too exhausted to argue. "We were compromised when you involved your American friend!" He watched the color drain from Saeed's face. "I don't know what happened in the woods, and Halil may have been telling the truth, but Nadeem and Waleed aren't coming back! Halil was lying about me profiting from the attack. You can believe me or not, but the goal is the same as before!" He hefted the satchel he'd carried across the border. "This is our most important companion now. All of the mission is in this bag, and it's not leaving my side. You two prepare to go. Saeed, get the truck started. Ghazi, gather what we'll need and tell me when you're ready to leave. I'll need help walking out of this hellhole."

CHAPTER 43

MARTY

Kurt could smell the burning camp on the swirling wind and knew they were close. He wanted to encourage Marty, but he was too winded to speak. He hoped Axe would be Axe and bull through the last hundred yards to camp. They were half dragging, half carrying Marty between them like a broken puppet, and Kurt knew just getting back to camp would be an achievement. *Then what? A burned-out cabin and three torched vehicles wouldn't do them any good. Christ,* he thought, *we even lost the cell phones! Tradition, my ass! What the hell were they going to do? Marty was near death, Axel was in no shape for this, and I'm not doing much better!*

As if to underscore their plight, Axel stumbled, and they all fell forward into the brush and fresh powder.

Kurt inhaled sharply, the snow shocking his face. "Dad, are you okay?" Axel pushed himself up from the snow and wiped his face. "I'm fine," he growled. "Just look to Marty." Kurt rolled onto his side and looked into the staring eyes of his brother-in-law.

Kurt panted in the cold, trying to focus. He reached out and shook his friend. "Marty...Are you okay?" Axel was alarmed by the tone in Kurt's voice. He rose to his knees and gently pressed two fingers against Marty's throat, feeling for a heartbeat. "He's gone, Son." Axel fell back into the snow again, trying to recover his strength.

"Goddammit!" Kurt said hoarsely. "I am going to kill those sons-a-bitches! Every fucking one of them!" Kurt's eyes burned with tears of rage, and he slammed his fist on the ground.

Axel sighed and pushed himself up again, meeting Kurt's eyes over their dead friend. "Maybe, but right now, we have two kids on their own back at camp."

Kurt got to his feet and helped Axel stand. "I don't want to leave Marty out here."

Axel brushed snow off his pants and glanced at Kurt. "I don't either, but Marty is dead, and we have to think of the living," he said tiredly. "Those bastards could be trailing us right now, and we need to keep our shit together." Axel produced a roll of orange surveyor's tape from his coat. "We'll mark this spot so we'll be able to bring him home later."

Kurt nodded and took the tape while Axel leaned against an aspen tree, still winded. Kurt finished tying the ribbon, snapping it off the roll, and letting the tape flutter in the wind. Suddenly Axel leaned forward, facing the trail to the cabin. Kurt forgot about Marty for a moment and focused on his father. "What is it? Did you hear something?" Kurt did a slow turn, trying to spot any threats.

"Do you smell that?" Axel said in a hoarse whisper.

Kurt sniffed the air and smelled something carried with the smoke from camp. "Cooking… food probably."

"That ain't food," Axel said flatly. "You get back to camp, and I'll stay here. I'm too tired to keep walking, and from what you said, there's nothin' back at camp anyway. You check on Rory and Jordan, and I'll make sure no one is following us."

"What then?" Kurt asked, slinging his rifle over his shoulder.

"Depends," Axel replied, "See what's back at camp, and if there's a way out of here, come back and get me, I guess. I suppose we could wait this out, but I guarantee you it's going below zero tonight, and I am too goddamned old for that shit." Kurt nodded. This night was going to be one hard bitch. "It's a long way back to the highway," Axel continued, "Hell, even the Swede's place is four miles of walking."

Kurt knew Owen Swenson was closest, but the snow and wind would make that trek all but impossible. "I suppose we can throw together some sort of shelter, but both of us know I'm going to have to make that hike sooner or later."

Axel took out a handkerchief and blew his nose. "Having discussed our options," He said, "I don't plan on sittin' outside tonight while those bastards over at Duchamp's are warm and dry." Axel folded the cloth before slipping it back into his pocket. "What do you think, Son?"

Kurt took off his cap and shook off the snow. "If anyone is going to sleep in the snow tonight, it's going to be those assholes." He put his cap back on and turned to leave. "I'll see what's up at camp and be back as soon as I can."

"I'll be here," Axel replied as Kurt started back to camp.

CHAPTER 44

RUINS

Aurora took the rake and went over to probe the charred remnant of the cabin for anything else they could use. The old wood stove and remnants of the chimney pipe jutted from the ashes, and their cook stove was recognizable, but the rest was a jumbled mess. She carefully moved smoking pieces of wood and looked through the wreckage. It was too much to hope that the coffee can with their cell phones might have survived, but she still searched the ashes. The rake made a metallic clink, and she found one of the enameled steel cups from the kitchen. She hooked it out of the fire and tossed it into the snow to cool. What else could she find?

Jordan picked up the cup and used snow to wipe the soot away. "Rory, this is perfect for getting water out of that big bucket." He went to her and stared into the smoking pile, hoping she would find something else. She suddenly stiffened, and Jordan watched her lean heavily on the rake and turn away.

He realized Rory was crying.

He looked closer at the pile of debris. A gust of wind cleared the smoke, and Jordan saw the charred corpse of Phillip Winters take shape in the glowing coals. Jordan almost cried out, unable to look away. Phillip's body was a shrunken mannequin of blackened flesh crackling with yellow fat, arms constricted in a boxer's stance, the hands burned down to stumps. Rory had raked across the body, exposing the milk-white ribcage, cartilage glistening amid the charred flesh. Jordan felt his stomach do a sickening roll. He tried to make out a human face, but there was only a charcoal skull with greasy, sunken eyes and a grinning rictus of teeth.

Jordan backed away from a scene he would remember for the rest of his days and fell to his knees. His mouth began to water with nausea, and his head felt like it would explode. Aurora dropped the rake and went to his side, supporting his forehead as he retched and gasped for air. Jordan crawled away from what had become Phillip Winter's funeral pyre and sat in the melting snow. "Dad and I walked right past the fire....We didn't even think of Uncle Phil in the cabin..." He faced Aurora with eyes filling with tears. "We could have saved him!"

"Don't say that, Jordan!" Aurora said sharply. "Didn't your dad say everything was burning beyond control when you got to camp?"

Jordan nodded, rubbing his eyes. "Yeah, but..."

Rory cut him off. "Your dad would have helped him if he could. Phillip was dead already, and no one could have saved him." She stalked over and stood above him. "Enough of this! There are men out there trying to kill us," she said roughly, venting her frustration. "Your dad and Grandpa Axe are still out there with Marty, so get it together!" Jordan said nothing but collapsed onto his side, facing away from her, shutting her out.

"Fine," she said, picking up the rake and throwing it on the smoldering embers of the cabin. "If you're going to be a little bitch I should just leave your ass here and start walking!"

"Shut up!" Jordan shrieked at her. "Don't call me that...Just shut up!"

Aurora was ashamed she had snapped at him. She didn't need another enemy in this mess, and she cursed herself for losing her temper. "I'm sorry, Jordan. I shouldn't have said that." She looked down at him, hoping he would forgive her. "You're too young for this shit....Maybe we both are."

Jordan didn't reply but rolled onto his back, blinking up at the gray sky and the flecks of snow still swirling through the air. He held out his hand to Aurora. "Pull me up," Jordan said, leaning forward.

She helped him stand, and he gave her an awkward embrace. Aurora smiled with tears in her eyes. "We'll be okay, Spud."

Jordan leaned against her. "If you say so."

They retrieved their guns and sat down on a fallen tree at the edge of the clearing. They waited in silence, both coming down from the fear that had them on edge. Now they were worn out and needed sleep.

Jordan nodded off, and his rifle almost slipped out of his hands. He snapped awake and was about to say something when they both heard sounds from the woods.

"Get down!" Aurora hissed in a loud whisper, hopping off the log and lying prone in the snow. "Someone's coming!"

Jordan dropped down and crawled to Rory's side. "Can you see who it is?"

"Shush!" Rory snapped, aiming her shotgun towards the sound.

Both strained to see something, anything in the gray woods that would signal salvation or danger. "Are you ready for this?" Rory whispered, not taking her eyes off the trail.

"Yes," Jordan replied, bringing his rifle to his shoulder.

They held their breath, waiting to see what would materialize from the mosaic of aspens.

* * *

Kurt knew anyone could hear him coming through the woods a mile away, so he didn't try to be stealthy. He was a little worried that Jordan and Rory would be jumpy and start shooting if he surprised them. *At least they would be alive.* It wasn't long before the smoke in the trees was thicker, and he recognized the familiar landmarks of camp. He unslung his rifle and slowly approached, watching the edge of the clearing for any movement. As he neared open ground, he surveyed the three burned-out vehicles and the dying flames of their family cabin. A lawn chair was straddling the fire pit with their old metal bucket steaming over a campfire. Rory and Jordan were nowhere in sight.

"Jordan!" Kurt called in a loud whisper. "It's Dad!"

Two figures popped up from under a snow-covered deadfall. They had Kurt in their sights the whole time. Jordan and Kurt stumbled to each other in the snow, and Kurt hugged his son.

"Where's Grandpa?" Aurora asked after a moment.

"He's okay, "Kurt replied, giving Jordan a fatherly slap on the back. "He was pretty worn out and decided to hang back."

"Marty's dead isn't he," Aurora stated quietly.

Kurt met Aurora's eyes and nodded. "He didn't make it. Axe and I tried to get him home, but he just couldn't hold on." Aurora looked away and pointed to the smoldering ruins of the cabin. "Phillip's in there. We found him in the ashes. I don't know if he was dead already or died in the fire."

Kurt walked slowly over to the ruins, and as the heat and smoke enveloped him, he recoiled at the sickly sweet smell of burned flesh. He understood now what Axel meant back in the woods. Surely anyone who experienced combat would never forget that smell. Kurt peered into the coals and blackened wood, making out Phillip's corpse. Kurt stared at the shrunken torso and teeth baked to chalk. The burnt skull was mis-shapen, but Kurt saw the neat round bullet hole just above the brow line. He turned away and rejoined Rory and Jordan.

"Phil didn't deserve to die like that," he said, shaking with anger. "Those bastards didn't need to kill anybody! What the hell did we ever do to them?" Kurt began pacing in a circle. "I mean, Marty screws up and shoots Tommy Duchamp, and they go psycho on us?" Rory and Jordan stepped back and let Kurt vent his emotions. "Those bastards are going to pay!" He said in a murderous tone. "No jail or even a trial! I'm talking gun to the head, pull the trigger and leave them for the ravens!"

"There wasn't much to salvage around here," Aurora said, trying to calm him down. "I checked the cars, and they're toast." She winced at her poor choice of words, but Kurt didn't notice. He had stopped pacing but was now staring into the woods. "We melted some snow to drink if you're thirsty," Rory said, hoping her uncle would snap out of his rage.

Kurt didn't reply. "Dad," Jordan said, pulling on Kurt's sleeve. "We melted snow for us to drink."

Kurt came out of his trance. "What?"

"There's some water to drink," Jordan said, pointing to the bucket over the fire.

"Oh," Kurt said, suddenly calm. "Good thinking, guys. I'm thirsty as hell."

* * *

Saeed returned from outside, the keys still in his hand. "It won't run. I can't get it started!" Ghazi could tell Saeed was on the edge of panic and was about to tell Ahmed, but he'd heard.

"What the hell do you mean it won't run?" Ahmed's voice boomed from the back bedroom.

"I don't know vehicles that well, but I tried, and it wouldn't start," Saeed stammered. "It just makes a clicking noise!"

Ghazi looked out the open door at the Suburban sitting in the snow like a worthless steel brick. "But we have to get out of here!"

Saeed glared at Ghazi with exasperation. "Don't you think I want to get out of here too, you stupid idiot? It doesn't run, and unless you're a bloody mechanic, you can go to hell!"

"Enough!" Ahmed limped out into the living area, leaning against the wall for support. "Is it the battery?"

"I don't know," Saeed said in a sullen tone. "Probably."

"Did you bring something to charge it with?" Ghazi asked hopefully.

"Oh, I forgot!" Saeed slapped his forehead. "I always carry a battery charger around with me!"

"Shut up, Saeed!" Ahmed's voice was like acid. "You've lost your standing to criticize Ghazi or me. Think! Would there be one in the vehicle? In this house or one of the sheds?"

Saeed shook his head. "I don't know, Ahmed."

Before the other two could react, Ghazi pushed Saeed out of the way and went to the door. "I'll look, but you two will have to come up with something if I don't find one!"

Saeed watched Ghazi begin rummaging inside the Suburban and feared they would all die here for nothing. "I'll check the other buildings." He said, leaving Ahmed alone in the house.

* * *

Kurt stood next to the campfire. He had some water and made the kids drink their fill. He used the steel cup to scoop more snow into the bucket and took up his rifle again.

"Okay, listen up," he told Rory and Jordan, "I'm going back to Axe. You two stay here and do like you did before – stay low and alert. If someone gets close to camp you don't know, don't hesitate - Just shoot the bastards." He paused a moment to let that sink in. "Understand?" Both nodded. "Good. Just keep the fire going, stay put, and wait for us to get back."

Kurt wasn't as confident as he sounded. A thousand things were wrong with this scenario, and it scared him how little he was in control and how high the stakes had become. That helplessness made him angry again. He was bone tired. They all were, and none of them would find rest any time soon. He murmured a small prayer and asked for the power to "let go and let God." Kurt had always scoffed when his mother said that. He figured the Lord helped those who helped themselves, but maybe this time, it wasn't up to him. Perhaps he had to count on God to get them out of this whole shitty mess.

* * *

Axel found a fallen tree just off the trail at the perfect level for sitting while he watched for trouble. His head pounded, and he had a terrible fluttering in his chest. Axel brushed away the snow and sat down to catch his breath. He'd been in worse scrapes than this, but that was long ago. At twenty, Axel was at the peak of physical stamina and mentally girded with a feeling of immortality. He felt the same as Kurt about dishing out some payback, but one thing about growing old was giving a shit about other people besides yourself. Axel poured a cup of lukewarm coffee and lit his pipe, taking a deep pull of sweet smoke before exhaling it into the wind. He sipped some coffee and felt better. Axel caught the sweet smell of burning flesh again. He'd been in too many bombed villages and napalmed battlefields to mistake the charred pork stink of a burning body for anything else. It must be Phillip, Axel thought, pulling on the pipe. *Poor Phillip was never really in tune with how things worked,* he thought. His middle son thought himself an idealist, but Axel knew Phil was just a little too weak to stand for anything and too arrogant to admit he didn't have all the answers.

Axel hadn't put everything together, but he figured a bunch of thugs showed up with Tommy Duchamp, and the shit hit the fan. *It had to be drugs, or Tommy screwed them out of money, or...*His train of thought faltered, and his mind returned to the cold and wind and the fact that they were up shit creek without a paddle. The only thing Axel knew for sure was that Tommy Duchamp was a disappointment to his father and managed to fail at pretty much everything.

Except getting mistaken for a deer. Tommy did that pretty well! Axel smiled at the dark humor. *Jeeesus...A brown coat!* Axel just hoped Tommy's friends weren't as stupid and hightailed it out of these woods before Axel and Kurt had to take the fight to them.

Axel shivered. It was getting colder, and they would soon have to make a move in one direction or another. He tapped the pipe against his boot and put it back in his pocket. Axel dumped out the last of the coffee and screwed the metal cap back on the bottle. *Hurry up and wait.*

* * *

Ahmed wasn't surprised that there was no means of charging the battery, which meant they had to bide their time. Either the Americans would come and root them out, or they wouldn't, and Ahmed would have time to find another way out of here. He looked through the dirty glass of the back window at the snow and trees they had come through the night before. He didn't know if the Americans had the spine to attack or if Halil had killed the ones he'd encountered, but this was not the time to let their guard down.

Ghazi knew very little about vehicles or how to fix them, but it was hard to sit by and trust Saeed to salvage their means of escape. Ghazi watched him retrieve a toolkit from the back of the vehicle and return to his work under the hood. Soon, Saeed came back to the cabin with the large battery from the truck. Ghazi hurriedly opened the door for him, and Saeed went directly into the kitchen. He placed the battery onto the countertop and opened the oven door. Ghazi watched him light the oven and slide the battery inside. Saeed turned the knob to high and closed the door.

"What are you doing that for?" Ghazi was skeptical that this could help anything.

"The battery is frozen, and our only way to get that truck on the road is to start it. Sometimes you can warm a battery, and it will come alive enough to start an automobile." Saeed took off his gloves and began chewing on his thumbnail.

Ghazi went back to watching out the side window for any sign the Americans were coming.

CHAPTER 45

KURT AND AXEL

Axel heard Kurt coming back along the trail and stretched, trying to will his body to do what was inevitably next. When Kurt joined him, Axel put his hand on his son's shoulder. "The kids?" Axel asked quietly.

"They're okay," Kurt replied, still catching his breath. "But Phillip's dead. Burned in the cabin."

Axel nodded but said nothing, disappointed he had been right about such a terrible thing.

"They shot him in the head," Kurt said quietly. He didn't add more because no words could blunt the regret they both felt.

"What a goddamned mess," Axel said, shaking his head.

"Yeah, well, Rory and Jordan are safe for now, but we're still in a world of shit. Are we going to visit the neighbors?"

"Just been waiting on you," Axel replied. Kurt nodded, relieved that Axel would come with him. "I'll lead, but you're running the show," Kurt said, starting back to where it all started. "Any advice?"

Axel gave him a tight smile. "Rule one: kill the other guy before he kills you. Two: No fight's the same as the last, and three: Don't be a goddamn hero."

Kurt couldn't argue with those rules, but it was probably too little, too late. He moved down the trail, keeping a slow pace for Axel's sake. Kurt wasn't conscious of it, but the softness of civility was dropping away to something primal with each step forward. Kurt underwent the change Axel had experienced so long before in the valleys of Vietnam; the terrible orthodoxy of kill or be killed. The gloves were off, and Kurt hoped he had the nerve to do whatever it would take to get them all home alive.

* * *

Kurt stopped well before the clearing. He waited for Axel to join him and then knelt, raising his rifle and focusing the scope on the Duchamp place. It had been quite a while since he'd been this far across the river, but he remembered the old farmstead well enough. The whitewashed siding was weathered gray, and the roof sagged in the middle. It looked like the snow load could take it down any minute. He could smell the fuel oil burner and saw a wisp of smoke streaming out of the chimney and into the wind. "We're here," Kurt said to Axel. "Now what?"

Axel was watching through his own scope. After peering through the trees for what seemed an eternity, he lowered his rifle and settled into the snow. "We wait."

Kurt stared at his father but didn't reply. Kurt's anger had dissipated with the exertion of slogging through the woods, and he was thinking more clearly, trying to reason the best way out of this. Something they encountered along the way also tempered his judgment. They had found a strange trail after they'd crossed the Joshua. Axel had spotted it and called for Kurt to stop.

"Son, look here," he said, motioning to the snow-covered tracks that ran along a north to south line." The snow's filled in since they came through, but there was something dragged through here by several people. Kurt could see the flattened strip where a sled was towed through the woods. He noticed multiple boot prints and broken branches marking where the group had passed.

"I don't like this," Axel said flatly. "There's nothing north of here except Canada."

Kurt wasn't sure what he meant. "Drug smugglers?"

Axel hesitated to answer. "Probably," he finally replied. "Doesn't matter. We're still going to Duchamp's, and I'll bet my ass this trail leads there too."

Kurt tried to think this through. Stumbling onto a drug smuggling operation would explain their situation and made him shudder at the stories he'd heard about the cartels and how they dealt with their rivals. "How many of them are there?"

Axel shook his head, "hard to tell, but more than the two of us. Our friends must have come over the border last night."

Kurt found that Axel was right. They followed the trail directly to the Duchamp place and saw it curve around the old farmhouse to somewhere around front. Kurt worried about how many they were facing and felt less in control so close to danger. He thought about the dead men with their light clothing and dark features. It didn't make sense that drug runners would be so unprepared yet aggressive in going after them. It occurred to him this might be a "one-off" crossing and something more sinister. *Terrorists? What the hell would they be doing up here? Yeah, the border was only a few miles away, but wouldn't it be easier to just cross in some remote spot in Texas? If they were terrorists, what were they bringing in? Weapons or explosives? It figures that goddamned Tommy Duchamp would be involved.* "I'm going around front to see what's going on," Kurt whispered to Axel. "I'll be back."

Axel watched Kurt disappear into the brush. He was proud of his son, but this wasn't some paintball game you could walk away from, and what the hell were they supposed to do if it was a gang running drugs? Axel shifted his weight and winced at the pain in his knees and hips. This couldn't go on much longer. If the bastards in the house didn't make a move soon, he knew Kurt would start something, and then all bets were off.

CHAPTER 46

THE SAFE HOUSE

"Saeed!" Ahmed hissed through clenched teeth. "What the bloody hell is going on?"

Ghazi went to the back bedroom. "He's heating the battery. He says that will make it work again."

Ahmed cursed under his breath. "Tell him we don't have much time!"

Ghazi nodded and went back into the front room.

Ahmed could barely contain his frustration. *What other things could go wrong on this bloody adventure? The only good thing was that the American "hunters" hadn't appeared, and they might still have time to get out of these woods.* He turned back to the bedroom window and scanned the tree line, looking for any movement. His hands were stiff from holding the AK, and he laid the rifle on the bed for a moment, flexing his fingers. If Saeed was correct about the battery, he had a clever idea. If the truck had a more complicated problem, they were out of options. He looked at his satchel, thinking of the cell phone trigger inside.

Ahmed didn't have many alternatives. He could send Saeed and Ghazi out into the snow to pull the sled along a road until they could hijack a ride, but that was no plan. They could seek another vehicle, but he knew from his aerial maps there weren't any farms or homes close enough to reach before they were hunted down. Fleeing back to Canada wasn't an option with his broken leg and another foot of snow to caravan through. *The storm was letting up, and there was a window of opportunity to escape if they could just get that bloody truck started!* He picked up the AK again and rested the barrel against the window sill while he waited for something to happen.

Saeed stood by the gas oven with the door cracked open, staring at the battery as if it were a sleeping child. He reached in and felt the sides of the battery. It was still cold as death, and Saeed began to fidget, tapping his foot and unconsciously chewing his nails. He thought of Thomas and felt like weeping. This situation was a horrible mistake, and he just wanted to leave this place and the others behind.

"Is it working?" Ghazi had come up behind Saeed and was trying to see past him into the oven.

"Dammit!" Saeed almost screamed like a child. "Don't creep up behind me like that!" He took off his stocking cap and ran his fingers through his hair. "I don't know. For all our sakes, it better work."

"Why did the battery go dead?" Ghazi meant no offense, but Saeed bristled at the question and the inference of blame.

"How the hell should I know?" He threw his hat on the counter and slammed the oven door shut. "Maybe Thomas left the headlights on, or maybe one of you imbeciles left the cargo door open last night, or maybe it's just bloody cold outside! It isn't my doing, but I'm trying to fix it. Why don't you go do something instead of bothering me?"

Ghazi backed out of the kitchen. These men were losing it. Both were barely in control of themselves, and that made Ghazi nervous. Ghazi tried to concentrate on watching the clearing and driveway beyond the disabled truck. The hand tremors were getting worse, and Ghazi gripped the Halil's Tokarev like it was a good luck charm.

Ghazi thought the pistol might be needed soon, and maybe that was okay, even if it meant shooting Ahmed or Saeed.

* * *

Kurt moved as stealthily as he could but knew anyone watching could catch a glimpse or hear him if they were outside. He was wearing brown camouflage, his orange vest discarded, but it was made for autumn and not snow. Kurt wove through the trees, slowly coming around to the front of the house.

A tan Chevy Suburban sat near the front porch with its hood up. Growing up in northern Minnesota, Kurt knew the truck was too cold to start. The Suburban's windows were coated with frost, and snow blanketed the roof, so it hadn't been driven since the storm. It was in good shape otherwise, so it wasn't some abandoned derelict. He scanned the yard with his rifle scope, spotting footprints to and from the porch. Someone was in the house, and they weren't leaving any time soon.

They were back to a stalemate.

He returned to Axel and described what he observed. "What do you think?"

Axel sighed and looked Kurt in the eyes. "I'd like to evict those assholes and sit in front of their oil stove until we're good and warm." He motioned toward the house. "Trouble is, we don't know what's in there waiting for us."

"Maybe we just need to speak up," Kurt whispered. "Let them know we're out here with guns, and tell them to give up or take to the woods."

Axel gave Kurt a withering stare. "Wise up, Son. This isn't like busting up some frat party. These sonsabitches hold the cards." He could tell Kurt wasn't listening. "Just take it easy," he said, putting his hand on Kurt's shoulder. "Our advantage is that they don't know what we're out here. You said their truck is out of commission, so maybe that's our bargaining chip."

Kurt turned to face Axel. "And how is that?"

"One of the batteries in our vehicles might be salvageable and have enough juice to jump-start their piece of shit. Your set of jumper cables will still work if the wires are intact."

Kurt stiffened at Axel's reasoning. "We give the murdering bastards a jumpstart, they hit the road, and we have a circle jerk until help arrives, is that it?"

"Yep." Axel ignored Kurt's sarcasm and continued. "I don't want to help them assholes either, but I'll eat the shit sandwich if it means we get through this alive."

Kurt pointed at the farmhouse. "Those assholes will be in the wind once they escape," he whispered. "They need to pay for what they did to Marty and Phillip!"

"They will," Axel replied tiredly. "Let the cops worry about it. I doubt those jokers will get far, and we need to get out of this situation soon. I think you should go haul a battery back here so we can try to negotiate our way out of this."

Kurt thought again about why the men might be here and why they had come in over the border. "What if they have something with them—Something that could hurt a lot of people? They were dragging some sort of sled. What if they have weapons or explosives? We're the only ones that can stop them." Kurt knew his father was listening. "I know you're worried about Rory and Jordan, but this is more than revenge. I think letting these bastards go might be something we'll regret for the rest of our lives."

Axel snorted. "I don't have much more life to worry about regretting anything," he replied. "And you're right; I am worried about the kids...*And you.* This is serious shit, Kurt, and I've seen what men can do to each other. I don't know what they're up to, but to assume they're some half-baked commando squad isn't worth your life. I'll take my chances that they'll fuck up before they can do any more damage. Hell, if they are some sort of terrorists, the FBI or CIA are probably waiting for them on the highway!"

"But you're thinking about it, aren't you?" Kurt whispered. "History is full of assholes that didn't recognize the opportunity to stop something terrible from happening. I don't want to be one of them!"

"Keep your voice down," Axel replied, "I hear you. They might be terrorists, but think of what you're asking of us. How are the two of us supposed to stop an invasion of the United States?"

"Dad, the kids are safe, they're warm enough back at camp, and if we can take these guys, we'll be home by suppertime."

"By 'take,' you mean kill?" Axel asked harshly. "Call it what it is. Remember my third rule of combat?"

"Don't be a hero," Kurt replied.

"That's right, Son. Every hero I knew in Vietnam died over there. I did some crazy brave shit in-country, but all of us who came back know that the real heroes, the ones who did the heavy lifting, are snug in their coffins, and you can bet their parents wish their boys had never signed up! Axel's voice was rising with emotion. "Maybe I'm a callous, cynical old man, but I've given enough to my country for you, Aurora, and Jordan to get a pass! Do you hear? You all get a pass from me!"

Kurt looked away in shame. He knew his father's beliefs came the hard way, and maybe this was something beyond their ability to stop. Still, it gnawed at him. "What about rule number one," Kurt blurted out. "Kill the other guy before he kills you?"

Axel scowled at Kurt and was about to say something, but the wind dropped, and both heard urgent voices from the house. They couldn't make out words, but something was happening. Both of them sank into the snow, waiting and watching.

CHAPTER 47

RORY AND JORDAN

Aurora was chilled to the bone. She and Jordan had taken turns standing watch while the other stoked the fire and warmed themselves. When it was this cold and windy, a campfire did a poor job of keeping you warm. Without a shelter to concentrate the heat, they were losing ground. She thought about building another fire in front of the outhouse where they could get out of the wind, but then they wouldn't see or hear what was going on. She wanted to know someone was coming in time to defend themselves. Jordan was shivering, and she went to his side and rubbed his shoulders through his coat.

"How much longer are we going to wait for them?" Jordan's voice trembled, and his teeth were starting to chatter. "It's been forever. What's taking so long?"

Rory brought him a little closer to the fire and threw another log into the flames. "It's only been a few hours, Jordan." She knew she was talking like an adult to a child, but it was true. She stared at the flames and shivered. Rory was tired of waiting too, and Jordan's questions made up her mind. Sometimes being sensible and following directions didn't cut it. She turned Jordan around and looked him in the eyes. "I think we need to go after them."

Jordan blinked. "The guys that killed Uncle Phillip?"

"No!" she replied. "Your dad and Grandpa Axe. But if we go, let's think this through. Nothing has changed, there are still bad guys out there, and we aren't soldiers. We both want to go home, but if we're not careful, we'll be in big trouble." She paused and made sure he was listening. "We'll go slow and catch up to Grandpa and your dad. But remember, there might be some bad stuff coming, and you can't freak out."

"I saw that guy you shot and Uncle Phillip, and I'm not freaking out, am I?"

Aurora frowned at her cousin. "I don't mean gross stuff; I'm talking about killing."

"I'll be okay," Jordan replied.

Aurora didn't want to say anything more that could spoil his confidence, so she left it at that. She took a look around the camp and decided there wasn't anything more for them to do but leave. Without speaking, both hefted their weapons and started on the trail to find Axel and Kurt.

They took it slow, Aurora often stopping to listen for danger. Following Axel and Kurt's footprints over the old walking bridge, she noticed the snow seemed to be ending, and the sky was a lighter gray as the storm dissipated.

"Have you ever been to Duchamp's place?" Jordan's voice was shaking, and Aurora wasn't sure if he was scared or just cold. She was both.

"No, but we'll be there soon," she whispered. "Grandpa Axe said it wasn't far past the Joshua." Jordan followed a little closer, and she could feel their tension increasing as they moved through the woods toward Duchamp's old farm.

* * *

Axel and Kurt strained to see movement around the farmhouse. The voices still carried when the wind slacked off, but no one had come outside.

A new sound caught their attention. This one was coming from behind them, following their trail. Axel tapped Kurt's arm and made a motion with his head to look behind them. Kurt nodded and slowly turned around to face the north. His apprehension turned to anger as he spotted Rory and Jordan approaching. He waited until they were close enough and let them have it in a harsh whisper. "What the hell are you two doing?" He grabbed Jordan's arm and shook him, glaring at both of them. "Why didn't you stay by the fire? You were safe there!" He pulled Jordan down next to him and squeezed his arm. "From now on, you do as you're told! Both of you!"

Axel gave his grandchildren a look that could melt steel.

Rory dropped down next to Kurt and, ignoring their glares, sized up the Duchamp farm. "We weren't going sit and wait at the camp," Aurora said flatly. "What's going on?" She asked. "Anyone in there?"

"Jesus, Rory, you are something!" Kurt muttered under his breath. "Nothing is going on…We can hear voices in the house, but nobody's been outside."

"What's around front?" she asked, "Do they have a car?"

"Yes, they have a truck, but it looks like the thing won't start." Kurt's reply made it clear he was not taking any more questions.

"Listen," Axel whispered, "We're waiting to see what happens. I know you want to get out of here, but let things shake out. These guys are bad news, and I don't want anyone else to get hurt, okay?"

Aurora nodded. She was sorry they were upset, but not sorry she was here with them. The four grew silent, straining to hear anything from the farmhouse.

"I can't see anything from here," Kurt whispered. "I'm going closer. Don't follow me," he said, looking at Jordan. Glaring at Aurora, he said, "Do what Grandpa says." He slowly crawled forward alongside the clearing.

Rory took Kurt's place next to Axel. "How are you doing, Grandpa?"

"Better than you if you pull a stunt like this again." His voice was rough, but she knew he had already forgiven her. "I'm holding up. How about you two?"

"We're okay," she answered.

"Just keep your eyes peeled and ears open," Axel growled.

"Got it," she whispered, watching the farmhouse. "Jordan, be ready."

Axel was surprised to see both Jordan and Rory carefully aim their weapons at the farmhouse and settle into the snow. He didn't comment but did the same, watching the clearing through his rifle scope. They might not be professionals, but he felt sorry for any sonofabitch stupid enough to mess with them.

* * *

Kurt crawled to the clearing's edge, surveying the house. He didn't want to endanger the others, especially the kids, but they couldn't sit out in the snow much longer, and he needed to do something. Rising to his knees, Kurt cupped his hands around his mouth. "You in the house!" He shouted. "You're surrounded! Come out with your hands up!"

He couldn't believe how corny that sounded.

Ahmed was startled by a voice shouting from the woods. He peered out of the bedroom window, trying to spot the source.

Kurt exhaled with relief. *I guess they're too chicken-shit to...*

A burst of automatic weapon fire erupted from the side window. The bullets raked the trees and brush over their heads, and they all instinctively flinched and flattened, their faces pressed against the snow. Axel recognized the distinctive pop and cadence of an AK-47 as it spit out 7.62mm rounds in a long random burst, showering them with bark and twigs.

Just as suddenly, it was quiet again. The men in the house weren't making any noise or trying to communicate. It was still a standoff. Kurt kept low and crawled back to the others.

"What the hell, Kurt!" Axel said as loud as he dared. "*Come out with your hands up?* Are you nuts? I taught you better than that!"

"I gave them fair warning," Kurt replied sullenly.

"Jesus H. Christ!" Axel was beside himself with anger. "They've got a fully-auto AK in there!"

"Now we know they're the bad guys, don't we? Still want to offer them a jump-start?"

Axel glared at his son. "Okay, smartass, they were laying for us," he said, "but talk about poking a hornet's nest!" Axel weighed their options. "Alright, we've got them pinned inside the house, and they know we're onto them. I guess we just stole the initiative."

"Great," Kurt replied. "How do we keep it?"

Axel thought for a moment. "We let the bastards stew for a while. In the meantime, we need eyes on the front, so they don't try to flank us."

"I did the right thing!" Kurt muttered as he started back to watch the front entrance.

"You probably did the right thing," Axel said to Kurt in a harsh whisper, "but was it the smart thing?"

Kurt let the question hang as he left Axel and the kids behind.

CHAPTER 48

THE SAFE HOUSE

Saeed and Ghazi were startled by the voice from outside, and they looked at each other, realizing the Americans had found them. Before either could react, a burst of deafening fire from Ahmed's rifle erupted from the back room.

Ghazi cautiously looked out of the living room window but couldn't make out anything. The raw fear from the border crossing was back, and Ghazi started for the bedroom in a near panic.

"Ghazi," Ahmed said in a low voice, putting his finger to his lips. "Go back to watching outside and keep quiet." He inserted a fresh magazine in the rifle and gave a weak smile to his new protégé.

Ghazi nodded and returned to the front window. *There were only three of those... Magazines? For the gun, and they won't last long if the Americans come at us!* No one had talked about it, but Ghazi knew the thing in the sled was at the center of this. When carrying out Ahmed's errand, Ghazi thought there would be more weapons or drugs in the sled, or maybe even money, because it was so heavy. But the sled only carried the machine gun next to a complicated thing with wires and strange parts. Ghazi was baffled. *It didn't look like a bomb, but what should a bomb look like? Is it a machine? Some sort of computer?*

Whatever it is, it probably cost the lives of Waleed and Nadeem, Ghazi reasoned. *It wouldn't take much for Ahmed to shoot me and close the circle!* It was hard to trust Ahmed after he'd killed Halil. *And what did Ahmed do to Mohammet, his own brother?* Ghazi didn't want to think about something so horrible.

Distracted by the sudden activity outside, Saeed was slow to notice the hot plastic smell filling the air and quickly shut off the oven. He opened the stove and turned away as a wave of hot air and the sharp smell of sulphuric acid washed over his face. The battery was hissing gently but didn't seem to be damaged. He flung open drawers along the kitchen counter, looking for an oven mitt, but finally gave up and took his leather gloves from the counter. They were too thin, and he winced as he pulled the battery out of the oven and up onto the stovetop before dropping it with a crash.

Saeed knew if this didn't work, their chances of escape were nil. *If they have no other options, will Ahmed trigger the bomb despite being in the middle of* nowhere? *I don't want to die in a place like this!* Saeed tried to put his fear aside. "Ghazi," he said, "I'm going to put this back in the truck and try the ignition."

Ghazi cautiously went to the door. "Aren't you afraid the Americans will shoot you?"

"Yes…I guess I am," Saeed replied, a haunted look in his eyes. "But what choice do I have?" Saeed picked up the battery and held it against his chest. "I have a spanner outside to reconnect this, and the keys are in the vehicle. Just hold the door and watch out for me…Please?"

Ghazi nodded and opened the front door, casting a furtive glance past the porch and along the tree line. Saeed scuttled down the steps and around the Suburban while Ghazi held the Tokarev, eyes flickering between Saeed and the woods

Saeed was out of sight, but they were both exposed. It seemed the Americans were allowing them to leave. "Come on….Come on…" Ghazi whispered like a chant, frantically trying to watch the area around the house. "Come on….COME ON!" Ghazi knew once Saeed started the truck, they could be out of here in minutes.

"What's going on?" Ghazi flinched at Ahmed's voice and turned to see him silhouetted against the gray light of the bedroom window. "Is Saeed outside?" He asked in a loud whisper.

Ghazi nodded and went back to the vigil, sure Saeed would be gunned down any second. But there was nothing. *Why aren't the Americans shooting at us? Maybe Ahmed killed them or at least scared them off?* There were sounds from the engine compartment, and Saeed pushed the hood down with a grunt, closing it with a dull click. He nodded to Ghazi as he went around to the driver's door and got into the truck. It seemed like an eternity as Saeed checked the switches and made sure there wouldn't be any added draw on the battery.

Ghazi heard the jingling of keys as Saeed inserted them into the ignition, and before Ghazi could even dread failure, the truck roared to life. Saeed leaned out of the driver's door smiling and giving a relieved thumbs up.

Allah was merciful! Ghazi smiled for the first time in days and turned to see Ahmed give a tired wave from the back room.

Saeed revved the engine. *I've done it! We're free to leave!* He took his foot off the accelerator, almost expecting the engine to die, but the Suburban ran smoothly, purring exhaust into the frigid air. He almost forgot the Americans were near. Saeed slid out of the truck and left the door open. He hurried along the Suburban's side, concerned about the depth of snow they would have to push through to the main road. Thomas had mentioned the Suburban had larger wheels and a lift kit, whatever that was. With the four-wheel-drive engaged and the bomb in the back for traction, they should be able to escape.

It was in the hands of Allah now.

CHAPTER 49

THE CLEARING

Kurt watched one of the men close the hood and get into the Suburban. Kurt spotted another one silently observing, crouched in the doorway, nervously scanning the area around the house. The men didn't look as formidable as they had in his mind, but he knew they might be dangerous just the same. They were both swarthy like the two dead guys, and Kurt decided they must be Middle Eastern. He checked out the one in the doorway. *Younger, no more than a boy. Could they be related to each other?*

Kurt brought up his rifle, but his resolve wavered. *Should I shoot them?* Maybe in an action movie, but these guys hadn't threatened him directly, and Kurt knew the court system usually punished vigilantes more than the criminals. The truck suddenly roared to life, and exhaust billowed around the Suburban like a cloud. *It's time to decide,* he thought. *It was tempting to follow his father's advice and let them go, but Kurt just couldn't kick this can down the road. How many more people will they hurt? And what about justice for Marty and Phillip?*

* * *

Aurora crept along, staying low and following the path Kurt had made in the snow. Axel told her to find her uncle and get him to come back to where they were waiting. Grandpa was usually right about these things, and she hoped she could convince Kurt to see it that way. The sound of a vehicle starting made Aurora hesitate. *The men in the house must be leaving! I have to reach Kurt before he does something he'll regret!*

CHAPTER 50

THE SAFE HOUSE

Ahmed was relieved when he heard the Suburban roar to life. The three shared a silent moment of triumph, but he knew they would only be safe when they'd put these woods, and the Americans, behind them.

Since Ahmed had fallen in the gravel pit, he'd pushed aside thoughts of his negligible future contributions to the mission. Now, when they finally had the bomb loaded and the opportunity to escape, the Americans had appeared to harry them, and he knew his best action would be to stay behind. Saeed and Ghazi could continue the mission without him. He'd killed his brother and a friend, and their deaths resulted from his arrogance and greed. Throughout their venture, Ahmed had held back, and someone else bore the sacrifices that had to be made. He could do no more for the mission, and with the trail of death left behind, he could never reap any reward from their great attack. Halil had found out the truth, and to become richer would be for naught.

Ahmed would put more than his wealth on the line this time. He had the AK-47 and could hold the Americans back to give the others time to escape. "Ghazi, come here," he called from the bedroom. "Hurry, we don't have much time!"

Ghazi appeared in the doorway, obviously tense and frantic to leave. "Come on, Ahmed, we have to go *now!*"

"Yes," Ahmed replied, picking up his satchel from the bed. "You and Saeed must leave, but I'm staying here to make sure you escape." With an effort, he tossed the pack to Ghazi. "Everything is in that bag. The primary target, the trigger device, and most importantly, instructions for setting off the bomb."

It was a bomb! Ghazi hefted the bag and started to unzip the main compartment to see what was inside.

"No time for that!" Ahmed said quickly. "Just take it. There are notes for everything, the safe house, secondary targets, and your contact in Minneapolis. Do not lose that bag! Now go!"

Ghazi stood in the doorway a moment longer, then turned and left Ahmed in the dark bedroom.

Ahmed felt an emptiness not unlike he had felt when he killed Mohammet. *What did I expect? Tears? A heartfelt plea not to sacrifice myself?* He knew, in the end, they were all expendable. *My enterprise and guile have carried the battle to the enemy and positioned us to strike a country that was the most significant threat ever faced by Islam. I may have been wrong to think of personal gain, but the new Caliphate will have new life because of me!*

But now, the moment had come, and it was a hollow victory. *Mohammet and I will not live to revel in the explosion and aftermath with the rest of Islam.* He should be ashamed at his bitterness, but they had worked so hard! Sacrificed so much! *Imam al-Qadhi and Mohammet rest in a sea of snow-covered cars in Canada, and Halil was driven to betrayal! For what? The mission? It was my pride! My actions brought them to their deaths, and their corpses lay at my feet. This jihad is nothing more than a testament to my failings!*

Ahmed steeled himself and waited for the Americans to show themselves.

Ghazi put one arm through the strap of Ahmed's satchel and went to Saeed. "Ahmed is staying behind. You and I are getting out of here." Saeed stared dully at Ghazi but didn't protest. He went to gather his gloves and hat. Ghazi put a hand on Saeed's shoulder. "Here," Ghazi said, holding out the pistol. "Take it. Maybe you should be the one to cover us. I can drive."

Saeed hesitated but took the Tokarev, slipping it into his waistband. "Ready?"

Ghazi nodded and followed Saeed to the front door. *Should they call out to Ahmed and give him some words of encouragement or a meaningful farewell?* There was nothing to say. Ghazi only wanted to leave this place behind, and if Ahmed stayed behind, it was Allah's will. Ghazi pushed aside any emotion or loyalty to Ahmed and focused on their escape. Saeed opened the door, and Ghazi cautiously followed.

* * *

Kurt made his decision. *This shit will stop here and now in one smooth move! I'll steal the truck from under their noses, blast back to town, and save the fucking day. The assholes will be stranded in the house, and Axel can lay low with the kids until I come back with the sheriff!*

Now or never! Kurt's resolve exploded into action as he rushed the house. He burst from the willow brush and ran as fast as the snow would allow, reciting his plan like a mantra: *Five yards of brush, thirty yards through the clearing, then jump into the truck, and hit the accelerator!*

Aurora heard twigs snapping ahead and raised up on her elbows, ready to endure Axel's wrath for risking her skin. She stared open-mouthed as her uncle burst from cover and bolted into the clearing, his strides kicking up snow behind him as he ran.

Kurt was halfway across when two men exited the cabin and started down the steps. "Stop!" Kurt shouted, as much in surprise as aggression. "Get back in the house!" He was too winded to say more, but he brought his rifle up to his hip and trained it on the two.

Saeed stopped next to the Suburban, stunned at the appearance of the American. His mind raced; *they were so close! Why hadn't Ahmed shot them down?*

Aurora stood up and began jogging toward the house, trying to catch up to her uncle. Kurt was alone against two of them, and she couldn't just stand by and watch.

Axel watched Kurt's attack unfold, and got to his feet, horrified to see Aurora break from cover and follow her uncle. "Rory! Get back to the woods!" he shouted, waving his arm to get her attention.

Saeed's mind raced. There was no escape from this other than surrender or retreat into the house. *We are so close to the idling truck and freedom from this wooded hell!* Saeed gambled that the American wouldn't shoot and pulled back his coat, snatching the pistol out of his waistband.

Kurt fired, and Saeed was knocked back against the Suburban, the unfired pistol spinning out of his hand into the snow beyond the porch.

Saeed lived just long enough to see the American lower his rifle and take one step forward before Ahmed fired the AK-47, dropping Kurt at Saeed's feet with a single shot to the head.

Aurora screamed as Kurt fell, her shock turning to terror as she realized she was stranded in the clearing like a sitting duck. She stumbled forward through the snow, trying to reach safety behind the Suburban.

"Dad! DAD!" Jordan stood up and brushed past Axel, struggling to reach his father's side.

Axel's legs felt as though they were made of sand, and he was panting with effort. "Jordan! Leave your dad – I'll help him—Just get to cover next to the house!" His voice was weak, and he wasn't getting through the blind grief driving his grandson to certain death. Another shot rang out, and Jordan spun around, clutching his arm before collapsing in the snow. Axel saw Ahmed's determined face glaring from the broken window, the muzzle of the AK-47 now pointed at Aurora.

Aurora heard Jordan calling for his father and watched him break from cover, Axel rising to stop him, calling his name. CRACK! Another rifle shot from the window, and Jordan went down. Axel stopped and began firing at the house, working the bolt and holding his ground.

Ghazi crouched on the porch, trying to stay behind the flimsy railing and out of sight. *Everyone is shooting now!* Saeed's body rested against the idling truck, and the American that killed him lay face down in a halo of red snow. Ghazi heard footsteps approaching the house and chanced a look around the railing.

Aurora caught the movement and was surprised to see a boy's face peering around one of the porch columns. She swung the shotgun around and fired, blowing a hole in the wood next to his head. Ghazi ducked back, scrambled to the other side of the porch, and dove over the railing into the snow.

Axel knew he hit the man in the window with his last shot but wasn't sure he'd killed him. Axel reached Jordan and knelt at his side. "Jordan, it's Grandpa!" Axel put down his rifle and touched Jordan's shoulder. You'll be okay, Spud. Just hang in there!

* * *

Ahmed grimaced with pain and struggled to rise. The old man had shot through the wall and hit Ahmed in the hip, knocking him off the chair. *Don't let it end like this!* Ahmed's mind screamed. *Please let Ghazi and Saeed leave this damned place!* Clenching his teeth in pain, Ahmed reached the window. The Americans were so close that he couldn't miss. Ahmed pulled the trigger, shooting the old man as he knelt beside the boy in the snow. The white-haired fool collapsed on top of the boy, and Ahmed emptied the magazine of the AK in a long burst, stitching Axel's body with a torrent of fire that caused him to jerk then go still.

Aurora whirled around in time to see Axel fall onto Jordan, their crumpled forms riddled with a vicious burst of machine-gun fire, snow, and dirt exploding into the air as the rounds strafed them.

"Grandpa!" Aurora screamed in anguish. Jordan and Axel weren't moving, their bodies a lifeless mass in the clearing. The machine gun didn't fire again, but in the sudden silence, she knew she couldn't survive this fight. They would shoot her down if she ran, and if she took the truck, she'd be dead before the wheels started turning. With the realization came a sudden calm. She was done running. They'd killed everyone she loved, and there was only one thing she could do.

My life will count for something. I'll make sure all our lives counted for something!

She strode purposely up the steps of the house and kicked the door open, rushing forward, looking for the murderer inside. She scanned the shabby living room and kitchen, swinging the shotgun, ready to fire at any movement. In the dim light, she saw a ragged man slumped in a chair at the end of a short hall, just inside a back room. The weak sun filtered through the window, and Aurora saw the black metal and wood stock of a rifle across his knees. This was no doubt the man who had killed Grandpa and Jordan. She slowly walked across the living room and into the hallway, approaching the killer. Aurora saw blood pooled under the chair and held back, watching with cool detachment as the man lifted his head to face her. He grimaced with pain, watching her approach as though he had been waiting for her.

It took all of Ahmed's will to raise his head to face the American. *It was a girl!* Her hair was a wild, tarnished gold, and her eyes ice blue. *Of course!* He thought bitterly. *What could be more American than a blonde woman-child to end this farce!* He worked to fit the last magazine of 7.62 rounds into the empty rifle. He wasn't thinking of Mohammet or Halil or the others who had fallen in their cause. He only stared blearily at the young woman now standing in the bedroom doorway, a shotgun at her shoulder, the round black hole of the barrel showing the way to paradise. As the magazine finally snapped into place, Ahmed realized he could still hear the Suburban idling outside. *Ghazi and Saeed hadn't escaped. It was all for nothing!* It took him several tries to release the bolt and chamber a round, the girl continuing to observe him without speaking. He raised the AK-47 unsteadily, trying to point it at the girl.

Aurora watched the man load the rifle and waited to see if he would be able to do more. She had her shotgun aimed at his chest, but as he tried to raise the AK, she turned the gun around, holding the butt-stock in her left hand and barrel in her right. She raised the weapon above her shoulder and took the last two steps to the man in the chair.

Ahmed was trying to aim, but the girl was upon him, her weapon raised and ready to strike. He squeezed the trigger as she smashed his face with the butt-stock of the shotgun, snapping him back in the wooden chair, the recoil from the full-auto burst pushing him over the tipping point, the bullets stitching a line of black holes in the ceiling, plaster dust falling like dry mist. Ahmed fell backward onto the floor, the AK clattering down next to him in a jumble of spent brass casings.

Aurora's eyes were like flint glittering in the weak light from the window. She stood over the man and struck him repeatedly until his breathing stopped and his body became still. Aurora backed away, feeling none of the horror or remorse she'd endured after shooting the man in the woods.

She'd been through too much to care about killing this monster.

Aurora went to the window and watched for any sign of movement from Grandpa Axe or poor Jordan. Shaking with the release of tension, she brought the Remington's bloody stock up to her shoulder and went back out onto the porch. There was one more out there. "Show yourself, you fucking bastard!" Aurora's voice was raw with emotion, channeling the frustration and loss she felt, standing alone after all the blood and death. "Just pop your head up! I'll make it quick! You won't feel a thing, I promise!" She waited on the top step, daring the boy to challenge her. She heard nothing but the low rumble of the Suburban and the rush of the wind through the gray trees.

Her mind was numb, and she wasn't aware how long she stood on the porch, her mind reeling from the jangle of nerves and raw instinct that had kept her alive. An inner voice was pleading for her to leave this place. *You're free and alive, and you should just go home!* Aurora pulled her hair back from her face and rubbed her eyes. She recognized the voice as hers from the past she'd left behind an eternity before. That place had Starbucks, and dances, shopping, and kittens, and nothing to run from or kill for. *I can go home!*

Tears welled in her eyes, and she fought the sorrow, knowing once she began to weep, she might never stop. She didn't want to leave the others behind, and what of the one still out there?

She threw her shotgun out into the clearing and walked stiffly down the steps, trying not to look at Kurt's body or turn around to see Axel and Jordan. She stepped over the dead man sprawled against the truck and stood by the open door of the Suburban.

Aurora climbed up into the truck and felt a wave of guilt, feeling the soft leather seat and the glorious heat blowing out of the dash vents. She tugged the door closed and sat in silence, letting the heat wash over her thighs, her hands, and caress her face. Aurora robotically looked at the dash and controls and prepared to leave. She made sure the truck was in 4-wheel-drive, put it in gear, and pushed the accelerator. The Suburban bogged down, tenuously plowing through the drifts, gaining speed and momentum as she held the wheel in a white-knuckled grip. *I just might make it!* The Aurora of yesterday dared to hope as the Suburban rolled smoothly through the new snow, taking her away from the nightmare.

The seatbelt chime startled her, and she reached back for the shoulder belt and clicked it into the buckle. All was quiet except the swish of the wind and the low rumble of the tires turning in the deep snow as she drove down the narrow lane to the county road. It was darker in the forest, and she switched on the headlights, the trees from a fairy tale with their cloak of new snow.

It is so beautiful…And I'm alive!

Rory wasn't sure where the lane met the county road and slowed the truck, making sure she didn't overshoot the turnoff. The rearview mirror was tilted downward, and when she adjusted it, a stark face was staring into hers.

Ghazi pushed the Tokarev into the hollow behind Aurora's right ear. "I won't hurt you!" Aurora stiffened, and Ghazi's voice became more strident. "Don't be scared! I'm sorry about what happened! I wasn't part of it. I just need to get away from this place!"

Aurora was too tired to be frightened. "Why do you have a gun to my head?"

"I need you to listen, and I….I don't trust you. You shot at me. You said you would kill me!"

Aurora was trying to focus on steering the vehicle as the Suburban came to the county road. "I don't have my gun now. Put yours away, and I'll take you to town. You can explain everything to the police."

"No!" Ghazi said quickly. "I mean, I'm here illegally. I just want to get to Minneapolis! My parents are dead, and I joined those men back there to cross into America. Please don't turn me in. I promise I won't hurt you!"

Aurora sank into the seat of the Suburban, realizing that another nightmare was just beginning. "Take that gun away from my head, ass-hole." Aurora's tone made Ghazi shrink back. "I'll drive you as far as I can, but don't threaten me again." Aurora would bide her time and wait for the next opportunity.

Ghazi watched the girl, surprised by how emotionless she was. The girl was strong and dangerous like Halil, and Ghazi wasn't sure how to manage this situation. The girl would cause problems later, but for now, they were heading south with the bomb.

That was all that mattered.

PART THREE – THE JOURNEY SOUTH

CHAPTER 51

THE CLEARING

Jordan remained still as long as he could, wedged tightly under Axel's body, hiding in plain sight. The warmth of Axel's corpse was fading as the wind coated them with fine snow blowing across the clearing. He knew Grandpa Axe was dead, but he hadn't dared to move until the Suburban drove away.

Jordan's right hand and wrist throbbed with dull pain, and he pressed the wound hard against his chest, knowing it was severe, but not daring to look at the damage. It seemed like a long time since the truck left. He had cried silently as the taillights flickered out of sight beyond the trees. *They must have thought they'd killed all of us and left me for dead.* He raised his head slowly, looking around the clearing. There was nothing but the sigh of the wind and the raspy call of a raven somewhere overhead.

He dreaded the pain that would strike when he went to stand, but Jordan struggled from under his grandfather's body and got to his feet. The sickening ache turned into a fresh torment of sharp agony. *Grandpa died saving me*, Jordan realized, looking down at Axel's body. He gritted his teeth and trudged across the snow to his dad, dropping to his knees next to his father, not daring to turn him over. Jordan's vision blurred with tears, and he struggled again to his feet and stumbled toward the porch steps. He reached the steps to the house and realized his rifle was lost when the bullet shattered his wrist. He cautiously stretched to see into the house. The door was half-open, and there was nothing but darkness beyond. He took one step, then another, his knees quivering with fear.

Jordan pushed the door open, trying to stay clear in case there was someone still inside. The door swung open with a rusty groan, and he looked around the jamb, ready to snap his head back if anything moved. There was no sound or movement, so Jordan took a bold step inside and pushed his back against the door until it closed. There was a bolt lock, and he chanced to take his left hand away from the wound to slam it into place. He surveyed the shabby house, gasping when he saw a body lying on the floor at the end of the hall. Jordan neared Ahmed's body and saw he was safely dead. Jordan shuffled back to the main room and stood next to the oil-burning heater, an amber flame glowing behind its glass door. He began to shiver uncontrollably as the warmth radiated around him, and when he peered through the window at the gray landscape, he began to sob. He had never felt so desperately alone.

* * *

Aurora drove slowly through the drifts on the county road, the passion and anger she'd felt at the house turning to self-pity. She fought back tears of rage and grief for the deaths of her family. *I'll be damned if I'll cry in front of this asshole!* Aurora took a deep breath and shut down her emotions. *I'm alive, and we're heading back to town. There will be an opportunity.*

Ghazi fought to stay awake, the warmth of the truck and the low rumble of the snow-covered road calling for sleep. *There wouldn't be any sleep for hours,* Ghazi thought. *I'll never make it that long. How do I control this girl?* They would be arriving at a town soon, and the girl would probably try something. She hadn't held back earlier, and her fierceness had made Ghazi terrified. *She is a caged tiger, and the moment I drop my guard, she'll spring!*

The wind scoured away the snow from the asphalt but left drifts along the way, and Aurora gripped the wheel, fighting to keep the Suburban on course. The sky was darkening, and the snow resumed. They were running with the storm, overtaking its path, and soon would be in the thick of it again. She was sure they were almost to Roseau, though the snow obscured any lights from view. Aurora knew she should force the issue, drive right into the most populated place in town, and make a run for it. She could get help and let them deal with the asshole in the back.

As if reading her thoughts, Ghazi placed the cold steel of the automatic against her neck. "Please don't be scared," Ghazi said in a steady voice. "I mean you no harm, but we will be coming to a town soon, and I can't let you do anything that would make me hurt you."

Aurora said nothing, focusing on the gray world ahead.

"I'm tired," Ghazi said. "I know you must be too. I want to rest. Stop here. There is no one else on the road."

Aurora didn't expect this. "Why stop?" Her fear was back again, the pistol barrel a harsh reminder of who was in charge. "We may not be able to get going again."

"We will get going again. "Ghazi said, irritated that the girl was arguing. "Just stop here!"

Aurora knew the boy wanted to control her more easily, but she was bone tired and losing the fight to stay awake. The road was empty, and with the snow and twilight, they might as well be on another planet. She didn't trust Ghazi but found herself stopping the truck in the center of the road. "How are we going to do this?" Aurora was unsnapping her seatbelt.

"Carefully," Ghazi answered, crawling over the top of the front seat and landing on the passenger side, the pistol still pointed at Aurora's head. "Get out."

Aurora frowned. "What? You're going to leave me out here?"

"No!" Ghazi replied quickly. "You'll need to be in the back seat so I can drive. Get out so I can make sure you don't do something stupid."

Too late, Aurora thought. *I let myself get into this mess in the first place.* "Okay, I'm getting out." She opened the door, and it almost flew out of her hands in the stiff north wind. The cold stung her eyes, and she gasped. The temperature was far colder now that darkness was upon them.

Ghazi went across the seat and hopped out next to Aurora, squinting against the cold and wind. "Get in the back." When Aurora hesitated, Ghazi prodded her with the gun. "Hurry, it's cold out here!"

Aurora scanned the landscape around the truck. Bleak, with no visibility past a hundred yards. Not the ideal environment to survive an escape attempt. She opened the back door and crawled up onto the seat. Ghazi hovered in the doorway, watching her. Once inside, Aurora saw the boy produce a zip-tie from a canvas rucksack.

"Your hands," Ghazi said, motioning with the pistol.

Aurora should have known this would happen. She held out her hands in front of her.

"No, put them behind you!" Ghazi knew this was a critical time. The girl could force the issue, and they would both pay.

Aurora scowled at the boy but turned to allow him to bind her hands behind her back. He smelled of sweat, stale smoke, and unwashed clothing. She grunted as he pulled the plastic tie. "Not too tight, asshole!"

Ghazi flinched at the insult but let it go. "It isn't too tight." To prove it, Ghazi ran a finger between her wrist and the plastic. "You'll be fine. You can sleep while I drive."

"How am I supposed to sleep in this situation?" Aurora was tired, but there was no way she was going to let her guard down.

Ghazi took a bottle of water from the bag and produced a pill bottle. Aurora watched the boy open it and shake out a single capsule. "What do you think you're doing?" She asked.

"Take this," Ghazi said, holding out the capsule in an outstretched hand. "It's my last one."

"No way!" Aurora snapped, trying to scramble away from the boy.

Ghazi lunged into the back seat and grabbed a handful of Aurora's hair, pulling her head back. She pursed her lips and tried to turn away, but Ghazi pinched her nose closed and, when she gasped for breath, slipped the pill far back on her tongue. Aurora gagged, and before she could spit it out, the capsule was down her throat.

"What the hell was that?"

"Just a pill to calm you down. I have a prescription for it." Ghazi held the water bottle to her mouth. "Drink some water; it will help you to swallow."

The capsule started to feel like a burning ember, and she reluctantly took a sip of water.

"You will sleep now," Ghazi said, pushing Aurora's legs out of the way and taking the satchel. Aurora fumed as Ghazi slammed the back door and got into the driver's seat, putting the bag next to him. She heard the shift engage, and the boy hit the accelerator. The Suburban spun in place, but the tires found purchase, and they lurched forward, moving south again.

"My name is Ghazi. What's yours?"

"Ghazi?" Aurora repeated flatly. "Go fuck yourself, Ghazi." Aurora stared out of the side window and ignored the boy's sullen glare in the rearview mirror.

* * *

Jordan slowly pulled his right arm away from his coat, yelping when the dangling hand remained glued to the fabric with congealed blood. He gripped the hand and peeled it away, sobbing with pain as it detached from the cloth and slipped out of his grasp, dangling on stretched ligaments and a strip of skin. The blood flowed fresh, and he panicked, letting go of the hand and holding his wrist tight, trying to staunch the heavy dribble spattering the floor.

Jordan knew from Boy Scouts that a tourniquet was the only way to stop bleeding from a wound like this. He went into the kitchen and found an old dog collar, slipping it over his pulsing wrist, and pulled it tight on his forearm. The blood dripped until the collar finally staunched the flow. *Now how do I keep it tight?* He again searched the kitchen and found an ancient first aid kit in one of the cupboards. Supporting the tourniquet and dangling hand, Jordan flipped open the metal case and scattered the contents onto the kitchen counter. There was a roll of white surgical tape, yellow with age.

Jordan awkwardly wrapped the white tape around the dog collar on his wrist and tore the strip with his teeth. He let out his breath in a sigh and wiped the sweat off his face. The pain was still there, but the bleeding had stopped. He felt lightheaded and sagged against the kitchen counter, wrung out physically and mentally. The pain muted in a few minutes, but Jordan knew it would keep tugging at the ragged arm and start the bleeding again.

I have to cut it off.

* * *

Aurora watched their progress from the backseat, sitting awkwardly, her hands zip-tied behind her. She waited for the lights of Roseau to appear, but at their slow pace, the miles dragged on. The storm must be bad if the plows hadn't ventured out. It was surprising the truck had made it this far. Her bound hands made it hard to balance, and soon she relented and lay on her side, the leather seat cool on her face. She fought sleep, but the drug overcame her, and she fell unconscious.

Ghazi's eyelids drooped, and it was getting harder to remain awake. They had to stop soon. The truck slogged on, the road discernable only by the high drifts along the shoulder. Ghazi snapped awake when the dull glow of city lights appeared out of the storm. According to the map from Ahmed's bag, this must be Roseau, the closest town to the border. Better be careful. *I'm here illegally, and I've got a hostage in the back seat.* As if to make sure, Ghazi looked back and saw the girl was asleep. That was a relief. Ghazi looked for a place to stop and rest. They had to get off the road in case someone came upon them, but it had to be secluded. A supermarket was ahead to the right. Ghazi turned into the lot and came to a stop next to the store's brick wall.

Soon, the truck would be covered with a skim of snow, and they wouldn't stand out.

Ghazi quietly undid the seatbelt and looked back at the girl. *In sleep, it is hard to imagine she almost killed me!* Ghazi watched the girl's chest rising and falling as she slept. Even after what went on back at the farm, the girl was pretty, and lying across the back seat, looked nothing like the vicious person that attacked them. That made it harder to think of what would need to be done. Ghazi got out of the truck and went to the back, wiping snow off the rear windows and peering in. The device was still in the same position they had placed it the night before. *What did you expect?* Ghazi took the opportunity to urinate outside and then returned to the truck. Settling back into the driver's seat, Ghazi thought only of sleep. The front seat wasn't comfortable, but it would have to do. Ghazi closed tired eyes and joined Aurora in sleep as the storm passed overhead.

* * *

Fighting the dizziness from loss of blood, Jordan tottered across the kitchen to the sink, dreading what would come next. He took the hunting knife given to him by his father and held it in his left hand. Jordan leaned forward, and grimacing with pain and fear, dangled the ruined hand down the side of the sink, the blanched skin and wiry ligaments stretched tight. Sweat bloomed on his forehead as he placed the knife against the taut flesh. His chin quivered as he sliced the tissue, the blade grinding against the enameled sink, his severed hand dropping into the basin, resting at the bottom like a crimson flower.

Jordan moaned as his vision darkened, and he collapsed onto the dirty floor in merciful unconsciousness.

* * *

Ghazi awoke with a start, groggy and disoriented. It was ice-cold inside the cab, and the rumble of a plow truck clearing the highway meant it was time to go. The windows were foggy with frozen condensation, and Ghazi started the Suburban and waited for the defroster to clear the windshield. The storm had passed, and the streetlights were newly brilliant in the sub-zero night.

There was time to review the documents Ahmed had placed in the satchel. Ghazi opened the canvas bag and scanned the papers in the light from the parking lot, some were printouts from website pages, and others were photocopied maps and photos of buildings and places Ghazi didn't recognize. After absorbing as much information as possible, Ghazi focused on a hand-drawn set of diagrams stapled together separate from the other pages. They showed a route south to Minneapolis with instructions for reaching a safe house in the metro area. The map listed roads, street names, and an address, but Ghazi knew it would be hard to follow. *The girl will help me.* Ghazi thought. *The medication should wear off by then.*

Ghazi drove the Suburban out of the parking lot and back onto the highway. The gas gauge was below half a tank, and the digital clock on the radio was blinking at 12:00. *Taking out the battery must have reset it. I wish I had a watch!* There was the cell phone in the satchel, but Ahmed was clear that it shouldn't be turned on until ready to trigger the bomb. The weight of such an ominous task was almost unbearable. *Why me? Why did I survive? Is this mission worth my life?* Ghazi instantly regretted the thought. *The prophet and the will of Allah must be obeyed! If my life is given in jihad, I will instantly find myself in paradise! But will I? I fear death because secrets will stand in the way of heaven.*

Ghazi knew it was a long way to the safe house in Minneapolis. They would need fuel before long, and unless the girl had money, they would be stranded when the tank ran dry. *What then? Do I steal another truck and continue? Do I abandon everything and hope I can disappear?* There would be a fuel station soon. It must be remote, or at least a place where I can refuel without any questions. Ghazi's mind processed the possibilities as the miles wore on. They were chasing the storm's tail, following in the ragged line of snow and wind. The passing landscape varied between the darkness of trees on either side of the highway to gray open fields which seemed to stretch forever into the night. An occasional yard light glowed in a farmyard, but the world seemed to have stopped until the storm passed.

There were small towns without traffic lights, and Ghazi passed through them at the same steady pace. The road improved, and soon Ghazi came up behind a plow truck with flashing yellow and blue lights. The Suburban followed the monster, snow swirling like a tornado as it cleared the road ahead. Few vehicles were traveling the highway, but when huge trucks passed, the Suburban was blasted with a gust of white that blotted out the road, making the headlights useless for what seemed like an eternity.

Ghazi and Aurora passed through several small towns, and after a few hours, Red River Falls was behind them. Sedated, Aurora was unaware as they crossed the bridge over the river of her hometown. Ghazi only noticed a bank sign that blinked 2:20 AM and -06F in stark white LED letters.

The fuel gauge needle moved toward empty, and Ghazi unconsciously slowed down, conserving fuel, knowing they would have to stop at the next gas station. Ghazi hoped the girl would remain unconscious. *If there are people around, the girl may try something.*

What will I do if she does?

CHAPTER 52

THE STATION

Aurora awoke when the Suburban stopped, and the cab filled with bright white light. She turned her head away from the windows and tried to open her watery eyes. She heard Grandpa Axe open the door to the truck and wondered why they had stopped. The rush of cold air into the cab brought her fully awake. She remembered. *Grandpa Axe was dead. Philip, Marty, Kurt, and Jordan were all gone!*

Her hands were bound. Panic rose like a cold wave, and she began to struggle.

The Suburban's door flung open, and the boy was silhouetted against the bright canopy lights of a gas station. Aurora screamed and kicked at him when he leaned into the truck.

Ghazi looked around nervously and lunged into the cab, holding her shoulders to calm her. "Please be quiet; I don't want to hurt you!"

"Get your hands off me, you asshole!" Aurora's voice was raw, and tears of frustration welled in her eyes. "Help! Somebody help me!" She struggled with her legs, twisting to the side, trying to get leverage against the back of the seat. Ghazi backed out of the cab and stood next to the Suburban while she struggled. Aurora realized the boy was standing outside in the wind, watching her. That meant no one was around, and that meant no help. She took a deep breath and leaned back in the seat. "What now, asshole?"

"Don't call me that!" Ghazi's voice sharp and menacing.

She glared at him but said nothing. Aurora realized the true nature of her captor was emerging.

"Money." Ghazi was shivering in the cold, eyes boring into hers, waiting.

"I don't have any money, you asshole!"

Ghazi leaned into the truck. "I think you do. All American girls have a credit card!" Ghazi's voice was suddenly full of rage, and Aurora knew he held the advantage for the moment.

"Just give me a minute!" Aurora's wallet had some small bills and a credit card Axel had given her for emergencies. She peered out of the windows. They were at some all-night gas stop in the middle of nowhere. Now, with credit card gas pumps, it was all automatic—no need for a cashier to watch over things.

Ghazi's patience was at an end. Even though it was early in the morning and they were alone for the moment, time wasn't their friend. Lunging into the cab, Ghazi slapped Aurora across the face and pushed her back down onto the seat. Before she could react, Ghazi took her legs and pulled her across the seat, rolling her over, her feet dangling above the ground next to the Suburban. Aurora felt the boy tugging at the back pocket of her jeans. "Get off me!" She felt his hands gliding over her thighs and along her hips. "Stop it, you asshole!"

Ghazi raised a fist and punched her in the back of the head. "Enough of your dirty talk! I've told you I wouldn't hurt you and all you do is make fun of me! Now give me your credit card!"

Dazed by the blow, Aurora's knees buckled, and she fell onto the icy curb next to the gas pumps. The boy was looming over her, his fist raised. "Where is it?"

"In my coat – in the front pocket."

Ghazi thrust into her coat pocket and pulled out her wallet. It was a feminine pink, and the harsh fluorescents reflected off rhinestones shaped in a heart. The boy's grubby hands repulsed Aurora, and she felt violated watching him go through her things.

"You piece of shit," Aurora muttered, trying to get back on her feet. "You're just a common thief!" She leaned forward to stand, and Ghazi slapped her hard across the face. Her knees weakened, but she kept her balance and staggered back, leaning against the truck. "You're gonna pay for that." Aurora hissed, glaring at the boy.

"Just be quiet," Ghazi said, stepping forward, glancing at the darkened convenience store to see if anyone would appear. Aurora edged around to the front of the truck, leaning against the grill. She thought the boy would hit her again, but she heard his feet crunching in the snow back to the gas pump and the nozzle being pulled out of the holder. There was beeping as he made the transaction, and the pump began to whir as he filled the tank.

The boy was hunched forward in the cold wind, his jacket collar up. He gripped the gas nozzle trigger in his left hand and put his right into the pocket with the pistol. She turned slowly, trying to balance with her arms behind her. The air was foggy with fine blowing snow, and the gas station seemed to be floating in a luminescent cloud. She looked at the darkened building. Night lights at the back of the store cast a blue-white light across the interior. No silhouette of a person holding a phone and looking nervously at the two people outside. Only blaze orange lettering stuck to the front windows that said: "Powerball Sold Here." She looked off into the distance around the station. She could make out a road sign on the highway and beyond, the dim yard lights of a farmhouse in the distance. The weather was clearing, but she had nowhere to run.

"I'm going to go around the back of the building to pee," she said to the boy. "Untie me so I can go."

Ghazi didn't want to leave the vehicle, and though they were alone, letting the girl out of sight wasn't an option. Still, the girl probably needed to go, and there was no need to have that smell in the truck if she wet herself. There didn't appear to be anyone in the store, and if the girl ran, she wouldn't get far. Still, she was too rebellious to trust. "Just do it right there," Ghazi said, pointing to where Aurora was standing.

"No way, you perv!" She shouted, stomping her foot. "I'm not going to pee in front of you!"

Ghazi set the trigger catch on the nozzle and started towards Aurora, pulling Halil's knife from a belt sheath. Before she could react, Ghazi spun her around and cut her plastic bonds, pointing the blade towards the front of the truck. "Just do it there. Please? I won't look."

Aurora was bewildered at the change in tone. She glared at the boy until he went back to the gas pump. Aurora tried to open the button of her jeans, but her fingers were numb, and she finally just wriggled her hips and got her jeans down far enough to pull her panties forward and relieve herself.

She pulled up her pants and straightened her coat, watching the boy for any sign of aggression. There were vending machines along the front of the building. "I want a can of pop. Give me my wallet, and I'll get us some." Aurora tried to sound confident but non-threatening. She didn't want the guy's alter-ego to show up again.

Ghazi stared at the girl with suspicion. A can of soda would be good, especially the caffeine, but it would be easy for her to run.

"Hey, I need some dollar bills!" Aurora stood in an offended teenage girl's posture and waited.

Ghazi looked beyond her at the vending machines. Even though they were alone, something could be hiding beyond the lights in the snow and darkness.

Aurora was about to chide the boy again, but he flung the wallet at her feet. Surprised, she knelt to pick it out of the snow, the rhinestones glittering on the pink leather. "Thanks," she muttered as she turned toward the store.

Ghazi stooped to pick up a piece of dirty ice from the lot and threw it at the girl, hitting the back of her thigh. She let out a little yelp and turned to deliver a fierce glare. "Get going!" Ghazi shouted, walking toward her, holding the pistol for her to see.

Ghazi suddenly stopped and looked back towards the road.

Aurora rubbed the spot on the back of her thigh where the boy hit her. She looked down at the ice chunk he had thrown and picked it up, flinging it with all her might against the front door of the station. The ice shattered with a dull crack but merely left a dark brown spot where it hit the glass. She cautiously looked back, expecting the boy to be coming to kick her ass, but he was stopped in front of the truck, looking at the highway beyond the station. She was relieved that he hadn't seen her lame stunt, but then, no alarm went off, so nothing gained either.

Aurora heard a car on the highway.

Ghazi tried to place the direction and distance of the sound. A vehicle was approaching from the highway! *Think! I can't leave the girl on her own, but if I go after her, the truck will be unprotected!* Ghazi stood paralyzed, the sound clearer as the vehicle neared the station, headlights suddenly materializing out of the snowy haze. The turn signal began to blink, and the car slowed down.

Ghazi jogged back to the truck.

Aurora watched the car turn into the lot with both fear and hope. *I should have planned for this! The asshole is running back to the truck!* Aurora bolted around the vending machines and plunged into the deep snow drifted along the side of the building. If she could get to a back door, she might be able to break in and make a call.

Ghazi tore the nozzle out of the truck and dropped it next to the pump. *Calm down! I'm panicking like a child!* Stooping to pick up the nozzle, Ghazi hung it back onto the pump as the new vehicle pulled into the pool of light under the canopy. The girl was gone, probably around the back of the building. *Maybe it's a good thing she isn't here to make a scene.* Sliding into the driver's seat, Ghazi started the Suburban but left the door ajar. The unwelcome car pulled up to the other side of the pumps, and Ghazi saw two women in front and a child in the back.

I don't want this! I could drive out of here and take my chances, but I can't let the girl stay behind to contact the authorities! Ghazi tapped the pistol barrel on the seat, looking at the building for any movement. *Where did she go?*

A middle-aged woman got out of the car and went around to use the pumps. Ghazi watched her warily from the truck, trying not to make eye contact. The back door swung open, and a child jumped out and bounded toward the store, following in the girl's fresh tracks to the vending machines. Ghazi began to panic. *Where is this kid going? Things are getting out of control!*

Aurora stayed in the shadows along the side of the building, watching the two vehicles under the bright canopy. The boy had gotten back into the truck, and a woman was filling the other car with gas. Just then, a young girl got out of the car and slammed the door, coming towards the building.

She's coming to use the vending machines!

Aurora's mind raced. She needed to get a message to the people in the car, but she didn't want the asshole to kill anyone. She pushed tighter against the building and moved closer to the corner near the vending machines.

The girl was wearing a lilac ski jacket with mittens flopping back and forth on the ends of her sleeves. Her long hair was raven black, and she was wearing tennis shoes that barely kept her feet out of the snow, even as she tried to follow in Aurora's footprints. As she neared, Rory saw she was a Native American girl of seven or eight. How would she get a message to her? She felt in her pockets for a slip of paper or something to give the girl. *The wallet! It had her driver's license and student ID. It could work!*

The girl was at the machine, feeding a dollar bill into the changer. Aurora wanted to whisper something, but the wind would snatch it away, and the girl would probably freak out if a voice from the darkness startled her. Rory carefully lined up her toss, like a game of horseshoes she had to win. With a flip, she arced the wallet out into the lot about ten feet behind the girl.

Aurora heard bottles clunking out of the machine and watched the child fumbling to retrieve them. The woman pumping gas was looking out over towards the highway, studiously avoiding eye contact with the boy and not focused on the little girl. There was an old woman in the passenger seat, and it seemed for a moment that she was looking directly at Rory. *Can she see me?* Rory wondered. The woman turned on the dome light and began digging in her purse for something. *A cell phone? The boy would kill them if he saw her making a call!*

Ghazi watched the little girl using the vending machine and tried to keep an eye on her and the two women near the car. The one at the pump wasn't looking, but the old woman in the front seat seemed too interested, glancing over at the truck. The seconds turned into a minute, and Ghazi was electric with tension. *What are they doing out here at this time of night? The old one is looking at me like I'm a criminal!* Ghazi's world shrank down to the view from the side mirror, the woman passenger, and the little girl at the vending machine. The old woman turned on the dome light in the car and began searching her purse.

Ghazi held the pistol close and opened the door wider, ready to jump out and shoot the woman before she could use her phone.

The little girl started shuffling through the snow back to the pumps with three bottles clutched against her chest, puffing her hair out of her eyes. Aurora watched as the girl came to the wallet sticking out of the fresh snow. The girl was concentrating on the car and walked past the wallet without pausing. Aurora was beside herself with despair. *Damn! How could she miss it?* She bit her lip and looked at the pumps. The boy was half out of the truck, focusing on the woman in the passenger seat. Aurora couldn't see it, but she knew he had the pistol, waiting to fire.

The little girl was halfway back to the pumps, and Aurora knew it would be too late if she didn't act. She came out from behind the building and quickly scooped up the wallet. "Hey, let's get going!" She shouted at Ghazi.

Shocked, the little girl dropped the bottles and turned to stare at Aurora, mouth open and brown eyes growing wide.

Ghazi hesitated when the American girl came out of the shadows, shouting something. The little child seemed to be talking to the girl. At the same time, the old woman in the car produced a tube of lipstick from her purse, flipped down the visor mirror, and began to apply it to her wrinkled mouth.

Lipstick! Ghazi looked at the old woman in amazement. *She almost lost her miserable life over a tube of makeup!*

Aurora dug into the snow, picked up the pop bottles, and held them out to the girl. Aurora knew Ghazi was watching them, and she hurriedly thrust the bottles into the child's arms. The girl was wary but took the sodas, flinching when Aurora stuffed her wallet into the girl's jacket. Aurora patted the girl's shoulder as she went returned to the Suburban. "You dropped something," Aurora whispered. "I put it in your pocket."

Aurora trotted to the Suburban and reluctantly went to the passenger side. The boy's face was red with anger. "Get in the truck," he hissed, climbing back in and unlocking the passenger door. Ghazi shifted into gear as Aurora climbed in, gunning the engine and driving past the native girl, her eyes following them fearfully as they left the lot.

CHAPTER 53

VANESSA WHITEBIRD

"Vanessa, what did that girl say to you?" Gloria Whitebird was driving west on Highway 2 on the way to Grand Forks for the big Black Friday sales. Her mother-in-law, Mary Broussard, was in the passenger seat, working her dentures and breathing through her nose in that loud way of hers.

"Nothing." Vanessa was eight, and like her mother and grandmother, was an Ojibwa of the Seven-Clans. They farmed on the White Earth Reservation near Bijou, and Vanessa was trying to hide the wallet the scary girl had put into her pocket. There was $28.00 in it, and that was more money than she had ever had at one time.

"What do you mean, nothing?" Her mother wasn't going to take that answer, and now Grandma Mary was twisting around to look into the back seat, letting Vanessa know she was interested too.

"She didn't say nothing!" Vanessa looked down at her lap as she spoke, the wallet back in her pocket. "She just helped me pick up the pop bottles and went off with that Mexican-looking guy!"

"Well, that boy was on drugs or something." Gloria had been a little scared for a moment when the boy was messing around in the truck and staring at their car, but then the girl had appeared, and she seemed more of a threat coming up to Vanessa the way she did. It was over before Gloria could do much worrying, and Grandma Mary hadn't even noticed what happened.

"They was casino people." Grandma Mary said as if to explain the whole encounter. Shooting Star Casino was in Mahnomen, not far from the gas station. "That place attracts a lotta weird people that show up at all hours!"

"Yeah, they was out late," Gloria replied, losing interest in the thread of conversation. She turned on the radio as Grandma Mary looked out the side window at the passing snowfields, the night clearing, and the stars appearing in the cold sky.

Vanessa Whitebird took the bills out of the wallet and quietly balled them up in her pocket. Then she picked a card out of its plastic slot and tried to look at it in the dim light from the dashboard. *Aurora Winter.* She was surprised that the picture looked like the girl from the gas station. There was a funny feeling in her stomach, and she wondered why the girl would give away so much money. Vanessa thought it was just a wallet in the snow, and the crazy girl just figured it belonged to me. *But why did it have all her stuff in it? She should tell Mom, but the girl gave it to her, and it was almost thirty dollars!* She struggled with it awhile, worrying she should tell, but feeling entitled to the money. Or what she could buy with it, anyway. Maybe she could say to Mama Gloria that the wallet was empty when she picked it out of the snow. Vanessa was drowsy, and soon she nodded to sleep, thinking of how much better the day would be now that she could buy something instead of just shopping.

* * *

Aurora knew what was coming and cowered against the passenger door as far from the boy as possible.

"You stupid bitch!" Ghazi shouted, shaking violently with tension. "What were you thinking? You almost made me kill them, and then I would have killed you!" Ghazi swung viciously and punched Aurora's shoulder. "You think you're so clever! Things are going to be different from now on!"

Ghazi mashed down on the accelerator, and the station lights receded behind them. They were again in the black night, following the ribbon of gray road.

"You're going to kill me, aren't you?" Rory spoke quietly.

"I will if you don't do what I say!" Ghazi replied.

"No, you're going to kill me either way. You just used my grandpa's credit card back there. I guess you're not stupid, so that means you don't care if they trace it." She stole a glance at him, but Ghazi's face was impassive. "That means you don't need me much longer, so why don't you just get it over with?"

"Be quiet." Ghazi's voice had lost some of its edge.

His tone sent a chill down her spine. She knew then it was true.

"So when were you going to do it?" She asked, almost to herself. "I mean, I'm your hostage, right? I'm not rich, so there won't be any ransom money if that's what this is about."

Ghazi glared at her. "This isn't about money! You Americans and your damn money…"

"Well, why then?" Aurora asked, staring at Ghazi. "Is it sex? Are you going to rape me? Maybe you're into little boys, or just like doing it with farm animals?"

Ghazi slammed on the brakes, and Aurora was thrown violently forward, banging her head on the dash and straining against her seatbelt. The rear of the truck slued around, and they came to a stop in a white burst of snow. Ghazi swung a fist at her head, but she ducked and pushed the release button on her seatbelt, clawing at the door handle. Ghazi lunged at her again, but Aurora pushed the door open and leaped out of the truck.

The wind and cold stung her eyes as she dove into the ditch. For a moment, she floundered in knee-deep snow, then staggered to her feet and climbed to the other side, plunging forward into the open field. The wind had swept most of the snow from the shallow furrows, and she pumped her arms and legs as she ran into the plowing. The farm she had seen from the station was about a quarter-mile off the road. *This is it. I have to make it!* With as much speed as she could muster, she ran. Her eyes adjusted to the darkness, and she saw a long driveway about 100 yards to her left leading into the farmyard. *I have to get to that driveway!* She couldn't go fast enough across the rough surface of frozen dirt. She focused on the goal, trying to control her breathing, willing the boy to abandon her. *Just give up and leave me alone!* She didn't dare turn her head. It wouldn't matter if he were right behind her; She would either make it to the farm or not.

She squinted her eyes against the stinging wind, breathing in needles of freezing air. Her heart pounded in her ears, and Aurora knew she couldn't keep this pace much longer. *The farm is closer!* She was heartened by the yard light twinkling in the clearing air and the small white barn next to a tidy brown mobile home. There was a car near the house, and she thought there was a light on inside. *The driveway is just ahead! If I can just...*

Ghazi tackled Aurora from behind, arms wrapped around her in a violent take-down. Both tumbled headfirst into the rocky soil, but Aurora's face smashed into the plowing, her front teeth snapping with a sickening crunch. Trying to breathe through her ragged mouth, Aurora inhaled a tooth still attached to a clot of tissue. She choked, desperate for air, but Ghazi held her arms tightly against her sides. Aurora was suffocating and helpless to clear the obstruction in her throat. Her vision darkened at the edges, but before blacking out, Ghazi rolled on top of her, and she coughed up the tooth, spitting it out and gasping for air.

Ghazi rose with a fist knotted in Aurora's hair, dragging her to her feet. They both stood panting hard from the pursuit. When Ghazi spun her around, Aurora saw the Suburban idling with its headlights throwing white light across the field. The truck wasn't far away at all. In a blur of tears, Aurora turned to look at the farm. It didn't seem any closer than when she bolted from the truck.

She never had a chance.

Ghazi started back for the truck, tugging her along behind, her hair firmly clenched in a fist, her hands on Ghazi's wrist, trying to lessen the pain she felt with every step as they stumbled across the plowing. Her mouth and nose were dripping blood onto the dark ground, and she was glad she couldn't see it. The fist tightened, and she let out another cry. He was tearing her hair out by the roots!

Ghazi was breathing hard, struggling to bring the American girl back to the truck. "Now...you will... behave... I think." Aurora was half-dragged into the ditch and back up to the roadside. In the red tail lights, Ghazi saw the girl's mouth was swollen and bleeding. She certainly wasn't pretty anymore.

This girl was brave to escape, but Ghazi felt no admiration or respect for her. There was only a decision to be weighed. *Do I carry on alone, or do I wait to see if I need her? Her life might protect mine. At least until I reach safety.* Ahmed and Halil worried about American drones that could fire a missile from above. The Americans would surely fire at the truck if they knew the girl was dead. The decision was made. *I will tolerate this girl, but there will be no more running!*

Ghazi pulled open the rear door of the truck and produced another plastic tie. "Your hands – in back of you - now!" The girl complied, and Ghazi was relieved she didn't put up a fight. Letting go of her hair, Ghazi slipped the band around Aurora's wrists and pulled it tight, securing her hands behind her back once again.

Aurora spat out a clot of blood as the boy pushed her face-first onto the rear seat. She wriggled forward, resigned to becoming a hostage again, the dark interior ominous as the mouth of a monster, swallowing her once more. There was still a chance, but next time she had to think before she acted. *At least I can catch my breath*. Aurora dug her knees into the upholstery, trying to get to the other side. Ghazi seized her as she lay face down on the seat, roughly grabbing her leg and pulling down her boot and woolen sock. In horror, Aurora heard him pull the knife from its sheath and felt the cold metallic snick of the blade cutting her Achilles tendon, the blade gouging deep into her leg. For a frozen second, she sharply inhaled, the shock and pain of this latest violation engulfing her, a horrid chill numbing her spine.

Rory cried out in anguish and despair but her screams were carried off by the cold November wind.

* * *

Jordan opened his eyes to darkness. The throbbing pain of his arm brought him fully awake, and he felt nauseous as he lifted his head above the kitchen floor. He sat up weakly, leaning on his good arm, waiting for the dizziness to pass. Jordan found a towel and tied two corners together to make a sling, wincing in the pain when he looped it over his neck and slipped his arm inside. He could still feel his missing fingers with each beat of his heart, the dying nerves still sending signals to his brain.

Maybe there's a telephone in here somewhere. Jordan searched the main room, but there weren't any cords or wall jacks. He dreaded going down the dark hallway, but if there was a phone, it might be in one of the bedrooms. Opening the first door on the left, he reached awkwardly around the inside corner until he found the light switch.

Jordan gasped and shuffled backward. Halil's body was like a bloody scarecrow in the stark yellow light, the face staring at the open door. Jordan stopped at the threshold, not daring to go further. The dead man's eyes were open, and his teeth were brown with dried blood. A rosette of black holes in the center of the chest showed how he died. *The man looked a lot like the guy Rory had killed... Yesterday?* It seemed like a lifetime ago. Jordan took a deep breath and leaned into the room. There were only bunk beds with rumpled blankets and some damp clothing hanging from nails.

Jordan backed away and stepped into the room with the other body, instantly chilled by the wind gusting through the ruined window. He shivered and walked forward, his feet crunching on broken glass and spent brass from the gunfight. Stepping around Ahmed's corpse, he went to a bedside lamp and pulled the chain, lighting the room in a warm yellow glow.

The fangs and red mouth of a timber wolf lunged at him, and Jordan ducked from the mounted head snarling above him, the eyes yellow and menacing. His heart raced, and he felt faint, the phantom hand throbbing with renewed pain. The dead man was lying on his back in a pool of dark blood, tangled in an upturned chair with one leg hanging over the seat. Sticks were wrapped around the other leg with duct tape. *This guy shot Grandpa and me,* Jordan thought. The dead man's face was swollen and bruised, and he tried not to look at it as he patted the jacket and pants, looking for a cell phone. There was nothing in the pockets, but Jordan found Ahmed's rifle on the floor and edged around the body to retrieve it. Jordan backed up to the doorway, the dull glass eyes of the mounted animals and birds watching him, hovering over Ahmed's corpse as though welcoming the latest addition to their menagerie.

Jordan shivered as the wind rose outside and swirled around him in the bedroom. As if to complete his terror, the mournful howl of a timber wolf drifted across the frozen woods, raising the hair on Jordan's neck.

He wanted to slam the door and leave the scene behind, but there was no door, and he fled back to the living room and stood by the oil burner, shivering as much from fear as the cold. He didn't want to spend the night here, but he knew it was miles to the nearest farm, and his spirits sank just thinking about going back outside into the snow.

What would Dad do?

He would probably find a way to block off that window so it would stay warmer in here. Then he'd get a blanket from the bedroom and get some sleep. He felt the loss of his father in a sudden wave and was almost overwhelmed with sadness.

What happened to Rory? He wanted to go outside and call for her, but he was afraid he'd find her body in the snow and have no hope of seeing her again. It was better to think that she had escaped in that truck and would send help. The thought of spending the night in this place was terrifying. He was old enough to know that dead men couldn't hurt him, but closing his eyes for even a minute seemed out of the question.

He dreaded what was going to be a long, painful night.

CHAPTER 54

MINNEAPOLIS

Ghazi adjusted the rearview mirror and looked at eyes red and sunken into dark circles. The journey was soon over, but Ghazi's right hand began to twitch uncontrollably. It was almost 48 hours since the last dose of the antipsychotic prescription from a Toronto doctor, and it wouldn't be long before Ghazi wasn't in control.

The girl moaned in the back seat, and it was another reminder that Ghazi would have to decide her fate soon. Sometime during the trip, the girl had stopped crying and must have fallen asleep as Ghazi followed the gray highway south. It was foolish to have kept her to this point. She was injured and probably mentally worthless for helping with directions in the city anyway. *I should have thrown her into the ditch after the scene at the fuel station,* Ghazi thought. *Now it will be harder to get rid of her.* Without realizing it, Ghazi began humming in a low monotone, unconsciously trying to stay in the moment and focus on getting to the safe house, knowing the medication was wearing off. *Maybe there would be a way to refill the prescription, but would it matter?*

Still, they hadn't lost much time, and it cost nothing to let the girl sleep before they reached Minneapolis. The Suburban headed south, still riding the storm's tail, the towns becoming more numerous, and the road was improving as the hours and miles passed. Ghazi drove through the city of St. Cloud and cut across to Interstate 94 for the final run into the Twin Cities.

They reached the edge of the metro area, and Ghazi retrieved Ahmed's hand-drawn map and directions from the satchel, but it was tense trying to control the truck and consult the map. The blustering snow made spotting the exit signs difficult until they were almost overhead.

More snowplows were out, their gigantic orange hulls almost invisible in billowing clouds of snow as they blasted along the road, their amber warning strobes flickering in the dark.

Ghazi kept left to head east on Highway 694 for what seemed an eternity until the exit for 94 split away to the south, leading to downtown Minneapolis. As the city center neared, the sky became a rose-gray in the reflected glow of a thousand lights. The tall buildings of Minneapolis appeared in the sky ahead like sentinels guarding the city. The Broadway Avenue exit was just ahead, and Ghazi nervously signaled and moved into the right lane, climbing on the exit ramp, stopping at the top, and signaling left. The tall buildings seemed to loom over the highway, and Ghazi's stomach tightened at the thought of navigating through such a large city.

Ghazi turned onto the overpass and looked over the guardrails at the highway below, sparse lines of cars braving the storm, white and red lights fading in and out of the blowing snow. The sign for Washington Avenue South appeared out of the gloom, and Ghazi overshot the intersection before the Suburban came to a skidding halt. *Slow down, you idiot!* Ghazi's heart was racing. *Another wrong turn, and you won't be able to find the safe house! Now follow Washington to...*Ghazi squinted at the map again. *Cedar then Riverside...But how far will it be?* The homemade map didn't show distance. The Suburban was too difficult to back up, so Ghazi made an awkward u-turn, dreading the appearance of a police car. Once back at the Washington intersection, Ghazi made a left to continue to the destination.

The Suburban drove deeper into Minneapolis through the gentrified Warehouse District and Gateway neighborhood. Ghazi tried to focus on the road ahead, mortified that a loss of concentration had almost caused an accident, or worse. Ghazi didn't notice the Vikings' US Bank Stadium on the right, its huge barn-like shape melding with the mass of downtown, the apartments, and storefronts crowding close to the freeway.

Ghazi passed over Interstate 35, feeling the press of buildings looming closer as the Suburban entered the inner city. Ghazi continued to follow Washington...*As it becomes Cedar Avenue? Now what?* Ghazi was confused by the street signs and slowed to a crawl. *This is now Cedar? How can that be?* Ghazi watched for the blue and white street sign above the next intersection…*Riverside!* The Suburban's interior was filled with white light as a delivery truck came up behind and blasted its horn. Startled, Ghazi pressed the accelerator, the back fishtailing as the wheels spun on the snowy pavement. The delivery truck fell behind as the Suburban increased speed, and soon it turned off onto a side street, its headlights no longer a blinding reflection in the mirror.

Ghazi tried to calm down and began to hum louder, taking quick breaths then exhaling in a monotonous drone. The map showed a left turn to head southeast on Riverside. Ghazi slowed down as the road became a residential street lined with cars on the left side, most snowed in so thoroughly one couldn't tell their color or make. Even with four-wheel drive, Ghazi struggled to keep the Suburban from bogging down in the ruts made by the few vehicles moving at this early hour.

It was difficult to see the address numbers on each building until Ghazi rolled down the passenger window and made out the number on a cracked transom window over a doorway drifted with snow. It looked to be an old block of apartments, but there were no footprints along the sidewalk and nothing stirring on the street. Pulling over to the curb about a half block past the building, Ghazi turned off the headlights, letting the truck idle in the early morning darkness. *The next challenge will be getting into the building and finding Ahmed and Saeed's contact.*

The rendezvous was another hurdle. *What will they do when I tell them all the others are dead? Will they trust that only I survived, and Ahmed placed the mission's success in my hands?* Ghazi turned the key, and the truck stopped, the engine ticking as it cooled in the sudden silence.

The time had come. Ghazi retrieved the pistol and pulled back the slide. The dull gleam of brass confirmed a chambered round. The girl wasn't stirring, and Ghazi hoped she would stay asleep through the next few moments. Not wanting to open the door, Ghazi undid the seatbelt and quietly turned, climbing half over the seatback, and hovering above the girl.

In the dim light of a corner streetlight, Ghazi saw the girl lying quietly on her back. Her eyes were closed, but it was suddenly very uncomfortable being this close to her. Ghazi took one last look outside the Suburban, trying to spot anyone who might witness what was about to happen.

Looking down again, Ghazi flinched and pulled back as though stung. The girl's eyes were open and staring in a silent plea.

Ghazi swallowed and quickly searched for something to put over her face. An orphaned coat was crumpled on the floor. The wool was rough and dry, and as Ghazi was about to cover Aurora's face, a solitary tear rolled down her cheek; her eyes resigned to death, but there was something more. *Is it pity?*

Ghazi draped the coat over Aurora like a shroud and aimed the pistol at her covered face. She didn't move or struggle, and after a moment of hesitation, Ghazi fired the gun into Aurora Winter's head.

* * *

Ghazi's ears rang from the shot, the smell of the gunpowder fouling the air. Nauseous, Ghazi's resolve collapsed. *I have to get out of here!* Clawing at the passenger door, Ghazi tumbled out of the truck into the snow along the curb, chased by the afterimage of the girl's haunting eyes. The shock of the cold was enough to refocus, and Ghazi stood quickly, expecting someone to be standing nearby, watching.

There was no one. The last snow of the storm fluttered in the light of a solitary street light like moths in summer. Nothing stirred, just quiet and darkness surrounded the Suburban. Ghazi took the satchel off the front seat and edged against the truck in the snow, peering into the rear window of the Suburban to make sure the package was still in place. "Killing the girl was too much," Ghazi whispered in the darkness, trudging to the apartment entrance. It was necessary, overdue even, but it was an empty, cruel end for both of them after so much had taken place. *Such a mountain to climb! The entire group lost! Except me, of course, and now I bear the mission alone.* Ghazi felt the stinging of tears and became angry. *Why am I crying? It is nothing but weakness! The girl wasn't your friend or even worth worrying over; she was an unbeliever!*

"Make me stronger!" Ghazi whispered to the sky. "Make me strong, Allah, for a few more hours, and it will be done!"

Ghazi wiped away the tears and sighed. *I just need to rest for a little while; no more talking to myself!*

Ghazi knew from Ahmed's instructions that a key would be hidden behind a loose brick next to the intercom panel. The temperature wasn't much warmer inside the building, and the musty smell of decay hung in the air. Ghazi began unconsciously humming again, setting down the pack and digging out a penlight. Flicking it on, Ghazi panned the circle of light on the ceiling and walls. The foyer was probably opulent at one time, but now the wallpaper hung down in water-stained sheets, and the terrazzo floor was littered with wind-blown leaves and chips of paint from the ruined ceiling, Ghazi's footsteps crunching as if walking on a gravel path.

Ghazi passed a row of corroded mailboxes, each labeled with faded names of tenants long since gone. Crossing the foyer to the stairway, Ghazi climbed the steps to the second floor, shining the light down the hall and spotting the next key hide. It was secreted inside a glass cabinet holding an ancient fire extinguisher. Ghazi slipped another hidden key out from under it and crossed the hall to apartment 210. Opening the door, Ghazi was grateful that the heat was on in this unit at least, but it made the lingering smell of decay that much stronger. There was enough light coming from the street outside to click off the penlight and cross the room to close the drapes on a single window. Ghazi felt along the wall and found a floor lamp in the corner and switched it on. The light filtered through an ancient lampshade with a sickly yellow glow. There was a threadbare sofa with one leg replaced by stacked bricks, a small kitchenette without any appliances, and a grimy table with two chairs in a back corner. A door next to the sofa was slightly ajar, and Ghazi looked inside to see a toilet and sink streaked with rust. It smelled worse in the bathroom, but it would be good to have indoor plumbing after so long. Behind the door was a mildewed tub, but a few clean towels were hanging on the shower rod, and a bar of soap sat on a shelf.

Ghazi returned to the main room and fell back onto the old sofa, staring at the ceiling, thinking of the girl's pleading eyes and the single tear. *Will I be able to face my death with such peace?* Ghazi tried to focus, but it was getting harder to concentrate without the medicine. The contact was supposed to meet Ahmed here in the morning. *What will they say when it's just me and no one else? Will they kill me and take the bomb for themselves?*

Ghazi's nervous humming was like an unbroken chant in the musty apartment.

CHAPTER 55

THE CONTACT

Suli Omar awoke in a small house twelve blocks from where Ghazi waited. Even though it has been over four years since she came to America, there was always a moment of disorientation until she remembered where she was. She didn't sleep well this night, dwelling on the task she was to carry out this morning.

She and her husband, Ali, lived in Kismayo and later moved to Mogadishu, Somalia, when Al-Shabaab insurgents grew in power. Following family, they applied for refugee status, and after a stay in New York and a short period in Detroit, they had moved to Minneapolis. Her husband Ali Omar joined two cousins and invested in real estate, and established several Halal grocery stores in the Metro area. They brought their boy and girl to America and began their new life in "Little Mogadishu," the local moniker for the Cedar-Riverside neighborhood. As the children matured, her daughter acclimated to America and progressed to university. Suli's son was very different. He was restless and angry and succumbed to pressure from Muslim groups recruiting fighters for the conflict in their home country. He left one night, traveling back to Somalia, and Suli feared he would never return.

Sometime later, Suli and Ali were notified by the Somali Outreach Center that a splinter group of Al-Shabaab was holding their son. In communicating through liaisons of their Muslim community, intentionally avoiding the American authorities, they learned that he could be ransomed if they would pay a tithe to his captors.

Ali agreed immediately, especially since the abduction appeared to be only an informal measure to ensure American Somalis did their zakat by contributing to the cause. Suli knew the words of The Prophet: "Whoever pays the zakat on his wealth will have evil removed from him." But Suli was ill at ease that they would be aiding a Wahhabi sect fighting the Sufi majority. After all, it was Al Shabaab's aggression that had forced Suli from her home. The Somali government wasn't much better, but it was academic now. Their son had been out of touch for months, and as long as Al-Shabaab held him, she and Ali knew his whereabouts. Suli realized it was almost impossible for her son to be safe there, but she thought they could control the situation with the money they sent overseas.

Then, just a week before, her husband told her that jihadists needed help in America, virtually in their backyard. This disturbed Suli greatly, and she questioned Ali's judgment in stepping beyond the financial support they were providing. Ali didn't admonish her or exercise the power he held as her husband. He just reminded her that she should be happy to do anything to preserve their son's life. Any argument was over before it could start.

Ali dealt with the communication and met with a man from their mosque who gave him a disposable cell phone and instructions to power it on only after the fifteenth of the month and let the voicemail answer if someone should call. The message would tell them what to do. Suli spoke the Somali language, but she could also understand Farsi, Arabic and was fluent in English. Ali designated her to carry out the task as part of the zakat ensuring their son's safety.

Yesterday morning, a call came in, and she almost shrieked when it rang, trembling as she held it through four…Five…Six rings. Then the terrible pause before the phone chirped to signify a message was left.

She tried to calm down as she waited for the message to play. A rough Somali voice said, "One must go to the high place tomorrow morning."

The "high place" was an apartment complex in North Minneapolis that Ali and his first cousin owned. They called it that because it had three floors, and the other property they owned nearby only had a single level. Both buildings were empty because they hadn't finished improvements to comply with the necessary city approvals. She shared the message with Ali, and he reaffirmed his decision that she should go alone.

* * *

Jordan gritted his teeth against the pain as he returned to the chair by the stove. He'd managed to block the smashed window with a seat cushion from the sofa, but he'd almost passed out from the effort. He braved going into the bedroom with the bunk beds and gathered up a blanket and a grimy pillow, stepping over the body on the floor and slamming the door behind him.

He was sweaty and feverish from exertion but felt better knowing his dad would be proud. Now he could stay warm while he waited for... *What?* Jordan didn't think anyone would be coming back here soon. Maybe ever. He wasn't even sure anyone would find him before he died but was pretty sure he was safe for a while.

He slid the pillow behind his head and awkwardly wrapped himself in the blanket, ignoring the stale smell of the wool. He was starting to realize how much harder life was going to be with only one hand. Another eerie howl sounded through the thin walls of the house, soon joined by a chorus of others as the pack of timber wolves rallied together in the forest. Jordan found that he wasn't frightened by them anymore. He felt almost elated to know there were other living things around him, and he wasn't truly alone.

He closed his eyes and listened to the howling, imagining their grey shapes coursing over the snow, the cold moonlight turning them into silver wraiths as they wove through the trees, chasing their prey.

CHAPTER 56

BLACK FRIDAY

Vanessa stood in front of the LEGO sets filling the aisle and tried to hold her ground against the other Target shoppers. She didn't know it was 5:40 AM, and the store was still in the midst of the opening frenzy of bargain shoppers that is the hallmark of the busiest shopping day of the year. Momma Gloria was in line to get a DVD player for $19.99, and Grandma Mary was somewhere, probably trying to find a place to sit down.

She reached out and took down the "Panda Jungle Set." She liked pandas, but then there was the "Vet Clinic Rescue," which was awesome too.

"Baby Daughter, don't run off like that." It was Grandma Mary in her loose jeans with the bingo jacket, and her hair pulled back in a gray bun, her face a pleasant maze of wrinkles. She unconsciously worked her dentures in her mouth, but Vanessa was still too young to be embarrassed by her. "Whatcha got there?" Grandma asked, sidling up to look.

"LEGO stuff." Vanessa knew the rules. She would have to wait until Christmas. Or until she could get to the checkout without being seen and get to the car and hide the LEGO sets (she had decided to get both) and drift back into the store like nothing happened.

"You gotta wait till Christmas, little girl." Grandma was a soft touch, but she would never let Vanessa pull something like this.

"I know. Where's Mom?" She hoped Grandma would leave to look for her.

She went back to get a cart. Is this the one you want for Christmas?" She pointed at the "Panda Jungle Set" Vanessa held too tightly in her hands, her little brown fingers clenched until the nails were white.

263

"I guess so, yeah, or whatever."

"Put it on your list, then." The old woman turned to go, and Vanessa's heart fluttered that she was going to get her chance. It wasn't like she was stealing or anything.

"I'm going to go find Daughter. You want to stay here?"

"Okay." Vanessa tried to sound like it wasn't a big deal.

Grandma Mary went by the other shoppers and disappeared around the end of the aisle. It was now or never. She snatched up the "Vet Rescue Clinic" and, tucking both sets under her arm like a football, started dodging shoppers to get to the checkout. Vanessa couldn't see over the shelves and panicked, unsure where to go. She spotted her mother, and her heart jumped. Her mom didn't see her, however, and Vanessa ducked past the throng pawing through the DVD movies, stealing a glance around the corner to see if the coast was clear, then bolted for the checkouts.

* * *

Jordan awoke, unsure how long he had been asleep. The wind still whistled around the cabin, but the wolves seemed to have moved on.

He slowly became aware of a new sound. A deep rumble from the woods was getting louder, and he was instantly on guard, his nerves taut. Jordan stood and tottered to the front window to look outside. The moon was a bone-white disc in the sky, shining down on the clearing, and he scanned the wood line around the cabin, frightened that he would see something moving in the shadows.

Jordan went to the front door and unlocked it, opening it just enough to watch the front yard and the driveway. The sound grew louder and his heart began to race as bright light played through the trees, coming closer until a plow truck appeared and lumbered into the clearing.

Jordan closed the door and retrieved the AK-47, hefting it in his left hand, wedging it under his armpit. He knew it was empty, but they wouldn't know that. He waited for whoever had found the cabin to make the next move.

* * *

Ghazi floated up from a dark pool of dreams, an indistinct image of men watching from below as Ghazi rose, their faces turned up to the surface. *Were they angry? Were they bitter?* The faces faded as Ghazi's eyes opened, but another part of the dream lingered. It was a twisted version of an even darker memory Ghazi thought was buried so deeply it could never rise again.

Ghazi stood stiffly and went to the window, sore to the bone with a throbbing headache. Careful not to pull back the drapes, only looking around the sides of the curtains at the street below. There was no one stirring, but Ghazi felt uneasy in the silence of the apartment. *The dream was only from the stress I'm feeling. Besides, nothing is honest in nightmares.*

Ghazi went into the bathroom and pulled the chain hanging down from the single bulb over a cloudy mirror. The door wouldn't latch, but Ghazi stripped anyway, hanging the smelly shirt and jeans stiff with grime on a tarnished wall hook. Lastly, the tight wrappings of beige Ace bandage came off Ghazi's chest in damp coils. It was like shedding a second skin, and Ghazi began to shiver uncontrollably. *Secrets shouldn't matter, but they do!*

Turning away, Ghazi pulled the shower curtain back and recoiled as a spider skittered across the tub. Turning on the faucets, Ghazi aimed the weak shower spray and washed the spider down the drain in a whirl of rusty water. Ghazi stepped in and almost screamed as the water hit naked skin. Gripping the bar of yellow soap, Ghazi scrubbed hard, muscles bunching and tense. The soap smelled antiseptic, and the water seemed to wash away the dark thoughts of the nightmare. Still, being awake didn't stop the image of draping the wool jacket over the girl's face, pulling the trigger, then dark blood spreading around the scorched hole. It was all the more terrifying now.

Another dead soul to greet me in the afterlife! I have misrepresented myself to everyone, even myself, and now I'm alone. Will I ever become clean again? Perhaps I failed even before I began!

Ghazi murmured a prayer and let the water roll across eyes that had seen too much.

* * *

Suli drove alone down the streets, following the rutted paths in her Toyota SUV, a sense of dread growing in her thoughts as she neared the apartment.

She stopped on the side street and looked around the neighborhood. A few people were shoveling out their cars, and one old man crossed the street with a bottle in a brown bag, gripping its neck like it would keep him from falling. She parked and went to "the high place," following a single line of footprints leading to the front entrance. Suli carried a plastic tote bin tucked under one arm, balancing it on her hip. Setting it down, she opened the lobby door, pushing the tote inside and locking the door behind her. *Now, where are they?*

Her question was answered by the trail of half-melted snow leading from the rough entry to the second floor. The building was musty and cold, and she was glad they didn't live here. She had done her time in the slums of Africa. They were trying to get above this.

Suli carried the tote bin to the second floor, breathing hard, trying not to make too much noise on the stairs. She followed the drying footprints to apartment 210 and knocked softly on the door. Suli waited for a moment and then used her master key.

Suli saw clothing on the floor and a single pair of wet boots cast aside near the sofa. Water was running in the shower, but she thought it strange there was only one person. Maybe more men were coming? Suli closed the door and walked across the spartan room, relieved to see the drapes were tightly closed. She sat on the arm of the threadbare sofa, and the bricks shifted, giving her a start. She smoothed her hijab and looked at her watch. It was just after four in the morning. She hoped she could be done with this and be able to get to work on time.

CHAPTER 57

JORDAN

Owen "Swede" Swenson stopped his pickup in the clearing of Tom Duchamp's place. He'd followed fresh tracks from the county road and down the driveway, but there was no sign of any vehicles. His headlights were mounted above a formidable red plow blade and illuminated the cabin and yard in stark relief.

There was a light on in the cabin, but no one seemed to be stirring. Owen didn't like this whole scenario, especially after what he'd seen at Axe Winter's place. Owen had a feeling whoever left that light on had something to do with the ruins of Axel's camp. *Tom Duchamp was long dead, and no one ever came up here anymore, so who could it be?*

He was still shaken by what he'd seen earlier.

The snow tapered off sometime overnight, and Owen figured he'd plow out Axel's driveway and stop in for some coffee with the boys before they went out hunting. When he'd come around the final curve in the drive, he stopped the truck and sat with his mouth open, shocked at the destruction. He got out of the pickup and waded through the snow to check out the burned-out vehicles and what was left of Axel's cabin.

The heavy smell of smoke still lingered in the air, which meant the fire must have happened yesterday. Owen wasn't surprised that he hadn't smelled or seen the smoke. He'd been cocooned in his house four miles away, enjoying Thanksgiving with his family. It was around 4:30 AM now, and the fire was completely out, so that meant Axel and Kurt were long gone. *What the hell happened here? Where did they go?* Their vehicles were cooked where they sat, and no one else had traveled into the camp. Owen took off his stocking cap and scratched his head. *If Axel called 911, I would have heard the sirens. This doesn't make any sense!*

Owen took one last look around and got back into the pickup. He lifted the plow blade and turned the truck around, heading back to the county road. When he reached the end of the drive, he noticed one set of fresh wheel ruts from Tom Duchamp's farm. Owen decided to take a look at Duchamp's next door.

Now Owen sat in his truck watching Duchamp's farmhouse, wondering what to do next. He pulled out his cell phone to dial 911 but put it back in his pocket. *What am I going to say?*

Owen got out and walked cautiously toward the house. The halogen lights on the plow cast his shadow across the porch as he approached. *Making me a perfect target,* Owen thought. He considered calling out, but something didn't seem right, and he kept quiet. As Owen got closer, he saw bullet holes in the siding and wood splinters scattered on the steps. He was so focused on the damage that he tripped over something covered with snow, falling headlong forward sprawling next to the steps.

"Darn it!" He spluttered, wiping snow off his face and getting to his knees. Owen turned to see what he'd tripped over, and the face of Saeed Alghamdi stared at him in the harsh light. He jumped to his feet and stumbled backward, almost falling over another body in the snow. "Jeee-sus!" He cried, sidling away from Kurt's body.

What the hell happened here?

CHAPTER 58

SULI AND GHAZI

Suli waited in the living room of the tenement. The sofa smelled of urine and worse, and she hoped she wouldn't have to wait much longer. This meeting was a simple errand, but she worried that it might turn into something dangerous. Suli wasn't a fanatic but did feel compelled to help the Islamic cause. Like many of her family, she perceived Muslims were targeted and unfairly persecuted throughout the world. If the brothers carried the battle too far or made war against the United States, that was just an unfortunate reality. Suli didn't hate the Americans, but she distrusted them and hadn't bonded with her new nation.

Suli heard the shower stop and water dripping in the silence of the apartment. Then the sound of curtain rings on metal and someone stepping out of the tub. She unconsciously looked up and realized the door to the bathroom had swung open. A nude figure appeared, standing with his back to her in front of a mirror fogged with condensation.

Suli froze, unsure of what to do. She looked away and tried to move out of the man's line of sight, but before she could stand, the figure raised a towel to the mirror and wiped away the moisture.

In the reflection, Suli saw something she didn't expect. The brown eyes looking into the mirror were that of a young woman. She seemed haggard with a drawn face below short-cropped hair. She had a boyish figure with narrow hips, and her breasts barely cast a shadow below dark brown nipples. Red lines circled her chest as though she had been wearing a corset. Only the tuft of pubic hair between the woman's legs was proof of her gender.

Suli was mildly surprised.

Ghazi was terrified. Her first reaction was to slam the bathroom door and lean against it as though holding back the world. Or maybe all that had happened in the last two days.

Ghazi had lied to Imam Al-Qadhi and lied to Mohammet. She had lied to everyone for months, including herself. What began as a fresh start in a new city had become a house of cards. She grew absorbed in the role of a young man and gradually displaced her identity. Ghazi knew she was an unattractive woman. Her nose was too big, her skin sallow, and she had an unappealing body. Most importantly, her gender made her subservient to all men. She didn't resent men, and her great deception wasn't a protest against her station; it was simply a way to participate in a life she felt entitled to live.

Whomever she was had ceased to exist, and she adopted Ghazi as her new name. Her build and features may have been a hindrance as a woman but suited her new role well. By binding her breasts and posing as a modest Muslim boy, it was easy to avoid questions and become part of the mosque community on Presque Street. It was only the will of Allah that raised the opportunity to join Ahmed and the others on their mission. She would be finally taking part in her jihad, doing the work of the Prophet, and earning her way to paradise!

But now, the deception seemed sordid and selfish. *Maybe it is right that I've been discovered naked with no illusions left!* She was a fraud, an amateur, and though she believed in all that she was doing, it was supposed to be within the framework of male leadership. She was the weak link, and now she was discovered, alone and vulnerable.

There was a knock on the bathroom door. The black woman was speaking, but Ghazi couldn't understand her. Ghazi picked the towel off the sink and wrapped it around herself. She opened the door but stayed inside the bathroom.

Suli met her eyes and smiled warmly. She spoke to the younger woman in Farsi.

Ghazi shook her head. "I'm sorry, I don't understand."

"Oh, English! Welcome, Sister!" Suli said, placing a hand on Ghazi's shoulder. "I am Suli. Where are the others? Where are the men?"

Ghazi shook her head in shame. "My name is Ghazi. I'm the only one."

Suli frowned, but the look of defeat in the girl's eyes told her not to pursue it. "That is all right, Ghazi, just a moment." Suli carried the tote bin to the sofa and pulled out an assortment of men's clothing

Ghazi came out of the bathroom shivering, wearing the wet towel around her waist and the shirt she arrived in draped over her shoulders.

"My husband told me to bring clothing for you," Suli said. I'm sorry that I assumed there would only be men.

Ghazi pulled a pair of jeans from the pile and held it in front of her waist. "A bit big, but they will fit," Ghazi said. "Are there any stockings?" She held a black sweatshirt against her chest and then slipped it over her head. Suli dug further into the bin, found a pair of white cotton socks, and handed them to Ghazi.

"I didn't bring shoes," Suli said, looking at the wet boots Ghazi had worn since the afternoon they left Winnipeg. "I am sorry."

"No matter," Ghazi said, returning to the bathroom.

Suli placed the rest of the clothing back into the bin and closed the lid. She went to the bathroom door. "We can buy something for you," Suli said. "The shopping places will be open soon. Some are open all night long."

I will not be alive long enough to need new shoes, Ghazi thought. "No, there isn't time," She said through the door. She was looking in the mirror and tried to recognize the young woman staring back. *I am hideous,* she thought, running her hands through her short dark hair, staring into her reflection. *Am I even alive?* She stripped the belt from her old jeans and considered Halil's knife. She shouldn't wear it anymore, but she would keep it for now.

Ghazi opened the bathroom door. "Thank you for these clothes, she said, embracing Suli tightly. "You are a blessed person." She released the Somali woman and picked up the sodden boots, leaning against the wall while loosening the wet laces.

Suli watched the young woman grimace as she put on the boots then stand for a moment with her head down, one hand against the wall. Suli was about to go to her, but the girl straightened up and retrieved the jacket from the floor.

"We must go now," Ghazi told Suli. "You can ride with me."

Suli's heart fell to hear that her errand wasn't complete. She did not want to accompany this woman to wherever she was going, but she owed it to her beloved son and must honor her husband's demands.

She had to assist this woman, but she would part ways with her as soon as possible.

* * *

Jordan waited in the dark hall, his heart pounding. A truck had stopped in front of the cabin, and the headlights lit up the clearing outside. He heard someone get out of the pickup and then footsteps approaching. Jordan heard a man curse but nothing since. *Were they waiting outside? Do they know I'm in here?* Jordan wished he'd shut off all the lights in the cabin. *What if they came for me? Maybe Rory was able to bring help?*

Caught between fear and hope, Jordan cracked open the door, squinting into the headlights of the pickup idling across the clearing. A man was walking away toward the truck, his hands in his pockets. He decided to take a gamble, stepping out onto the porch, trying to keep the AK pointed forward. "Hey! Who are you?" Jordan's voice sounded like the scared boy he was.

Owen turned around, obviously startled by the voice from the cabin. A young boy stood on the porch, a machine gun tucked under one arm, the other in a sling around his neck. In the headlights, the boy's face was deathly white, his eyes squinting against the glare. Owen was surprised to see the assault rifle and put his hands up. *This kid is the shooter!* Owen thought. *He's off his rocker, and I'm the next victim!* "Hold it there," Owen called out. "I'm...I was just here to check on the place. I'll leave you alone!"

Jordan didn't expect the man's reaction and lowered the rifle. "Who are you?" Jordan asked again, his voice cracking.

"I'm Owen Swenson. I live up the road a ways. Who are you?"

Jordan's arm was tiring fast, and he let the AK-47 clatter onto the porch. "I'm Jordan Winter."

Owen frowned. "You're Kurt's boy?"

Jordan nodded. "Yes, "Kurt was my dad," Jordan said, his throat tightening. "He….He was killed."

Owen put his arms down and cautiously walked back toward the house. "You didn't shoot him, did you?"

Jordan's eyes widened. "No! We were attacked! They burned my grandpa's cabin. They killed everyone!" Speaking drained Jordan's strength, and he sagged against the porch railing.

Owen quickly reached Jordan's side and helped him down the steps. "I'll take you home and get you looked after. "What's happened to you?" Owen asked. Your arm broke?"

"I got shot," Jordan replied tiredly.

As he helped the boy up into the cab, Owen was shocked to see the boy's right hand was missing. "When did you lose your hand?"

"I had to cut it off."

Owen was stunned that the boy was alive. Owen's mind raced. "You cut it off?"

"Yes!" Jordan snapped. "Please just get me out of here!"

Owen nodded and got Jordan buckled into the passenger seat. "We'll go right to the hospital."

Owen made a wide turn and pressed the accelerator, rolling on the newly plowed drive back to town. He called 911 for an ambulance to meet them on the road to Roseau. He lowered the phone and looked over at Jordan. "Who the hell attacked you guys, anyway?"

He waited for a reply, but Jordan had already fallen asleep.

CHAPTER 59

RESURRECTION

Aurora opened her eyes in darkness; pain followed her awakening like a dull current running through her body. She couldn't see anything, and she moved her head to shake off the weight pressing against her face. The bloody cloth clung to her cheek with congealed blood, sending a fresh wave of agony through her as it tore free. Her scream was only a wet mewling sound absorbed by the cloth over her mouth. She realized with horror that she could barely hear the sounds she was making.

Everything came back in a sickening wave. The camp killings and the trip south. The boy, Ghazi slitting her ankle and the long ride, fading in and out of consciousness. The memory of him looming over her with the gun was terrifying, but seeing the cold intent in his eyes meant it was over, and she could do nothing more than pleading with her eyes. Aurora thought of the wool coat pulled over her face, the pressure of the barrel against her cheek, then the hammer blow of the bullet shocking her into oblivion.

Aurora coughed and gritted her teeth to keep from crying out. Her hands were still tied, but she could feel her fingers and toes, her ankle throbbing. That pain was bearable compared to the fresh wound in her face. She exhaled and felt her breath coming through the hole in her cheek, setting off a new wave of nausea.

The bullet must have entered her mouth and out the back of her jaw. A cold shiver went down Aurora's spine as her tongue explored the gap in her upper molars where the bullet had passed, leaving a massive hole in the right side of her mouth. Her face throbbed with pain from the bullet wound and the damage to her front teeth from before. Her head felt swollen and full of cotton, and she just wanted to pass out. *I have to stay awake,* she thought. *I could bleed out before anyone would find me!*

Aurora tried to listen for any activity from the outside, but the dullness in her ears made it impossible to recognize any familiar sounds. She slowly shifted her body to lay on her stomach, the jacket still covering her head. *He must have run away and left me for dead.* She winced as her cheek came to rest on the leather seat of the truck. She needed to get her hands free, but she was alive. *I am alive!*

Aurora lay still for a full five minutes, willing the pain to subside. She thought of just screaming for help over and over until she was rescued or died, but some instinct told her to stay quiet and only trust herself. *I have to get my hands in front of me so I can see what I'm doing.*

Aurora gritted her teeth and arched her back to bring her legs up behind her. She fumbled with the bootlaces and got them untied and loosened down to the toes. The right boot was filled with dried blood and clung to her stocking. She gently worked her finger around her ankle, trying to avoid the wound while she peeled the leather away from the blood-soaked sock. She finally pushed the right boot with her left toe, succeeding in getting it off, the boot dropping to the floor of the truck with a soft thump. *Halfway there!*

Now she would have to pry the boot off of her left foot. She tried to ignore the sickening motion of her foot, imagining the slit in the back of her ankle opening like a red mouth as she struggled. She kept up the pressure, grunting with effort and pain, and when she began to see flashes of light behind her eyes, the boot dropped to the floor with the same soft thump as the first.

She slowly turned on her side and pulled her legs up tight against her chest, reaching down with her arms as far as she could. Her wrists made it past her heels, then over her knees, and her hands were in front of her.

Aurora waited for the wave of pain to subside, then slid the coat off her face. *She could see! It was like waking up all over again!* Rising on her elbow, she cautiously raised her head above the seat and looked outside. Her vision was blurred, but she could see they were parked on a snowy street somewhere. She almost expected that psycho Ghazi to be standing outside the Suburban, but everything was dark and quiet. She dropped back down, head throbbing, trying to think where she could be and what time it was. *What day it was, for that matter.* Just as she had felt in the gas station earlier, so much had happened in the last 24 hours she couldn't piece things together. She shivered suddenly and became aware of how cold it was in the truck.

She sensed something wasn't right and sat up again, peering out the back. Someone was coming down the street. *She should call for help!* She almost reached for the door handle, but something about the way the figure walked with hunched over shoulders made her lie down again. The footsteps in the snow were coming closer, and Aurora pulled the jacket back over her head, feeling the cold, wet spot of blood against her wounded cheek. She was hyperventilating and focused on getting her breathing under control. *It has to be Ghazi!* The boy was coming around the truck, past the back door, and she could hear the key sliding into the driver's door.

Oh shit, oh shit, oh shit...

The door opened, and a rush of cold air swept over her, chilling her to the bone. She held as still as she could, knowing the boy was looking at what he thought was her dead body. She worried he would notice that her boots were off and lying on the floor, but before she could panic, the boy climbed into the driver's seat. She could smell laundered clothing and the antiseptic smell of soap instead of the sweat and stink of her captor. *Maybe it isn't Ghazi, and she could risk asking for help? But who else would have the key?* She couldn't believe this was happening. She clenched her fists and silently cursed herself. *You idiot! How could you have gotten back into this mess? You almost made it, and now you're stuck again!*

The driver opened the passenger door, and someone else got in.

Whoever these people are, they don't know I'm back here. Or at least that I'm still breathing, Aurora thought. *I won't fall asleep this time. This time I'll be ready!*

* * *

Owen Swenson sat in the waiting area of the ER at the County Hospital. He finished the last cold swallow of coffee and rubbed his eyes. He'd called Jen Winter and told her that Jordan had a hunting accident but was doing well. He couldn't bring himself to tell her the whole truth about Kurt and the others. Owen would let the Sherriff do that. He scanned the magazine he was holding, but he couldn't concentrate. He set it down and stood up to walk around.

The Sheriff was standing in the hall talking to the doctor that checked Jordan into surgery. Owen approached the men and waited with his hands in his pockets.

"This is the gentleman who brought the boy in." The doctor said, putting his hand on Owen's shoulder. As I told you, Sheriff, Jordan did an excellent job of first aid, but if it wasn't for Owen, he might not have made it."

"Good job, Mr. Swenson." The Sheriff shook Owen's hand. He knew most people in the county, including Owen and Axe Winter. "What did the boy tell you?"

"Nothing much," Owen replied, genuinely sorry he didn't know more. "He was pretty exhausted when I found him, but he did say he got shot, and his dad, Kurt Winter, was dead."

The Sherriff took Owen aside. "For some reason, Mr. Swenson, there are some heavy hitters from the FBI coming up from St. Paul for this interview, so you and I have a little time to visit the site and get an idea of what happened out there."

Owen nodded and took his stocking cap out of his pocket. "I'll take you there. Let's go."

The Sheriff keyed his microphone and called for two of his units for backup, then followed Owen Swenson out to his plow truck.

Owen told the Sheriff as much as he knew about Axe Winter's camp on the Joshua. He described the scene as he came into the ruins of the cabin and the burned-out cars, then told him about going over to Duchamp's place and discovering two frozen bodies before Jordan appeared.

The Sheriff listened with growing concern. *Was this some land dispute or maybe a war over meth territory? That didn't explain the FBI's interest.* "You said the boy was carrying an AK-47 when you first saw him. What do you make of that?"

Owen shook his head. "I don't know," he said honestly. "I think you're just going to have to ask him when he wakes up. I know it's official business, but why would the FBI be involved? How did they even know this happened?"

The Sheriff shrugged. "I think they know more about this than I do. My guess is we're only a stone's throw from Canada, and the Feds caught wind of an illegal crossing. The deaths you reported went over the wire, and now they're coming up to close the loop." He shifted in his seat to look at Owen. "Of course, that's just between you and me, right?"

"Yep," Owen said, keeping his eyes on the road.

They bypassed the Winter Camp entrance and went directly to the Duchamp place. Owen was nervous about returning to the scene. Thoughts of bad guys lying in wait, or worse, being a possible suspect in the murders made him regret he'd ever come over to plow this morning. *No good deed goes unpunished!* Owen down-shifted and took the last turn into Duchamp's, making sure the two deputies were right behind them as he led them to where he found Jordan Winter.

CHAPTER 60

VANESSA

Gloria Whitebird and Grandma Mary sat across from Vanessa in the mall food court, trying to determine how baby daughter had the money for not one but two LEGO sets. Not to mention buying toys for herself just before Christmas!

Gloria sniffed out the plot when she spotted Vanessa in the check-out line, and now Vanessa was pleading her case. "The money was in the crazy girl's wallet. She just said I dropped something and put it in my pocket!" Vanessa figured it would be finder's keepers.

"You think that girl at the gas station was crazy?" Grandma Mary was looking through thick glasses, her eyes magnified behind the lenses in a way that would make Vanessa giggle any other day.

"Probably," Vanessa said with a casual shrug.

Gloria shook her head at Vanessa. She picked up the pink wallet and looked at it with a frown on her face. "Aurora Winter," she read. "The girl is from Red River Falls. She's got a hunting license in here and a picture of her dad, maybe?"

Vanessa sensed something had shifted. Somehow there was a bigger thing here than LEGO sets.

"She'll be needing it probably. It's got her license, and it's a nice wallet too." She handed it to Grandma Mary and took a sip of coffee. "Still don't make it right that you spent her money, though." She looked over the cup at Vanessa with disapproval.

"I swear she gave it to me!" Vanessa was stung that the story could still swing back into her like a boomerang.

"Well," Grandma Mary said, "She don't have no phone number in here, so I suppose we'll have to mail it to her."

Gloria was still glaring at Vanessa, and the little girl had a revelation. "You know," Vanessa started with hopeful hesitation, "The crazy girl looked a little scared. Maybe she was trying to get me to help her or something?"

Grandma Mary snorted and looked off into the mall and the crowd of shoppers passing their table.

"Whatcha mean, Daughter?" Gloria was thinking the same thing but didn't want to say it.

"I dunno, maybe she wanted us to call the Sheriff or something." She stared down at the table. "She seemed kind of scared."

Grandma Mary took the wallet, turning it in her wrinkled hands. "Did she really just give it to you, baby daughter?" Vanessa didn't look up but nodded weakly. "Well then, let's find the police and give it to them. They can see what it's about." She slipped the wallet into her jacket pocket and slowly stood up. Gloria finished her coffee and stood too, slipping on her coat and putting her purse over her arm. "Come on, Baby Daughter, you can tell a policeman what you told us."

* * *

Officer James Nichols was sitting in his Grand Forks squad car outside of the Target store attached to the mall, buckling his seatbelt and getting ready to go off shift. Nichols had broken up two fights between women shoppers fighting over the last PlayStation and the same pair of red Nike's, respectively, and just finished processing his seventh shoplifter. He'd had enough of Black Friday and was ready to go home and get to bed.

There was a light knock on the side window, and he met the eyes of a young Native American girl standing next to the car. He rolled down the window and saw two women standing behind her, probably mom and grandma.

Vanessa thrust out the wallet, holding it under the officer's nose like she was daring him to bite it. "I found this over in Minnesota this morning," She said quickly. The policeman frowned, and Vanessa thought she'd better get it out fast. "This girl," she said like a question, "gave me this wallet this morning and told me I dropped it, but it wasn't mine, and when I looked in it later, it had her license and stuff, and some money, and I think maybe she was in trouble and trying to tell me to get help!"

Nichols stared at the wallet, and then he looked at the girl and the two women. He took it from the girl and flipped it open. "Aurora Winter," he said aloud. "She just gave it to you? Why do you think she was in trouble, was there a note?"

The mother and grandmother started talking simultaneously, the little girl joining in, relating a story about getting up early and getting gas and casino people and a weird young guy and a crazy girl who may or may not be in trouble. He was tired and ready for the shift to end, but this was the kind of thing that could spell trouble if not taken seriously. "Let's go into the mall and talk," he said, rolling up the window and securing his squad.

Later, Nichols finished his report and put his notepad back in his pocket. He told the women that he would look after the wallet and not worry about the money but expect a call if this Aurora Winter wanted her cash back.

The sun was just starting to lighten the sky to the east as Officer Nichols left the mall and went back to his cruiser. He transferred the data and went into the driver and vehicle database. Bringing up Aurora's driver's license, he saw no hits for warrants or violations on record, but something pushed him to look further.

He pulled up the Minnesota Bureau of Criminal Apprehension and got the number for the Northwest part of the state. He felt stupid following up on this, and he hoped he could wrap it up before 06:30 when overtime would kick in, and he'd have to explain himself. The BCA dispatcher answered, and he gave her the information for one Aurora Winter. She put him on hold, and he watched the endless stream of Black Friday shoppers walking past the squad car and into the mall. His radio let out a burst of static, and he turned down the volume.

The dispatcher was back. "Officer?"

"Yes," he said, shifting in his seat, holding his cell phone tighter to his ear.

"I am going to transfer you to Agent Sundgaard; he has some questions for you."

"Wait," he said quickly, "Who is Agent Sundgaard?" But he was back on hold.

"This is Sundgaard," a surprisingly awake voice said.

"Um, yes, this is Jim Nichols. I'm with the Grand Forks Police Department." Nichols felt nervous about this call for some reason.

"Yes," Sundgaard replied. "I understand you have information about Aurora Winter?"

Nichols gave a much-abbreviated version of Vanessa's encounter and ended with the data on Aurora's License.

There was silence on the other end for a moment, and Nichols waited for the big brush-off.

"Wait one," Sundgaard finally said.

Nichols could hear Sundgaard relating the details in a loud voice like he had someone else on a speakerphone across the room or was speaking to a group of people. *This early in the morning?*

"Nichols?"

"Yes, I'm here," Nichols replied.

"The one who retrieved the wallet, this girl, Vanessa, is she still there with you?"

"Um, no," Jim Nichols replied.

"Jim, I think you'd better try to get the girl and her mother somewhere we can question them a bit more. I'm going to give you my direct line, and when you find them, call back, and we'll fill you in on the Amber Alert." Sundgaard gave him the number and hung up before Nichols had a chance to ask anything more.

Officer Jim Nichols of the Grand Forks, North Dakota Police Department, radioed his dispatcher that he was continuing his shift indefinitely but would be unavailable for the time being. He then called his supervisor and left a voicemail about the call with Agent Sundgaard and an Amber Alert for Aurora Winter. Nichols got out of the squad and went back into the mall, dialing the number Gloria Whitebird had given him, hoping it was a cell phone and they hadn't gone too far.

CHAPTER 61

THE OBJECTIVE

Ghazi hunched her shoulders against the cold dawn, walking back to the truck. There was a dusting of snow on it, but the weather had cleared for the most part. She could hear some traffic in the distance, and there were several lights on in the old houses and dilapidated apartment buildings along the street. She listened to the Somali woman locking the building door behind them.

The end would be coming very soon. Ghazi patted her front pants pocket and felt the outline of the cell phone. The pistol was heavy in the light jacket, but she had cinched her new jeans too tight to stick it in the waistband. Her stomach was empty, and her head throbbed with a pain that wouldn't go away. She should have asked the Somali woman if she had something for pain.

What would it matter? Ghazi thought to herself. *My headache will be gone soon enough.*

Ghazi wanted just to keep walking past the truck, down the block, and keep walking until she fell dead. She thought of the ugly, worthless girl in the mirror and the pretty, dead girl in the back. *Ahmed and Mohammet had a purpose. The others who died before they could realize their dream had a purpose, including the girl. But isn't Ghazi dead too? She thought of the nightmare again. Wasn't I dead even before Winnipeg? Maybe I never really existed. I can only hope that if I set off the bomb, I will be allowed to live again in a better way.*

She found herself at the driver's door of the Suburban, robotically opening it with the key. The girl's body was a dark form on the backseat, and Ghazi tried not to think of the final moments before she fired the pistol. Getting in, she opened the passenger door for the Somali and started the truck. The knife Ghazi placed under the seat, but the gun stayed in her jacket.

Suli snapped her seatbelt as Ghazi pulled away from the curb and started down the rutted street. It was cold in the truck, and Suli sat stiffly, resisted the urge to turn up the temperature control. Ghazi took a folded sheaf of paper from her jacket and handed it to Suli. The document was damp, and Suli took care to unfold it gently lest it tore. The girl pointed at a location on a simple map of the metro area.

Suli looked at the diagram and nodded. "Yes, I know this place well."

Ghazi nodded curtly. "Turn the page."

Suli carefully flipped to another page stapled to the first.

"And this place," Ghazi asked, "can you take me there?"

Suli frowned. "This exact spot? Why would you have to go there?"

Ghazi shook her head in tired frustration. "That isn't important. Can you find it when we get there?"

Suli was chastened by the rebuke and thought again that others were counting on her besides this strange young woman. "Yes, I think so." She quickly added, "It is part of the place you want to go." Suli traced the streets and shapes they formed, thinking of the right and left turns they would need to make once they arrived. Suli nodded again. "Yes, this will be a spot we can find."

Suli waited for Ghazi to say more, but she focused only on the road. "Will this errand be all you need of me?" Suli looked down and waited for some sort of outburst. The girl didn't seem to hear, but before Suli could ask again, she nodded without taking her eyes off the road. Suli was relieved and felt better knowing this trial would be over soon. She leaned forward and watched for the signs that would lead them to the Minneapolis suburb of Bloomington.

Ghazi didn't know why the bomb had to be in that spot. She had never been to the target, so she had to trust that Saeed or someone had scouted the area and decided that was the best place. Perhaps she would understand when she got there, but the Somali woman would have to guide her.

In just the first few minutes since leaving the apartment, they were already on a busy highway and heading directly into the heart of downtown. They were nearly back among the towering buildings studded with amber and white lights.

If this Somali woman did something erratic or jeopardized the mission somehow, Ghazi would place a call to the package and hope the damage was acceptable.

* * *

Aurora stayed as still as she could, trying to imagine where they were. After hearing the conversation between the people in the front seat, she was sure one was Ghazi. Aurora shifted a little, trying to get more comfortable. Her wounds had settled into a bearable ache, but she needed a doctor. It felt claustrophobic under the wool coat, and the smell of blood was stronger now that it was warm in the truck. *Keep it together*, she thought to herself, feeling nauseous. *Don't make a sound. The only reason I'm alive is that they think I'm already dead!*

Aurora chanced a peek from under the coat, pulling it slowly down from her face until she could look out the window on the other side of the truck. *Skyscrapers!* They were in a big city, and after a moment, her eyes adjusted to the sights, and Aurora recognized two of the buildings and knew she was in Minneapolis. The sky was lightening, but Aurora wasn't sure of the time. She watched the towering offices as they drove down the highway, amber sodium street lights shining into the truck every few seconds as they passed exits and overpasses. Aurora looked at the buildings for a moment longer, thinking they were the most beautiful structures she'd ever seen. She took a last breath of clean air and burrowed under the bloody wool coat again.

* * *

Suli navigated for Ghazi, guiding them to merge onto Highway 94, over the Mississippi River Bridge, and head west to a tangle of roads coming out on Interstate 35 to Bloomington. The sky was beginning to lighten, and Suli looked at her watch. It was 6:36 AM, but she set it to run fast by six minutes to make sure she was on time to the cardboard plant for her shift. Her husband thought it was silly to fool herself. "You and the clock both know what time it is. Who has more sense, I wonder?" They had laughed at the joke, but now Suli wondered if she would ever laugh again.

The maps weren't the only thing Ghazi had in her pocket. Suli had seen the blue metal of a gun when the girl had put on her jacket. She was up to something that Suli might have to answer for later. She knew little about the laws in this country, but it seemed the police were very active. Still, there wasn't much that happened without cause, and perhaps, more importantly, Suli knew America was a nation of laws and had seen far more kindness than violence in her time here. Either way, if it meant keeping her son alive long enough to untangle the mess in the homeland, she would do it.

She saw the green sign with white lettering with the blue and white Highway 494 sign coming up and let the girl know about the lane change, hoping this zakat would be her last.

* * *

Ghazi shifted to the right lane anticipating the exit. She was jittery from being off her medications for almost two days, and her mind was starting to wander. The road improved, and they picked up speed, joining a rush of cars moving south. *These Americans were so ambitious. The biggest storm in years, and here they were, bustling like ants rebuilding a shattered nest!* The Somali woman seemed to be nervous, and Ghazi slowed down, focusing on the taillights of the cars ahead. "How much farther?" Ghazi chanced a look at the Somali woman.

"Not long," Suli said. "You will be impressed when you see it."

Ghazi didn't care about that. "Why are you helping me?"

Suli was taken aback by the question. *How much should I share with this woman?* "My son is being held for ransom in Somalia. I have been told that helping you will allow him to go free."

"Do you know of Ahmed or Mohammet Abu Sharim?" Ghazi asked.

"No, are they your friends?"

Ghazi thought about that. "No, but I was with them when they died."

"Oh no, Sister!" Suli was genuinely sorry that lives were lost in this girl's jihad. Ghazi looked away, embarrassed at the Somali's show of concern. Suli placed her hand on the girl's arm. "Were they the men who were to be with you at the rendezvous?" Ghazi nodded but said nothing. "Forgive me, Sister, but why were you posing as a man? Why do you keep the name, Ghazi? The feminine form is Ghaziyah."

Ghazi didn't want to speak of her past, but the woman's kindness compelled an explanation. "I was running away, as I am still. Ghazi was my younger brother. He was just eight when he died, and I took the name to honor him."

"How horrible!" Suli was beginning to understand the depth of sadness in this young woman.

"I killed him," the girl known as Ghazi said in an emotionless voice.

Suli wasn't sure what the girl meant. "You killed.... *Your brother?*"

"And my parents," Ghazi replied. "I was just back from hospital that afternoon." Ghazi's said in an emotionless voice, thinking of that night and forgetting about Suli and the bomb. "I went into the kitchen for a knife, then to my brother's bedroom. He was sleeping, but he woke up when I stabbed him." Ghazi remembered the boy's eyes were wild like an animal after she slit his throat. *He must have been so sad to see his sister standing over him with a dripping butcher knife in her clenched fist!*

She waited until the boy's neck stopped pulsing blood, then continued to her parent's bedroom, pushing open the door silently and crossing to the bed.

"My mother and father looked very old with their gray hair and wrinkled faces. I bent forward and blew in my mother's ear, and she opened her eyes, smiling at me."

"I slit my brother's throat while he slept," Ghazi told Suli in a clinical voice. "Then I woke my parents and stabbed them many times."

Suli was shocked into silence, her skin tingling with horror. How could she reply to such an admission? *Who would set me on a path to aid this horrible person?*

Ghazi smiled. "There was so much blood that I didn't think it would ever stop. I left the next morning and became Ghazi, reborn in Winnipeg and now redeemed by this holy jihad. You are the first I've told since that day."

Suli was mortified. "I....I don't know what you want me to say."

Ghazi turned calmly toward the Somali. "You will say nothing, of course. You won't need to ever tell anyone about what I've done."

"Of course I won't," Suli said quickly, shrinking back from Ghazi. "Sister, why did you kill them?"

"I don't remember," Ghazi said with a sigh.

Suli began to panic. If she reproached this girl, she would likely lash out in her insanity. Suli cleared her throat and tried to keep her voice from betraying her fear. "You have been through much, Sister. Know that Allah forgives the righteous, and your path can straighten by your confession. Atonement will allow you a way to paradise!"

Ghazi didn't acknowledge the woman's words and seemed to forget what they had been discussing. "Is this the exit we need to take?"

* * *

Aurora felt as though frozen in a nightmare. Learning of Ghazi's true identity was like a punch in the stomach, but the chilling confession stunned Rory with its depravity. *Ghazi tried to murder me, but what he...She had confessed was beyond insane! The other woman surely must know it too? How could anyone listen to Ghazi's madness and react so calmly?* The woman had a foreign accent, but Rory couldn't understand her role in all of this without seeing her. Her image until now was of a mature, compassionate woman, but maybe she was as heartless as Ghazi. Aurora heard fear in the woman's voice. *Is she trapped just like me?* Could she become an ally Aurora could trust to aid her escape? *How do I let her know I'm alive without triggering Ghazi into killing us both?*

Aurora knew she had to try.

CHAPTER 62

THE MALL OF AMERICA

"If you do an internet search for Mall of America, or MOA, it was described as a 'city within a city.' It had what every mall has; restaurants and retail stores. The smaller merchants operated kiosks in the broad aisle ways, standing like islands parting the stream of shopping humanity that flowed past. As mundane as a mall can be, the visitors came to MOA by the hundreds of thousands every year, rivaling the big theme parks. It even had an indoor amusement area, a gigantic roller coaster generating screams heard throughout the mall and a mild chlorine smell from the water rides.

Shoppers were seen looking up or down, marveling at the multiple levels, each with its flow of people circulating with or without purpose. They came from all over the world, and one could see Japanese visitors snapping selfies to northern Europeans who blended in very well until they spoke to ask for a table at a bistro or buy tickets at the multiplex. Schwarzenegger and Stallone were on hand back in 1993 when Planet Hollywood opened but didn't return to Minnesota when it closed ten years later.

Like all malls, it was a jigsaw puzzle of capitalism, the number of missing pieces dependent on the economy and who could make rent every month. Anything you wanted in a mall was at MOA times ten."

Excerpted from "Fallout – Surviving in a Dark New Age" by Miriam Glenn - published in the St. Paul Pioneer Press

Ramon Martinez stopped his MOA parking lot security vehicle at the crosswalk. He had started his shift an hour early for Black Friday, and he sipped the tepid coffee he'd brought with him from his night job at the cab company. He set the travel mug in one of the cup holders and watched the shoppers crossing from the parking ramp into Macy's entrance. The sky was starting to lighten, but it was dark enough for the yellow strobes on the light bar of his SUV to reflect off the faces of the people who glanced at him.

The cold was brutal, and he turned up the heat. His father still lived in Juarez, making concrete blocks. He could see his father's face creased and dusty and the smile that would appear when he came home to his family. Ramon sent some of his money home, but less now that he had little Rose. Ramon's mother was staying with him and his wife. She worked too, and they were thinking of buying a house. Two jobs were difficult, but they needed the money, and as his father would say, "*Usted puede ser joven y sabio, pero es bueno tener una espalda fuerte.*" Roughly translated, it meant: "You may be young and smart, but having a strong back doesn't hurt." Ramon's back was hurting this morning.

The last stragglers made their way across the walkway, and Ramon drove forward. He was there to make sure the parking areas were safe, but mostly he helped people start their cars if they left their lights on in the winter or breaking up groups of teenagers loitering in the ramps. There was never anything too exciting, and if he did see anyone break into a car or get violent, he called it in, and the Bloomington cops from the sub-station in the mall would take care of it. Ramon liked this job.

He saw the gas gauge was hovering over empty. The night shift usually filled the tank before Ramon took over, but they were off their schedule with the holiday and the storm. That was okay; he would drive around the main building one more time, then fuel up at the gas station on the Northeast end on the airport side of the outdoor parking lot. Ramon could get some fresh coffee. He would need it— it was a long time until five o'clock.

Chapter 63

MOA

"Outside the MOA, past the sea of parking and a vast IKEA store, sprawled the Minneapolis-St. Paul International Airport. The Lindberg and Humphrey terminals emerged from the storm like battered cities, their refugee travelers crowding every corner. The busiest holiday for air travel and the backlog from the storm meant thousands wandered through the concourses or slept on the floor. Many waited in queues for food, tickets, baggage, or loved ones. Planes swarmed the airport hive arriving and departing in the crisp morning air. Record numbers of aircraft queued nose to tail on runways shut down for hours; commuter jets darting into the sky, while their jumbo cousins lumbered into the air, bound for Amsterdam or Tokyo's Narita airport."

Excerpted from "Fallout – Surviving in a Dark New Age" by Miriam Glenn - published in the St. Paul Pioneer Press

Ghazi drove the Suburban higher and higher inside the east parking garage, circling the perimeter ramp, the rising sun flashing through the concrete pillars as she passed. At each entrance to the parking lots, the police in their bulky winter coats and neon green and orange vests waved her on, higher and higher up the structure. "How many vehicles can there be?" Ghazi asked glibly. Suli remained silent, too frightened by Ghazi's change in tone to risk upsetting her.

The rumble of a jet plane taking off from the airport startled both women, and Ghazi instinctively reached for the pistol in her jacket. She felt as much as heard the airliner roaring overhead, and when she realized it was only a plane and not a threat, she forgot the gun and forced herself to take a deep breath. The Somali woman was wringing her hands, and Ghazi saw her cheeks were wet with tears. Ghazi ignored the woman's distress and continued to follow the cars ahead, rising still higher in the ramp.

They reached the highest tier, and a policeman with a heavy face-mask and stocking cap was just ahead, waving the cars off the ramp and into the parking structure. Ghazi's heart beat faster as she approached the turn. The Suburban had tinted glass, and Ghazi hoped it would conceal the girl's body as they passed near the traffic cops.

Suli was in anguish. She wanted desperately to signal one of the policemen and escape this nightmare, but that would mean failure and perhaps losing her son forever. This girl was insane and would never believe Suli could remain silent about such a horrendous murder. She wiped the tears from her cheeks and tried to think of a way out of this.

Ghazi followed the line of cars as each made the left turn, the concrete tunnel of the ramp giving way to open air, the rising sun blaring in the dawn sky. She lowered the sun visor, her eyes watering at the sudden brightness. Ghazi hadn't seen the sun in many days. That seemed like a lifetime ago when Mohammet was alive and befriending her, thinking she was a brother in the cause. *Wasn't it just a fantasy for me?* She thought. *A lark to see if I could make it across the border? Surely none of this would actually come to be?*

* * *

Aurora braced herself as the Suburban drove into the parking ramp. Slowing for sudden turns and accelerating again jarred her wounds and tormented her with waves of pain. She could tell the sun was up as light filtered through the wool jacket in a red haze. The sounds outside the truck seemed to echo like they were driving inside a cavern, but maybe it was just her damaged hearing. She desperately wanted to shrug off the jacket and see where she was but stayed as still as possible, hoping for a miracle.

Ghazi followed the cars ahead as they began to turn into open parking slots one by one, like a rehearsed dance, so eager to reach their "Mecca" to spend, spend, spend! She and the Somali woman both leaned forward as they neared the parapet of guard rails at the end of the lot. They could see for miles beyond the parking ramp, and Ghazi realized this spot was ideal. The shopping mall would soon be packed, and the airport congested with holiday travelers. This vantage point overlooked the entire metro area, the skyline's distant spires glittering in the morning sun. She was about to thank the Somali, but a horn blared behind them, and she quickly moved over to let the cars behind them pass. After some jockeying, Ghazi backed into the last space, tight against the open railing of the parking ramp.

* * *

Rory squinted when the light filtering through the jacket suddenly became brighter; they must be out of the tunnel and in the open. The Suburban slowed to a stop, and she could hear voices outside. *They were in a public place, but where? The woman had told Ghazi she would be impressed when she saw it, but what did that mean?* A car horn sounded behind them, and the Suburban jerked forward again. Rory braced against the pain as the Suburban backed up and came to a sudden stop. The driver shifted into park, and Rory strained to hear any sounds that might signal salvation.

Suli's nerves were so taut she felt she would scream. The insane girl had pulled against the concrete of the parapet so tightly Suli wouldn't be able to open the passenger door or even crawl out if she opened the window. Suli doubted there was any righteous purpose for the girl being in this place. Suli wasn't part of the girl's plan, but she knew the Americans wouldn't see it that way. For the first time, she wished she was at her job, standing in the mindless processing line, pulling cardboard off the stamping press, and setting flattened boxes onto a table for binding.

Ghazi still held the wheel to mask the tremors in her hands. The morning sun streamed in from the passenger side, and the Somali shielded her eyes. Ghazi watched Americans opening their car doors, laughing families pouring out, the doors slamming, and the chirps of alarms as they hurried across the lot. A young couple walked in front of the truck, holding hands. They stared as they passed, likely because of Suli's hijab, but quickly turned away and joined the shoppers filtering into the mall.

Suli looked out over the parapet at the sun glinting off a thousand vehicles going to and fro in a frenzy of traffic. "Will you be going inside?" She asked in a wavering voice. "I can go with you if…"

Ghazi closed her eyes and began to hum, rocking in her seat, still gripping the wheel.

Suli frowned, the girl's actions startling her. "What are you thinking, Sister? Why are you upset? I only asked if you were going inside!"

Ghazi hummed louder and pounded a fist against her forehead.

"Stop that," Suli snapped, suddenly disgusted by the girl and her actions. "You should be ashamed of yourself!"

Ghazi opened her eyes and slowly leaned toward the Somali until their noses were almost touching. "What did you say?"

Suli instantly regretted her words. "I'm sorry, I didn't mean to upset you!"

Ghazi turned to face forward again and resumed her monotone humming, her eyes closed and a strange smile on her face.

Aurora heard Ghazi's outburst and the other women's admonition. *This is my last chance*, Rory decided, pulling the bloody jacket from her face.

Suli noticed a sudden movement behind her and gasped as a bloody face emerged from under a jacket on the backseat, a finger raised to its ruined lips, hands bound together. Suli stared speechless at the poor soul, trying to make sense of what she was seeing.

Aurora pleaded with her eyes and willed the black woman to do something. *Anything.*

"Sister, what have you done?" Suli stammered, reaching into her parka to call her husband. "Ghazi, who is this person in the back seat?"

Ghazi swung Halil's knife, ramming the blade deep into Suli's gut. The Somali woman gaped like a fish and doubled over, the pain overwhelming any instinct to fight back. Ghazi pulled out the blade and jammed the knife upward into her throat, pushing down on the back of Suli's neck, holding her firmly while she bled out onto the floor.

No! No! No! No! Aurora ducked back under the coat, trembling and breathless. The attack shook Aurora to her core. Ghazi had killed the woman without any warning, and *if I hadn't distracted her, she might have lived! Now Ghazi knows I'm alive!*

Ghazi turned and leaned over the seat, almost expecting to see the girl sitting up, staring with her ice-blue eyes, but the bloody jacket with the scorched hole and the girl's body remained as they were. Ghazi sat back down and sighed. *It was unfortunate that the Somali had noticed the girl's body, but it was ridiculous to think she could be allowed to live after she had shown such disrespect. And after all that I've been through!* Ghazi wiped the knife on the Somali woman's coat and pushed the body down onto the floor.

Ghazi took Ahmed's phone out of her pocket and held it in her lap. There were no more barriers to setting off the bomb, and a simple call would complete the mission and strike a blow for all of Islam. Ghazi pressed the power button and watched the screen flicker to life. She had a bleak hope that she would be forgiven for her deceit and find paradise, but her uncertainty was like hovering over a dark abyss.

There may be another way, a soothing chorus of voices spoke. *You were to die a martyr, but other people planned that for you.*

The voices were so familiar! Her mother and father? Mohammet and Ahmed spoke to her. I even hear my brother, Ghazi! Their whispers melded into a soft cadence, and she felt euphoric that they were here with her.

You are not known, the voices said in the same soothing tone. *You could still walk away and start over. You've done it before.* Ghazi closed her eyes and let the voices speak as though listening to music carried on the wind, her headache ebbing away. *You can become an American and thrive! It was Allah's will that the American girl and Somali woman joined us in death. They are here with us now!*

Ghazi smiled. *Yes, she could hear their whispering voices among the others!*

You must live! Whispered the chorus.

Ghazi felt tremendous relief. *The dead had enabled her to shed the past, cross the border and start a new life!*

The voices faded, and Ghazi's mind darkened again. She imagined cold fingers of bone caressing her neck, the lifeless girl just behind her, ice-blue eyes staring through the shroud of the coat into her murderer's soul. And beyond the girl was the bomb, a living thing watching Ghazi with cold cat eyes. It had a soul, and if it had a soul, it had a memory. It remembered the ones who had sacrificed their lives for this moment. The two women Ghazi killed were merely additional offerings to the monster straining to be unleashed. It was time to decide. She was drawing nearer to the abyss. Ghazi put the cell phone on the dash.

Will you disappoint us? The whispering chorus seemed urgent, accusatory.

Ghazi suddenly became angry and slammed her fists on the steering wheel. *Don't mock me! I've come too far to lose my nerve!*

There is no need for martyrdom, the voices murmured in her mind. *You can leave the bomb here and trigger it from a place of safety. Who would know to follow you? Who could trace a trail erased by fire?*

Yes, Ghazi thought. *I can serve Allah and live on to serve again. It isn't necessary to end my life!* She slipped off her seatbelt and pulled the door latch with a new purpose. The door hit a car next to the Suburban with a metallic thud, and she smiled, the euphoria returning. *I dented the car, but soon there will be no dent because there will be no car!* Leaving the door ajar, she walked around to the back of the truck, giggling at her little joke. Snow drifted into the corner of the parking stall, and she felt the familiar cold seeping through her boots. She wrenched open the double doors and let them swing wide. She saw the flat black of the sled and the rope handles polished from hours of pulling it with gloved hands.

Aurora thought her heart would explode when she heard Ghazi open the door and get out of the truck. Rory held her breath, listening to Ghazi's footsteps on the frozen ground, sure she would tear open the door, rip off the wool shroud and finish her. She listened as Ghazi went around to the back and opened the rear doors of the Suburban. Rory shivered as the icy air filled the truck, but it felt clean and fresh, washing out the stink of death.

Ghazi could barely pull herself into the back of the truck, sore from the last two days. She crawled forward and lay next to the sled, catching her breath. Raising her head, Ghazi looked to see if anyone was nearby. No one was in view, and she hooked her heel in the far rope handle like a stirrup and pushed her leg straight. *Oh, the thing is heavy!* She tried again, moving the sled half a foot each time. Soon, she was able to get behind it and shove it to the edge of the tailgate.

She considered if the fall would damage it, but there was a cushion of snow, and hadn't they tested the thing enough already? *Maybe it's a dud, and I'm starring in a comedy!* She giggled again, making one last push until the sled and its contents gently slid away and stopped in the snow at an angle, leaning against the truck. Ghazi crawled out and jumped down next to the bomb. She would have to drive forward and let the package slide away of its own accord.

Ghazi looked around again for witnesses and then had a chilling thought. *Wouldn't there be cameras everywhere?* She quickly looked up and all around. Nothing resembled a surveillance system near the Suburban. *They must have chosen this spot with care!* She got back into the truck and shifted into drive. Ghazi let her foot off the brake and felt the package fall away, the Suburban shuddering as the weight came off the back.

Ghazi quickly went around the back again and closed the rear doors, surveying the sled. It rested in a shallow crater coated with a light dusting of snow. She gave it one final look and then got back into the Suburban, slipping the cell phone off the dash and putting it back into her pocket.

Halil's knife, still painted with Suli's blood, rested on the center console. Ghazi casually slipped it behind the driver's seat, letting it fall to the floor, out of sight. Leaning over the Somali woman's corpse, she dropped the pistol into the glove compartment. There was a roadmap inside, and Ghazi took it out, spreading it across the steering wheel. She scanned the area around the mall and found the best escape route. Ghazi draped the map over the Somali woman's body and shifted into drive, accelerating across the lot towards the exit ramp, humming in a steady drone.

CHAPTER 64

FLIGHT

Aurora felt the Suburban gain speed and chanced to peek out from under the coat. They were leaving a parking ramp, a gray concrete ceiling blocking the sun. *Now, where are we going?* She wiggled her toes and saw them move in the wool socks. She turned her head to the left and spied something she couldn't believe. A wicked-looking knife lay just inches in front of her face. Aurora turned on her side and snagged the knife in her bound hands, almost rolling off the seat and falling to the floor. *That was too close- I have to be more careful!* Rory wriggled back from the edge and wedged herself against the backseat. She ignored the blood on the handle and turned the knife in her hands, desperate to cut the plastic zip tie.

Ghazi found her way out of the ramp much easier and faster than the trip to the upper level. The Suburban was one of a few vehicles leaving the mall. The euphoria returned, and a sense of relief washed over her. She increased speed and watched for the signs she knew would be coming up soon. *Find Highway 494 going east and leave the area as fast as possible!* The bomb might be found soon, and Ghazi didn't want to be caught in the area if it was. She had no idea how big the explosion would be but felt safer by the minute as the Suburban cruised away from the mall.

The sun was completely up, and she batted down the sun visor. Another jet launched from the airport and joined several others crossing overhead, their white bellies crisp against the blue sky. The deep rumble receded as it climbed, and she thought of the terror the passengers would endure if the explosion tore them from the sky. *Would they know they were going to die as they plunged to the ground, or would the plane explode and snuff them out?* It would be as Allah willed it.

299

* * *

Ramon Martinez blew on the cup of fresh coffee as he drove up the southeast ramp. He often stopped, allowing shoppers to back out of parking stalls or walk to and from the mall. Ramon looked for anyone hovering near a car up to no good. Years before, he and his brother had foolishly stolen cars over two summers back home, and no matter how fast the thief, it was easy to spot when you knew what to look for.

Ramon drove the white security SUV steadily higher in the ramp. There were five levels with wide entrances filled with cars pouring in. Bloomington police stood at the main ramps, and Ramon waved to one policewoman in a heavy coat and a face mask under her uniform trooper hat. No way to tell if she was pretty.

He reached the top tier and looked out past the IKEA store and hotels toward Richfield and the airport. He could see planes taking off and many circling to land. He knew it was the busiest day for travel as well as shopping. That and the delays from the storm made things pile up, and now that the weather was clear after such a blizzard, everything and everyone was catching up.

He sipped his coffee and drove to the end of the row. In one of the last parking spaces, wedged in a drift left by the snowplow, was a black plastic box of some sort. He stopped to look it over.

Ramon thought it might be one of those fishing huts Norte Americanos used up here and shook his head. Driving onto a frozen lake, drilling holes, and setting up a tent for a stupid fish was ridiculous to Ramon. But, just the same, those fish houses were valuable, and someone would like to take that home. It probably slid out of the back of a truck when they pulled away from the parking space. It wasn't that out of the ordinary; people left many things behind. Laptop bags that slid off the roof, pet carriers, sometimes with the shaken dog or cat still inside, and once, a baby in a car seat! There was a procedure for dealing with this type of thing, and he knew he should follow it.

He put the SUV in park and looked in the rearview mirror to see if he was blocking anyone. He leaned forward to see if there was a camera in this corner of the lot. They might have this on video and see what had happened. He couldn't see any cameras facing this corner. He reached for the radio handset but thought for a moment. To hell with it. He pulled his gloves out of his pocket and unlatched his seatbelt.

Ramon wasn't sure if this was anything serious, but he had to report it and get someone to claim it or wait to see if he should pick it up and take it to storage or straight to lost and found. He got out of the truck and stepped into the wind coming across three states and most of Canada. *Es demasiado frío* -too cold! Ramon zipped up his uniform jacket and adjusted his collar. He patted his pockets for his stocking cap but remembered he had left it at his other job.

He would check it out, *Rapidamente.* He half slid, half walked around the front of the idling SUV, and skidded over the icy concrete. Crouching down, he brushed the snow away from the black plastic, now sure it was a fishing shelter. The snow was melting on the top, and there were beads of water forming despite the frigid wind across the parking ramp.

Ramon leaned down, putting one gloved hand over his ear against the wind, and tried to lift it by the rope loop. *Madre Dios, the thing was heavy!* He slipped and skidded his way back to the SUV and keyed his radio. Ramon didn't mention the "B" word because he didn't think it could be a bomb. It seemed a long way to the store that anchored the northeast corner of MOA, and if it were a bomb, it wouldn't do much damage in the parking lot.

He also knew this could turn into *a grande situation* emergency plan fiasco with Ramon in the middle. He didn't want to cause problems on the busiest day of the year, but his training required reporting it immediately, no matter how *insignificante.* So Ramon decided he would just have to wade through the *las tonterías* and get someone senior to check it out. He wished he'd just kicked snow on it and kept driving.

* * *

Ghazi merged onto Highway 494, heading east. It was the fastest route away from the blast and led straight out of the metro area. She would have to dispose of the bodies, but that could wait. The bomb was her insurance. *Once it explodes, I'll be a needle in a haystack!*

The whispering voices echoed in her head again. *You are driving with two dead bodies!* There was an urgency in their tone she didn't expect. *How will you be rid of them?*

"What does it matter?" Ghazi said aloud, "The Americans will investigate, but assume I died along with everyone else and quit looking!" The voices in her mind became shrill. *The Americans are already looking for you! You must abandon this vehicle soon!*

Ghazi hadn't considered that she might already be in the crosshairs. The voices would surely know, observing her from the afterlife. "Let me explain," Ghazi whispered aloud. "Anyone looking for me will soon be dust! I only need to go a few more miles. Just a little more distance and I promise I'll use the phone!"

Aurora became more alarmed at Ghazi's ranting. She was having some sort of breakdown, and that meant she was liable to do anything. *Ghazi could drive into a concrete wall and take me with her!* Aurora sawed at the stiff plastic tie, her hands cramping up to where she could barely put pressure on the blade. The Suburban hit a bump, and the blade nicked her arm, the cut beading with blood. Tears of frustration welled in her eyes, but she adjusted the knife in her grip and began again.

The road began to curve, and Ghazi followed along with vehicles of all colors and sizes. A small bus was ahead, and a semi-truck was passing on her right. The highway was covered with dirty slush and each passing car kicked up road salt in a mist that collected on the windshield. Ghazi turned on the wipers, pressing the button to spray washer fluid to clean the glass. It was smearing badly, and she felt the first stirring of panic. The highway continued to curve, and Ghazi gripped the wheel tighter, trying to hold her lane and see through the gray haze of the windshield. The road straightened, and Ghazi was driving directly into the sun, the smeared glass turning to solid silver, and she lost the highway in the glare.

Ghazi lowered the side window, leaning out to see ahead. In the side mirror, she saw a maroon and gold Minnesota Highway Patrol cruiser appear in the left lane just a few car lengths back. *"This can't be happening!"* She whispered to herself. Her heart raced, and Ghazi began to sweat, her stomach knotted with tension. Looking through the windshield was useless, and she took her foot off the gas pedal, slowing the Suburban as she clenched her jaw and gripped the wheel.

"Come on…Come on!" Ghazi whispered, hoping the patrol car would continue past. She fumbled again with the washer fluid knob and held it down. The pump whined, and just as Ghazi was about to let up, a spray of fluid shot unevenly across the windshield, and the wipers smeared the grime aside. She could see again! Ghazi almost cried with relief, wiping cold sweat from her upper lip. She looked in the side mirror again, and the cop was still there, using a microphone clipped to his collar. He seemed distracted by some other errand, and Ghazi relaxed her grip on the wheel, relieved he wasn't paying attention to her.

Rory chipped at the zip-tie with the knife, wearing it away with agonizing slowness. It seemed to be working, but her wrists were raw, and it was excruciating to keep pressure on the blade. *What will I do when my hands are loose?* She tried not to think of anything beyond freeing herself.

Ghazi was approaching the South Roberts Street exit. She thought of turning off and leaving the patrol car behind, but she didn't want to abandon the highway. As if reading her thoughts, the patrolman triggered his lights and siren, motioning for Ghazi to pull over, swinging in behind the Suburban.

Aurora stopped sawing at the plastic tie when the siren sounded. *It was right behind them! She had to signal for help!* She let the knife drop onto her chest and waved her bound hands in the window above her head.

Ghazi was stunned. *What have I done to cause the patrolman to come after me?* The Suburban was in the far right lane, blocked by a solid line of cars to her left continuing east. *This is the wrong lane!* Ghazi bit her lower lip and began to hum again, holding her speed as the routes split off from the looming exit. There was an opening to her left, and she began to merge into the lane, but a white delivery van cut into the gap to avoid the patrol car, and she was trapped.

Ghazi overcorrected, speeding up to take the exit, and didn't see a Volkswagen Jetta to her right. She brushed the side of the car and cried out, pulling back on the wheel, the Suburban swerving dangerously.

Ghazi was frantic. *I need to get on the other side of this overpass and trigger the bomb!* Whether it was far enough away made no difference now. *Make a move!* The exit ramp was upon her, and she pulled hard to the right, punching the accelerator to gain distance from the patrol car.

Aurora frantically waved her arms above her head, daring to hope the police car would overtake them. Ghazi's driving became more erratic, and when she hit the car next to them, Rory knew it was only a matter of time. *I just have to stay alive until the highway patrol catches us!*

Ghazi could only see flashing red and blue lights in the rear window and knew the patrol car was too close to evade. She thought of the cell phone and its single number waiting to trigger the bomb.

You were foolish to put the phone back in your pocket! The voices seemed to be laughing at her. Ghazi became angry and smashed her foot on the gas pedal, accelerating up the ramp.

The damaged Jetta pulled onto the exit ramp and immediately became stuck into the snow piled along the shoulder. The Suburban was still gaining speed, and Ghazi kept her foot pressed on the accelerator, desperate to put the ramp between her and the explosion.

The Jetta's driver began to get out to survey the damage, but the Suburban slammed into the door, ripping it off and flinging it across the ramp in a shower of orange sparks and broken glass.

Ghazi swerved hard to avoid the crumpled car door in the middle of the ramp but overcorrected, and the Suburban slued into a horrible skid. Ghazi's world seemed to slow in time, prolonging each disastrous second. The trooper's siren was a constant shriek as the Suburban yawed sideways, the back end nearly rising off the road. Ghazi watched helplessly as the truck hurtled toward the cross-traffic moving along the Roberts Street overpass ahead, the commuters blind to the juggernaut that was about to launch into their path. The Suburban spun faster and harder, heading for the roadside as they roared up the ramp. Ghazi screamed and fought the skid, straightening the truck too late, the back wheels catching the shoulder and slinging the front into the dirty roadside like a jackknife snapping shut, an explosion of snow spattering down like hail.

Ghazi sat stunned for a moment as the engine stalled. She trembled with adrenaline and tried to restart the truck. *The bomb will take care of everything if I can just get to shelter on the other side of the overpass!*

Aurora was thrown off the seat onto the floor when the truck began its skid on the exit ramp. The siren's wail made Aurora's head throb, and she lay on her back panting, feeling as though an enormous bell echoed in her brain. Her vision blurred with sudden vertigo, and Aurora rubbed her eyes, willing her vision to come back into focus. She suddenly realized her hands were free. *The crash must have broken the zip tie!*

She rolled onto her belly and pushed up from the floor, pulling her legs under her. She found the knife, gripping it tightly as she rose to her knees.

Ghazi violently twisted the ignition key, trying to start the truck, but it was no use. *This is the moment!* The voices shouted. *You must act—The police are on top of you!*

There would be no more running and no more future. Ghazi's thoughts collapsed into the reality of the moment. She tried to spot the patrolman in the side mirrors, but he wasn't visible. Ghazi reached up and twisted the rearview mirror to scan behind her and gasped at a vision from hell.

The dead girl's face was a nightmare of blue-black bruises, and her clenched teeth showed through a ruined cheek. Her matted blonde hair was red with gore above eyes staring through a mask of blood, wide and fierce with hate.

Ghazi opened her mouth in surprise. "You're alive?"

In that horrible second, the girl's crystal blue eyes fixed on Ghazi's reflection with deadly purpose.

Aurora attacked.

Ghazi instinctively ducked forward, covering the back of her neck. Aurora brought the knife down hard, and the blade tore into Ghazi's shoulder, sending a shudder up Aurora's arm and causing Ghazi to cry out in pain. Ghazi rolled to her left and pressed hard against the driver's door, the knife pulling free as she dodged. Aurora drew back and gripped the knife in both hands, unsteady on her week knees, kneeling and lunging over the seat. She swung down again and smashed the knife back into Ghazi's shoulder, the blade finding its mark but deflecting on bone, traveling down her arm until it tore free at the elbow and lodged in the leather seat.

Ghazi screamed in pain and surprise. *How can this be?*

Aurora tried to pull the knife free, but it was deep in the seat cushion, and she struggled to work it loose.

Ghazi leaned forward, trying to pull the cell phone out of her pocket, groping with her left hand, her right arm useless at her side. Blood poured from her sleeve and dripped on the seat as she finally tugged the cell phone out of her jeans.

She was severely injured and knew this was her last chance to trigger the bomb. *Concentrate—This is your test of faith!* She remembered their great purpose, the sacrifices made and the journey to America, and all the killing that led to this moment.

The bomb is the key to everything! The voices screeched. *It will sanctify your actions and even the score for all of us!* The whispering didn't matter now. There was only the bomb and trigger in Ghazi's hand.

She powered up the phone as Aurora freed the knife from the seat.

* * *

As Ramon Martinez waited for direction from his supervisor, one of the mall's maintenance trucks pulled up behind his SUV. Ramone sighed and got out. Walking back to speak with the driver, Ramon explained the situation, and both he and the guy from maintenance went over to the black box resting next to the rail of the parking ramp.

The maintenance guy pulled up his collar and kicked the sled with his foot. "It's a portable fish house."

Ramon nodded, squinting against the wind. "Si. Yes, but what do we do with it?" Ramon was cold again and wanted to get going.

The maintenance guy shrugged. "I guess we'll put it in my truck and take it down to lost and found."

* * *

Aurora wrenched the knife free and brought it up again for another blow. Ghazi struggled to pull away, holding something in her left hand. Rory tried to hold her back, ready to duck away if she saw Ghazi's pistol, but it was only a cell phone. Ghazi was desperately pressing the buttons with the thumb of her left hand. The LCD screen came alive, and Aurora was confused. *Why is she making a call instead of fighting for her life? Wait....The thing she shoved out of the truck and her ranting! She must have planted a bomb, and this phone will set it off!*

Aurora tried to reach over the seat and grab the phone, but Ghazi held it away, using her thumb to move the cursor to the single phone number stored in the menu. Aurora fought to get leverage, but her injured leg buckled, and she couldn't hold on. Aurora made another desperate lunge but failed to knock the phone out of Ghazi's hand.

There was only one way to stop her! Aurora reached around the girl's neck and pinned her back against the headrest, slashing down with the knife. Ghazi screamed in surprise, but Aurora's effort was too weak, and the blade didn't penetrate Ghazi's jacket.

Ghazi struggled to breathe. "Allahu Akbar," she whispered, trying to pry Aurora's arm away from her throat and make the call with only one hand. "Allahu Akbar....*Allahu Akbar!* Ghazi whispered over and over.

Aurora watched in horror as the cursor hovered over the phone number, and Ghazi pressed SEND. Aurora made a fist, weakly smashing the side of Ghazi's head, and bit her ear, trying desperately to distract her. Ghazi continued the chant, holding the phone at arm's length, her words louder and more insistent: *"Allahu Akbar...Allahu Akbar!"*

The trooper approached the Suburban and saw two figures struggling inside. He drew his pistol and called for backup.

Aurora and Ghazi knew nothing but the struggle for the cell phone. Ghazi pressed the SEND button, again and again, shouting in a frantic cadence, *"ALLAHU AKBAR! ALLAHU AKBAR!"*

Aurora's strength was ebbing away, but with one last effort, she brought both hands around Ghazi, locked her wrists, and pulled with all her might, the blade finding its mark, sliding deep into the base of

Ghazi's throat. Ghazi's breath left her with the searing pain of the knife, and her vision darkened. She couldn't speak, watching the phone slip from her grasp and fall to her lap, the bright screen showing one word; CONNECTING...

The trooper pulled open the door, his gun at the ready, but nothing could have prepared him for the nightmare inside. The driver slumped over the wheel, a hunting knife buried in her throat, while a frightening creature hunched over the body, its face a ruin of blood and gore. The trooper waivered with one hand on the door and didn't notice the cell phone as it slid off Ghazi's knees and onto the floor next to Suli's body.

"No!" Aurora cried in a voice filled with sorrow. She gave the knife a final tug and felt the girl's muscles relax in death, slumping forward against Aurora's embrace.

The trooper lowered his pistol. "Aurora! Let go of the knife! You're safe now!"

Aurora didn't hear the trooper, only thinking of the cell phone connecting with a bomb Ghazi had placed somewhere in the city.

After all of the sacrifices we made to stop them, how did I let the bad guys win?

* * *

Ramon followed the maintenance man over to the fish house, glancing across Highway 494, jet planes glittering in the rising sun in the sky over the airport. His wife will laugh at him tonight when he tells her about the great crisis.

But she would never see him again.

Ramon stooped to help the maintenance man lift the fish house and heard what sounded like a cell phone ringing inside. He frowned, and as he tilted his head to hear over the wind, there was a muffled click, and the air around Ramon Martinez went white and black at the same time.

* * *

The trooper gripped Aurora's shoulder, trying to let her know she was safe. "Aurora, let go of the knife!" Aurora slowly relaxed her grip and fell back onto the seat, defeated. The trooper was surveying Aurora's injuries when a blinding flash startled him.

In another millisecond, their surroundings lost all color and definition save for the darkest of shadows in the purity of the whitest light imaginable.

The inside of the Suburban glowed, and the trooper staggered back, feeling as much as seeing the light burning around him. Then the shock wave struck, the nuclear blast knocking him off his feet and causing him to tumble along the ramp until he came to rest in the center of the road.

Aurora shut her eyes tight against the blue-white light, but the brilliant afterimage remained. As Aurora rubbed her eyes, trying to regain her sight, the vehicle shuddered and jerked forward as the blast washed over the truck. Aurora was whipped backward and then headfirst into the front seat when the Suburban came to a stop. She crumpled to the floor, moaning in pain.

The trooper staggered to his feet, feeling faint and struggling to stay conscious in the miasma of air that seemed too solid to breathe. A wave of nearly unbearable heat washed over him on the roadway with the sickening smell of ozone and burnt earth lingering in the wind. Aurora and the chase were forgotten when he became aware of the hundreds of cars littering the highway, disgorging their wailing passengers in stumbling groups dazed by the nuclear flash or hobbled by injuries. Some limped from car to car, trying to help whoever they could, while the staccato blasts of ruptured gas lines and exploding electrical transformers sounded like gunfire accompanied by the low rumble of collapsing buildings to the west.

A deafening roar overhead made him duck instinctively as a destroyed airliner blotted out the sun above the overpass, the fuselage and tail in flames, oily black smoke roiling in its wake. He watched it do a slow roll upside down, then plunge into the ground beyond his vision, a gigantic fireball blossoming upon impact.

He shook his head to clear it. *Why am I here? There was an accident, and I drew my weapon… The Amber Alert and the Chevy Suburban!* He realized with horror that his pistol was gone and spun around in a panic, hoping he wasn't staring down its barrel. He froze in place, witnessing a terrible vista he would never forget.

An angry red and gray cloud was spewing upwards like a dirty geyser, towering over the land like a god made of fire. It was as though the sky collapsed on itself in a display of madness made visible. The dawn sun reflected in blood red, and a nimbus of impossible color and brilliance played through the mushroom cloud. The trooper watched in helpless awe as it rose thousands of feet into the sky, born by the heat of a hundred suns, the dirty brown at its base fading to a bright white at its peak, moving outward in a hellish corona. Now he understood what had happened.

"Dear Lord," He whispered. His legs weakened, and he fell to his knees, tears rolling down his burned cheeks as he shook with fear and despair.

Aurora was in agony and trying to stay conscious. The air was like the sickening vapor from an arcing wire, and her chest ached just trying to breathe. She clawed her way upright and saw the trooper on his knees on the ramp ahead, staring into the sky.

Aurora opened the rear door of the Suburban and spilled out onto the pavement. Her chin impacted the icy road, and she struggled to remain conscious, enduring fresh waves of pain. Aurora rolled onto her side, crawling across the pavement as best she could, wanting only to get away from the truck and beg the patrolman to take her to a hospital.

The trooper seemed to be in a daze but slowly noticed her when their eyes met. Aurora tried to form words with her ruined mouth, but she could only extend her hand toward him in an unspoken appeal.

The trooper rose and began to stagger toward Aurora as she closed her eyes and fell into blissful unconsciousness.

CHAPTER 65

AFTERMATH

"The world now knows about the terrible ordeal of Aurora Winter and her family. What is not known is how a small cadre of terrorists could pull off such a massive attack on the most powerful nation on earth. They were self-funded and not affiliated with any state sponsor, named terror group, or political movement. Sadly, the simplicity of their plot and the limited scope of their communications left intelligence agencies one step behind.

Possibly it's too soon after the event to be definitive, but our actions before and after are disturbingly like September 11th and we seem to be reliving a terrible nightmare. Aurora Winter and the terror cell led by Ahmed Abu Sharim were players in the final act, but the stage was set long before, produced by cultures clashing over the soul of the free world.

The morning of November twenty-ninth, 148,568 individuals fell. There are easily ten times that amount injured in the blast, and everyone is aware of the grisly death notices that continue to mount daily. Already we have lost more Americans from this single event than Vietnam and the Korean conflict, but the final count may never be realized. In a nuclear conflagration, generations are affected, and the cost of this attack will echo long into the future.

Of the 148,568, it is estimated that over 96,000 died in the initial blast. Their hearts didn't just stop beating; they ceased to exist. It took less than a second for 96,000 minds to cease thinking, for their bodies to vaporize, for their very beings to be erased. For the 96,000, there is no physical trace to mourn, no body to be laid to rest. Not knowing is the hardest, and closure is elusive for many loved ones who continue living with grief. The bomb did not discriminate, and the dead include all races, ethnicities, and religions. Time will tell if the incident will bring us closer as Americans or further tear our society into tribal factions.

Now we debate the differences between restraint and cowardice, prudent response, and effective retaliation. The President will address the nation in a televised ceremony to honor the fallen at Arlington National Cemetery this Friday. The world will be watching."

Excerpted from "Fallout – Surviving in a Dark New Age" by Miriam Glenn - published in the St. Paul Pioneer Press

EPILOGUE

It was a bright April morning at Arlington National Cemetery.

Aurora and Jordan sat in the back of a black Towncar parked along one of the service roads to the South of the Memorial Amphitheater. Aurora's iPhone and earbuds were on her lap, but she was tired of noise and words, and the quiet backseat with tinted windows was a welcome respite from the ceremony. The crowd had dispersed, and there weren't as many people on the walkways and milling around the plaza. Aurora looked out over the rolling green expanse with the rows of crisp white tombstones. It was so beautiful yet terrible at the same time.

She glanced at Jordan, trying to make eye contact, but he was lost in his thoughts of his own. Her cousin was red-eyed and worn out from the stress they'd endured.

Jordan was self-conscious about his missing hand and hadn't been fitted with a prosthesis. It was too soon physically, and he wasn't ready to move on just yet. She guessed he wanted to be with her instead of his mother or any of the family.

Aurora knew she and Jordan had shared something no one else could understand. Aurora caught her reflection in one of the side mirrors and looked away. She wasn't used to the puckered scar around her right cheek and jaw, the lines of the initial plastic surgery still pink and sensitive. She had dusted on foundation and took extra care, but the dimpled skin cra-tered in, and she often put her hand to the side of her face or pulled her hair forward when she spoke to anyone. She had new front teeth im-plants, but she didn't often smile anymore, so maybe it didn't matter.

Her cane rested on the seat next to her purse. It was as fashionable as a cane could be, wrapped in a printed field of sunflowers. She needed it less and less, but it was too early to trust walking without it. The Achilles tendon had been cut, not torn, and the delay between the injury and the repair was too long for a rapid recovery. Even more troubling was the trauma to her inner ear from the bullet wound meant to kill her. It affected her balance, and the doctors were still observing her for neurologic damage. Her physical therapy was getting easier, but it was still a daily struggle.

Aurora and Jordan were both very aware of their scars and how it made everyone uncomfortable to be around them. It was comfortable with Jordan because they didn't need to talk about the events that changed their lives without anyone asking questions or trying to console them. They could hold their grief and ordeal close until time could catch up, and their memories dulled until life was bearable and they dared to think about something more. For now, there was a dark curtain just ahead, and the future was something unplanned they stepped into day by day.

Aurora glanced at the driver in the front seat. He was some sort of government security guy, but she wasn't sure if he was Secret Service or a rent-a-cop. The man just looked forward out of the windshield at some spot in the distance, his eyes covered with wraparound sunglasses. He sensed that Aurora and Jordan didn't want to talk, and his silence was gratifying.

Aurora thought about the ceremony. She gave a very brief eulogy for Grandpa Axe, and though many praised her, she felt she should have done a better job. It probably didn't matter because the President gave his speech right after, and that's what people wanted to hear. She didn't remember most of it. She thought it went on too long, and he was too much of a politician. She knew he didn't write it because his speechwriter, a woman with a gray flannel suit, bad hair, and too little makeup, had come by the Hyatt hotel when Aurora had checked in the day before to "get her take on things." Aurora told her story to the woman and tried to answer blatantly partisan questions without losing her temper. Aurora was disappointed to see the writer's expensive pen merely hover above a cheap steno pad without taking any notes. Aurora realized the story was written already, and the speech would only reflect the administration's spin.

The woman's words, spoken by the President, focused on key terms like sacrifice, rebuilding, and hope. The President said, reading from his teleprompter, "Their efforts were courageous, inflicting a heavy toll on the attackers, holding a line unseen but marked with their blood and America's loss of innocence." Aurora felt the speechwriter was shooting for a job in Hollywood.

Aurora sat in the front row with Jordan and the remnants of her family. Her mother and a new boyfriend were relegated to the row behind them. That was okay. Aurora guessed there was too much distance between her and her mother to bridge easily, and she didn't have the strength to work at it. At least not right now.

Vanessa Whitebird, the Native American girl she gave the wallet to, was there with her grandmother. Too late, the wallet found its way into the hands of the FBI, who issued an Amber Alert about the time Suli Omar took her last breath. The state trooper who witnessed Ghazi's death and rescued Aurora was there too, looking pale and haggard. She guessed maybe they all did. It had been a very long, harrowing winter.

The President awarded several citations during the ceremony. He gave Aurora and Jordan the Medal of Freedom. Kurt, Philip, and Marty received theirs posthumously, and Grandpa Axe was awarded the Medal of Honor. They told Aurora that he earned it between his service in Vietnam and dying to protect his country decades later.

Aurora was struggling with the praise she received that morning. It was in such contrast to the criticism and schadenfreude the world media had enjoyed at her expense. Interviews and panel discussions often twisted her role in the tragedy, alluding to her failure to stop Ghazi and maybe even a reluctance even to try. Many found her circumstance fascinating and fertile ground to plant their own daydreams. In them, they would have easily overcome Ghazi, defused the bomb, and saved the day.

For others, there was contempt for Aurora, spawning rumors of her complicity in the plot or having a secret affair with Ghazi. It seemed every special interest group had stepped up to carve off a piece of Aurora's story to "shed light on their cause" or their perennial favorite: "raise awareness." Ghazi had a Facebook page and a loyal following which wasn't bad considering she was dead.

Aurora bore it all stoically, merely answering the questions truthfully and without embellishment. Avoiding the ambush interviews when she could, but trying to be available to tell her story and let everyone know about the special people who had died in the latest skirmish in the newly accelerated war on terror. The ones whose deaths were soon eclipsed by the thousands killed by the bomb.

Anyone at ground zero ceased to be. Anyone behind concrete or a sturdy structure within the first mile died the next day or maybe the day after, but no more. The rings of devastation (a term virtually all news networks quickly adopted) were consistently used in a rifle target image with its bullseye centered on the Mall of America. The rings radiated out like ripples in a pond and represented the death toll from the "Twin Cities Bomb," or the "Minnesota Attack." The fact that the deaths were premeditated murder and carried out by a quasi-Islamic terror group fell away from the main story at some point. Now it was sliding into a politically correct slot somewhere between a school shooting and a destructive hurricane. It also happened in flyover territory, meaning it was less of a disaster for the media and elites in Washington and New York.

In listening to the daily chatter of the political class, there was a collective sigh of relief, knowing that Saeed Alghamdi would have been flying east with the bomb in his Cessna.

The elites knew it could have been their charred shadows burned onto concrete in Manhattan or Chevy Chase instead of some hockey mom flashed in silhouette on a Bloomington Wal-Mart.

Aurora noticed a gray-haired man in an elegant dark suit approaching from the Plaza area. He seemed to make eye contact with Aurora despite the tinted glass and walked toward the town car with an easy stride, one hand in his pocket, and a steady manner that radiated confidence and power. The driver or guard rolled down the window well before the man arrived at the vehicle. As the man neared, he smiled professionally at the driver and leaned in with his hand on the driver's shoulder, speaking very quietly in his ear. The man must have been a big shot because the driver nodded and popped the lock on Aurora's side of the car.

She pulled back a little, not sure what this was all about. The man opened the car door gently like one might enter a hospital room. He stood on the grass of the boulevard and leaned in tentatively. He met Aurora's eyes and smiled. "Hello, Aurora. My name is Preston Royce."

He didn't make an effort to get into the car and or extend his hand; he just continued to smile. Aurora nodded slightly, and his smile widened. The man looked over to Jordan. "Hello, Jordan, It is truly a pleasure to meet both of you."

Neither replied.

"Aurora," Royce said in a smooth voice with just a hint of New York, "may I speak with you for a moment in private? I promise it won't take long." He moved back to let her get out of the car, watching her pensively as she hesitated, then grinning when she expertly wielded her cane and smoothly got out of the Towncar.

Aurora turned and tossed her iPhone to Jordan. "I'll be right back. Listen to some music if you want." Royce gently closed the door behind her and nodded to the driver. He began walking slowly in the direction of the Tomb of the Unknowns and politely waited with his hands in his pockets while Aurora caught up. She moved to his right, shielding him from the damaged side of her face. They fell into step together and began walking the footpath near the Memorial Amphitheater. The trees were newly leafed and sun-dappled along the path as they strolled past Romanesque columns and multitudes of headstones radiating from the plaza down the soft green hills.

Aurora didn't speak, hoping this didn't turn into some sort of mild interrogation. Royce didn't look the type to shake her down, but she was ready for him if he did. She noticed that no media people were in sight. No Paparazzi or Washington media with the disheveled preppie look they tried so hard to cultivate. She realized this guy must have some creds to make the parasites disappear.

"It is a beautiful day, Aurora. I'm very sorry for your loss and the trouble that found you, but I'm glad we have this chance to talk and get to know each other a little."

Aurora matched the man's leisurely pace, perfect for a casual conversation on a spring morning. "I'm not trying to be impatient or rude, but what do you want, Mr. Royce?"

"You're not rude, just direct," Royce replied with a smooth voice. "I want to see what you're all about, Aurora. I know a great deal about you and your experiences, but I wanted to talk to you directly."

"To see what I'm all about," Aurora replied. "Sounds like the speechwriter they sent to get my take on things the other night."

"You're popular," he replied. He sensed Aurora's wariness and changed the subject. "I was stationed in Minnesota for two years back in the '80s. Do you plan to stay in Minnesota after you graduate?" He turned slightly to watch her answer the question.

"What do you mean stationed? Were you in the military or something?"

He smiled again and looked into the distance. Aurora answered his question with a question. It was good that she wasn't intimidated to make an automatic reply. "No, I was FBI in St. Paul."

"So you're with the FBI?" This was another interrogation, just a different approach.

"No, not for many years," he replied. "I'm not officially with anyone right now. I guess you could say I'm a talent scout for the right people."

Aurora frowned and watched the cracks in the footpath as they walked along. "The 'right people,' meaning the candidates or the people you represent?"

Royce smiled. "I asked if you would stay in Minnesota after you graduate."

Aurora let it go. "I've had offers from several schools, but I haven't thought much about it since last November. I suppose I could go to U of M, but I'm thinking about someplace away from there. I don't have much to keep me there now, and for that matter, I don't know if school is the answer. I've thought about the Marine Corps or maybe the Army." She stole a glance at Royce, but he was impassive.

"What would you want to pursue if you did go into the military?" Royce's question was refreshing in that he didn't instantly reject the military option.

"Whatever will protect me in every way; physically, emotionally, and financially. I never want to be helpless again, Mr. Royce." She didn't look for his reaction this time.

Royce stopped and turned toward her. "I think that's the most profound thing I've ever heard from someone your age, Aurora. I know you'll do well, but I think we should discuss your future from a more pragmatic viewpoint. Would you consider being part of something larger? Something that will make a real difference?"

She faced him and took off her sunglasses. "What, and make the world a better place? Should I wish for world peace? As you can see, I'm not a beauty queen, and I don't think like one either." She looked away and unconsciously touched her scarred cheek. "Part of being safe from harm is not being anyone's fool. I'm not sure I can help you, Mr. Royce."

Royce said nothing, merely began walking again, knowing that Aurora would follow.

"Aurora, I've studied you professionally, and you won't believe me, but I might know more about you than you do. I know what you're likely going to do in the next five hours, five days, and five years. I understand your personality, and I know your weaknesses, and most importantly, your strengths. It isn't magic, and it isn't good or bad, but I am accurate, and it's what I do. I want you to work with me."

"Join your team, you mean?" She allowed herself to smirk. "I'm being recruited for what organization, exactly?"

Royce stopped and shaded his eyes, looking at the rows of tombstones. "Look at them, Aurora," he said, making a sweeping gesture with his arm. "Single headstones stretching into the distance until they melt into each other in a single blurred white line of sacrifice." Aurora looked across the field of graves and followed each row to its vanishing point below the skyline of Washington. Royce turned to her. "A line of sacrifice that points to that city of fools across the Potomac. Not recruited, Aurora. More like groomed for more."

"And what is this going to demand of me?" She asked, meeting his eyes. "There's no free lunch Mr. Royce."

"First, call me Preston, and second, you're right. There is no free lunch. But sometimes a meal is worth paying for."

She thought for a moment then replied, "I think you have the wrong person, Mr. Royce. I'm damaged goods and probably not worth your effort."

"I'm sorry you feel that way. You did the right thing at every turn. You didn't shrink from danger, and you stubbornly stayed in the fight to the end, and you survived. The bomb was beyond your knowledge."

"Haven't you heard, Mr. Royce? I was the very last line of defense. I was the one that didn't stop that looney toon from turning half of Minnesota into a wasteland. I couldn't prevent them from getting a nuke, and I didn't allow a bunch of thugs to enter the country and kill my family, but I get my share of the blame!

"Yes, I fought back, Mr. Royce. I fought back hard, but it wasn't enough. In the end, it all came down to me, Aurora Winter. I dropped the ball, and thousands died. 'Why didn't you talk some sense into that crazy bitch? Why didn't you drive her off the road and into the ditch? Why didn't you set off the bomb in the wilderness and save the big city? I am the latest excuse in a long line of scapegoats, Mr. Royce, and I don't deserve it."

Royce looked away from Aurora as they walked. To her, he seemed lost for words or embarrassed by her outburst. When he spoke, he sounded different, less formal, with no trace of sympathy. "You've thought about this a lot, haven't you?"

She bristled at his change in tone. She looked at the white skyline of Washington DC, shimmering like a mirage above the green horizon. "Mr. Royce, I've had plenty of time to think about this. I've had time to view damn near every one of the 2.6 million hits that come up when you google my name, most of them negative, and I've had enough face time with would-be biographers wanting to tell my story that I have a good handle on what's real and what's fiction.

"Today I was standing in the center ring of a shitty little circus while politicians stood on the bodies of my dead family and crowed about patriotism and sacrifice. In short, Mr. Royce, I feel pretty underappreciated, and it pains me to talk to you about it. Do you get it now?" Her heart was beating faster, and she felt out of breath. "If you're looking for a hero, Mr. Royce, it isn't me. I'm tainted. I didn't defuse the bomb, and I didn't save anyone. I'm just a stupid, stupid girl who was tested and found wanting. So they can all go fuck themselves as far as I'm concerned!"

Royce didn't reply, but a park bench came into view, and he gently touched her arm.

"Aurora, let's sit down for a while."

She hesitated, then followed him and sat down heavily on the end of the bench. He stood for a moment with his hands in his pockets, considering her. After a moment, he sighed and sat down next to her. He leaned forward with his hands clasped, elbows on his knees. He gave her some time to calm down and then turned his head to look at her. "Aurora...."

"I'm sorry," Aurora began.

"Stop," he said quickly. "I like the Aurora who isn't sorry." He put his hand gently on her shoulder. "Everything you've told me is true and heartfelt, and that means you're the real deal. Let me tell you a story," Royce began. "My father was a bricklayer in Queens, and he taught me never to look back. He had setbacks, but he never quit. He told me many times that he tried to hit all the hard spots so my sister and I wouldn't have to." Royce smiled at that, and Aurora thought Royce had probably hit a few bumps in the road himself.

"He's been gone for over twenty years, Aurora, but there are many things I remember him telling me, things that come out at just the right time."

Aurora listened as Royce continued.

"He and I would do a chimney and fireplace occasionally, and one time, this couple in Belle Harbor wanted this big fireplace with a big chimney which meant lots of work for my dad and me. Belle Harbor was a big deal neighborhood, and my dad took his time splitting the stones and working out from the center, mirroring the rock until it reached the sides and weaving around the corners. We worked many days on that job, and at its end, I remember hauling the last of our tools out to the van and my dad talking to the homeowner. She wasn't paying him as agreed and told us her husband was away on business, but the check would be in the mail. My father took a lot of pride in his work, but he didn't make a scene over money. He just told her that the fireplace wouldn't work until she paid. I thought dad was just giving her the needle, but he knew she was one of those people who needed to experience things firsthand before things sink in, so we left without a check.

Aurora stopped worrying about her outburst and began to listen intently, curious now.

Royce leaned back and crossed his legs. "So sure enough, that October, when their house was done, these uppity types decided to have a party and show off that big stone fireplace. About a minute after they lit their fire, the whole place filled with smoke!" Royce smiled at the memory. "It was probably so dark the day maid couldn't find the silverware! Next, they speed-dialed my dad. I happened to be in the kitchen when they called, and when they screamed at him over the phone, he didn't laugh or give them a hard time. Dad just said if they wanted their fireplace to work, they could pay him, and he'd make it happen.

They must have offered cash because the old man and I went over there that evening with an extension ladder and got their fireplace working. We got into the van after he'd helped them air out the place and made sure they weren't too angry, and on the way back, I asked him how he'd pulled that off. He told me he always cemented a clean plate of glass about halfway up the chimney, and when Dad got paid, he dropped a brick down the chimney and smashed the glass. If they didn't pay, the glass stayed, and the smoke backed up into the house." Royce smiled wistfully and looked at Aurora. "That was an elegant solution, Aurora. You pay. It works. You don't, it doesn't, and if you try to get around it, you won't even see what's blocking the way!"

Aurora didn't react, but Royce could tell she was still with him.

"I'm all about winning, Aurora, and you've been tested and had a bad outcome. That means you're angry and hurting and hungry for payback. On top of that, you're smart and see things the way they are."

"So what?" Aurora thought the story was interesting but didn't see where this was going. "Just cut to the point, Mr. Royce."

"The point is I want you for my group, and I know you will want to join us, but I need to let you come to that conclusion. I don't have time to do a sales job on you, Aurora, and I don't think I would be able to anyway. You're past that now, and I can only hope that you'll see where I'm going."

Aurora said nothing, just looked at the rows of tombstones.

"But that's not the end of my story," Royce said, looking into the distance again. "The crash of Flight 587 destroyed the house with the chimney in Belle Harbor soon after September 11th. That house and that chimney aren't there anymore. That was the incident that brought me into the fray."

Aurora frowned. "Not 9/11?"

"I was in the business, but I was visiting my daughter at her school when the planes went into the Trade Center. My first real blooding was flight 587. The official NTSB report came back pilot error, but let's just say I took care of the actual cause. It's a smaller world now, Aurora. You know that because people from the other side of the earth changed your life forever. I am telling you now that you can have the opportunity to change lives on the other side of the world and some much closer. Most for the better, but the ones you can't change, you will end."

Royce stood up and held out his hand to Aurora.

She looked into his eyes and saw something there that made her disregard her pride and take his hand. Royce gently pulled her to her feet, and they started back to where they first met.

They didn't speak for most of the way back to the car. They didn't need to.

When they came around to the south side of the amphitheater, they could see Jordan standing next to the town car, speaking with his mother and the driver.

"Mr. Royce, what exactly do you want me to do?"

"Graduate high school," Royce replied. "Be a kid. Do whatever you want for a while. After that, the military isn't a bad place to get your bearings."

"Then?" Aurora asked, knowing there was something more.

"Then," Royce said, not unkindly, "I want you to take a full scholarship to a school we agree on; we'll talk line of study later, and then join me in the big game." Royce stopped walking. "This is where I leave you, Aurora," he said, handing her a plain white business card. "Don't lose it because you won't be able to Google me," he said with a smile. "We'll talk again, I'm sure."

Aurora looked at the card and saw only his name and a phone number in black type.

She glanced up and saw he was already halfway back to the memorial, walking at the same leisurely pace. He didn't look back.

She put the card in her pocket and made her way back to the car.

After so much helplessness and the numbness that followed, there was a spark forming in her mind. The dark curtain that kept her thoughts of the future contained was opening for the first time since November, and a lighter path began to form for the days ahead.

She tucked the cane under her arm and walked the rest of the way to the town car in a careful but confident stride.

AUTHOR'S NOTE

First, thank you for getting this far! I appreciate anyone reading my stories, and I hope you enjoyed it. Aurora will be back for another ad-venture as soon as I can write it, but it's hard to keep up with her.

If you enjoyed DARK FRIDAY please take a moment to post a review on Amazon or your bookseller's site.

I'm always open to your comments and questions and I hope you'll share them with me at www.kdwentzel.com

KD Wentzel – June 2021

www.ingramcontent.com/pod-product-compliance
Lightning Source LLC
Chambersburg PA
CBHW030602180626
46816CB00005B/1647